# OUT OF THE CLOUDS OF DECEIT

David Canning

Matador
9 Priory Business Park,
Wistow Road, Kibworth Beauchamp,
Leicestershire. LE8 0RX
Tel: (+44) 116 279 2299
Fax: (+44) 116 279 2277
Email: books@troubador.co.uk
Web: www.troubador.co.uk/matador


ISBN 978-1780883-403


British Library Cataloguing in Publication Data.
A catalogue record for this book is available from the British Library.


Typeset by Troubador Publishing Ltd, Leicester, UK
Printed and bound in the UK by TJ International, Padstow, Cornwall


Matador is an imprint of Troubador Publishing Ltd

*For Paul*
*More like my brother than my friend*

# Part One

# 1948-1949

## *Chapter One*

Aiden found himself kicking his heels at Kings Cross and wondering whether he had been greedy with the butter ration. Everything around him looked grimy and it was no warmer on the concourse than it had been outside the station. The air was insidiously damp and raw. When he had left the house earlier this morning the sky had been oppressively grey and overcast and the cold had lost no time in penetrating every seam and fold of his clothes until it had chilled him right through to his bones.

The trains were hopelessly erratic and overcrowding seemed depressingly normal, so Aiden had allowed himself plenty of time in case not just one, but two connections should fail; amongst his many natural anxieties was a fear of being late, besides which it had been repeatedly emphasized to him during his training that he had a responsibility to set an example to his crew and with his news he felt that this was now more true than ever before.

He had been visiting his mother. It had been the first time he had returned home since the funeral. With his news had come an unlooked for, but welcome, forty-eight hours leave. The visit had been virtually unannounced as there had been no opportunity to telephone her until he had reached London to catch a train for the final leg of his journey.

~~~~

Aiden had pushed the backdoor shut against the foggy, sulphurous night-air; the door always stuck against the frame when the cold weather came. The kitchen had smelt of cooking; the comforting, unfresh but homely, smell of cabbage and boiled potatoes that never seemed to totally leave the kitchen during the wintertime months, but also the inviting and much less common smell of meat frying.

With the collar of his greatcoat still turned up, he had stepped across the kitchen and kissed his mother lightly on the cheek. His mother had remained standing over the stove serenely stirring the contents of a saucepan. It had been as if he had never been away, and in truth he had not really left the parental home in any definitive sense.

"I was sure you'd be hungry," his mother had said, smiling at him in answer to his kiss.

"But Mum…" Aiden had begun, but with kindly exasperation.

"We'll manage," she had replied without even the slightest hint of concern.

Despite the lateness of the hour and the lack of notice she had received of his impending arrival, before allowing herself to think of anything else she had cooked him a meal; her son had been coming home and she would have considered doing anything less as a dereliction in her duty as a mother.

"And gravy!" Aiden had exclaimed looking into the saucepan, but his tone had really indicated an appreciation of his mother's care rather than any genuine surprise.

"It's only sort of gravy, of course. It's mostly cabbage water and browning!" she had replied, still smiling at him. She was really a very ordinary woman.

Having hung his greatcoat over the newel post in the hallway and dropped his kitbag at the bottom of the stairs, he had returned to the relative warmth of the kitchen and sat at the table where his mother had already laid out his knife and fork.

"How was your journey?" she had asked as she dished up his dinner.

"Oh, you know, cold mostly."

His mother always opened the kitchen window a little whenever she was cooking, whatever the weather happened to be, and she had also parted the curtains an inch or so to allow for ventilation. From where he had sat Aiden had seen that a thin, soft band of condensation had formed around the edges of the panes, like cold beaches on a deep, black lonely sea.

"Did you manage to get a seat?" she had asked as she carefully drained the fat from the frying pan into the pint pudding basin that served as a dripping bowl, taking care to capture the final few precious drops.

"Coming up was a bit crowded, but the train from Charing Cross was pretty empty really."

He had received his news late that afternoon in an interview with his presiding squadron leader. A transport to the station had been due to leave and he had barely had enough time to collect up his kit if he had wanted to catch it. Besides which, it had been nearly teatime and many aircraftmen had finished their duties so there had been long queues for the telephone kiosks on the airfield.

Rush hour had long-since finished by the time Aiden had finally crossed London and reached an almost deserted and very cold Charing Cross. But being a man who was inwardly anxious about many small matters, he had checked for the time of his train before he had found a phone box and telephoned his mother, his breath steaming even in the closed kiosk, to say that he was arriving home and that he had some news to tell her.

"I've put a hot water bottle in your bed."

Although she had not been indifferent to the news which had precipitated his visit, her primary concern as it had always been had remained his comfort. But tired from his journey and from the emotion of the afternoon, he had actually wanted nothing more than his bed and he had eaten largely to please her, although the small portion of liver had been an unexpected treat.

He had been content to be back in the familiar kitchen, it was like safely drawing breath, although there had been a draft from the open window. The kitchen had not changed since his last visit and had seemed pleasantly set; as if now that she was on her own his mother would see no reason to alter it in any way.

Between mouthfuls, and managing to sound quietly jubilant, Aiden had then said, "I've been posted. I have to report to my operational conversion unit the day after tomorrow."

"Oh, I see," she had replied, indulgently. "But you know what I'm like; I don't really know what all that means!"

A part of him would have liked her to have asked if there was any more news. But then, he had reasoned to himself, as if he had been jealously hoarding something of the sweetest value he had deliberately said nothing to her on the telephone which would have indicated that there *had* been anything more.

"Bombers, it means I'll be flying heavy bombers." Already, he had felt a pride in being able to say that. Aiden had smiled up at his mother; long ago he had thought that he had outgrown her and that he must surely know more about the world than she, but he still craved her pleasure in his achievement.

"Oh, I see," she had said again, but this time thinking abstractedly of children she had sounded vaguely worried.

During the war she had been mildly ashamed of the views of Bishop Bell, Bishop of Chichester, whose speech in the House of Lords against the allies' bombing campaign had been so widely reported. She had thought there had been such a surfeit of wickedness in the world which had had to be stopped. These bishops, she had thought, and those fashionable Hampstead poets she had heard report of, were quite out of touch with everyday people whose daily lives seemed a world away from such noetic niceness. But she had also been secretly relieved that Aiden had been too young to play any part in such a necessary yet monstrous thing.

"And that's not all," Aiden had continued brightly. "My papers came through! I've been commissioned!"

This news had been of much greater interest to his mother as she could equate this with him doing well or with generally getting on in life and although not ebullient in her congratulations, Aiden had recognised that she had been deeply pleased for him.

The following morning his mother had woken him with a cup of tea. "I've put the kettle on the gas. Can you make do for a wash and shave?" There had been no question of a bath; coke for the boiler was in short supply again. She had continued, "Let me have anything that needs a wash."

Aiden had not taken advantage of his mother in any real sense; it was more as if both he and she had slipped effortlessly and comfortably back into the roles they had both played before Aiden had joined the RAF. It was as if not enough had changed for these roles not to simply continue.

"You don't have to, you know," Aiden had half-heartedly and ineffectually protested. Besides his mother's determination, like the majority of his peers he craved the continuing existence of a well-regulated domestic life and he had therefore felt content to let his mother look after him even while knowing that it involved a degree of sacrifice on her part.

Although it was not a Monday, she had washed his clothes as she had always used to, boiling up his shirts, scrubbing the collars on the draining board, running the clothes through the mangle to squeeze the water out and then hanging them over the coke boiler to get what was left of the heat.

"There," she had said, hanging up the last of them, "I daresay they'll be dry enough to iron this afternoon."

Aiden had nothing in particular that he had wanted to do with his time at home and, apart from walking muffled-up through the dismal cold to the parade of shops at the top of the street to get himself a newspaper, he had been content to stay around the house. He had found a peculiar satisfaction in watching his mother carrying out her workaday tasks. It was, he had decided, not so much nostalgia - as much as, say, the balneal smell of the open airing cupboard reminded him of the smell of being safely in his childhood bed - but more like a sense of voyeurism, as if he were witnessing something secretly delectable but that he did not have the necessary sanction to seek out and engage in.

After a late lunch of tinned sardines, Aiden had built a fire in the dinning-room grate, wondering when his mother had last used it, partly so that the room might be warm enough for them to sit in later - other than the kitchen, the dining-room was the only room in the house which his mother might heat - but also because she had wanted to finish drying his clothes on the clotheshorse in front of the fire.

For their evening meal his mother had improvised hamburgers from grated potato, oatmeal and a tiny amount of meat which they ate with winter greens and root vegetables. Aiden had briefly toyed with the idea of looking up some of his old friends, but then he had deliberately spent too long with the evening newspaper spread-out in front of him studying events which were only of limited interest to him for this to have been viable. So having consulted, and then assiduously rechecked, the railway timetable for his journey the next day, they had sat in the easy chairs in front of the fire in the dinning room and had switched on the bakelite radio in good time so that it should warm up. Then at half past eight they had listened to Tommy Handley and It's That Man Again and which had always made his mother laugh.

As they had sat together, listening to the radio, the room had finally seemed cosy; the thick curtains had been pulled tight shut over the french windows against the draft and the fire had now warmed the room reasonably. Aiden reflected that without his father the family seemed defensively small and lacked the comfort of a tribe. For her part, his mother had felt content to minister to Aiden sensing that the purposeful covenant would cease once Aiden found himself a wife.

~~~~

Across the station from where Aiden now stood, a short train of grubby carriages in charge of a black tank-locomotive, the anachronistic yellow lettering on the side of its water tanks barely visible through a layer of grime, crawled slowly alongside a platform, the connecting rod of the engine's driving-wheels rising, falling and slowing like the elongated foot of some fabulous beast. As it came to a halt the locomotive suddenly let off steam with a deafening whoosh which sounded all the greater in the relative quiet of the early afternoon gloom, the sound reverberating loudly around the cathedral-like train-shed.

Pigeons, startled and disturbed at the sudden noise, jolted into the air, like a mass of erratically blown envelopes, the fluttering of their wings briefly illuminated in the dim shafts of light straining in through the filmy glass of the station roof. The great swirling cloud of white steam and grey-black smoke billowed higher and higher reaching up to the panes of grimy glass high above the platforms and adding to the layer of dirt and soot which dulled everything on the station: the retaining walls; the steel-work high above the heads of the travellers; the backs of the wooden benches and roofs of the newspaper kiosks; the window sills and panes of waiting rooms and the parcels office; and, which even permeated clothing making cuffs and shirt collars absolutely filthy.

As abruptly as it had started the engine stopped venting and the last of the steam and smoke dispersed like a winters-breath about the station and the pigeons, cooing softly to each other, re-entrenched to their streaky, feculent perches. An occasional carriage door slammed shut, and a handful of passengers made their ways towards the ticket barrier. Aiden watched them, wondering about their lives: a middle-aged woman in sensible shoes keeping one eye on the concourse clock, with one hand holding the hand of a boy, the other hand a girl's, all three of them dressed in warm coats and with the boy's long grey school socks visible below the hem of his coat; a middle-aged man with a small, nondescript suitcase, his scarf carefully layered between his overcoat and his neck; a young woman walking quickly, seemingly impervious to the cold as if quite distracted by her own pleasant thoughts. Presently, they had all surrendered their tickets at the barrier and had dispersed in different directions across the concourse and Aiden remembered that he was very cold indeed and looked about him for the refreshment room.

With a cursory backwards glance at the pasty-faced girl whose job it was to dole out refreshments and who was now disinterestedly counting copper coins into the till drawer, he managed, by focusing his attention on his cup to the exclusion of virtually everything and everybody else about him, to keep his cup level and his arm steady and constant relative to the rest of his body as he walked away from the serving-counter. He manoeuvred carefully between the tables, half expecting the sudden jolt of his heavy kitbag as it slid off his shoulder and which would cause him to spill his tea. Reaching an empty table he lowered himself awkwardly, consciously keeping the upper part of his body upright until his cup was level with the tabletop.

He then carefully slid the cup onto the table. Easing his kitbag off his shoulder and carefully taking its weight in his now free hand, he placed the bag down onto the floor beside him and then, with a feeling of something like relief, sat down. Although an improvement to being out on the concourse, it was not particularly warm in the refreshment room and there was condensation on every window.

There was still a long time to wait before his train was due. He stirred the hot, sweet orange-brown tea, then cradling the cup between his hands, partly for warmth and partly because that was his habit, he found himself thinking about his father.

His father had been a mild and compassionate man and who had had a sweet tooth. Eking out the chocolate ration had been a constant concern to him and Aiden fondly remembered him sitting at the kitchen table carefully dividing up his precious ration, making it last by measuring out a meagre amount for each day. It had been a serious business and if the small bar fractured unevenly spilling tiny irregular shards onto the table, he would frown, quite unconsciously, and dab at them gently with the end of his moistened finger, anxious not to waste even the smallest amount.

But Aiden thought his father would have been proud of him. Being in uniform would have been too simplistic a reason for his father's pride. But being a man who understood duty as being a transcendent manifestation of care, he would have recognised and approved Aiden's earnest desire to live up to his responsibilities. Although being a man of many small anxieties, Aiden secretly worried whether he would ever be able to measure up to what he thought was expected of him. And then he had not really known what had been expected of him at the funeral. Amongst the dark trappings he shyly, and with uncertainty, intuitively received from all those around him the generally favoured mixture of ceremony and sorrow, and was left seriously wondering whether remembering the chocolate ration was too trivial or un-weighty a thing to be considered a legitimate part of his grief.

Only now, having almost finished his tea did Aiden look properly about the refreshment room. Firstly he glanced back at the counter, idly wondering whether in fact the girl was not as plain as he had first thought her to be. Then, looking around the main body of the room for the first time, he noticed that there was a man of about his own age sitting at the table next to his who, like Aiden, wore blue-grey uniform. Reserved and not at all naturally gregarious, Aiden would not have sought out company to merely pass the time, but the other man struck up a conversation with him.

"You seemed miles away," he said, offering Aiden a cigarette.

"I didn't even see you there!" Aiden replied casually, accepting it.

"Where're you off to?" The other man struck a match and held it up to the end of Aiden's cigarette. Neither of them showed any curiosity that they should be on the move, transitoriness being a fact of their lives.

"OCU." Aiden exhaled the first breath of smoke, the sulphur-and-potassium smell of the match still pleasantly pungent in his nostrils. He intuitively knew that no explanation of the abbreviation that tripped so easily and proudly off his tongue would be necessary; the implications of shared service experiences and a common technical language were seductively comfortable, but mostly he had greatly surprised himself at just how relaxed he was with this casual conversation.

"Me too," the other airman said as he held the match up in the air, waving it exuberantly until the flame was extinguished. Then, reaching across the gap between the two tables, he offered Aiden his hand. "My name's Dennis."

Aiden offered his own hand. "Aiden."

Dennis then stood up and, bringing his cup with him and pushing his kitbag with his foot, he crossed over to Aiden's table and sat down opposite him.

"Heavies?" Dennis enquired hopefully.

"That's right!" Aiden had instantly warmed to Dennis; he seemed just like himself and talking to him was refreshingly and remarkably effortless.

"Then I guess we must be going to the same place," Dennis said, as if a perfectly satisfactory conclusion had been reached. Then, with a note of obvious excitement in his voice, as if he were completely thrilled at the prospect of what lay before them, he continued, "I wonder what we'll be flying?"

Aiden paused before replying. He carefully knocked the ash off his cigarette into the ashtray, taking his time to formulate what he was going to say and, more importantly, thinking what Dennis might say to him in return.

"Actually, I received my papers at the same time as the posting." He did not know if it should matter if it turned out that he had been commissioned but Dennis had not been.

"And me! I was going to sew the badge on in the train."

Aiden's mother had already insisted on performing this small duty for him.

Aiden felt a sense of relief pass over him and he said evenly, "I expect when we're operational we'll end up flying Lincolns, but I don't suppose we'll go straight on to them."

It would have been disappointing if it had turned out that Dennis and he were not of equal rank; it would have seemed like a spoiling of innocence as they were so obviously starting out together.

"Lancasters then, if we're lucky!" Dennis exclaimed loudly, but then shot Aiden an uncertain, almost guilty look as if he were worried that he might have said too much.

"Perhaps we'll end up in Coastal Command." Aiden smiled easily. Aiden and Dennis both knew well enough that quite apart from being used to address the bomber gap until more modern designs could be brought on stream the Lancaster was being pressed into a number of peace-time roles, notably maritime patrol.

"Well, I don't know about that." Dennis said with uncertainty and frowned. But Aiden found that he rather liked the idea of flying along, mile after mile, high up in the sunshine over the craquelure sea, the bright light gleaming on the newly-applied grey and white paintwork of the aircraft.

Then presently, markedly at odds with his earlier apparent enthusiasm, Dennis unexpectedly lowered his voice and asked conspiratorially, "Were you thinking about the posting just now? Quite honestly, between you and me, I find it all *dreadfully* nerve-racking."

Dennis unconsciously played with the teaspoon in his saucer, repeatedly twisting the handle so that the convex back of the spoon was uppermost, and then twisting it back again to its more natural resting position. He frowned, as if by speaking in this way he had somehow placed himself at Aiden's mercy.

"I know," Aiden quietly agreed. But feeling indescribably comforted, elated even, that Dennis appeared to feel as he did, he tentatively continued: "I always seem to worry about such silly things. I always have done, you know, at school, during training, everywhere. Whereas other chaps don't seem to be like that at all, they're able to just get on with things…"

Aiden heard his own voice trailing off weakly, as if he were aware of how unshielded and feeble he must sound. But Dennis, almost imperceptibly, nodded his agreement as if he were ashamed to admit to it, and then sounding like a man who was fearful of ever finding loving grace said, "It's more than just something being new, isn't it, of being a new boy?"

"It makes you feel so awfully vulnerable." Aiden almost whispered, the back of his neck and ears burning, his eyes focused intensely on his empty cup.

Had he been minded to, he could have recounted a litany of such awkwardness and embarrassments from his earliest memories right through to the present day. But Aiden knew that if he were to recount such apprehensions to anyone else they would sound extremely trivial, and more importantly, to admit to having such concerns seemed somehow questionable or dubious as if he were inadequate and insufficiently manly. He had not even been able to speak of such things to his father, despite him having been the gentlest of men, and Aiden attributed this inability to connect with him as having been contributory to his sense of being isolated or set apart from other men that he invariably felt.

Awkwardly, and wondering if he were alone in having such feelings, Aiden looked up and smiled encouragement at Dennis. "But as it happens, I was thinking of my father just then."

"Well, if he's at all like mine I expect he worries about you flying."

"It's only me and my mother, now," Aiden offered.

"Oh, I see. The war I suppose?"

Aiden thought it quite natural that everybody should assume his father had been killed in the war.

"No, it wasn't the war. I mean," Aiden stumbled on to say, thinking an explanation was called for, "he was actually in a reserved occupation..."

But Dennis startled Aiden by suddenly exclaiming, cutting right across Aiden's reply, "I lost Tommy. He was my brother. And I'm all they've got left now, so they tend to worry so!"

"In the war?" Aiden asked softly.

But he surprised Aiden by loudly clearing his throat and replying very matter-of-factly, "Yes, but it was a silly accident, really."

They lapsed into a kind of mildly astonished silence as if each of them had been taken aback by the extent to which they had revealed to the other something deeply private about themselves. Presently, and with a shy look at each other, they each glanced towards the counter, then extinguishing their cigarettes and shouldering their kitbags in a curiously unconsciously synchronized action, they went in search of their train which they calculated ought to be in at the platform by now.

~~~~

Aiden and Dennis were the only passengers from their train who alighted at the country station that afternoon. There was a smell like damp cabbage stalks in the cold Lincolnshire air and for a moment they stood on the platform to get their bearings. Huddled in their greatcoats and stamping their feet, they wondered whether they would ever feel warm again; for the whole of their journey the heating in the railway carriages had persistently failed to work. As the train drew away into the distance, the carriage wheels click-clacking over the rail joints and the contact of the wheels on the rails making a sighing noise like perpetually sad mermaids, they walked towards the station building.

Under the blanket of damp, cold air, the station and its

surroundings seemed as if they had been stupefied. As if they had been abandoned, two or three solitary goods wagons stood silently in the sprawling goods-yard, their red-bauxite-coloured bodies virtually indistinguishable from the colours of the dirty track sleepers, yard hoist and goods-shed. A flatbed lorry, drab and mute, had been parked outside the empty coal merchant's office, roughly-folded coal sacks piled unevenly in the coal-dust on its back, and a shovel leant against the coal staithes as if it had been forgotten. Against the deep oppressive stillness of the afternoon it seemed as if they were the only living souls on the station, until the sudden clunk of a signal being re-set and the diminishing oscillations of the cables which connected it to the signal box beyond the throat of the goods-yard, suggested the possibilities of lives they could not see.

"I can't see anyone here to meet us," Dennis said carelessly.

Each of them had simply been told that transport would be waiting for him at the station and if travelling on his own, each would have desperately worried about appearing foolish as he would not know what the transport was and where he should look for it.

From time to time during the train journey they had even wondered out loud about the transport. Their wondering would have appeared to a casual listener as being something of no more than idle curiosity but in reality they had both known that each of them had felt the same sense of gnawing unease.

"Perhaps they're outside." Aiden replied in the same easy manner. With the intuitive comfort that he could now always share his secret apprehensions with Dennis without fear of opprobrium, Aiden felt sufficiently venturesome to think he could even make a joke of it if he had wished; relieved, he thought he must have at least now appeared to be acting as other men would in the same situation.

"I shouldn't get your hopes up," Dennis said nonchalantly, swinging his kitbag up and onto his shoulder. "They've probably forgotten all about us!" The two men laughed loudly together as if making a show of their indifference.

As they came closer to the station buildings, the smell of an unseen coal-fire mingled with the smell of the damp cabbage stalks and they could see an ordinary aircraftman, propping himself up against the peeling cream paint of the ticket barrier and watching their progress.

"This way, sirs," he said disinterestedly, as they gave-up their travel warrants.

Secretly relieved, and hoping that he had seen the two of them laughing together, they followed him out to the station forecourt where a standard airforce lorry was parked immediately outside the entrance to the booking hall.

Aiden and Dennis squeezed up in the cab of the lorry with the driver where they were only marginally warmer than they had been on the station. As it ground its way out of the station forecourt, they initially sat in awkward silence, but then, in an attempt to appear as if he and Aiden were totally relaxed and old hands at the game, Dennis continued the conversation they had been having in the train.

"So that's why you joined up, seeing the Tempest shoot the doodlebug down?"

"It didn't shoot at it," Aiden replied but then hurriedly added, "It was all wrong really, the Tempest shouldn't even have been there; it was behind the balloon barrage. But having seen it happen, all I really wanted to do was fly!" And suddenly worried about the overt enthusiasm of his final sentence, he stole a quick sideways glance at the driver.

"Flipped it over with its wingtip, I suppose? You used to read about that sort of thing in the newspapers." Dennis tried to keep the wonder out of his voice, but he involuntarily let out a long, low whistle before adding: "that must have been really something to see!"

They were still boyishly excitable and believed themselves extraordinarily lucky for actually receiving pay for having adventures and were weighed down with the niggling belief that their commissions had therefore somehow been unwarranted. So they secretly feared the judgement of men who laboured indifferently and they therefore felt a little intimidated by the presence of the aircraftman. But their driver concentrated on the road before him with an apparent indifference to his passengers that he could have been born with.

"No, I think that must have been the intention, but the Tempest actually collided with it!"

Such weapons had seemed to belong to the pit of another world and Aiden had watched it approach with fascinated horror, the hairs on the back of his neck on end. June 1944 had been a month of heavy cloud, driving rain and leaden skies which had made the buzz bombs all but intolerable. But as he had watched it approach, a well-maintained, oiled sound like an urgent, growling purr had joined with the saw-edged sound of the flying bomb. With an overwhelming impression of power and speed, the Tempest had appeared as if out of nowhere and banked incisively towards the bomb.

Aiden had expected to hear the deafening thump of cannon shells, but the aircraft had approached closer and closer, but still the pilot had not fired. Then the two shapes had merged together into a complex cluster of points and indeterminable motion and had then suddenly sprung violently apart again; each had acquired an unexpected trajectory. For two or three seconds the metallic drone of the flying bomb became louder as it described an upwards arc into the air and then it became quieter, its hot glowing exhaust pointing skywards as the bomb tipped down towards the ground. In collision with the short stubby wing of the bomb, first the Tempest's skin had been torn, exposing and then breaking the longitudinals of the wing's frame. With the supporting laminar flow of the air interrupted, and its rugged loveliness broken forever, the Tempest had also spun down towards the ground.

Miraculously, the pilot, who had seemed to be not much older than Aiden, had managed to walk away from his crashed aeroplane and had seemed physically untouched by the incident. By the time Aiden had run to the scene, the pilot had been standing serenely in front of his broken machine, inevitably holding a cup of tea provided by a well-wishing local house-holder, seemingly oblivious to the destruction around him and exuding a remarkable inner stillness, as if he had been occupying a private celestial space. Aiden had felt as if a great tension had been released, as if he had witnessed a tremendous personal battle being won, and that all the pilot's energy had been spent in a most marvellous and noble endeavour.

"Collided!" Dennis exclaimed. "Whatever happened?"

The event had been something beyond the merely exciting, a sudden, essentially private, revelation; something red-animal. It had been about wilfully disregarding the tilt of the scale-beam and drawing upon some deeper knowledge hard-wired into the soul, and made umbilical by the experience of generations. The experience had left Aiden with a feeling of replete peacefulness and he now felt reticent about trying to describe what he had seen, and especially what he had felt, on that day, so with one careful eye on their driver he simply replied:

"Oh you know, bit of a mess really. The bomb made a tremendous crater and the Tempest went down, but the pilot got out alright."

Having left the station forecourt, they were now passing through an unattractive village which was strung out along the road as if it had no heart or soul. It consisted mostly of small brick-built houses whose gardens seemed full of bicycles, bits of grey disintegrating wood, rusting garden implements and rubbishy sheds. The whole village seemed closed-up, silenced by the cold and invading damp.

"Is that why you joined up?" Aiden then asked, "Something about the war?"

"I suppose so. I wanted to pay them back!" There was something boyishly excitable about Dennis, with his matter-of-fact excitableness. "You see, we were very nearly bombed out."

Fearing that the conversation had already strayed too much into the personal, Aiden cast about for a safe change of subject.

The village left behind, they travelled slowly through a dreary, monotonous landscape of dull fields which they glimpsed momentarily through gates set into the thick hawthorn hedges that defined the field boundaries as far as they could see, a seemingly endless expanse of stalks of brussels sprouts and root vegetables. The unrelenting flatness of the landscape was broken only by an occasional bleak, fingery tree that dripped persistently from the heavy, wet air.

Then presently they arrived at a junction and they forgot all about trying to make tempered conversation for the aircraftman's benefit.

Glimpsed through a barbed-wire-topped chain link fence, the agricultural land suddenly gave way ahead of them to a grey-green sweep of grass, as capacious as a beach, and a bright, wide expanse of concrete that ran away into the distance. It was as if a malignant sadness had been chased away by trumpets and sunshine. After the dank claustrophobic lanes the wideness and evenness of the scene seemed clean, purposeful and on the cusp of familiarity.

Turning to the right, the lorry followed the lane, which shadowed the perimeter of the airfield, for about a mile before gaining the airfield buildings. Here Aiden's apprehensions were further appeased for the aircraftman brought the lorry to a halt in front of a brick-built administrative building and announced indifferently, "The Duty Officer said you were to report to him first. This way please, sirs." and deftly handed them into the vestibule of the building thereby saving them from the necessity of having to ask where they should go.

## Chapter Two

Having been allocated their living quarters and unpacked, Aiden and Dennis sat in the mess talking and drinking mugs of tea wiling away the unexpectedly empty dog-end of their arrival afternoon. Aiden felt the airfield to be peculiarly evocative; it could almost have been holy. It was as if there were deeply comforting ghosts everywhere and he found it easy and gently thrilling to imagine the mess hall empeopled with airmen.

Of necessity, it had been built to house hundreds of men at a single sitting but Aiden doubted whether a fraction of that number now ever sat down here together. It was a functional, lofty place but the opal-glass spheres suspended above the tables cast sufficient light only to illuminate the diners' meals, leaving their soft, smooth faces in a half-shadow. The lights failed also to penetrate the gloom above them so that the flaking paint high up on the ceiling was invisible in anything deeper than semi-darkness. Large metal-framed windows, the panes now covered in condensation, were set along one wall of the room, windows of Elizabethan proportions separated by solid concrete mullions.

Earnestly, he fondly imagined the wartime bomber crews eating together here before flying on operations, as if with the immediacy of danger communal eating had become a soothing, soughing wave of sensory comfort: the purl of knives and forks making continuous fall on plates; the rhythmic chink and swirl of cups being stirred; the occasional scrape of a chair being pushed back, plates pushed away and cigarettes lit. He thought he could catch the even hubble of their conversation and arrogate to himself the haze of blue tobacco smoke drifting over a sea of blue-grey uniforms and the faces of the airmen bobbing away like flecks of foam on an illimitable tide. But at this hour in the afternoon most of the serving counters were cold and closed up, the occasional rattle of cutlery and the faint stewy smell of institutional cooking coming from the unseen kitchens being the only indicators that the evening meal was plausibly impending. Outside, the gloomy November light was now failing rapidly.

"It still seems unbelievable that we're here!" Dennis was leaning across the table and speaking enthusiastically in a loud whisper; despite the presence of a number of other people in the mess hall, it seemed to both of them almost irreverent to raise their voices overly much.

"Flying heavy bombers from a wartime bomber base!" Dennis continued.

"The whole place seems magical." Aiden smiled indulgently at Dennis; he felt more awed than excited.

"It seems wrong really, but I feel almost guilty when I say that. It's as if I have to pretend to everyone that I'm not really that excited about it." But the excitement Dennis felt was palpable; as if his glands pungently exuded it into the air about him.

"I could tell mother didn't much like the idea of me being on bombers."

Aiden was pleased that no one else was sitting close to them.

"But being keen would have seemed natural enough in the war, wouldn't it," Dennis said, almost wistfully.

Aiden felt uncomfortable with this line of discussion. He also thought it seemed a little impudent to be so *excitable* about it; he knew somewhere deep in his bones that the reality of flying bombers in the war must have been so very much more faceted than they could possibly imagine.

"We ought to be careful what we say, you know." He said warily. Quite apart from his awareness of popular sentiment, he was concerned as to how far the insidious post-war political distancing from the allied bombing campaign might have spread; perhaps it was even felt on the airfields either as wounding treachery, or even, perhaps, it suddenly and coldly dawned on him, as a sly opportunity to further careers, all of which seemed to him to be an unimaginable step away from the wonder of flying.

"I suppose so," Dennis replied, tracing nothings on the table in front of him with his forefinger, before casually slipping the conversation back towards the topic they had so frequently found themselves returning to throughout the day, "You still wanted to join up even after the war had finished? And I guess you weren't thinking of flying bombers especially?"

It was as if at some subconscious level, getting this part of the story straight in their own minds was of fundamental importance, as if there was some truth to be had which somehow continued to elude them or defied adequate articulation.

"I think it was because of Spitfires, really. They always seemed so glamorous, didn't they?" Aiden replied lightly.

Glamorous was a woefully inadequate word to describe what he had felt, but because in such a context it was such a believable word – with its distinctive elliptical wing, its power and agility, the Spitfire remained the ultimate chivalric icon of victory - he had used it quite deliberately so as to avoid any reference to his deeper feelings, but with no intention to mislead. Besides which, he would have been content to fly anything that had been offered to him.

"And I was set on it by then," Aiden added. Although it was less sleek, less feline, and had an altogether less knowing shape than the Spitfire, after witnessing the Tempest downing the flying bomb Aiden had become completely air-minded and had joined the Air Training Corps as soon as he had been old enough, but he felt too embarrassed to admit to Dennis to having signed-up for aircrew selection on his eighteenth birthday, brim-full of boyish enthusiasm. "What about you?"

"Oh, it's a case of bugger Bexley!" Dennis replied amiably. "I thought there must be a bit more to life than hanging around at home. Didn't your parents mind?"

"My father spent his war as a draughtsman and although he never went on about the Germans or anything, in fact I think he felt rather sorry for the ordinary Germans, I think he felt he had missed out on something. Rather like missing out on an adventure, despite all the disruption and horror of it all."

Aiden thought that his father had been secretly thrilled that he had been sufficiently daring to join the airforce, understanding the private validity of such a path; although he also had no doubt that he would have been immensely frightened for him if the war had still been in progress. He was also convinced that his father would never have talked about any of this to his mother, intuitively understanding that she would not understand that mere exhilaration was almost coincidental to his son's needs.

~~~~

Each of them had been expecting communal living, a barracks or a dormitory, such as each of them had experienced while they were training. But on understanding that they were to share a room together, it had seemed as if there had been a disturbance in their fields of tempered expectations. It was like a feeling of fey recklessness that had made each of them simultaneously incredulous at their luck in the unexpected privacy of a room to themselves and, at the same time, elation at the inevitable justice of being together.

Although essentially utilitarian, when they had been built the airfield buildings had been extravagant in their provision of accommodation but now room upon room remained empty. Within such rooms there were bare mattresses on the metal-framed beds and the bare walls were pockmarked with occasional holes made by the drawing pins where pin-up posters and smudgy home photographs had once been placed. There was an unnatural quietness when the doors of these rooms were shut fast and Aiden never lost the sense that this emptiness was inappropriate, and like an empty school classroom he felt there should have been voices, laughter, movement, or even misery in them to indicate precious life.

Unpacking their kitbags was in actuality rather as it would have been anywhere else, whether sharing or not, each spreading his clothes out on the taut blanket on the bed before him, carefully folding and re-folding his uniform shirts to keep the creases sharp before carefully placing them on the shelf in his locker, and checking that the small but essential items such as boot polish, matches, needle and thread had not been forgotten. The whole process had seemed to take hardly any time at all. But having a room to themselves allowed for less of a sharp demarcation regarding how some of their personal items were placed and in some small way they were able to set about making the room their own.

More experienced airmen would have treated living out of these rooms indifferently, and Aiden and Dennis having very nearly reached operational status both recognized that their time here would pass quickly, but being together, it felt like an adventure.

The darkness of their room at night was never total; a thin strip of yellow light from the corridor outside their room was continuously admitted through the gap underneath the door. This appealed to Aiden as it reminded him of the hallway light at home; although he would never have told this to anyone but Dennis.

In the following weeks they slept here like brothers; it seemed quite natural to them that as they talked together in the dark before they fell asleep, sharing confidences and reviewing with each other the fresh experiences they lived each day, that they should be lying facing each other across the narrow runnel that separated their beds. It was like the excitement and intimacy of camping.

On one occasion Aiden asked Dennis about how his family came to be almost bombed out. Dennis's words tumbled out in a seemingly unstoppable torrent as if his family had suffered a serious loss, and not just experienced a lucky escape.

"It was in the Blitz. We only just managed to get down to the Anderson before the bombs started to fall. We were counting the seconds between each one, you know, how one used to: one, two, three… But then Tommy tripped on the path and was the last one in and before we shut the door there was this sort of incredibly loud wumph noise and it felt as if the whole shelter lifted up. Tommy was literally blown off his feet and next door had a direct hit!"

Then Dennis paused, took a deep breath and then said quietly, deliberately, "That's it really. That's all there is to it."

It was the safety of the campfire.

"And you decided to join the RAF to get back at them?" Aiden asked gently.

Dennis replied with an air of detachment, nonchalance even, "Well, that came a bit later, I suppose."

"It would have been natural enough, wouldn't it?

In the dim light, Aiden could see that Dennis was lying on his back staring up at the ceiling.

"At first I just wanted to kill Germans."

To hear Dennis say this sounded jarring; he seemed so youthfully innocuous that the idea of Dennis killing anything seemed quite ridiculous.

Occasionally, and without it striking them as being at all ghoulish, they would speculate upon the previous occupants of their room. They wondered how old they would have been and what aircraft they would have flown. Romantically, they wondered how many of them had penned sad and moving letters to wives, girl-friends, brothers, fathers, someone uncompromisingly dear, to be collected up by the Committee of Adjustment along with all the other possessions of a missing airman, and forwarded in the event of the letter writer having failed to return from an operation.

~~~~

There was little activity on the airfield during these first few weeks; cold wind and rain swept over the airfield in great erratic patterns and people dodged between doorways in a futile effort to keep dry. Stepping into the vast hangars from outside was like passing into the comfort of order, but the overlaps of the giant hangar doors were not quite sufficient to totally prevent the wind from occasionally whistling in and reminding those within of the powerful elements outside.

But inside, where the Lancasters were being made ready for their new crews, the hangar lights, hung high up from the steel-work which supported the roof, cast a harsh but business-like light and the cables of inspection lamps snaked though hatches and panels in the aircraft so that pools of soft welcoming light flooded out of the aircraft at unexpected places. Within this glow, men in overalls worked together industriously and purposefully; the sounds of tools, the calls and chatter of men, the smells of grease, lubricants and hot solder a mixture more heady than incense lingering in a great cathedral or dusk falling on a busy fairground.

Workbenches were placed next to each aircraft. Scaffolding towers, hoists and gantries sprouted up around the engine nacelles the better for the mechanics to access and service the engines. Metal panels were stripped away from the airframes and placed to one side, allowing the electricians to access wiring looms as thick as a man's arm, and fitters to access the control surface linkages. Engine parts were laid out carefully and labelled with engineers' pencil or neat cardboard tags whilst awaiting re-assembly. The individual registration number of the aircraft from which a panel had come was marked on it in chalk to allow for later identification and re-fitting. Each worksheet, requisition and form were brought together to make a meticulous record of the work performed on each aircraft.

But eventually the wind subsided, the slanting rain stopped and the oppressive blanket of low, dark grey cloud lifted. A wash of pale sunlight, hardly sufficient to cast a shadow, occasionally shone through a feathery rent in the now thinner and lighter cloud highlighting the almost unnatural cleanness of the aerodrome, such had been the ferocity of the rain: the individual stones of the aggregate in the aprons of concrete hard-standing stood out like pebbles on a mountain stream-bed; and the rows of mortar between the courses of bricks on the sharp, damp airfield buildings were strangely picked-out as if they had been made anew.

Upon completion of its overhaul, each silent Lancaster was pulled out of the hangar, tail first, by a small but powerful blue-grey tractor-tug and the mechanics completed their last checks and adjustments before firing-up the engines. Witnessing this almost unimaginably exciting event was like being present at a fiery Promethean birth.

Sitting in the pilot's seat, the small sliding-glass panel in the cockpit canopy open, the better to listen to the tick and roar of each engine as it burst into life, the flight sergeant who led the ground crew looked critically out at the engines as if not yet quite daring to trust that they would work.

Being closest to his vantage point, the port engines were generally fired-up first. There would be a slight whine from the inner port engine as the flight sergeant, leaning slightly forward towards the aircraft's instrument panel but all the time looking over his left shoulder out towards the engines, operated the starter. An isolated cough from the engine would be followed by several more, and at each fitful cough puffs of blue-grey smoke discharged from the engine's exhausts and dissipated in the cold winter air. The propeller would start to turn, very slowly at first, but then as the fuel and air mixed and ignited in each cylinder in the correct proportions the pistons started to drive the propeller shaft less erratically and the propeller started to revolve more quickly. The coughs joined together to form a continuous resonating sound increasing in pitch from deep, dark notes to a loud even tenor, like a powerful motorbike, but much, much louder. The propeller turned faster and faster and despite the flame-shroud over the engine's exhausts, spurts of yellow and orange flashed dramatically out along the engine housing. Opening the throttle, the engine raced, the propeller turning so fast that the yellow-painted tips of the blades described a yellow circle in the air around the propeller's spinner. Then with more smoke and flames, the outer port engine was started, the noise adding a harsh discordant, jarring note to the running of the first engine. Looking out across the flight engineer's station to the starboard wing, the flight sergeant then started-up the starboard engines. One after the other they added to the deafening cacophony, a raucous, untempered sound of boiling, popping urgent noise. But then the engines were synchronized and the blades on the airscrew optimised. The cacophony became a smooth virile, purring sound sending shivers down one's spine; the Lancaster a sleek, living, puissant thing.

Flying the Lancasters was an adventure. For the young men who were not yet clear of their boyhoods, and who now flew them, this was the closest they could probably come to the thrill of learning about God, about comradely dependence and respecting something solitary and wild inside themselves.

Each and every time they flew them it was only with the greatest difficulty that their self-discipline prevented them from simply losing themselves to the open sky. Each time one of them opened the throttles wide and his aircraft gathered speed and momentum as it rolled down the long runway at the start of another flight he could feel the deep resonating power of the aircraft as if he were in communion with it. Each time his aircraft rose so effortlessly into the air, at such a seemingly slight touch of the marvellously tight and responsive controls, each of them felt humbled.

Risking a reprimand, they would occasionally engage the superchargers. One day of high, thin grey cloud with a bright powdery light which gave unusually good visibility, Dennis and Aiden were flying their Lancasters together. From their home airfield they had headed southeast into the light wind, gradually climbing up higher and higher over the flat, dull agricultural land. Flying out over the Wash they had then turned northwards towards the bombing ranges at Wainfleet Sands with the intention of following the East Coast for some miles before turning south west to fly the third side of the triangle back to their aerodrome. Far below them and far away in the distance where the sweep of white sand all but disappeared from view, the whitewashed walls of a cottage, close to the foreshore, stood out in the sharp light. Aiden knew instinctively what Dennis was going to do. Dennis engaged the superchargers on the engines of his aircraft and, taking the cottage as his marker, put the Lancaster into a long shallow dive. Aiden felt a delicious thrill run through his body, butterfly wings in his stomach and an almost imperceptible tremble in his fingers as his left hand reached out towards the instrument panel. And with the anticipation of excitement, the adrenalin coursing through his veins quickening his heartbeat and his breathing, he engaged his own aircraft's superchargers.

Instantly the revolutions of the engines increased, their sound now louder and higher in pitch. The whole airframe vibrated and buzzed. The aircrew's ears filled with the sound of scary, random creaking as the metal stressed and strained. With a sound like an angry insect, a slide-rule moved slowly across the navigator's table propelled by nothing but the pulsation of the metal beneath it. The aircraft leapt ahead. With a slight forward movement on the control column, the wavy line of the beach and the white-topped waves below them instantly started to rush up towards them. The Lancaster gathered more speed. The rapid approach of the foreshore and the white cottage was dangerously mesmerising. Destruction might be only seconds away. The speed was exhilarating, intoxicating. The throb of the engines increased to a fever pitch. The creaking and groaning of the airframe increased like a violent storm. The cottage was looming up large in front of them now. The flight engineer called out suddenly "Two-ninety, Skipper", and Aiden knew he was now edging the machine beyond its design limits. The Lancasters roared over the cottage at little more than roof top height, shaking it to its foundations.

Instead of throttling-back and gently climbing to resume their normal flight path, they pulled up sharply and banked hard to starboard. The aircraft lurched violently. The engines' pitch changed as the engines laboured against the interruption to the aerodynamic flow of air over the wings and tailplane as the ailerons and elevators operated in response to Aiden's positive and assured movement of the control column and pedals. Where there had been sea and sand previously they could now see white cloud. Disengaging the superchargers, the aircraft described a wide arc out over the sea, then, carefully formating their aircraft together, they reduced their speed and sedately turned towards the cottage once more to complete a full circle in the niveous light.

Looking back to the shore, they saw a man who evidently had trouble walking emerging stiffly from the door of the cottage. He was holding the hand of a little girl, and about them a dog ran around barking wildly. As they turned towards the cottage for this second time, the man dropped the little girl's hand and both he and the little girl began waving excitedly at the approaching Lancasters. The man stood with difficulty and waved with something of a size and shape that suggested a tablecloth. Aiden and Dennis flew their aircraft low, but at a stately speed, over the cottage and resumed the intended course of their journey. The man and the little girl continued waving until they were out of sight; Aiden and Dennis felt like kings.

~~~~

In the evenings, there was not even the possibility of a woman penetrating the officers' mess. It was therefore possible for the men to regain something of the particular feeling of intimacy that may sometimes exist between men, which they may have experienced with their fathers, the feeling like teeming expectancy that is rightly present between brothers.

"Being coned in the searchlights was a real gut-wrenching experience."

Aiden and Dennis had fallen into conversation with two of the instructors. Their instructors were older pilots, all of whom had flown the Lancaster operationally in the war. Although in years they were not much older than they were themselves, it seemed as if their experiences qualified them to belong to an older generation and Aiden and Dennis found them powerfully congenial company.

"We'd all seen it happen to others before, of course," the instructor continued. "Planes suddenly illuminated and then hit by shells from the ground. First you'd see balls of flame come from the engines, then from the fuselage, and then you'd see it going down and down until it disappeared into total blackness again. Poor devils, you'd think. And then the first time that beam lit up your own aircraft you'd think that was it! You thought your number must be up!"

The officers' mess was a large, comfortable room that encouraged conviviality. There was a soft, calm background hum of relaxed conversation and here and there men sat quietly reading newspapers.

"Bill's right, you know, flak was a real bugger," the other instructor agreed, his tone implying that he had more to add. His listeners respectfully waited for him to continue. "There would be great red fire-flashes and orange explosions lighting up the cockpit," he said quite undramatically. "And each time the plane was hit there was a huge hollow bang and the whole kite would shake violently. A direct hit would destroy a plane, of course, often instantly in a huge explosion where nobody had a snowball's chance in hell of getting out, but most damage was caused indirectly by shrapnel from exploding shells, penetrating the fuel tanks or the hydraulics or by just killing men, of course."

There was a comfortable silence as Reg, the other instructor, finished speaking; an instinctive, empathetic condolence existed between pupils and instructors. Aiden's glass was now empty, but feeling enormity about them he intuitively felt that it would be disrespectful to attract the attention of the steward to order more drinks and so he remained sitting in attentive silence; he understood that it was the older men's experiences that determined the warp and weft of such a conversation.

The thrilling congeniality of such evenings was beyond the experience of both Aiden and Dennis. Neither of them had ever previously imagined the possibility of sharing real intimacy between men, especially men of different ages, in this way. Dennis, the more forward of the two of them, ventured to ask, "But men got out, didn't they?"

"Most didn't." Bill spoke in a kindly, softly informative manner; there was no intention to shock the younger men. "On the Nuremberg raid I saw a crewman bale out of a crippled Lancaster, only for the top of his parachute to be caught by a stream of burning petrol from the ruptured wing tanks. The parachute quickly burnt to nothing and the man fell earthwards from twenty-two thousand feet."

Having passed through fire, the older men freely offered the younger the benefit of their knowledge and experience, but not for any aggrandisement of their own deeds or actions. So unspeakable had been their experiences in the war that the opportunity to talk in truly sympathetic company was cathartic for the older men and therefore a meaningful bargain existed between them and the younger men. And although they spoke of the unimaginable daily horrors they had endured, it was as if the soft rosy glow of maleness now protected them and would now keep all of them safe.

Aiden suddenly found himself thinking of his mother and how she would find the subject matter of this conversation abhorrent, but then imagined that his father would have understood the need.

"Nuremberg was particularly bad, wasn't it?" Dennis asked quietly. There was no need to ask which Nuremberg raid Bill had been referring to.

"There was so much carnage I felt I was overlooking the end of the world," Bill replied, avoiding eye contact with Dennis. Nursing a sense of shocking betrayal, the men who had flown bombers operationally in the war felt more than most the importance of a defining set of beliefs and values and through their rectitude Aiden and Dennis learnt about loyalty, integrity and honour.

Reg then said, "Make no mistake, flight crew was the most dangerous job of the war. The attrition rate was something terrible."

"In that raid alone, in just seven hours, six-hundred-and-seventy aircrew died, more than all the men the RAF lost in the entire Battle of Britain."

"Yet they're heroes while we're made to feel ashamed."

"We're not saying the Fighter Boys weren't brave," Bill quickly asserted, "but they never had to live with the sort of terror we did." He then went on to explain, "I once took a Group Captain from Fighter Command, a veteran from the Battle of Britain, Spitfires, as a guest on a bombing run over Berlin. We were in the last wave and as we approached the target we looked down on a scene of absolute chaos: myriad searchlights, hundreds of small clouds of smoke from shells, the crack of lights from exploding bombs and a carpet of fires below. Aeroplanes were silhouetted by the light of battle, some on bombing runs surrounded by bursting shells, others diving away, some in trouble. The Group Captain had seen nothing like it. "Bill, surely we're not going in there!" he yelled as I steered towards the coloured marker for my bomb run."

Bill paused. He was now sitting forward in his chair with his arms resting on his knees looking down at his cupped hands. At that moment a steward arrived with a tray of drinks. He discreetly placed a glass in front of each of the four men, and cleared the empty glasses before slipping quietly away. Aiden was taken by surprise, but looking up Reg caught his eye and smiled.

"So I held out my hand to my companion," Bill continued, without daring to look up at them. "You see, I knew how terrified he must have been. He took my hand and wouldn't let go as we made our bombing run."

The group of men fell into a velvety silence as Bill finished speaking. Eventually Bill looked up, his arms still resting on his knees and managed a weak smile at them, his jaw still tightly clenched shut.

"But how could you cope with it."

"The daily terror, you mean."

"The main thing was a sense of hope and support," Reg said. "Getting a proper send off was important. The adjutant, the ground crew, lots of Waafs, and perhaps even the padre would all be there to see you off on an op, all huddled round a small caravan at the end of the runway, mugs of tea in one hand and all waving."

"Oh, the Waafs!" Bill exclaimed and laughed; with the soft camaraderie he had now regained his composure. "We were all warriors, especially the pilots, so you were never short of a popsie!"

"And then, of course," Reg said, "we relished debriefing for its sense of cosiness and companionship; it really felt like we'd come home. The padre and the girls were all there to welcome us back with rum and chocolate. We'd sit at a circular table and in the middle there was always a big bowl of raisins and currents and packets of cigarettes, Thames cigarettes, the cheapest you could buy in those days, of course!"

At that moment there was an outburst of raucous laughter from a group of men who were gathered around another of the tables further down the room. Bill smiled broadly at the sound and nodding his head towards the group said, "Oh yes, and then there was roistering, of course! I suppose it got a bit out of hand sometimes, but pranks built comradeship, killed time and were a way of blowing of steam."

Aiden thought there was something ancient and ritualised in the way the older and younger men shared. It was as if the older men had opened wide their arms, unashamed of their scars, their wounds, and, as if for the first time, the novice men with their skimpier acquaintance with danger and pain could openly and honestly delight in their passions and enthusiasms. As their instructors, the older men would carefully weigh up the character of the younger men, asking themselves whether they thought they had learnt enough about their wildness to understand the necessity of balanced risk-taking.

These evenings were magical. It was the old men in the flickering firelight telling you a story that you were in yourself.

## *Chapter Three*

"They're still sopping wet!" Dennis remarked gloomily as he removed his socks from the tepid radiator. He had left them there as long as he could in the vague hope that they might dry off enough for him to wear them this morning. "But there's nothing to be done," he continued, "I'll just have to wear them like it, I suppose."

"No spare pair?" Aiden replied.

"These *are* my spare ones." Dennis frowned and held up the offending pair of socks gingerly between the thumb and forefinger of his right hand as if he were holding something mildly disgusting. "I wanted clean ones last night; but I'm not sure why we bother, really."

"Forget it. You just try too hard, that's all," Aiden replied sympathetically.

As he spoke, Aiden tilted his head so that his chin pointed angularly upwards as he struggled to fasten the top button of his shirt. The shirt was new and as his fingers struggled to push the hard round button through the stiff eyelet, the left corner of his mouth suddenly twisted in the direction of the tilt forcing the fleshy part of his cheek into a thick plicate-shaped fold so that one could guess what his face might look like when it was older and care-worn.

"It'd be nice just to have the chance to try!" Dennis sat down heavily on the edge of his bed and looked intently and disdainfully down at his pair of socks where he held them in his hands.

"I'm sure there'll be others." Aiden wanted to console him, and although he had no more experience in these matters than Dennis to draw upon he nevertheless also wanted to reassure him.

"I hate these socks. I mean, just look at them!"

"And what did I tell you?" Aiden continued, unable to keep a note of quiet jubilation from entering his voice. As Dennis had come off far worse than he, to spare him any embarrassment Aiden was deliberately trying to make light of last night's debacle, but he was also in good humour; after a break of several days they had both been rostered to fly again this morning.

"But you haven't even looked outside yet," Dennis rebuked him mildly.

"I don't need to."

Aiden had awoken earlier than was necessary this morning and although he could not have said what it was exactly, the growing steel-blue light had had a particular quality about it and the air a different feel from yesterday, perhaps a subtle change of barometric pressure, which had sufficiently confirmed to Aiden that the premonition he had experienced last night, that this morning would be clear and fine, had been correct. Aiden had then reached out his hand and pushed down the small black metal lever on the side of the clock which turned off the alarm.

It had been Aiden's clock, but over time it had come to be fraternally considered as being held in common. It was a round, enamelled-metal casing, perched on a tripod of insubstantial looking legs. It had pressed-steel keys and machined knobs projecting from its back plate to wind it and to adjust the time. It was a solid familiar that provided a comforting and homely backdrop to the night. But the alarm was a violent jarring noise that would rip them violently from sleep with their hearts pounding, and fully expecting Dennis to be out of sorts this morning he had therefore thought it kinder to wake him gently.

"Damned if I know how you can tell. But it still feels bloody cold to me. It's only February, after all, and I'm going to catch my death in these things!" Dennis made a grimace as he eased a sodden sock over the hairy toes of his right foot and negotiated it over his heel with some difficulty, adding glumly, "God, that's disgusting."

Once Dennis had been awake, he had not even needed to speak for Aiden to have known that he had been correct. Having pushed back his blanket and silently swung his feet out onto the linoleum-covered floor, preparatory to standing up Dennis had given a feeble, involuntary sigh and placed his hands on his knees, his elbows slightly bent and turned out, disinclined to check the curvature of his posture.

"Come on, breakfast will buck you up." Dennis's moods were naturally more volatic than Aiden's and Aiden therefore felt quite certain that Dennis would soon bounce back to his normal self. "And get a move on for heaven's sake, or we'll be late," Aiden added; he was keen to be flying again. "If we catch it from the CO we won't be allowed anywhere near town for a month!"

"They're not just wet, they're too small." Dennis complained, irritably, now easing the other sock a quarter of an inch at a time over the joint with the great toe on his left foot.

But then, as Dennis pulled on his boots, Aiden asked quietly, "Alright?" The single word, unfurling like a petal, was weighed with concern. Dennis nodded as he finished lacing his boots.

"God, that feels horrible!" Dennis complained as he stood up and started down the corridor after Aiden.

~~~~~

"Porridge! Why is it always porridge?" Dennis complained bitterly. "An egg would be nice."

Aiden and Dennis had sat down at one of the tables in the officers' mess-hall and were now steadily unpacking their metal trays, each of them placing their breakfast items on the table: cutlery, porridge, toast, jam and the ubiquitous tea. Their movements mirrored each other's, like a curious and moving incident in an unfamiliar ballet.

Having finished unpacking his own tray, Dennis reached over the table in their accustomed way to take Aiden's tray from him. Taking it, he placed both it and his own, but with a loud clatter, on the chair beside him. Aiden flinched at the sound and several other people looked around at them. The morning light was now hard and unforgiving so that they could see clearly the flaking paint on the ceiling high above them as if they were seeing it afresh after emerging from a long illness.

"Steady!" Aiden spoke quietly, wary of attracting attention.

"Or bacon." Dennis spoke harshly and loudly as he mechanically stirred his tea. Glancing around, Aiden was relieved to see that the other people who had been disturbed by the sound of the trays had turned their attentions back to their own breakfasts and conversations.

"Find something to take your mind off it." Aiden's voice was insistent, but not much above a whisper. He was certain that the subject would not be considered seemly.

"It's all very well saying it!" Dennis dropped his own voice to little more than a conspiratorial sibilance. "Nobody ever tells you just how much you'll be driven by it, just how much it distracts you! Bugger me, but sometimes I can't seem to think of anything else!" Still stirring his tea, Dennis let out a long involuntary sigh, "Surely, this can't be normal!"

It was a tremendous relief that they could at least articulate their thoughts to each other about this most unpublic subject, however haltingly it had to be done; both of them felt painfully isolated on his own and therefore had no real credible measure of the validity of his own feelings.

"I think," Aiden said, dipping his spoon again into his bowl of porridge, "that we're all in the same boat." He spoke as if articulating an unlikely or unexpected thesis. Looking sharply around in case he could be overheard, he continued, "I don't think we're actually any different from the others."

As each of them usually felt an uncomfortable gap or gulf between themselves and the other men of the squadron, neither Aiden nor Dennis felt particularly comfortable with this notion.

"I'm just saying that I don't think human nature changes very much. And it worms its way through all of us!" Aiden added.

"But nobody really *says* anything about it, do they? Dennis made a grimace at his porridge. "Well, they do, of course, but it's all just bravado, nonsense, nothing else."

It seemed to be that more or less every gathering of airmen provided examples which illustrated the point; often alcohol-fuelled in smoky pubs, but equally on the sports field, in the mess at mealtimes, even kitting-up before a flight, goatish comments echoing around the locker-lined crew room.

"We may not join in much with the bragging, the innuendo, but neither do we really distance ourselves from it, do we? There's a bit of each of us inside us which would like it to be so."

"As I said: its just talk, isn't it?"

"The problem is that you just don't know what people *really* think, do you?" Then, quietly and slowly, as if he were reluctantly admitting to something he thought should be quite shameful, Aiden said, "And another thing. Despite what we say, I'm sure we'd *both* see how far we could get if we actually had the opportunity." Aiden was uncertain yet whether Dennis *had* made a simple mistake with the girl, or had actually taken a calculated action.

"Well perhaps." Dennis spoke as if such an idea was unpalatable. "But doesn't that simply make us hypocrites?"

But Aiden felt relieved at Dennis's answer; talking in this way seemed infused with the gentle comfort of shared sedition. He put his spoon down in his now empty bowl and without looking up at Dennis spoke carefully: "I don't know. The question just doesn't seem enough, if you see what I mean." Aiden thought he needed the sensibilities, or at least the language, of a poet to adequately explain the deep contradictions that he felt. "But even though the urge is so powerful," he continued, "I guess people like you and me are too frightened of disgrace and approbation to say what we really feel inside and so we carry on continuing to pay lip service."

"Perhaps everyone's the same. We'd never know, would we?" Then Dennis's eyes almost imperceptibly darted to the left and to the right before he hissed: "And it's so damn inconvenient, you know, physically. Nobody ever tells you how to deal with it, do they?"

"Not your parents, that's for sure!"

The idea was quite ludicrous to them.

"Mine gave *me* a little book to read, from the church of all places."

Then with a facetious look, Dennis said: "But I do seem to remember a talk once, at scouts, I think it was. We were told that it was best to sleep on our backs and keep our hands out on the sheet in front of us. Didn't know what the silly bugger was talking about; I can only have been about eleven or twelve at the time!"

Aiden smiled at Dennis and although not exactly returning the smile, Dennis met Aiden's eye and his shoulders perceptibly relaxed as if a measure of the tension in his body was finally beginning to dissipate after the upset of the previous evening. With a greater degree of good humour than he had previously been able to muster this morning, Dennis then added as if from nowhere, "And it's freezing in here as well!" Which was really a comment about sharing and for a moment they sat in a companionable silence.

It did seem uncommonly cold this morning. Their own room was never terribly warm when it was cold outside – one could curve one's hands over the top of the radiator and tuck one's fingers down in-between its cast iron verticals and the dull warmth would do no more than barely permeate the joints of one's fingers, or gently warm the palms of ones hands – but the officer's mess was usually reasonably warm.

Dennis eventually broke the silence by saying, "And I thought things had been going pretty well." There was a note of resignation in his voice.

"We managed to talk to some women, which is more than we usually do!"

"Do you think we'll ever understand them?" Dennis's voice was now tinged with melancholy.

"I think the more interesting question is do you think they'll ever understand us?"

"Doesn't that amount to much the same thing?"

"You'd think so, wouldn't you?" Aiden countered. "But we're always so scared and afraid of looking like idiots, and desperate even, that we never stop and ask ourselves that particular question. She didn't understand you – she listened, but that's not the same thing - and I don't really think she could be bothered to try."

Dennis reflected for a moment before saying slowly, "Well, maybe. But I felt *so* humiliated. I thought I must have made some sort of dreadful mistake, that I'd misread the signals." He then added vehemently, "Damn it all, it was one hell of a shock!"

By now, Aiden was convinced that Dennis *had* simply made a mistake.

One of the instructors, passed close behind them carrying a laden breakfast tray. As a reflex action to his proximity, Aiden and Dennis mechanically glanced up at him. Aiden waited for him to have passed and to have gained a seat in the full light of the windows before he said seriously, the events of the previous evening having also been revelatory to *him*, "I wonder if Bill and the other older chaps had to fly off on operations feeling so uptight about it all. After all, some of them weren't much older than we are now!"

Giving a sigh Dennis began toying with his toast and replied, "Having heard him talk, I have the feeling Bill's popsies, as he calls them, wouldn't have left *him* feeling particularly frustrated!"

"But hang on! They were warriors!" The thought had suddenly struck him that implicit in the idea of a warrior was something deliciously antinomian, as if the warrior was not to be bound by the common moral law.

By now there was a general drift of men getting up from the tables and starting to make their ways out of the mess-hall to kit-up for the morning's flying. Aiden looked at his watch. "Time to get going, I suppose."

But sometimes, when Aiden found himself looking at an attractive woman, it seemed as if he were caught up in a deep and powerful current. Her form and her movement an absolute delight to him, so that, involuntarily catching his breath, each glance at her would seem as if it were weighted with all the irenic possibilities of a lifetime. At such times he suffered tremendous, almost overwhelming, temptation to yield to such a woman, to completely surrender, to place himself totally in her hands. But all this seemed remarkably at odds with the appeal of the warrior.

## Chapter Four

Aiden and Dennis had been glad of their greatcoats. In the short time the early evening bus had taken to reach the local town, the wind had turned to the east and the temperature had grown appreciably colder, although the rain, which had been persistently falling all day, had been at last starting to die down. The bus, its green livery appearing a nondescript brown under the dull streetlights, had terminated in the market square. Aiden and Dennis had alighted from the elderly, rather worn-out single-decker and pulled their coats tighter about themselves.

As they crossed the square, the wind worrying at the inky surfaces of the puddles until they looked like spoiled varnish, Aiden turned and saw the bus driver, who was not a young man, climb down wearily from his cab and walk awkwardly and stiffly around the bus to join the conductor inside for a smoke before they started on their next journey. Glancing back again before turning out of the square, Aiden had a final glimpse of the two men sitting comfortably together, exhaling smoke through their nostrils and gently laughing. Aiden felt certain that it was the laughter of familiarity and contentment and he had a sudden impression of the dignity of the two men sitting together in the bubble of amber warmth. Momentarily, he thought longingly of the comfort and familiarity of the officers'-mess and despite valuing such times for their dizygotic intimacy, he wondered whether their persistence in visiting local pubs was truly worthwhile.

There was a brooding, inky darkness behind the plate glass windows of the silent and closed-up shops they passed as they walked. A memory of pressing his cheek up against such a window late one winter's afternoon a number of years ago when he had been a child had stayed with Aiden. He and his mother had been waiting a long time for a bus. He had forgotten now where they had been and what they had been doing. But reprimanded for fidgeting he had sulkily crossed over the pavement and had peered into the window of the shop closest to them.

At first he had been unable to see anything, but as his eyes had become accustomed to the dimness, he had seen that the shop window had actually been packed full of things. It had been bric-a-brac mostly, the detritus of uneventful lives; chipped salad platters, candle sticks, jugs that nobody wanted. But a painting had attracted him and had held his attention. Thrust at an awkward angle behind an ugly dark-green vase so that part of it had been obscured, it had been of a small boat being tossed upon a tempestuous sea. Other than for the boat's gaily painted tiller, the painting had been dark and moody and Aiden had continued starring into its depths until his mother had called him away when their bus had finally arrived.

"We won't be flying if this lot keeps up," Dennis remarked, the paltry light from the street lamps shimmering on the glistening pavements beneath their feet.

"It'll be fine tomorrow. You'll see!" Aiden replied brightly.

But then Dennis looked up in the direction they were walking and suddenly said, a note of acute alarm in his voice, "Oh! It looks like we've got to run the gauntlet again."

Immediately ahead of them the lights of a cinema gave out a feeble glow. It was a flea-pit cinema, the sort of place where the plush on the arms of the seats had been worn smooth and everything had long since been stained a dirty nicotine brown by drifting cigarette smoke.

There were a number of people outside of the picture-house, many of them even younger than Aiden and Dennis, their faces joyful in the insufficient light. Where the sickly yellow light streamed out from the foyer onto the pavement, girls with chemical perms, cheap coats and unartfully applied makeup stood in familiar pairs, threes or fours, giggling coyly behind their hands while boys in cheap suits and spivvy overcoats circled, calling out to them in sparse coarse greetings, catcalls and whistles.

"All right there, flyboys?"

At the sound of the girl's voice, something instantly churned in the pit of Aiden's stomach and left behind it a residual discomfort.

"We should at least have crossed over and walked on the other side of the road," Dennis muttered under his breath.

By now the drops of rain had found their way through Aiden's close-cropped hair and formed tiny rivulets of water which coursed over his prickling scalp and ran down the back of his collar adding to his discomfort.

"Do you fancy taking me and my friend inside?" she taunted them.

Out of the corner of his eye Aiden saw Dennis looking fixedly ahead; he was sure that they both felt equally harrowed and that they had both secretly feared the trauma of having to rebuff, or, the most likely course of action, to simply ignore the comments they knew would inevitably be directed at them as they walked past the cinema.

"What's the matter, not good enough for you?" Her voice sounded raucous, primordial and canny. She was plain and her skin had an etiolated pallor but if she was attractive in any way, the fact simply did not register with them; it was as if she was of another species. "Don't you want to *come* with me?"

The innuendo was lost on Aiden, but not on her cohorts who were instinctively alive to her actions and who, following them closely with their feral eyes, seemed to collectively snigger, or leer, at Aiden's and Dennis's discomfort, the girl apparently gaining kudos or prestige for such contumelious daring. This was tribal, but to Aiden and Dennis, it was something verging on the preternatural; even as they had approached the cinema she had seemed to have had some sort of sixth sense that Aiden and Dennis were of a different mould from her.

She then said, "In the dark we'd be that cosy inside that big coat of yours." Adding, knowingly, as if in some sort of appeal to her friend, who stood next to her, "There's plenty that would, isn't that right?"

Half a head shorter than the girl, vaguely twisting her body as if she had been trying to pivot around on one leg only to be prevented from doing so by the traction of her feet against the pavement, the friend remained silent, an expressionless stare on her half-vacant face. The question was really an affirmation of a truth that was self-evident to the girl's peer group.

Paradoxically, the cinema was a place Aiden and Dennis imagined they would happily go to with girlfriends, and that they could even safely write home about going there. But, frightened, as if panicked in another country, they dismissed even the idea of initiating a meeting with the sort of girls they saw outside the cinema here; it appeared to them as if they inhabited an abhorrent, treacherous world of tricks and half-meant words. And even meeting girls somewhere where public-ness and noise offered insurance against the embarrassment of being rebuffed, such as a dance hall or palais, their lack of knowledge of the etiquette of striking-up acquaintance, their inexperience of achieving a temporary balance of words of flighty meanings, would still have been terrifying to them; although the need to try remained a desperate animal craving that grew until it seemed to possess them both physically and mentally demanding to be sated.

Aiden and Dennis walked on, letting themselves look neither to the left nor to the right. Once beyond the cinema, Aiden suddenly became aware of his deportment – how he was walking in a stiff and exaggeratedly erect manner - and of his breathing, of how shallow it had become, and of how refreshing the sharp air passing over his tongue and teeth now felt, especially the molars and premolars towards the back of his mouth.

Just inside the door of the public house, thick beige curtains made up three sides of a small square, the fourth being made by the door itself. The construction was intended to keep what little warmth there was in and to keep draughts out. The curtains billowed voluminously as they entered, letting in a swirl of cold damp air. Shutting the door behind them, Aiden and Dennis squeezed into the tiny space enclosed by the curtains and absent-mindedly wiped their feet on the grubby mat. Dennis, knowing the right knack from experience, tugged the curtain in front of him to one side and the curtains parted reluctantly, the curtain rings grinding along the pole with a sound like a worn-out machine part.

The saloon bar was shabby but familiar. The carpet on the floor was worn threadbare in places with black shiny patches at those points where it carried the heaviest traffic - immediately in front of the bar and near the door - and an inadequate fire burnt in the hearth. But having both been brought up in a class who did not drink, at least not publicly, the privacy the saloon bar offered over the public intuitively appealed to Aiden and Dennis; there was never any question of forfeiting this privacy by drinking in the public bar to save the extra penny or so they paid on each pint in the saloon.

Tilting his head back and raising his eyebrows a fraction, the corpulent landlord silently requested their order.

"Two pints, please."

"How on earth do they know?" Dennis complained, still agitated from their encounter with the girl outside of the cinema. For a while they could not shake off the sensation of having been unsettled and it would not have surprised them if the girl and her friends had theatrically appeared through the door having followed them all the way to the pub merely to ridicule them again.

"Thanks." Dennis picked up his glass, and slipped his change into his pocket without bothering to count it.

The landlord turned back to a conversation he had evidently been having with a crony at the end of the bar and which he had interrupted in order to serve Aiden and Dennis. The man, the only person at the bar other than Aiden and Dennis, sat on a bar stool nursing a glass of scotch, a small black water jug with the legend Black and White reproduced on the side of it had been placed conveniently on the bar almost in front of him. Positioned to the right of his hand was a large ashtray into which he deposited the ash from the end of his cigarette with a slow deliberate rolling movement. The newspaper, open at the racing pages, had been spread out between the two men.

To cover his lingering embarrassment Dennis asked the rhetorical question, vaguely indicating the mostly empty tables and chairs in the body of the room, "Do you want to stay here, or shall we sit?"

There were few other customers. Other than the man sat at the end of the bar talking to the landlord, the only other people were a seemingly impenetrable knot of young men and women who talked in low familiar voices and who occupied the two tables closest to the fire, but most of them remained huddled in their coats.

"I'd prefer to stay here. But if it's any consolation, I expect she's completely forgotten us by now."

Not even bothering to loosen their greatcoats, they remained standing where they habitually stood.

"But only after a jolly good laugh at our expense, I expect!"

Despite what he had just said, Aiden had a lingering, irrational sense that the attack had been strangely and savagely personal.

"My parents should have warned me about girls like that." Dennis continued, attempting to lighten the atmosphere.

"I expect they probably did," Aiden replied, with a weak smile.

"They can't all be like that, can they? Take them, for example," Dennis said quietly, gently inclining his head towards the group by the fire. "You simply can't imagine that they'd carry on like that."

Aiden had already noted that the group was mixed – something he still found quite novel when compared to the pubs at home; he considered pubs more properly the preserve of men - and he had also noted that they all seemed remarkably comfortable together. He could imagine that they had probably all known each other for years having grown up here together in the town, and consequently had lives that were interwoven with threads of commonality and history. From the way they dressed, talked and carried themselves Aiden felt quite certain that they were from the same sort of background as he and Dennis were from.

"Oh well." This quiet interjection from Dennis was not meaningless, but was a part of the etiquette of personal conversation between them, and as such indicated that Dennis thought the subject closed or exhausted for the time being.

But Aiden wanted to continue with it. "Don't forget we're outsiders here and soon we'll move on to new squadrons!" He spoke quietly so that Dennis alone would hear. At that moment the murmur of the contemperous conversation at the tables was enlivened by a burst of relaxed laughter. "So we'd hardly be good prospects from their point of view, would we?"

Although privately questioning of the universality of the moral laws that seemingly bound Dennis and he, it would never have occurred to him to impugn the purity or intentions of the type of girls they were now talking about.

"Oh well." Dennis said, taking a mouthful of beer.

The group at the tables continued talking and the landlord and his crony continued their conversation. The landlord stood in front of the shelves which contained bottled brown and light ales and was slowly and mechanically wiping a pint glass with a grubby tea towel, his manner suggesting that he were pondering some sort of intractable problem. After a moment, Aiden and Dennis overheard the words "by a length or more, by all accounts" following which the landlord said quietly "put me down for five bob then" and the man duly licked a dirty stub of pencil and surreptitiously wrote something in a small, dog-eared notebook as the landlord inverted the glass he was holding and reached up to re-home it on the shelf, just above head height, above the bar, his expression now once again as inscrutable as it usually was.

"Did I tell you I joined the ATC on my sixteenth birthday?" Aiden said, offering something personal to draw them closer together following the earlier upset; it felt as if they had been viciously mocked. At the end of the bar, the man slipped his notebook back inside his pocket.

"No, but you told me you'd signed-up on your eighteenth. It all sounds rather too keen to me!" Dennis smiled back at Aiden uncritically, indulgently and then, at last undoing his greatcoat, turned back to face the bar, adopting their more usual, relaxed, drinking position. Aiden also turned around to face the bar, mirroring Dennis's movements.

But apropos of nothing, Dennis said bitterly, "I suppose a lot of people must really hate Christmas." Aiden had previously noted how Dennis would revert to the subject of Christmas, especially when feeling dejected or doleful. "Christmas was pretty beastly, really."

Dennis lapsed into silence. From the other end of the bar, they heard the Landlord quietly ask "One for the road?" and the stock comic reply of "I don't mind if I do".

Aiden remembered parting from Dennis on Charring Cross Station on Christmas Eve, each to catch his own train back to his own parental home. They had waved to each other cheerfully as they had been carried along on the tipsy afternoon crowd, office workers for the most part revelling in their rare early release, but Aiden now wondered if he had been guilty of not having seen some awful dread or sorrow in Dennis's eyes.

Sounding full of anger, Dennis continued, "You'd think by now they could move on, wouldn't you? After all, lots of people have lost someone!" And Aiden had the impression that Dennis had momentarily forgotten that he too had lost someone.

The man at the end of the bar mixed a little water from the black jug into the shot of amber liquid in his glass, the liquid briefly taking-on an opaque tincture as the water mixed with the spirit with a tumbling or rolling motion. Away from the bar, the level of noise from the group sitting near the fire suddenly increased as a number of empty glasses were pushed across the tables and members of the group began to hunt through pockets or handbags and all seemed to be saying something at once.

"Gosh, she's quite an eyeful!" Dennis said appreciatively; the increased level of activity had drawn his attention to the group once again.

Aiden said, sharply, "But you simply can't imagine what it must be like for them to lose a son, it must be the worst thing of all!"

He felt embarrassed the instant the words left his lips. It was a trite cliché but he did not know if his own experiences of grief were transferable and reacting to Dennis without thinking through what he was saying, it was as if he had been eager to say something which reduced Dennis's experiences to something nugatory or at least less consequential than Dennis clearly felt them to be.

The girl who had caught Dennis's attention snapped her handbag shut. Then holding a ten-shilling note that she had taken from her purse, she leant across the table the better to hear something someone else in the group was saying to her.

"No, I guess not," Dennis replied absent-mindedly, distracted. Dennis was frequently drawn irresistibly by the appearance of a woman he had merely glimpsed, casually abandoning the track of their conversation in the process.

Dennis, completely captivated with her, watched as she and another girl from the group got up from the table. One of the girls pushed her chair back with the calves of her legs as she stood up, the chair scraping on the threadbare carpet, while the other girl, with greater meticulousness, half turned and moved her chair, lifting it by the chair-back to create sufficient space for her to squeeze out. Each of the girls then removed and folded their coats and placed them with deliberate care, one on top of the other, on one of the chairs.

Thick in conversation and carrying nothing but their purses, the two girls walked jauntily and mesmerically in step together across the void between the tables and the bar. Aiden and Dennis both fell silent, watching them approach with a kind of fatal fascination.

As they walked, the two girls seemed intent solely upon each other, their heads angled closely together as if the better for the exchange of confidences, and one of them brought her right hand up to her face, her thumb and first two fingers hovering over her lips, as if she were whispering some morsel of delightful gossip to the other. Both Aiden and Dennis surreptitiously admired the comeliness of the girls' figures, and Aiden noted that one of the girls wore her cardigan open despite the chilly ambient temperature.

The two girls arrived at the bar close to where Aiden and Dennis were standing, and then, without any undue hurry, one of them pointedly leant over the bar the better to attract the landlord's attention. Her skirt, which was of a rich, densely textured material and, unusually, looked brand new, clung to the smooth, perfectly rounded contour of her backside as she stretched herself forward.

The sight awoke an intractable consuming lust in Aiden such that he felt physically unable to avert his eyes from her. He had appreciated the form of women before, of course, but this moment was a real shock and a revelation; it was deliciously subversive. It felt as if he were experiencing a physical hunger. In an instant, he was lost to the astonishing appeal of the taste, feeling, perfume and unctuousness of flesh. It was not *she* necessarily that so thoroughly transfixed him, but the limitless power, depth and unexpectedness of the emotion.

Having given their order, the girls continued their conversation apparently completely indifferent to Aiden and Dennis, who, ensorcelled by the girls' physical beings, furtively watched them, feeling secretly petrified in case they should be caught-out looking. While they waited, the girl who had leant across the bar retained a provocative pose leaning her elbows on the bar with her hands cupped under her chin while the other girl absent-mindedly held her ten shilling note in her loosely clenched fist, her thumb bending the brown note over her index finger as she talked.

Running true to form, the landlord remained taciturn as he served their drinks, placing each one on the bar in front of the girls as it was poured. There were more glasses than the two girls could comfortably manage between them. So, the landlord having turned his back towards his customers and stepped up to the cash till with the ten shilling note in his plump hand, each of the two girls dexterously encircled a number of glasses between the outstretched thumbs and forefingers of her own hands. Picking the glasses up in this way, they managed to carry all the drinks but their own back to the tables.

"Should have asked for a tray," Dennis muttered to Aiden as they watched the girls carry the drinks, set them down and then start back towards the bar again.

Arriving back, the landlord dropped a few coins into the hand of one of the girls and then turned back towards his sentry-go at the end of the bar. Instead of starting back to their group of friends with their own drinks, the girls unexpectedly pulled up two barstools and proceeded to sit on them less than square-on to the bar, as if forming a quarter circle in front of it, so that they were more or less facing Aiden and Dennis. As the girl with the gorgeously rich skirt slowly eased herself onto the barstool her skirt rode up and Aiden's eyes instantly and involuntarily flickered towards the few inches of stockinged leg that had been revealed above the girl's knee. There was a firm luxuriousness and a raging voluptuousness about the shape of her thighs that caught away Aiden's breath and that made him giddy for carnality. He was certain that his darting look had been noticed, but her face showed no hint of a reprimand.

"I suppose there's no prize for guessing where you two come from." The girl spoke matter-of-factly but Aiden thought he detected the slightest of smiles playing about the corners of her mouth, but whether this had been through a sense of her own facetiousness or pleasure at Aiden's perceived interest in her, he could not be certain. "Do you boys fly, then?"

Aiden – heat rising up his neck, face and ears so that he seemed unnaturally hot and unusually conscious of the glands in his neck - felt that the shock of being addressed directly by such an unattainably attractive girl was rather like if someone had jerked backwards on a hook attached to his intestines. But before Aiden could find his own tongue, Dennis, sounding hoarse and awkward, said:

"Yes, we're on Lancasters but we caught the bus in this evening."

Dennis coloured as he uttered the words, but the girl continued speaking with perfect equanimity, as if he had made her a perfectly measured reply, "We've seen you in here before, but since you've never spoken to us, we thought we'd come over and speak to you!"

Dennis gave a nervous cough and said awkwardly as if he thought it necessary to redeem himself in the girls' eyes following the lameness of his reply, "Our squadron's an operational conversion unit, you know."

"So, what exactly is an operational conversion unit?" She measured-out her words slowly, as if she were carefully weighing out individual sweets to make up a valuable ration, adding, "And what is it that you convert?"

As if with practised ease, the girls listened attentively, their drinks untouched in front of them, as Dennis self-consciously embarked upon an explanation.

It was as if Dennis had been pixilated by the dizziness of promised carnality, and it dawned on Aiden that the girls had practised this conversation before; he was both jaggedly exhilarated and deeply shocked at where such conversation may lead. Looking back to the table from which the girls had come, he was surprised to see that the rest of the group had long since turned back to their own conversations and seemed quite oblivious to the activities of the two girls.

"So you're both pilots!"

There was an unmistakable timbre of excitement in her voice, as if the discovery genuinely impressed her. For Dennis had, haltingly at first, but then with gathering enthusiasm, begun to explain what they did. The girl who had spoken, evidently the more forward of the two, now sat more upright on her barstool, shifting her position as she sat, so that she shuffled forward slightly on her buttocks, her head remaining stationary as her attention fixed on Dennis. The movement, coupled with her erect posture, necessarily twisted her hips and torso backwards and forwards an eighth of a turn once or twice, and therefore in so doing emphasised the prominence of her breasts.

And as Dennis continued to speak, it was as if all his inhibitions and tongue-tiredness left him. He spoke eloquently, loquaciously, about the wonder of flying. He spoke about the awesome power of a heavy bomber, of the sights, sounds and smells of the Merlin engines firing into life: the smell of cordite from a cartridge start; the cloud of blue-grey smoke discharged from the exhausts like a wild escaping animal; the deep, sinewy, puissant sound of the harmonised engines. He spoke of the almost mystical communion, or conjunction, between a pilot and his machine. And as he continued to speak he became delightfully alive and animated. Without a hint of his more usual self-consciousness, his hands became an adjunction to his speech, not to simply illustrate his effusion, but as a natural extension of it; his whole body seemed to dance with vivacity and his eyes sparkled with rare crystal clarity like sunshine over seaside water. The girls encouraged him through their attentiveness, every so often adding words or simple interjections of surprise and wonder. And as they made slight and subtle changes to their posture, which provided a focus for his attention, he spoke of the necessity of taking measured risks and of soaring for perfection in the company of other men. Glancing up, Aiden noticed the landlord and his crony say something to each other and nod in their direction.

Then without warning, Dennis placed his hand upon her knee.

Two of his fingers slid slightly under the hem of her skirt. She tensed and there was a deep, mordacious silence lasting no more than a split second before her hand stung across his cheek very hard indeed.

## Chapter Five

Having kitted-up, Aiden and Dennis were walking to where their aircraft would be waiting for them. Flying generally cleansed their minds of distractions and made them feel noble again after a disappointment, as if they could imagine they were in service to a purpose greater than themselves, but this morning Dennis remained out of sorts.

The giant doors of the hangars stood open. The runnels between the concrete floors of the hangars and the concrete apron outside, in which ran the metal rails for the doors to slide open and closed on, were unevenly watermarked and discoloured a red-oxide brown colour. Aiden and Dennis, walking in the bright sunlight, casually glanced in at the vast empty spaces as they passed. The insides appeared curiously dark, hollow and hushed; since first light the ground crews had been making the Lancasters ready. The hangars were arranged alongside a wide curving taxiway each end of which connected with a straight, broad concrete apron. This apron ran parallel to the main runway and as they walked they could see the Lancasters lined-up on it ahead of them side-by-side, wing-tip to wing-tip.

This morning there was a hint of menace about the Lancasters; against the fulgent blue sky they appeared hunched and smiteful like outspread god-hands and against the unusually bright winter sunshine their brooding silence contrasted strangely with the industry of the aircraftmen who busied themselves on and around them.

"I think we need a new place to drink after last night's debacle," Dennis mused as they crossed over the taxiway, and adding before falling silent, "perhaps Lincoln would prove more sinful."

In marked contrast to last night it was now extremely cold, the air bone dry and everything seemed brilliantly crystal clear. A sharp frost, hoary and unmelted in the bright sun, covered every horizontal and sloping surface exposed to the deep clarion sky: the roads and pathways, the grassy mounds banked against the wartime shelters, the roofs of buildings. Here and there on the wide expanse of dazzlingly bright concrete, puddles, the only evidence remaining of yesterday's persistent rain, had frozen black and hard. In places, boot-shod feet had attempted to dent and smash the icy surfaces, but had made little impression leaving only marginal scores and scratches and the occasional scattering of tiny fragments of ice, rough and irregular like pummelled and pulverised quartz.

Breaths streaming, Aiden and Dennis resumed their conversation.

"At least you had your face slapped by an attractive girl!" Aiden said; so far this morning they had focused almost exclusively on Dennis's feelings following the violent end to the conversation with the girls.

"I'm not sure that's any consolation." Dennis's gaze remained on his feet as he continued speaking, "I can actually feel my feet squelching in these socks as I walk; it's really quite horrible."

"Actually, I think she was dangerous." Aiden said with conviction, as if he were savouring the idea of her.

"Not our finest hour. I suspect I won't be writing to tell mother."

Letters between them and their mothers were economical and had a peculiar quality of innocence, each of them instinctively understanding that their mothers would have preferred to keep their sons close to their pillows. Each could imagine his mother saying things like "Oh, he's found himself a young lady, *how* exciting!" but in such a way that somehow seemed to imply that this had been an inevitable yet curiously asexual event, which denigrated their sons' efforts and yet was somehow something that they could in some peculiar matriarchal way, if not share the credit for, enjoy the glory of.

"I don't really understand what they wanted from us." Aiden admitted.

"That sounds like the understatement of the year!"

"But they didn't really want to *hear* what you said. But perhaps," he said in a more contemplative fashion, "that's because you described a place where no woman counted, a world where men are happy just being themselves, a monosexual world." Then he added, hoping that Dennis would understand what he meant by it, at some level understanding that the vocabulary of admiration, of deep friendship, has been hijacked by lovers and is frequently used superficially, "Actually, I loved seeing you so incredibly jubilant about it."

They walked on in silence for a while before Aiden finally took a deep breath and said, "Last night, when you spoke about your family, I didn't intend to trivialise what you said."

It had been on his mind and he had been looking for an opportunity to broach the subject since breakfast; it would be intolerable if anything remained unsaid between them and he was running out of opportunities as each step they took brought them closer to the point where they would separate and each would go to his own aircraft. Dennis seemed to be contemplating what Aiden had said but made no reply, so Aiden continued, "I *do* understand how difficult Christmas must be." Then, prompted by his own awkwardness, he added, "It's difficult for all of us." but instantly wished he had given Dennis the opportunity to make that particular reply to him.

By now they had crossed over the taxiway and reached the broad expanse of grass which they had to cross to reach their aircraft. The Lancasters were straight ahead of them, no more than about two hundred yards away. It was as if the hangars and the curving taxiway formed protecting arms about them. Their boots crunched on the chalky whiskers of grass.

Dennis stopped quite suddenly and turning to Aiden said sadly, "It's the commonplace things, isn't it. It's paradoxical, but it seems as if the commonplace can only ever be private. You can't really share such things, can you, despite them being so very important?"

Aiden felt a soft wave of relief pass over him. What Dennis had said inferred beliefs held in common, as if such beliefs had previously and always would predicate the commerce of conversation between their selves. Aiden felt himself vindicated for bringing up Christmas

– there seemed to be no territory that Dennis was not prepared to share with him - and began to feel easy once more as they resumed walking side-by-side.

A short way ahead of them they could see members of the flight crews milling about the aircraft. Some were noisily disembarking from a lorry in which they had cajoled a lift. Others carried small battered-looking leather cases containing maps, meteorological charts, flight plans and their navigational instruments. Generally, the men gravitated into small groups based upon crew membership, laughing, chatting and smoking, each man bulky in his flying suit and his bright inflatable life-jacket.

Aiden still needed to validate the feelings *he* had experienced last night. The lust he had felt for the girl in the pub had been epiphanic and he needed Dennis to not only appreciate the thrill and exhilaration it had caused him, but how it had made him feel a tremendous zest for life and, most surprisingly, and disconcertingly, how he had felt no shame at any of those feelings. But already, at their approach, the knots of aircrew were breaking open to receive them and Aiden realised there was now insufficient time to broach the subject. But feeling certain that there was no gulf between Dennis and he, it no longer seemed imperative to continue talking about it at this moment.

Reaching the point where they would separate, Dennis also seemed to feel the need to follow-through his own train of thought with Aiden alone. Glancing quickly in the direction of the Lancasters, once more he stopped and turned so that they were almost facing each other and said bitterly, "Why is it only women's tears? Why do we always assume it's *our* emotions and feelings which are at fault?" He sounded brittle, as if he would smash into a thousand pieces. He gave a great heaving sigh before continuing, "My father says things like "your mother misses your brother" as if his own feelings aren't legitimate."

Aiden did not know what to say in reply. But this sense of inadequacy could not overwhelm his sense of being greatly privileged at sharing this degree of intimacy. It felt quite unique amongst men. Then, as if he had suddenly gained a shocking new insight he said compassionately, "That's why you joined-up, isn't it?"

Dennis gently nodded his head in agreement, "All those terrible, ruthless, commonplace things."

Dennis sighed and his shoulders finally relaxed as if his words had in themselves been cathartic, purging him of hurt. For a moment the two friends looked tenderly at each other, holding each other in kind communion. Then Aiden reached out his hand and gently, gingerly even, placed the palm of his hand on the outside of Dennis's upper arm, just below his shoulder, curving his fingers around the thickness of his limb sensing the warm, feeling body of his friend through his thick flying jacket. Raising his other arm, he would have drawn Dennis towards him and embraced him but, self-consciously, awkwardly, he refrained from doing so and dropped his arm back down again. To even the most observant on-looker, the gesture must have appeared as merely amiable and commonplace. Dennis smiled softly at Aiden before they parted in warm silence to join their respective crews and aircraft.

~~~~

It was as if the exceptionally cold weather had got into everything. Their rooms had felt cold when they had woken, at breakfast-time the mess-hall had seemed unusually cold, and the frost had even penetrated the cockpits of their Lancasters, the very centres of their working days. The meticulously gradated instruments on the panels around them that measured the pulse and life-fluids of the airplane were doltish with a thin film of ice, the control column sported a delicate tracery of white lace and the seats in their flight stations were cold and hard, chilling their lumbar regions as they tried to settle to their work. The cold air tingled in their nostrils and the aircraft had a cold, other-worldly feel about it as Aiden and his crew, their movements restricted in their cumbersome flying-suits, set about making their aircraft ready for the morning's flying.

They were still far from completing their list of checks when the engines of one of the other Lancasters in the line fired into life cracking open the morning silence with a waspish crackle from the fire-spitting exhausts as the fuel in the cylinders of the cold engine blocks caught on the spark.

Aiden looked up, mechanically placing his index finger on his clipboard at the point he had reached on the checklist even though he knew the routine by heart. The aircraft of the squadron all looked virtually identical, but from his vantage point he could see from the large identification letters painted on either side of the blue, white and red national roundel on the side of the fuselage that it was Dennis's aircraft. The flight engineer sitting on his fold-up seat beside Aiden casually remarked "They're quick" without even looking up, as he wiped a film of ice off an oil pressure gauge with his gloved hand; after a few weeks of circuits-and-bumps, cross country navigation flights, low level and emergency flying procedures they all felt like old hands at the game.

Aiden resumed his work, but in-between marking off each completed instrument check on the chart that he was balancing on his knee in order to leave his left hand free, he periodically glanced out of his cockpit and along the line of aircraft. Dennis's aircraft, the only one to have started-up so far, was already edging forward out of the line, guided by an aircraftman who was waving a pair of batons backwards and forwards rhythmically but unenthusiastically. When it had moved forward a sufficient distance to provide for a broad turning circle so that its great wings would not collide with other aircraft, it began to turn to starboard and inch its way along in front of the line towards a holding point where the concrete apron curved round to meet the head of the runway.

Aiden now started-up the engines of his own aircraft. One-by-one they rasped into life. As each one fired-up it added another layer of harsh noise to the cacophonous din which now made unaided speech quite impossible for the moment and drowned out the sound of Dennis's aircraft which had now reached its holding position. Presently, Aiden synchronised the engines and the decibel level on the flight-deck dropped to a loud but bearable level and Aiden returned to the pre-flight checks; the engines required a few minutes to reach their operating temperature.

Suddenly, a green Verey light, fired from somewhere near the control tower, described a broad arc in the bright morning sky in front of them. The light burnt with the intensity and brightness of flaming magnesium as it drifted back down to earth. On the signal, Dennis's aircraft began its take off run along the runway.

As they watched, the Lancaster built up momentum, the engines roaring, the throttles fully open. Like a winding through his soul Aiden knew the intimacy and excitement of being on the flight deck at that moment. He knew exactly how the airframe would vibrate and creak with the tense, singing pitch of the engines. He knew the mingling, heady, smells of leather and hydraulic fluid. He knew the intoxicating adrenalin rush as the huge aircraft sped faster and faster along the runway approaching and then passing the point of no return. Above all, he knew the sense of joyously reciprocated dependency as the pilot and his flight engineer, their hands overlaid, touching, on the throttle levers between them, felt the vibrant life pulsing through the aircraft.

The aircraft continued to pick up speed. From their own flight deck Aiden and his crew could sense rather than hear the build up of power as the aircraft grew faster and faster as it raced down the runway. When the aircraft was almost level with them, the tail wheel left the runway, but the main wheels of the undercarriage stayed resolutely on the ground. The elevators on the tailplane flapped ineffectually until without warning the main undercarriage legs beneath the inner engines finally buckled and splayed out. Instantly, the leading edges of the wings slammed hard into the runway, the propellers buckling into the concrete, with great trails of sparks spreading out behind the broken wings as the engine nacelles scraped along the ground. Fractionally later the fuselage fractured in front of the main spar and the nose section crumpled sickeningly into the concrete.

Aiden and his crew watched in abject horror, each one of them isolated in their own bubbles of existence, cut off from the feelings of the other men by the spongy noise of their own aircraft's engines that surrounded them. There was a split second of paralysis during which the aircraft ground to a halt rotating slightly from its original compass so that the nose and wings pointed at a diagonal to the direction of the runway, then an enormous searing flash as the plane was engulfed by fire. Dennis's aircraft had not been carrying much fuel, but it was enough; on the impact fuel had been thrown forward over the hot engine nacelles. A deep yellow ball of fire tinged with intense oranges, berry reds and black puffed slowly and majestically into the air over the broken aeroplane, the intensity of the fire shattering every panel of the cockpit canopy.

The aircraft was totally engulfed in flames long before the fire engines and the unnecessary ambulances, ringing their feeble bells, were bumping even half way across the airfield. On the flight deck of Aiden's aircraft there was shocked silence until someone simply said, "Fuck". And as he looked he knew his friend was being consumed by fire, reduced to charred flesh and bubbling fat.

## Chapter Six

It was an ordinary semi-detached suburban house a short bus ride away from his own home. With the exception of the house next door and this one, the road it was set in appeared to have been largely untouched by the war, although most of the houses looked careworn due to the continuing difficulty in obtaining maintenance materials. The next-door house had been rebuilt and Dennis's house showed evidence of considerable repair following the wartime blast, especially the windows and a broad spread of new roof tiles.

Aiden stood in the porch-space on the front step. There was a small net-curtained side window beside the front door and two silver-topped milk bottles stood a little to one side of the threshold. The ceiling of the porch-space was formed by the over-thrust of the smallest bedroom and the brick-built side protected callers from the worst excesses of the weather and drew them into the house. The garden was well-tended with bright spring narcissi in the flowerbeds beside the garden path and brilliant forsythia below the front window.

Aiden knocked on the door. Naturally, he had written that he was coming, but the house seemed singularly hushed. Presently, Aiden thought he caught a glimpse of movement through the side window, as if someone had quickly peeked through the net curtain, trying not to disturb it as they did so.

"You must be Aiden." The door was opened by a remarkably shapeless looking woman. "It's *so* good of you to come."

Aiden was taken aback; he had not expected her to speak quite so brightly. "Mrs Goodman?" he replied, holding out his hand to her. Dennis's mother stood several inches shorter than Aiden. She had unexpectedly deep rich auburn hair held firmly in control by a recently applied permanent wave.

"Oh. Oh yes!" she said sparkishly, as if she had been taken by surprise by Aiden offering out his hand to her. Dennis's father, an amiable-looking man, hovered hesitantly in the background. Glancing down as she invited Aiden to come inside, she seemed mildly surprised to see the milk bottles on the step and suddenly stooped to pick them up. Then, having stepped back inside the hallway, murmured vacantly "I'm so sorry" as she quickly put them down again just inside the front door so that her hands should be free to take his coat from him.

She fussily ushered Aiden into the front room, insisting he take the armchair closest to the fire. Dennis's father silently followed Aiden into the room while Dennis's mother bustled off down the hallway towards the kitchen, cradling the milk bottles in her arms. Mr Goodman took the other armchair which was squeezed into the corner of the room on the other side of the hearth.

The front room was plainly kept for best. A coal fire hissed comfortably in the grate but looked as if it had only recently been lit and even though the weather outside was quite mild there was a distinct chill to the air in the room. A standard lamp stood in the corner and a large radio-gramophone, the lid of its polished walnut cabinet shut down flat, took a central and prominent position in the middle of the wall opposite the window. A half-empty coal-scuttle stood on one side of the hearth, a set of fire-irons on the other, and everywhere was clean and immaculately dusted.

There was a framed photograph on either side of the clock on the biscuit-coloured mantelpiece; each one was of a boy in uniform. Aiden instantly recognised the portrait of Dennis, proud in his new officer's uniform, whilst the other was a snapshot of a figure dressed in the fatigues of an army private who was standing between Dennis's mother and father. Judging by the background of a pebble-dashed wall and what looked like a kitchen window, Aiden thought the snap had probably been taken in their own back garden, and most likely by Dennis. All three figures were smiling for the camera.

After a few moments Dennis's mother returned to the front room, profusely apologising as she did so.

"Cup of tea?" she said chirpily, "or perhaps you'd prefer a glass of sherry, or something stronger?" She then added in a playful, teasing manner which seemed painfully inappropriate to Aiden, "I know what you boys are like!"

"Tea would be fine, thank you, Mrs Goodman."

Aiden imagined that if there were indeed 'anything stronger' in the house it would probably have been left over from the funeral; he sensed that Dennis's parents were the kind of people who would ordinarily have drank nothing more than perhaps a glass of sherry or ginger wine at Christmas and perhaps on other special occasions. But quite apart from being sensitive to their feelings, Aiden had no inclination to drink this early in the day – it would have felt too much like *drinking* - and he felt that to do so would have been in some way, which he could not properly formulate to himself, disloyal to the memory of his friend.

"Lovely! Right, I'll be back in a jiffy!" So saying, Dennis's mother backed out of the room leaving Aiden and Dennis's father sitting together awkwardly.

After a moment, Dennis's father broke the silence. "It's completely broken his mother up, of course." He spoke thickly, as if the effort was difficult for him.

Aiden did not know what answer he could possibly make but instinctively feeling a reply was expected, contented himself with the neutral, "I would have come before, Mr Goodman, but I'm afraid I couldn't get leave."

Even on the bus journey this morning Aiden had still had no clear idea of what he wanted to say to Dennis's parents and he was not even totally certain why he was making the visit, although a deep conviction remained inside of him that it was the right thing to do.

"We've lost both of our sons now, I suppose you knew?"

"Dennis told me that he had lost his brother," replied Aiden, and then added gently, "in the war."

"It was a silly accident, really." Aiden was startled to recognise the same words as Dennis had used when he and Dennis had first met, but the tone of Dennis's father's voice was much more pained, stretched and thinner. "Such a waste!" Mr Goodman fell silent again.

Feeling he was inadequately equipped for the conversation, Aiden could do no more than punctuate the silence with a perfunctory, "Indeed."

Other than with Dennis, the emotional had been never more than merely latent in conversations between Aiden and members of his own sex. He deeply wanted to contribute more to this conversation than mere platitude or superficial sympathy and had assumed that by drawing on his own memories, feelings and emotions in some way he would be able to do so. But he now found that in actuality this was no trivial task; it was as if each man had feelings of undeniably solemn magnitude but Aiden was floundering in his attempt to find any words with which he could connect them together.

"You never expect to bury a son, let alone two." Mr Goodman was staring into the depths of the glowing fire, as if something elemental could give him comfort or meaning. Speaking quietly and deliberately, he continued, "It's the most desolate thing in the world. You fear these things, not just as something you know is always a possibility, like something you can coldly calculate the odds on happening, but as something deep and trembling inside your soul. Nothing can prepare you for the reality of it. It really feels like the end of everything."

Weighing-up his thoughts against those of Dennis's father, his own seemed puny, insignificant. But perhaps, he supposed, one reason why he was here, focused on the comforting fire in the grate, was to try and find some meaning or sense in Dennis's death. Aiden cast about for something to say, and for a moment nothing he could think of seemed sufficiently grown-up, but then he plumped for saying, "Dennis probably told you, most of our instructors flew Lancasters in the war. And one of the things which seemed to keep them going in all the death and destruction was the camaraderie. Only," Aiden added haltingly, "it seems to me that the word doesn't really adequately describe what they felt. And I think Dennis thought he had found something rather like it."

Dennis's father did not reply, but remained staring into the fire. Afraid of trespassing on his emotional pain but at the same time feeling uncomfortable with the silence and thinking he should not be trying to simply explain away Dennis's death as if he were tying it up into a neat package, Aiden added, "But back then, I suppose, there was a purpose."

Aiden was not certain whether he had earned the right to speak in this way. But Dennis's father looked up from the fire and with a fleeting half-smile at Aiden said without any trace of bitterness or resentment, "In war you expect to bury valiant heroes. Being knocked down by a bus in Piccadilly doesn't make you a hero."

Protectively, Aiden's mother had tried to dissuade him from calling on Dennis's parents. She had said that as their squadron leader had already formally visited there was no need to call to offer condolences. Then in a final attempt to appeal to his sensibilities, she had further said that as the funeral had been and gone it might upset them more by visiting. But, as uncomfortable as visiting was proving to be Aiden was immensely glad that he had come. Dennis's death had struck Aiden violently, shocking him with the deep realisation that he was not indestructible and that active participation in the sadnesses of life therefore seemed as desirable and necessary as relishing in the joyous events.

Dennis's father continued speaking but in a way that suggested he and Aiden could have been fully equals: "I remember thinking when the boys were small, how easy it would be... and it would only take a slip or a moment of madness, but that's the other side of responsibility and love." He paused for a moment then visibly steeling himself he said, "I understand you saw it happen."

Aiden took a breath before saying, "Something happened on take-off. The aircraft didn't clear the runway as it should have and because of the pressure that put on it the undercarriage collapsed." Dennis's father nodded slightly as if he were clearly expecting Aiden to say more. Of course he would have been told all this, Aiden thought. He continued, "But then, of course, there was the fuel it was carrying; his plane was engulfed by fire almost straight away." But he hesitated before saying, "It must have been quick, but not instant, I'm afraid."

Dennis's father visibly winced and Aiden thought of his own torturing image of Dennis burning.

"Was there no chance of him getting out?" Dennis's father's voice was hardly above the level of a whisper.

Aiden spoke fragilely, "None at all, I'm afraid."

Aiden imagined that part of fatherhood must be the need to live and re-live such an unspeakably awful event in one's mind. Indeed even Aiden found himself repeatedly imagining the horror of it. Clothes and flesh on fire; screaming uncontrollably with no shred of your dignity left; no longer having control of your own body; stickily vomiting or shitting yourself in wild desperation; knowing that it was impossible to get out and that your life was about to be painfully extinguished. But no matter how much the thoughts possessed him, he knew that his imaginings must be very short of the horrible reality.

Swallowing hard, Dennis's father said, "I'm sorry, it must be hard for you as well. Thank you for not sparing me the truth; I'd rather not have to live with half-truths, however well intentioned or kindly meant."

Aiden wondered exactly what his squadron leader had told him. Intuitively, he understood that Mr Goodman would not want his wife to know the details of how Dennis had died and knew they would not talk about it again. The two men resumed their silence, each of them busy with their own introspections. The hiss and singing of the coal in the grate and the gentle, rhythmic ticking of the mantel clock lulled and comforted each of them.

Presently, there was a click as the door handle made a quarter turn. The door unlatched but sprung open no more than an inch or so. Virtually at the same time there was a slight bump and the sudden chink or rattle of china cups and saucers as if a number of them had been violently jarred together. This was followed immediately by something that sounded like the clicking noise made by someone's tongue against their hard palate and a split second later by a short sigh of defeat. The door swung open and Dennis's mother entered the room in a curious sweeping, arc-like movement, the result of pushing the door open with her backside at the same time as carrying a heavily laden tea tray.

"Ah, here's Mother with the tea." Mr Goodman's demeanour

changed as she crossed the room towards them. She had forgotten to take her apron off.

"There!" she said triumphantly, setting down the tray on the coffee table.

She perched on the edge of the settee, unconsciously smoothing down her skirt over her thighs, and looked up at Aiden with wide bright eyes and a curious look on her face like a startled rabbit. "Well, this is nice," she announced to the world in general and then turned her attention to the tray, looking it over as if she were pleasantly surprised to find that all the necessary items were actually present on it after all. "Milk? And help yourself to sugar, Aiden, dear."

Aiden carefully took the delicate cup and saucer that she held out to him. Setting the saucer down carefully, he took a sip of the tea then cradled the cup in his hands; the air in the room still felt chilly and he was pleased for the warmth the cup afforded him.

"Do have one of these, Aiden. They were always Dennis's favourite." Dennis's mother stressed the first syllable of the word "favourite" pronouncing it with a noticeably rising inflexion. She offered him a plate of delicate-looking fancy cakes which looked thoroughly overwhelmed by a tyranny of pink icing. Aiden dutifully took one of them and carefully peeled away the paper case which came away from the cake like a collapsed concertina.

"It's so good of you to spare the time to come and see us."

"It's the least I could do, Mrs Goodman."

"I mean, I'm sure you don't get very much leave do you? I'd expect you'd sooner be spending it with your friends. I'm sure you've got lots of things you'd rather be doing." Dennis's mother chattered on incessantly. "Young people are all so interested in everything nowadays, aren't they?"

"Not at all. I wanted to come, really."

"You shouldn't have come on our account," she added, pleasantly but vacuously. "I'm sure you don't want to spend your time with a couple of old fuddy-duddies like us!"

Dennis's father seemed resigned that she should lead the conversation and once again fell into quiet contemplation gazing into the fire, nursing his tea, and occasionally glancing up making sympathetic eye contact with Aiden as if they were co-conspirators in some masculine way. He restricted his contribution to the conversation to an occasional neutral word or two generally uttered in unnecessary support of his wife's questions, or assertions at those points where he instinctively understood she nevertheless expected them of him. Aiden imagined that he had probably been conducting himself in conversations in this manner for many years, perhaps, even, ever since he had married.

Dennis's mother had an apparently insatiable desire to hear of all the small doings of Dennis's life and in between pressing more pink cakes on him and urging him to take more tea - assuring him it was no trouble at all to "pop along and top up the pot" - she ceaselessly bombarded Aiden with questions.

"And what about the food, is it alright?"

"It's not too bad, really, Mrs Goodman," Aiden answered noncommittally.

"Oh, I see!"

Aiden quickly realised that Mrs Goodman said "Oh, I see" rather a lot, emphasising the word "see" in such a way that was peculiarly suggestive of the penny finally, and at long last, having dropped. He found also that generalisations were insufficient for her and he found himself talking at some length about their day-to-day existence.

"But you don't go hungry, do you?"

"No, Mrs Goodman. They look after us well enough!"

"And how about breakfast?" she said, looking mildly upset, "Dennis always *so* enjoyed a good breakfast."

By answering her specific questions he found that he was concentrating more on the domestic: where and when they had eaten their meals; how the room they had shared together was furnished, and whether it had been warm enough in cold weather; and, the laundry arrangements that existed for them to have their clothes washed and ironed.

"But tell me one thing, Aiden dear, however do you all manage to eat your breakfasts while wearing those heavy flying suits and those great big yellow things you blow-up?"

In reply, Aiden had revealed to her the existence of the crew room with its rows of sturdy metal lockers which held their flying kit and in which they could stow items they had no need for during flight. She professed herself indebted to Aiden for clearing up this little mystery for her, and, perhaps inevitably, added as she did so, "Oh I see!"

She was immensely interested in Dennis's likes, dislikes and appetites and asked about their 'outings', as she quaintly called them. Aiden talked about visiting the local towns and even mentioned the occasional glass of beer but he took care to leave out the times when it had felt good to revel in excess. She went on to ask about any "particular young lady friends" Dennis may have had, and Aiden was glad he could reply truthfully that there had been none.

Eventually her torrent of questions slowed, reduced to a trickle and then dried up completely. As Aiden had been speaking, she had seemed sadly elated with his account of their everyday lives and how Dennis and he had spent their time together, seemingly setting great store by it as if her own construct of her son was determined by quite different factors than those which would have been chosen by Aiden and perhaps by Dennis's own father.

But now, she sat staring into the middle distance looking quite spent. Without changing her posture, and as if she were lost in her own sad thoughts, she took a handkerchief out of the pocket of her apron and slowly wiped her nose, first beneath the left nostril then the right, a process she absent-mindedly repeated three or four times. Aiden, weighing her silence and the sufficiency of the stillness, judged that it would be a mistake to offer anything more to her about Dennis, and so thanking her politely for the tea, he rose to take his leave.

Taking his cue from Aiden, Dennis's father also stood up and then crossed over to the door and held it open for him. As Aiden passed through into the hallway he glanced back into the front room; Dennis's mother had hardly moved. She sat, slightly forward on the edge of her seat so that her thighs inclined gently down to her knees which projected proud of her shanks, her feet turned slightly to one side and tucked-in hard against the settee. Her upper body was hunched and rounded and she nursed her now compacted and damp handkerchief between her hands as they lay on her lap.

As they stood in the hallway and Aiden pulled on his greatcoat, Dennis's father said, "I'll walk to the gate with you."

At the end of the path the two men paused, both of them seemed reluctant for the meeting to be at an end. Aiden casually glanced along the street. A baker was carrying his large cloth-covered basket up the garden path of a house a few doors away but otherwise it was virtually deserted.

"You were very kind in there. There're some things his mother would find terribly hard to hear."

"Yes, of course," Aiden replied neutrally. As it had been tacitly understood that Dennis's mother should be spared the details of Dennis's final moments, it seemed to have been an unnecessary thing to have said.

"I'm sure there's a lot more you could have told us." It sounded as if Dennis's father wanted to hear more, but Aiden was uncertain as to what sort of truth it was he wanted, or needed, to hear about his son. Seeing this uncertainty in Aiden's face, Dennis's father said, "I mean about how he lived."

Aiden began slowly, sensitively feeling his way for something to say that was honest but carried little risk of upsetting him. "He had a tremendous capacity for life."

But Mr Goodman interrupted him in a kindly, avuncular manner, "You needn't worry, I expect the two of you got up to all sorts! But I've never been foolish enough to think fathers and sons should try to share such things." He then added, as if he were voicing a regret, "But I suppose it *is* right there should be a distance." As if it cost him a considerable effort, with his jaw tightly shut, the briefest of smiles passed across his face and Aiden was fleetingly reminded of the look on Bill's face as he had described the raid on Berlin. "You see, even in death she needs to cosset him, to keep him safe. But I need to know that he was growing up alright, that I had done something right by him along the way."

"We never did anything stupid, but I think he'd started to live beautifully." Aiden did not know what else to say.

The baker strode back down the path of the house where he had been delivering bread, whistling indifferently to himself and swinging his wicker basket in time to his step. The hinges on the rear doors of his van creaked as he pushed them closed having put the basket back inside. The baker then marked something off in a dark-blue notebook, placed his pencil behind his right ear, unconsciously smoothed back his slicked hair on the right hand side of his head, and then climbed into the cab of his van.

"You see, he couldn't seem to speak to me anymore. Not since Tommy died." Mr Goodman spoke sadly and painfully. But then he asked intently, "Do you think he was *like* you?"

"Yes, I think he was." Aiden was surprised at the question, but felt privileged in being able to reply truthfully. "Actually, I think we were remarkably similar, and he and I could really talk, that seemed so unusual, so rare between men, like we were no longer cut off."

"Well if he was turning out like you, then I must have done something right."

Aiden sensed that the compliment was heartfelt and felt a connection between the two of them that would have proved impossible sitting in the front room just a few minutes ago.

"He felt more like my brother than my friend." He said proudly.

The two men stood quietly together as the baker's van started up with a gravelly noise and pulled away from the kerb.

"Then it seems especially cruel that you couldn't have come to the funeral."

"I would have come if I could. But we did say goodbye to him in the mess. It's just the way it's done in the service; it's not really callous."

Aiden had had mixed feelings in the mess on the evening of the funeral. The very public-ness of the wake or revel was not just a celebration of Dennis's life but it had seemed a necessary and by merciless contrast an ultimately sobering reminder to the men of their own mortality in the particular environment in which they had all chosen to labour. But, Aiden, cherishing Dennis as he had, had also craved the sad intimacy and dark trappings of the funeral setting as a desirable legitimisation and commencement of his longer grief.

Then becoming anxious because he saw no reason why Dennis's father should understand, Aiden added, "I think it's a way of endorsing what we do, but really only for ourselves."

"Yes, of course, I understand that," Dennis's father replied softly, reassuring Aiden.

Their conversation had reached a sense of satisfying closure. To bring it to a conclusion Dennis's father said conversationally, as he held out his hand to Aiden, "I expect many of the men who flew bombers in the war prefer to keep themselves to themselves don't they?"

Aiden firmly grasped Dennis's father's hand. "Some of them talk with the other men in the squadron, but not much to anyone else; a campaign medal would've been something, I suppose."

Dennis's father nodded his head and the two men remained standing together with a static, solid handshake between them. They could feel the warmth in each other's flesh and to Aiden it instinctively felt that the handshake connected them both to something ancient, deep and strong.

Aiden traced his steps back along the streets of quiet semi-detached houses to the bus-stop outside the chemist's in the High Street where he waited with his hands thrust into his coat pockets for the bus which would take him back home again.

As he stood in the queue of Saturday morning shoppers and families intent on Easter visits to relatives, he thought about Dennis's parents. He thought about them letting the fire go out in the front room and returning to nurse their private despair in the familiarity of the warm kitchen, and of washing and putting away the best china cups in the sideboard, uncertain of when they would have the heart to use them again. He could vividly imagine them sorting Dennis's clothes - woollies, shirts and trousers - for hand-me-downs to pass on to someone who had need of them. Or, the more likely outcome he thought, they would be returned carefully folded to the chest of drawers in Dennis's untouched bedroom where they would remain for all the foreseeable time to come, the naphthalene-smelling moth-balls rolling over the lining paper as the drawer was finally and sadly pushed shut. Bitter-sweetly, he imagined Dennis's father half-heartedly 'going to do a bit in the garden' once the effervescent exhortations of Mrs Goodman to look on the bright side, or some other similarly inane saying, had become too much for even the most stoic soul to bear; how unspeakably and utterly disappointing to understand that with the death of your only sons you will have nothing more to add to the continuum.

# Chapter Seven

Aiden looked up as the bus approached, partly to confirm from the black and white destination blind that it was the correct one and partly to gauge how crowded it was. When the bus stopped, the queue moved forward with a peculiar shuffling motion, each person swaying slightly side-to-side like the motion of plastic balls bobbing in a current of water and when his turn came Aiden stepped onto the platform at the rear of the bus unnecessarily holding out his hand to the grab rail. The conductor was standing on the platform in front of the cavernous under-stairs luggage compartment where one or two large cases and an awkward-sized brown paper parcel had previously been stowed by passengers. As the queue edged forward, each person finding his or her seat, Aiden glanced inside to confirm his initial impression that it was reasonably full, and then mounted the stairs to find a seat on the top beside a window; the upstairs was relatively empty and Aiden did not want a crush of people around him at the moment.

Within a few moments of the bus starting away from the stop, the conductor passed along the upper deck taking new fares. Aiden held out a half-crown and stated his destination. The conductor, leaning his lower back against the seat diagonally opposite from Aiden's and splaying his feet out to steady himself against the motion of the moving bus, smartly turned the handle on the side of his ticket machine, which hung down from his neck on a leather strap, to issue the flimsy, purple-printed slip of paper. Aiden absent-mindedly took his ticket and change and turned to look out of the window. The spring sunshine, reflecting off the cream-coloured ceiling of the bus, pleasantly filled the space around him with a watery light.

Ever since he had been a boy, Aiden had enjoyed travelling on the upstairs of a bus; it allowed him an unusual perspective on everyday living. He had never wanted to make the everyday exciting; he had never been a child who craved excitement for its own sake, it was rather that an alternative view of everyday things reinforced his liking for, and contentment with, the domestic.

Heavy with his thoughts following the morning's visit, he slipped easily and gratefully into this comfort of everyday, familiar things: open boxes of vegetables laid out in front of a greengrocer's shop, with small mountains of early cabbage and mounds of earthy potatoes; a glimpse of hats and coats hanging up on pegs in the tiled hallway of a house where the front door momentarily stood open; a cat lying on a garden path stretching itself luxuriously in the sunshine alongside a mellow-coloured wall. He particularly enjoyed watching the passengers alighting from or ascending to the platform on the bus, his particular vantage point affording him a particularly unusual view which clearly distinguished those who wore hats from those who went bareheaded. It somehow felt wonderfully indulgent to have such a perspective and Aiden let all the desiderative images simply wash over him as if they could cleanse and purify him in some way.

It was almost lunchtime when the bus reached the stop at the top of the road in which he lived but instead of crossing the road and making off home, he turned and started to walk the length of the short parade of shops that served the day-to-day needs of people who lived close by.

The morning had affected him in an unexpected way. Whilst he would not have been surprised at being upset emotionally, he actually felt tired and unexpectedly drained and wanted to snap himself out of this mood before he returned home; undoubtedly his mother would be expecting an account of his visit, and Aiden wanted to be able to guard against straying into the territory of the confidence which he now felt existed between himself and Dennis's father. Entering the café at the end of the parade where a side road joined the main thoroughfare he thought he would feel brighter for a cup of tea and also give himself some time to collect his thoughts.

The café was almost deserted and the floor seemed gritty beneath the tread of his feet. A disinterested girl serving at the counter, who seemed to have been left in sole charge, carelessly poured him out a cup of tea from a large metal teapot, indifferently announcing to the world in general as she did so that the "sugar's on the table." Carefully taking his tea so as not to spill more of it into the saucer than was already there, Aiden went and sat down at an empty table. He took off and folded his greatcoat letting out an involuntary sigh as he did so and tried to force himself into being more mentally alert.

Aiden sipped his tea. It was stewed and not hot enough. At the table next to him, two girls sat lolling indolently over their empty cups. Aiden had the impression that they had been sitting there for some time as if they were simply whiling away their free Saturday morning by choosing to have nothing better to do. Both of them had looked up and casually glanced at Aiden as he had sat down, their eyes quickly reverting to the table in front of them. One of them rested her elbow on the table and cupped her chin in her left hand, her head leaning slightly to one side so that the skin covering her cheekbone was stretched tight but forcibly puffed-up beneath her eye. Her smooth fingers – but Aiden noticed she had close-cropped nails - rested just below her left ear. The index finger of her other hand traced imaginary nothings on the table before her. Looking at her twice you realised she was pretty.

"Her hair was a complete mess; it looked like she'd been dragged through the proverbial hedge backwards."

Her companion seemed to be in the middle of recounting an anecdote about someone who they evidently both knew.

"I suppose she'd been mucking about again."

Both girls half-smiled in a distracted, dreamy sort of way as if neither of them seemed to find the incident terribly surprising.

It suddenly struck Aiden that he did not really know the sort of thing that his mother would want to hear about Dennis's mother and father. Besides which, he was beginning to doubt whether any words that he could find would satisfactorily convey to her the comfortable ordinariness of them that so appealed to *him*; that seemed to be something peculiarly internal, inaccessible to another through the medium of slippery words.

"It's just like August bank holiday. You remember! One moment we were all on the Palace Pier having a lark and deciding about lunch and whatnot and the next she'd gone off with them without a word to any of us."

Judging by the way the girls wore their clothes, the pallor of their skin and their overall disposition, they seemed to be of a decent enough sort.

"She gets into hot water in the office as well, you know." The prettier of the two girls said.

But it was not just the way they wore their clothes that attracted Aiden; they somehow gave the impression that they thought of themselves as being slightly daring.

The prettier girl continued indifferently, still with her chin in her hand and tracing patterns on the table in front of her, "She'll have to watch it. She was late back from lunch again the other day. If she gets the push she'll be in a fix."

"She'll have to be careful in other ways," the other girl said knowingly.

"Oh, I think she's careful enough *like that*." the prettier girl said with emphasis. "It's not as if a girl doesn't have a choice, not if she's smart and knows what's what!"

Presently, having picked up their empty cups and saucers, the plainer looking of the two girls walked over to the counter and pointedly pushed the dirty crockery to one side as if she were making it absolutely clear that it had been finished with. Then with exaggerated politeness she asked the puffy-faced girl behind the counter for two more teas. Although the girl obliged, pouring the tea into fresh cups from the same large metal teapot from which she had filled Aiden's cup, this time she was not merely indifferent but discharged her service with a surly, disdainful expression. She then made a great show of noisily returning the teapot to its usual place.

Thanking her with excessive courtesy the girl placed the correct coins on the counter while at the same time shooting a deeply wicked glance at her companion back at the table. She then picked up the fresh cups and returned with them to their table and as she sat down the two girls smiled at each other self-complacently.

To Aiden's surprise, the girl with her chin cupped in her hand suddenly looked up from the table and addressed him directly: "Do you fly, then?"

He caught his breath; it was the second time that day he had heard echoes of previous conversations and this time it felt terrifyingly macabre reminding him as it did of the final evening he and Dennis had spent together.

It took him a moment or two to realise why she might have asked him the question; wearing uniform had become habitual, he had a pride in the service and out of respect he had also wanted to wear it when visiting Dennis's parents. And then taking himself greatly by surprise, he suddenly felt in abnormally, extravagantly high spirits as if a weight had been miraculously lifted from him, and he felt a sudden rush of wonderment and excitement.

Feeling that he must surely have the measure of her, he leant back in his seat to achieve a more dramatic effect and drolly tapped the wings on his uniform tunic as if the answer to her question should have been quite obvious. Then leaning across to the other table he offered cigarettes to both of the girls. The plainer of the two girls refused in a detached, practised manner that seemed to suggest that she knew Aiden had only included her out of politeness and that she did not intend to intrude. But the other girl, the one who had spoken to Aiden, accepted and sat back up straight, looking attentively at him.

"Yes, I fly," Aiden answered her, taking a cigarette out of the packet for himself as well. He then asked her boldly and with sharp directness, his clear interest in her all but excluding her companion from his consideration as if she were simply not there, "What's your name?"

"Margaret," she replied without hesitation, looking at him intensely as she waited with an obviously assumed coolness for Aiden to light her cigarette for her. She then added in such a pert or prurient tone as to entice his greater interest, "And I'm sure I'm going to have to know *yours*!"

# Chapter Eight

The train had barely started to slow down as it approached their station before Aiden had jumped up from his seat. Ever since they had changed trains at the junction he had anxiously peered out of the window at the name board at each stop they had come to even though there had been no real danger of being carried along too far. Margaret watched him from the comfort of her seat with quiet amusement and an air of unmistakable self-satisfaction.

Aiden lifted their suitcases down from the luggage racks. First his own rather travel-worn affair – the middle of the handle had been worn to a dark smooth chocolate-brown – followed by Margaret's somewhat less shabby case, and placed them ready on the floor of the carriage. Then, swaying rhythmically with the decreasing motion of the train as it slowed down into the platform, he leant forward towards the carriage door. He poised his fingers ready on the tongue of the door catch with his thumb tucked behind the edge of the casting so that the mechanism would be released by squeezing his thumb and fingers together. Even before the train had come to a complete halt, he opened the door which then swung wide open and banged into the side of the carriage. As it stopped, he seized his own case, stepped over the wooden running board directly onto the platform and placed the suitcase down. At the same time he spun around, extending out his arm to take Margaret's case.

"There's really no need."

Margaret stood in the open doorway of the compartment evidently enjoying his agitation and fluster. Although his attentions still flattered her, today she considered his offer to be unnecessarily gallant; s*he* considered her capriciousness to be a part of her own charm, and she also knew that Aiden remained rather uncomfortable with her occasional, and unpredictable, acts of independence. So relishing the situation, she joked, "This way we'll look much more like a married couple!" as she stepped down from the carriage, holding onto her own suitcase, and took his arm. As Margaret spoke, her free arm linked through his, she consciously leant against him and with a look of mingled amusement and affection she turned her head towards him, giving the unmistakeable impression that she was more in charge of the situation than he.

Aiden felt vaguely vexed by her joke, almost affronted, wondering if Margaret could seriously assume that he would be any less attentive when they were married. But, anxious not to do anything which could possibly spoil the day, he felt disinclined to remonstrate with her; he believed he would have no right to try to persuade her if she should change her mind. Therefore he merely picked up his suitcase, glanced along the platform towards the way out and said, "This way" trying to sound as decisive as he thought Margaret expected him to be.

They walked on in silence for a few steps as the train departed for its next stop, its electric motor making a threnodial whine as it disappeared down the line, leaving the station to its usual quietness. Only a handful of travellers had alighted from their train – many of them women carrying shopping bags or neat parcels, and who were returning from shopping expeditions in the larger town where Aiden and Margaret had joined the train - and in dribs and drabs they were making their ways towards the ticket barrier. Once more, Margaret turned to look at Aiden and said, impishly, "It's hardly Brighton, is it?"

Aiden made no response and remained looking resolutely ahead. Apart from the other passengers from their train, the only other activity on the station was the loading of a number of wickerwork baskets full of racing pigeons into a grime-encrusted utility wagon in a bay platform on the other side of the station. Aiden could hear the dove-grey birds gently cooing to each other as the baskets were manhandled from a flatbed truck into the wagon.

Rather relishing the situation, Margaret continued, speaking nonchalantly as if doing no more than making a simple throwaway comment, "For some reason, I always imagined being taken to Brighton for a dirty weekend!"

"But this is what we agreed, isn't it?" Aiden, suddenly cross and flushed, replied. He imagined her checking into somewhere shamelessly extravagant, such as the Grand Hotel or the Metropole, with her attentive, suave escort taking charge of all the arrangements with a sickening, practised ease. He imagined this man's accomplished consideration of her and how willingly she assumed the role of his lover. He tormented himself with the eager, lascivious look exchanged between the two of them, the over-plush surroundings lapping them up and somehow conniving at their illicit behaviour.

"Of course it is, Aiden, dear," she answered calmly.

"Well then!" he said, exasperated.

Margaret had readily agreed with his suggestion as to where they should go for the weekend. They had both wanted to go to somewhere anonymous, and they could just as easily have lost themselves in London, but somewhere quiet had seemed preferable and altogether more agreeable. But her needling of him now seemed to imply a criticism, as if she really craved greater excitement than Aiden could possibly offer her or as if she might secretly be holding out for somebody more amoral than he and was merely amusing herself until such an opportunity presented itself to her.

"Well what?" she said quietly.

"It's just that when you put it like that it sounds so, well, sordid, I suppose."

"But that's what we're doing, isn't it! Besides, a girl needs to have a little bit of imagination!"

Uncomfortable with the notion that Margaret could be motivated by unmediated physical desire or sexual curiosity, the possibility that Margaret may have considered such a liaison more concretely, perhaps with someone from her past and about whom she had not told Aiden, induced a feeling of burning jealously and he wanted to loudly confront her as if she had in fact betrayed him by actually being unfaithful.

"But this is different," he protested fretfully. "After all, we are going to be married, aren't we!"

"You might change your mind," she said, playfully. Then, waiting a second or two to maximise the effect of her words, she added, "Or it might be that you have me here on false pretences. You might say that to all the girls just to get your wicked way with them!"

Ever since first meeting her he had pursued his relationship with Margaret with the utmost, almost a religious, intensity, almost to the point of mental recklessness, and so that all his other purposes were temporarily forgotten or at best made subservient to it. She had seemed an unimaginably lucky find and feeling bleakly empty when apart from her he had even said that nothing else mattered as long as they were together. And, snatching at her words like a winterbird greedy for bright berries, he was all too ready to misinterpret her manner, always feeling that the very worst was inevitable and so the slightest word from her could bring him instant emotional turmoil, plunging him into the deepest, blackest despair. And her teasing deeply wounded him, seeming to imply that she did not reciprocate his seriousness and that she had overplayed her innocence.

Weighed-down by despondency, he could not possibly respond to her in any light or frivolous manner and could only blurt out rather foolishly, "You know you're the only one I've ever wanted! Perhaps it's you who's changed your mind!"

They stopped walking and stood facing one another in a wounding intensity, their suitcases hanging dead-weight in their hands at their sides. Two middle-aged women with respectable hats and sensible-looking shoes – who apart from Aiden and Margaret were the final passengers from the train – were walking composedly towards them along the platform.

Afraid of being overheard at a moment of emotional crisis, even by people who were complete strangers to them, Aiden and Margaret remained silent until the two women had passed. Not until they had reached the ticket barrier, some twenty-five yards distant from them did they speak again and seeing Aiden in such turmoil, Margaret now relented.

"Oh Aiden, don't be such a silly ass! Of course I haven't changed my mind! How could you possibly think that!"

On the strength of such adventures as having visited Brighton on the previous August bank holiday, Margaret thought of herself as being more worldly than Aiden and consequently that she therefore had a steal on him in matters of emotion. She had visited Brighton with her girl friends from the office where she typed for a living and had happily linked arms with them, strolled in the bright sunshine showing off her new clothes and for the pleasure of being looked-at. She had flirted harmlessly with young men who were also down for the day, before finally swaying contentedly home, tipsy, in a crowded train late in the evening.

From experiences such as these she concluded she was only gently teasing him, something she had observed that lovers often do. And although she sounded cross and hurt as if she were speaking from a sense of frustration that Aiden could have taken her so seriously, she also felt guilty that she had misjudged the situation and had not seen the upset coming and was genuinely sorry that she had hurt him.

"I could never love anyone but you! Please tell me you know that?" she continued, almost pleadingly.

After a short pause Aiden sighed and spoke hesitantly and quietly, "I suppose so."

He could not yet meet her eye again and remained with his head bowed focused on one of the tarnished locks on his suitcase where the lacquer, which ordinarily protected the metal, had been worn away. He worried that admitting he did know that she loved only him was a tacit admission of his foolishness and inexperience, and that as a consequence Margaret would think the less of him for it.

"Well then," she said softly. But there remained a disconnection between the two of them.

"But what you said made it all feel... Oh I don't know, as if what we're doing is thoroughly reprehensible..."

But Margaret cut him short, saying soothingly and earnestly as if she had no doubt of the truth of it, "All that matters is that we love each other. Isn't it?"

They stood looking at each other for a moment or two, before Margaret, understanding the reassurance Aiden habitually gained from her physical touch, once again slipped her arm into his and gently started them walking once more, slowly along the platform towards the ticket barrier.

At the ticket barrier, Aiden briefly fumbled in his pocket for their tickets which, once he had found them, he handed to the ticket-collector who had been standing quietly watching their progress along the platform. The ticket-collector casually checked to see that the outward portion of the tickets had been correctly clipped and looked at Aiden and Margaret with barely concealed wry amusement.

Outside, the station approach was almost deserted. A single taxicab waited silently at the rank in the sunshine and a solitary man, almost invisible in the afternoon shadow under the awning outside of the ticket office, consulted the bus timetable. As Aiden and Margaret walked down the slight incline of the approach, Margaret pulled her light summer coat closer about her. She had imagined that it must be warmer at the seaside than it had been at home, but the breeze blowing in off the sea made it feel noticeably cooler. Not wanting to ask Aiden to stop walking, she awkwardly pulled at the lapels of her coat - which she had neither buttoned nor belted upon leaving the train - whilst hunching one shoulder after the other in an effort to bring the material closer about her.

At the junction where the station approach met the main road, they crossed at the Belisha and continued walking until they turned into a side road which looked promising. The road was straight and broad and a few hundred yards ahead of them it looked as if it disappeared into an infinite blue void of stunningly bright clear blue sky, as if the road was taking them to the edge of the world. Aiden and Margaret hurried on towards the end of the road, to the esplanade, and to the sea. Ahead of them they could see gulls wheeling in the clear air, describing great arcs and turning sharply and unpredictably this way then that, their wings catching the light from the golden sun, their plaintive mewing peculiarly refreshing. At the end of the road, Aiden and Margaret paused to get their bearings and both of them inhaled deeply, savouring the primeval saltiness of the air. Aiden worked hard to put the upset behind him.

They had come out towards the far end of the esplanade and

instinctively they turned away from the main seaside centre with its brightly painted shops, its cafés and amusements. Being the very tail-end of summer, the little seaside town was almost entirely empty of holidaymakers so that without the oppressive crush of crowds the wide esplanade had a peculiarly spacious and unreal feel about it as if it were somehow connected with an illusion or a sleight-of-hand. At this end of the esplanade the coloured lights, which looped gaily between the lamp posts during the summer months, finally gave out and a bank of straggly grass reappeared above the pebbly beach beside the road in place of the tidy strip of municipal flower beds and lawns which ran alongside the esplanade for much of its length.

Where the road began to curve away inland they chose a guesthouse which looked discreet and respectable. It was a large, imposing bay-fronted house on three floors with a garden path which was edged with sorrel-coloured rope-twist tiles. The front garden was not large and seemed overshadowed by the business of the house and where Aiden and Margaret stood together before the front door there was barely room for them to stand next to each other, the path being overhung by a large hydrangea, the oriental globe-like flowers of which were still healthily in bloom. Elsewhere, the garden seemed jumbled and dusty, and full of russets, reds and earthy browns. Margaret reached out and gently touched the dry foliage with the tips of her fingers.

Aiden swallowed once or twice to ease the tight, constricted feeling in his throat. He took a deep breath before he stepped forward and rang the doorbell and then stepped back again to stand beside Margaret. Out of the corner of his eye he could see Margaret looking determinedly ahead. As they waited for what seemed like an age, Aiden noted the intricate pattern of different coloured tiles on the doorstep and the inset of coloured glass above the door which appeared to have some sort of vague nautical theme. Presently, the net curtains in the bay window beside them that gave out over the front garden twitched slightly and a moment or two later the door was opened by a late middle-aged woman who was wearing severe-looking clothes. She wore a necklace of costume jewellery about her neck where her skin was no longer as taut and firm as once it had been.

There was an uncomfortable, high-pitched trilling in his ears as Aiden nerved himself and guiltily enquired of her if there were any vacancies, feeling certain that they were bound to be turned away in disgrace; it seemed inconceivable to Aiden that they could fool anyone. The landlady was no taller than Margaret but she had a formidable presence. Taking her time, during which Aiden felt his colour rising, she looked Aiden and Margaret carefully up and down, her nostrils flaring slightly, before saying in a measured tone that seemed to imply she had her reservations about them, that yes, she did have a room she could let them have.

While Aiden signed the register, Margaret took care to proffer the cheap bright ring which she was wearing on the third finger of her left hand at an awkward and unnatural angle as if it were proof of her status and mitigation of their own proditory glances at each other. This had been her idea, and when buying it from Woolworth's she had felt quite daringly, tightly, dissolute. Aiden bent low over the side-table of dark, polished wood that served as a desk in the hallway and gently blew upon the inky marks he had scribed so that they should not smudge and then handed the scratchy pen back to the landlady. The landlady picked up the register and holding it almost at arm's length as if she were presbyopic, carefully scrutinised the entries while at the same time carefully explaining about the bathroom arrangements and the hours for breakfast.

With a final glance down at Aiden's worn suitcase, the landlady handed them a room key with a terse "I lock the front door at ten-thirty sharp", and had then retired to the sanctum of her private sitting room. With her departure, Aiden felt as if he had passed through some terrible ordeal but Margaret desperately wanted to giggle. But amongst her dusty aspidistra, her cats, and the ticking clocks with their pearled hands, as long as the appearance of respectability was reasonably maintained the landlady did not particularly care; she had been widowed for a number of years and had managed to keep a guest-house throughout the war, despite the general absence of holidaymakers, and consequently prudery amused her.

Although the air was distinctly chilly through a lack of continuous occupancy, their room was clean and homely enough. Relieved of the anxiety of registration, they instinctively set about making the room their own until they should leave it again. It was a passionless, necessary and deeply settling ritual; it was a benison of moving shoes and folding clothes. They neatly lined up their shoes in pairs on the snuff-coloured linoleum, Margaret's creamy-coloured sling-backs next to Aiden's polished oxfords. They took clothes from their suitcases, smoothed out the travel-creases and placed them neatly in the chest of drawers. Sliding shut, each drawer made a loud booming noise, echoing around the sparsely furnished room and Margaret noted with approval how each drawer had been lined with a single thickness of brown parcel paper. They stowed their suitcases safely on top of the wardrobe, arranged their sponge bags on the dressing table and wondered where to put the towel which had been left on the end of their bed. Aiden felt curiously shy about hanging his own clothes in the wardrobe next to Margaret's, and as he went to hang a loaded hanger on the clothes rail inside of it, he asked Margaret if it would be alright. She, her face colouring, sitting on the edge of the bed as she hid her nighty beneath her pillow, said that of course it would.

"What shall we do now?" Margaret said presently, distractedly teasing loose a few strands of hair from the bristles of her hair brush, before she placed it on its back on the dressing table in front of her.

"I don't know. It's still a bit early for dinner." Aiden came and sat next to her on the bed. Uncharacteristically, she tensed slightly as he sat down. He leaned back and stretching out his arms behind him and placing his hands palm down on the eiderdown, he added cautiously, "What do you want to do?" The eiderdown was cold to his touch.

"I'm not sure, really." Margaret sat looking down at her hands in her lap; her right hand was resting loosely in her left. She had curved the fingers of her right hand up to meet her thumb and was now absent-mindedly clicking her thumb-nail against the finger-nails of her index and second fingers in turn.

"We haven't even got anything with us to read," he said lightly, attempting to make her smile.

Ordinarily, Aiden relished the deliciousness of running his fingers down her back and now with her before him he would have liked to have reached up to her, gently feeling the ridges of her spine through her thin cardigan and revelling in her subtle intake of breath as his hand traversed the length of her back, enjoying that he had an effect on her, but presently he held back. More sensitive than usual to even the mildest hint of a rejection, he imagined her twisting her back and shoulders away from him at his touch, so instead, he sat back quietly trying to get the measure of her mood.

"How lovely to be able to see the sea!" Margaret suddenly exclaimed, getting up from the bed and crossing over to the window. She stood staring intently and gravely out across the road to the sea as if she were lost entirely to her own thoughts. But then, after a few moments, she turned around to face Aiden as if she had now quite dismissed the sea, "No, I think it will do us very nicely!"

She stepped back over to where Aiden was reclining semi-supine upon the bed and stood in front of him. Sitting up, Aiden took her hands and cradled them between his own feeling their warmth and soft loveliness. Bending down, she kissed him gently, affectionately, on the top of his forehead and said, "It's all very us, don't you think so?"

Aiden said nothing in reply, not certain that he would ever have the full measure of her, but, sighing softly to himself, he brought her hands up to his lips and held them there savouring the clean soapy smell of her fingers, as if he were the armourer to his memory, and was delicately equipping it so that one day it could protect and comfort him.

Presently, she carefully extracted her hands from between his and gently slipped her right arm around him pulling him closer to her. She placed her left hand on the back of his head so that they nestled together as if she were making a warm protective cocoon about his head by wrapping herself about him. They clung together with a life-affirming sensuality for a few moments before Margaret said lightly, "Come on, let's have a walk before we eat. But let's go down quietly, that woman gives me the shivers!"

Outside, they turned in the opposite direction from the way they had come when they had first arrived. The road, which had already been gently climbing up away from the level of the sea-front, now began to curve away inland. Initially there was an open space of rough, springy grass between the road and where the land fell away to the sea, a no-man's land for walking dogs and flying kites, but before very long both sides of the road were lined by substantial, sometimes even fanciful-looking, houses which Aiden supposed were mostly now guesthouses.

But not much further on they came upon roads which were laid out like any other place they knew; avenues of modest, well cared for, houses and villas. Aiden and Margaret felt their spirits uplifted and turned this way and then that along the avenues without having any particular direction in mind until turning a corner they unexpectedly found themselves back at the esplanade. Brought up short, they hesitated for a moment before turning down a short side street.

"This must take us back in the general direction of the station," Aiden quietly reasoned, as much to himself as to Margaret.

"Perhaps there're some shops somewhere we could look in until tea time." Margaret spoke matter-of-factly.

"Let's keep going down here and see what we can find." Aiden spoke quite brightly; the afternoon was not yet quite finished but he was starting to feel anxious about finding somewhere suitable where they could eat.

"This looks like it might be a cut-through," Margaret said, looking ahead of them to where the street terminated in a tee-junction. "It looks as if it might be a bit busier down here."

When they had very nearly reached the end of the street, a bus suddenly flashed passed across the junction in front of them suggesting that they may indeed have reached a busier road. It was so close and unexpected that it startled them as if it had come out of nowhere and the unfamiliar corporation colours of the bus added to the impact. Aiden and Margaret instinctively turned the corner to follow its direction. The bus slowed down and came to a halt at a bus-stop half way along the High Street. But apart from the bus, the road was almost empty of vehicles, the pavements empty of people and all the shops were now closing.

As they set off walking once more, Margaret half-heartedly looked in one or two of the shop windows, but it felt as if they were intruding upon private routines as shop awnings were retracted and goods stowed safely back inside, so that before long Margaret gave up even the pretence of interest.

Aiden actually felt quite relieved that the only restaurant they passed was not yet open for the evening; it looked reasonably expensive and he was uncertain about Italian food. He was careful, not niggardly, and he was unaccustomed to taking charge in such places. Reaching the end of the High Street the shops played out and there seemed to be nothing for it but to turn back towards the seafront once again.

"I suppose there's always fish and chips," Aiden said, disappointed that he had failed to find somewhere special for them.

"I wouldn't mind," Margaret replied giving Aiden a smile and squeezing his hand.

Presently, having walked a short way along the seafront to where the shops were less workaday and more holiday-like, but were no less closed or in the process of closing than those they had just walked past in the High Street, they found an anonymous-looking cafe. In answer to Aiden's question, the proprietor chattily said that they were not too early for him to do them an evening meal and in fact by this time of year he generally started to close up quite early as there was not so much demand.

The café had a warm, homely atmosphere. The air was moist from the steam of cooking and an urn gurgled occasionally as the water inside it was kept continuously at boiling point for whenever teas and coffees were required. From time to time there was a comforting "wumph" noise as the water geyser cut in as a sink-full of hot water was drawn for washing-up and then a rattle in the water pipes when the tap was turned off again. Aiden felt comfortable here; the food was like the food he would have eaten at home, or in the mess at an airfield, or in a Lyons Corner House on a visit up to Town.

The large plate-glass windows of the café looked seawards. Across the road the beach and the sea were still bathed in the early evening sunlight, but the cafe was now in shadow as the sun sank lower behind the town. Aiden and Margaret, sitting facing one another at a table in the window, felt as if they were in their own pool of softness, the velvety-keen light illuminating the world around them. On the beach, near to the water's edge, an elderly couple were walking, their shadows lengthening but sharply defined in the sunlight.

"Do you think that that will be us in years to come?"

Aiden looked up from his teacup. At the start of their meal they had been quietly full of conscious small talk but during the course of it their conversation had dwindled until they were sitting in companionable silence. Good-humouredly, he replied, "I don't know about retiring to the seaside. It seems rather too much like the full circle."

He looked out and beyond the beach and the elderly couple. The blue of the sky intensified and deepened towards the horizon so that it appeared that the sky and the sea merged seamlessly together so that as they sat in the café it appeared as if they were on the edge of a fathomless void. But Aiden then added pensively, "But perhaps that's the appeal."

"I'd be happy as long as I had a garden." Margaret spoke with quiet intensity and Aiden was uncertain whether the statement was conditional in some way. What was left of their tea was now almost cold and, having finished their desserts, they had pushed their dishes away to one side.

"I think he wants to close up." Aiden nodded in the direction of the proprietor who was putting cutlery away behind the counter and the urn was now silent.

"We'd better be on our way, then."

It seemed indecently early to return to the guesthouse so they sat huddled together in the leeside of a shelter that sat prominently on the promenade. The saltiness of the sea air had made the paint of the bench they were sitting on blister and flake prematurely.

"I shouldn't really like to live in a flat." The business of setting up home was at the heart of marriage to them, an equal purpose, and a topic each of them would periodically return to.

"A lot of people are pleased just to get a roof over their heads, these days, no matter what," Aiden replied amiably.

"But we *will* be able to get a little house, won't we, when we go into married quarters?" She sounded kittenishly vulnerable and Aiden reciprocally felt warmly protective towards her.

"I expect so. I'll find out about it when I get back. There'll be a lot of forms to fill in, I expect."

"It's dreadfully exciting, having our own little house and getting to know all the other wives and you off flying!" Margaret then asked him sympathetically, "Was it difficult? Getting away, I mean?"

Aiden had telephoned his mother from a call box at the aerodrome to tell her that he had some leave, but that he would not be spending it at home. There had been a short silence before his mother had spoken again. And when she had she had managed to convey a sense of hurt and deep disapproval in an exceedingly economical manner, as if she now considered him to be a changed moral being.

"I said that I was spending my leave with friends." It had been the first time in many years that cross words had passed between Aiden and his mother and he felt that it had irrevocably set him apart from her.

"And what did she say?"

"She didn't believe me."

"Perhaps you just shouldn't have mentioned it; it would have been a lot easier." She then added, a little brighter, "Daphne's covering for me. She thought it was a bit of a scream, really."

It had not occurred to Aiden that he could simply not have mentioned his leave to his mother.

"Perhaps it makes it easier having a sister," Aiden said pleasantly. He had a warm mental image of Margaret and Daphne laughing and giggling together, titillated at the piquancy of the plot they were hatching and hooded by their own risqué-ness.

"Hiking, of all things!" Margaret clearly seemed to think that the idea of her hiking was incongruous, and Aiden equally found it difficult to imagine such a thing. Margaret then exclaimed proudly, "Mum and Dad don't suspect anything!"

At the end of the telephone call to his mother, Aiden had put the receiver down feeling ashamed of himself and for a moment had remained standing in the telephone box, as if in shock.

"We're as thick as thieves, really!" Margaret continued. It was now getting quite chilly and Aiden could feel the warmth of Margaret's thigh pressed against his and her hands soft and warm cradled inside his own; she seemed wonderfully alive. With her warmth he began to think of the taste of her moist mouth and of the animal perfume of her flesh.

"Mother made me feel like such a dreadful fiend," Aiden said quietly. But feeling ashamed had been an insufficient counter to his overwhelming desire not to jeopardize this ever-longed-for chance of full carnality.

Margaret paused for a moment and then turning her head to look at Aiden she said softly, "Oh Aiden, darling, I'm so sorry. Have I upset you again, rattling on like that? It's just my way of talking, you know."

Aiden smiled at her. "It's not that. I wasn't expecting to feel so guilty about it, that's all. But I didn't want you to see how dreadfully anxious I feel, or to think I'm ridiculously feeble." They sat peacefully together for a few moments with Margaret's hands held comfortably within his before Aiden added, "And another thing. I hadn't expected that just making the decision to come away together would make me feel so unconditionally bound to you."

"And I didn't fully understand the implications of *my* choice before this afternoon." Margaret spoke as if she were making a confession.

Aiden felt constructively empty. It was as if a lot of clutter had finally been swept away and he was a peaceful, clear empty vessel waiting to be filled-up with the vital fluid of his life. He felt that with their decision, their choice, they had been granted permission to live in a kind of necessary suffering. Presently, Aiden said quietly, "Shall we go?" It was as if all the tempestuousness of the day had now been nullified.

As they had approached the guesthouse, partially screened by the front border of shrubs - spindly viburnum and spiky firethorn - they had gradually fallen silent, their conversation slipping away as if they were attempting to make themselves unnoticeable. Aiden opened the front door with as little noise as possible, turning the brass handle slowly as if he were trying to sense the movement of the catch through his hand in order to anticipate any snag which might produce an auditory alarm of their arrival. Crossing the hall to the stairs, Margaret exaggeratedly placed her forefinger on her pursed lips in a pantomimic exhortation to silence, but then mounting the stairs she noisily stubbed her toe on a stair rod and a fit of the giggles got the better of her and even Aiden had difficulty restraining his laughter.

"It's cold in here!" Margaret spoke matter-of-factly, but not as if she were making any complaint. Their room felt chillier than the air outside had felt as they had walked back along the esplanade, and a large, unwieldy, convector heater had now been placed in the room. Larger than a suitcase, it squatted on the linoleum near the window.

"That wasn't there before!" Aiden exclaimed.

"Ah, there it is," Margaret said, reaching in front of Aiden to the dressing table, to pick up her sponge bag and turned to go out along the hallway to the bathroom.

Placing the heater near the end of the bed, Aiden found that the flex would just about reach to allow him to plug it into the socket beside the wardrobe. He turned the black Bakelite dial on the end of the heater until the embossed arrow on the casing of the heater pointed to the word max. The heater made a low buzzing noise as the electric current coursed through the tightly wound element that could be seen by looking down at an angle through the gauze-like grill on one side of the grey casing. After a few moments the element began to glow bright orange and there was a faint smell of scorching dust.

By the time Margaret returned down the landing from the bathroom, the convector had still not taken the chill off the room and Aiden was already in bed.

~~~~

The next morning Aiden awoke early to the distant soughing of the sea. The windows were knocking quietly and irregularly in their sashes as the sea-breeze squeezed in between them causing the curtains to billow gently out into the room and then back again rhythmically and mesmerically like the breathing of a deeply contented sleeper. Aiden lay quietly for a moment, letting the soothing sounds and motion lap over him, and then cautiously he eased himself out of bed and crossed quietly over to the window.

After the relative dimness of the bedroom, slipping into the gap between the curtains and the window was like stepping into an envelope of hard bright light. Aiden took care not to let too much of the light back into the room behind him. Standing there was like being poised between two worlds. Pushing the net curtains apart he looked at the sea. Always the sea, he thought; it had been the last thing he had heard before he had fallen asleep last night. From where he stood the waves breaking on the shingle beach were hidden from view and he could only sense the perpetual movement of the water. Further out, where the grey was deeper, the sea looked calm and benign. He thought of the irresistible primeval deep, of the unexpectedly captivating fullness of the round swell. He imagined being caught and carried along by its movement like an overtaken bather, his entrails like ice and his strength taxed until he was unable to grip the rocks to haul himself clear, but still exhilarated and with his senses sharply acute.

From somewhere nearby a church bell began to call worshippers to the early morning service. Matins, he absent-mindedly thought it would be. The sense of relief that he had experienced before finally falling asleep last night had now given way to a feeling of replete peacefulness and it was with no great sense of passion or longing that he assumed that Margaret and he would now make love from time to time when they had the opportunity. He did not have an insatiable, overwhelming lust for her body and it had not been until she had climbed into bed and nestled close beside him and they had lain together, frightened and motionless, that he had begun to feel any real sense of urgent desire. And then he had been clumsy; beside himself with his fear of failure he had hurried in case he should lose his momentum. Now Margaret lay sleeping peacefully undisturbed by either the sea or the church bell.

Aiden knew that Margaret would never be more than routinely attractive to him; but there were women he did find deeply attractive, sexually. There were murderously carnal revelations that could come unlooked-for when walking behind a woman in the street, or sitting in a railway carriage compartment that could produce an all-consuming lust. But simultaneously they were also objects of enormous momentary regret so that it was like making acquaintance with black fathomless grief. Now that Dennis was gone, he could not imagine ever talking to anyone of such longing and despair. It was like a great solitary seabird journeying over the rolling, surging sea. For ever out of sight and desperate to make land-fall, its wings beating relentlessly and battling against fatigue, the seabird was doomed to remain on the wing until death overtakes it or it fails and falls into the unforgiving sea below. It was a solitary and thankless journey and especially now, an unbearably private struggle.

# Part Two

# 1957

# Chapter Nine

"Oh for goodness' sake, whatever next!" and with a sigh of exasperation Margaret tossed the letter onto the kitchen table beside the envelope which she had carefully slit open a few moments earlier.

She had been carefully reading the letter for a second time, the creamy sheets of paper held loosely between the fingers of her right hand and her thumb which she had pressed over the fold to keep the pages opened out, until the crash of the plate had distracted her. The kitchen faced east and by standing in front of the sink where the daylight was strongest, the pages had caught the light and warmth of the sun so that they had glowed in front of her as if theurgically illuminated.

Although the morning was not hot, Margaret wiped the back of her hand across her brow and then squatted down to pick up the pieces of toast, the backs of her thighs resting against her calves so that her bottom very nearly touched her heels. Miraculously, the plate had not broken. It had slipped from the table and fallen to the floor almost vertically, performed a half turn on its rim and settled on the floor with a dull "clunk" noise, the air inside its shallow concave shape magnifying the sound.

"I'm sorry, Mummy."

Mark looked crestfallen. The poached eggs had landed upside down beside the leg of the table. One of them had ruptured and globules of the thick yellow yoke had splashed across the lino tiles from a gaping wound in the white, the sudden evacuation leaving the smooth round egg sagging in the middle as if it had been suddenly deflated. Mark's lower lip began to curl outwards and his eyes started to water.

"Never mind, dear!" Margaret looked directly up at him and

managing a smile for his sake, tried to sound unconcerned. Then addressing Aiden as she picked up the plate and reached across and placed it on the draining board, she said, "Would you get me the dustpan and brush."

"Let him have mine," Aiden said appeasingly. "I haven't touched them yet."

Afraid that he risked her momentary disapprobation, he nevertheless glanced surreptitiously down at Margaret's exposed knees and let his sight flicker into the dark triangular space formed between the tautened material of the front of her skirt and her peach-toned thighs. He had already noticed that the handwriting on the envelope belonged to Daphne.

"But you can't go without your breakfast!"

"It's okay, I'll get a tea and wad on the way."

Aiden lifted up his own plate and reaching across the Formica-topped table placed it in front of Mark who brightened up considerably at the sight of the replacement breakfast. Mark carefully, studiously even, picked up his knife and fork and with a look of intense concentration meticulously fitted them into their proper places between his fingers.

"Will you cut my toast for me, Mummy?"

Aiden pushed his chair back just far enough to enable him to swing his legs out from under the table and stand up. The kitchen was cramped and the kitchen chairs mis-matched. He turned around and stepped out into the hallway. Each time the dustpan and brush were needed, a screwdriver or light bulb wanted, Mark's pushchair had to be moved out of the way of the door to the under-stairs cupboard and then back again once the items wanted had been taken out. It was inconvenient and partially blocked the hallway but having only recently arrived at the posting they were still in rather a muddle and had not yet found anywhere else for it to go. Mark had really outgrown it; the red fabric seat had stretched to the contours of Mark's body, the thick hem along the front of the seat had frayed and the paint had worn away along most of the footboard exposing the underlying dull silver-grey metal.

Holding the dustpan and brush in one hand, Aiden pushed the

cupboard door shut with his other. The coats which hung on the inside of the door in their usual place swung sideways with the motion of the door swinging back closed and the door hinges squeaked momentarily before the door finally latched, leaving an ear of fawn-coloured raincoat cuff caught between the cupboard door and the frame.

"In a moment, Sweetie," Margaret said gently, and then to Aiden, more matter-of-factly, as he awkwardly manoeuvred the pushchair back into place, "You could have mine, they're nearly done."

Over on the gas stove, a thin jet of steam escaped from beneath the flimsy aluminium lid of the egg poacher where it failed to fit snugly over the main body of the pan.

"No, I'd better be off: we've got some sort of special briefing this morning and the Old Man will have a fit if I'm late. Here we are," Aiden said. The short loop of hairy string which passed through a hole in the end of the handle of the brush and which was ordinarily used to hang it on a nail in the cupboard, hung limply across the fleshy ball of his thumb as he handed the dustpan and brush over to Margaret. "I should be back in plenty of time for tea," he continued and then added conversationally, "Any particular news from Daphne?"

Margaret slid the ruined eggs onto a piece of newspaper before dropping them into the peddle-bin along with the pieces of toast she had already picked up. She then dropped onto her knees to sweep up the smaller pieces and the crumbs.

"Now I'll have to wash the floor. It's all greasy from the butter," she said, irritated, brushing carefully to avoid the butter marks and the egg yolk. "I don't know what we're having yet. We'll pop along to the shop later." Then without looking up from her sweeping she added, "They're moving. They're buying the house in Enfield."

"But that's on the other side of London," Aiden said lightly. As he spoke, he unconsciously lifted his chin up and stretching his neck he turned his head slightly to one side and then to the other so that his collar would sit as comfortably about him as it might do. As he did so, he loosely placed the thumb of his left hand on one side of the knot in his tie and his forefinger on the other and gently made to push the knot up towards his Adam's apple, but there was no travel in it.

"It's more convenient for them," Margaret said quite sharply. "Ted can walk to his office from Liverpool Street!"

Ever since he had been demobbed from the army, Daphne's husband had worked as a buyer in a small commercial office somewhere up towards Shoreditch. And now saying that he had had all the excitement chased out of him and chiefly just remembered being cold and uncomfortable in the army, he mildly absorbed himself with the weights and grades of the paper and cardboard that he bought on behalf of the company he worked for and took satisfaction in quietly marking the passing segments of the clock until the time came at the end of the afternoon to pull on his hat and coat and hurry off in time for his regular train.

"Well, I suppose so," Aiden said, wanting only something innocuous to say in reply. "I was only thinking it's a long way from your Mum and Dad."

"They'll still be able to visit at weekends."

"It'll be a bit of a trek, though, won't it? Tube and two trains each way, if not a bus as well at the other end."

Aiden instantly regretted having said this. This present move was the second since he had been posted to the squadron, having previously converted to fly the Canberra bomber at Bassingbourne. At that time the squadron had been based at Wittering, but they had then been moved to Western Zoyland where they had stayed until just a few weeks ago. However, it had been his fourth, no fifth, posting Aiden thought since he and Margaret had married.

"Well, I wish we had a house like that," Margaret said without looking up, an unmistakable edge to her voice. "And don't forget there's your mother to think of as well."

The imminent danger of another accident saved him from having to reply. "Here, I'll do that," he said quickly to Mark, putting down his almost empty teacup.

Mark had been waiting patiently for Margaret, but by now the sight of the golden-brown buttered toast and steaming eggs had got the better of him. With a look of fierce concentration on his face,

Mark had stuck his fork into one of the slices of toast and was dangerously using his knife to try and prize or lever the toast into manageable sized pieces.

Aiden moved behind Mark and reached out his arms so that Mark was enveloped between them. With Mark's head resting softly back against his chest, he gently took Mark's knife and fork out of his hands and by cutting the toast into inch-wide strips then turning the plate through ninety degrees and cutting again, he cut the toast into neat squares. The appearance of the whorl of healthy, soft fine hair on Mark's head engendered a feeling of the greatest tenderness in Aiden, a feeling that would unexpectedly surprise him at odd moments, no matter what he happened to be doing at the time, and he lingered behind Mark's chair for longer than he needed to, privately relishing the moment.

"There we are," he said handing the knife and fork back to Mark separately, so that Mark took them from him carefully one at a time. He added with evident pride, "You can cut the eggs yourself, can't you, because you're such a clever boy!"

Mark meticulously cut himself a small piece of egg which he positioned centrally on a square of toast. Then using the fork as if it were a miniature shovel, he carefully transferred the egg and toast to his mouth. Mark started to eat carefully, his jaw working slowly and steadily.

Implying that Aiden and Margaret were not, Margaret then said defiantly, "Then they'll be settled!"

Aiden paused for a moment and then bent down and gently kissed Mark on the top of his head, savouring the bakery-day smell of his hair. "Be a good boy for Mummy today, won't you."

Mark barely seemed to notice Aiden's goodbyes and continued eating his egg resolutely. But Aiden did not need reassurance from Mark and Aiden was a sufficient certainty in Mark's life for his indifference to be only apparent. Aiden therefore picked up his tunic from the back of his chair where, as he habitually did each morning, he had put it when he had come downstairs for breakfast, and sliding first his right arm into one of the sleeves and then his left into the other sleeve, he pulled it on up over his shoulders and fastened the buttons at the front, and without further thought of Mark turned towards Margaret.

Irritated that she had not asked him about the briefing, he picked up his cup, swallowed down his last mouthful of tea and circled around to the other side of the table. Bending down as Margaret simultaneously lifted her head up from her sweeping as if she had anticipated the gesture, he mechanically kissed her lightly on her lips and said more brusquely than he had intended, "I must be off. I'll see you later then."

~~~~

"Can I get down now please, Mummy?"

So that they came out cleanly, Margaret had turned her own two eggs out from the poacher by carefully running the rounded end of a knife blade around the edge of each of the whites in turn as they sat in the shallow cups she had lifted out from the top of the poacher, her fingers protected from the heat by a tea towel. A dribble of warm translucent margarine, a barrier to prevent the eggs from sticking, had dripped onto the toast along with the eggs as she had tipped up each tinny hemispherical cup in turn. Margaret sat at the kitchen table opposite Mark eating her breakfast. Quite apart from her sense of irritation with Aiden, she had a vague, indefinable feeling of malaise, which could only be partially mollified by devoting her full attention to Mark.

"Are you quite sure you've finished?" Margaret spoke in a quizzical, kindly way, but with her eyes wide open in an expression of mock surprise; she had a parent's instinct that for a child of Mark's age the comic should be overt or even clownish.

Mark smiled cherubically back at her, his naturally ruby cheeks glowing with pleasure at her joke and at his own ability to share in it. Looking at the crusts from his toast, he said, "I don't want those. They're too hard."

"Alright then, Sweetie, just this once." Margaret smiled at him indulgently as the familiar phrase issued from her lips. She did not consider such gentle inconsistency to be a foible as she thought her own connection with Mark to be rightfully more enchanted than Aiden's. "Do you want to go and play in the garden while I clear away?"

Wishing to keep her milky boy perpetually away from harm, it was as if she was attempting to enter into a conspiracy with Mark, a conspiracy that would keep him as an integral part of her own dreams.

Predictably, Mark's answer was to neatly place his knife and fork together on his plate and then twisting his body around in the direction he wanted to go, he gleefully propelled himself off his chair and hurried out into the garden, leaving the backdoor wide open behind him. Margaret sat for a while, finishing her tea.

Tea with breakfast was invariably the second cup of the day. Generally, a moment or two after the heart-stopping clamour of the alarm pulled him from sleep – they still used the same alarm clock that he had brought with him when he had joined the service - Aiden would sleepily swing his legs out from under the bed covers leaving Margaret lying motionless as if she were insensible to the impossibly loud bell. With his eyes still heavy with sleep, he would pull his dressing gown on over his pyjamas tying the ends of the stripy cord together and go downstairs to the kitchen and put the kettle on, the "pop" of the igniting gas and the smell of the spent match a comforting start to their daily routine.

As he set the cups on a tray he would hear Margaret crossing the landing to the bathroom above him and then back again, so that by the time Aiden returned slipper-footed to the bedroom she would be awake and waiting for him. Sitting-up in bed together in the early morning drinking tea, hot and sweet, was a treasured time; a time when their conversation was unashamedly and reassuringly domestic. But by now, having attended to the needs of Aiden and Mark before her own, Margaret's tea was no more than lukewarm. An ingrained habit of economy prevented her from discarding it and making herself a fresh pot and besides which she took a certain perverse satisfaction in the fact that her tea was cold but Aiden's had not been.

The morning was just about warm enough to leave the back door open and Mark continued to play outside in the garden while

Margaret cleared the breakfast things away. Every now and then as she cleared the breakfast plates and cups from the table, or put the salt and pepper away in the oblong raffia-work basket where they lived together with some other kitchen odds and ends, she would automatically glance out of the kitchen window or the open door to check what Mark was doing.

As Margaret stood with her hands in the sink, the spring sunshine streamed in through the window striking the faery-shaped peaks of washing-up-water bubbles so that they sparkled with an exceptional brilliance. The light refracted through the larger bubbles into liquid rainbow-pane images that danced before her eyes like so many slippery cats. The detergent smell seemed intensified in the warm air and as she turned around, her wet hands dripping soap-suds onto the floor, to pick up the egg poacher from on top of the gas stove to place it beside the sink, the kitchen seemed momentarily darkened after the brilliance of the sunlight which flooded the sink and draining board. Slipping the lid of the poacher into the hot water, she glanced up again and out into the bright garden. Mark was driving his pedal car back up the garden path, his feet working furiously but the inefficient metal linkages which drove the wheels limited his progress to a mere crawling pace so that the sideways movement of his body generated in opposite action to his pedalling seemed incongruously at odds with his forward motion.

Margaret thought that even on a bright day such as today the garden was bleak. The concrete path launched at a perfect right angle from the kitchen door and ran down the length of the garden and stopped abruptly at its end. A low chain-link fence separated their own garden from the one next-door, as was next door's garden separated from the next one and so on; the gardens of all the married quarters were identical, bland and monotonous. A narrow bed of friable earth separated the path from the fence and in which a token handful of daffodils and bobbly grape hyacinths grew pitilessly in spring.

Margaret propped-up the wet lid of the poacher against the breakfast plates on the draining board. A film of water ran off it, formed up into a tiny rivulet of water which then ran along the draining board and down into the gap between the washing-up bowl and the sink. Having immersed herself once more into her domestic routine, she now felt cross with herself for having taken her irritation out on Aiden.

"You need to come in and clean your teeth in a moment, Sweetie!" Margaret called out to Mark as he stood up awkwardly in the well of his pedal car, stooping slightly forward with his knees bent so that he could stand in front of the seat. The pedals only propelled the car forward and Mark had learnt by trial and error that standing up in the well and lifting the front of the car off the ground by the steering wheel, whilst the rear wheels remained on the ground to swivel around, was by far the most effective way to turn the car at each end of its journey up and down the garden path.

Margaret now turned her attention to the top plate of the poacher, the part of it she most disliked cleaning. From where she had cracked the eggs into the cooking cups, prizing the halves of the smooth egg shells apart with her pink thumb nails, lines of egg white had streamed across the surface and had subsequently hardened on the dull aluminium surface as the eggs had cooked.

"And we must wash your face before we go along to the shop," she added, thinking that she could wash over the kitchen floor before they went out, that way it would dry while they were gone.

The hardened egg white was stubborn and where Margaret rubbed the wire wool of the scouring pad on the aluminium the surface bloom dulled and the pink foam from the pad dripped into the water below, contaminated with streaks of grey. The gritty foam from the pad worked its way under her fingernails, sensitising her skin and the steel wool scratched and bit into the ends of her nails which were already vulnerable and softened from prolonged immersion in the hot washing-up water. But because such petty self-mutilations to her field of beauty were complicit in her quiet conspiracy she worried over them less than if she had been unattached. Perhaps, Margaret thought, she would find time to drop Daphne a line this afternoon; she had always confided in Daphne.

Leaning over the sink to look out of the window, Margaret was in time to see Mark's head bob up as he stood up to turn his car around once again.

"Time to come in now," she called out. "And shall we take your pushchair with us to the shop?"

"No. It doesn't fit me anymore," Mark called back peevishly.

Margaret did not know whether to be disappointed with herself; she had always counted on her instinct that they surely *must* settle properly once they had a family and at first she had believed she had managed things so well.

Having turned his pedal car around, Mark headed off along the garden path again; he knew Margaret would tolerate him at least one more journey to the end of the garden and back again before he need listen out for any rising sharpness in her voice. Margaret tipped out the washing-up bowl, the dirty grey water rushed down the plughole leaving a detritus of crumbs and small limp fragments of rubbery egg white in the bottom of the bowl. A second or two later she heard the water rushing into the concrete drain gully below the kitchen window. She rinsed away the crumbs and turned to dry her hands on the kitchen towel. To go shopping with Mark without the pushchair was rather limiting; his walking pace was much slower than Margaret's. She therefore wondered if they might as well catch the bus into town.

"Come along in now. And it's warm enough to put your sandals on."

Margaret untied the bow behind her back which secured her apron, and draping the apron over the back of a kitchen chair, she dismissed the thought of the bus as she did not want her domestic routine to be upset.

~~~~~

They walked together along the pavement, his soft fleshy hand safely enveloped within Margaret's, and as anticipated their progress was indeed painfully slow. Mark generally had no sense of urgency, abandoning himself to his innate sense of wonderment and the freshness of his surroundings and Margaret generally thought that it was better to indulge him. With infinite application he would take whole long minutes to examine a leaf that had blown into his path; he would be mesmerised into rapt attention by the progress of bicycles, fascinated by the never-ending circular motion of each rider's feet, their socks and shining shoes incongruously exposed by bicycle-clipped trousers; or he would marvel at the cars and the drab dark blue lorries that made their way along to the aerodrome's main gate. But this morning, however, Mark dawdled because of his sandals.

After she had supervised Mark brushing his teeth, Margaret had patiently spent what had seemed like an eternity persuading and cajoling Mark into his new sandals. Eventually he had allowed himself to be persuaded on the strength of a vague promise of seeing what they could do when they got to the shop. But still he did not like them and would not be made to like them. As they made their way along the main avenue, only reluctantly would he take Margaret's hand and he wore an indissoluble scowl. Mark dragged his feet, petulantly trying to scuff the sides of the soles as he walked.

Most of all Mark disliked the shiny buckles. But the buckles and indeed the sandals in their entirety were suddenly forgotten. At the sound of the loud bang Mark instantly stood stock-still. The bang was followed immediately by a short fizzing noise, as if an unseen firework rocket had ascended weakly into the air, then by the low hollow drone of a jet engine starting up. As the pitch and volume of the engine increased, there was another bang, and then another, as engine after engine was cartridge-started. The mixed harmonics of jet engines in various stages of starting up resonated sickly through their bodies until after a few moments all the jet engines reached the same even, shrill, and ultimately intensely satisfying note. Mark turned and craned his neck in the direction of the giant hangars, the roofs of which were visible in the middle distance over the tops of the horse chestnut trees that lined the avenue.

"Is that Daddy?" Mark cried out loudly in wild excitement. Mark found all aeroplanes exciting, but especially jet aeroplanes. It was almost, but not completely, incidental that his father flew such craft, and for all Mark knew all fathers walked out of the kitchen after eating poached eggs on toast for breakfast and went off to fly fast jet aircraft.

"It might be, Sweet Pea."

At the sound of the jet engines being starting-up, a bolt of guilty stomach-churning horror had suddenly and forcibly struck Margaret; she did not known whether Aiden was due to fly today or not.

Always resolving their differences before they parted from each other, like newly-committed lovers might do, had remained an imperative for Aiden and Margaret long after it would probably have ceased to matter to other couples. And earlier this morning, fuelling his lingering sense of somehow having been wronged, Aiden had petulantly thought that he would not volunteer such information. But this was the first time she had ever forgotten to ask him when she had not known his movements for the day and therefore she now started to worry that she might have started to love him less and, superstitiously, that her thoughtlessness would bring awfulness and bad luck on him.

"Come along, let's get on to the shop." With an effort, Margaret managed to keep the tenor of her voice calm and even. "We've got to find something nice for Daddy's tea."

"Can't we wait? We might see them take off!" Mark demanded excitedly, if unrealistically; Margaret knew from living on the domestic margins of an airfield that the running up of engines might not indicate that any aircraft were imminently air-bound.

"But we won't be able to see them from here," Margaret replied patiently. The rows of leafy trees that lined the main avenue and the rows of utilitarian service houses which fronted the well maintained roads effectively hid any aircraft on the apron in front of the hangars from their view.

"But we might do, Mummy!"

Equally, the shallow climb of an aircraft departing the runway would be hidden from them until perhaps for a brief moment or two it would be visible in the distance, way beyond the airfield's boundary, a thin haze of black smoke spreading behind it from the jet tail pipes, as no more than a glistening speck, its tailplane and fin a tiny diminishing cross, until it was lost to naked sight just a few short seconds later.

"No, Mark, we really have to get on," Margaret said insistently and made to take a step forward but Mark jerked his hand out of Margaret's and flouncing his shoulders from side to side resumed the scowl on his face; Mark would have stayed to see an aeroplane no matter how small a speck it appeared in the sky.

But Margaret did not want to see Aiden's aircraft take off. She did not want to be reminded of the dangers that were ever present in his daily life, and she wanted to be distracted by her domestic routine until she knew that Aiden was safely back home again. Intuitively taking her contentment with her own daily purpose as her yardstick, she wanted to use the argument of her necessary application to their domesticity and the attendant petty sacrifice of her beauty to transition him away from the proximity of daily hazards; to hold a hand roughened by housework currently seemed to her to be having the better part of the bargain that existed between them.

~~~~

"Can I go and look at the sweets, Mummy?"

The vague promise of seeing what they could do when they reached the shop had evolved into something considerably more definite in order to secure Mark's co-operation in continuing their slow progress along the road to reach the shop and even then Mark had still dawdled at the unlikely prospect of seeing jets fly.

The shop was the only place on the airfield where provisions of any kind could be bought. It was housed in a long hut that had been prefabricated out of concrete sections and had a small grey tarmacadamed space between the shop and the pavement where bicycles and pushchairs might be left.

"I suppose so. But don't touch anything, though, wait for Mummy."

Margaret spoke with an air of resignation as Mark eagerly made his way along to the counter at the other end of the shop where a small set of stepped wooden shelves set at child-eye height displayed cardboard cartons of pastels, tubes of fruit gums and foil-and-paper wrapped slabs of chocolate. Enticed, Mark's step was now considerably more lively than it had been at any other time since they had left home earlier.

The entrance doors had been hooked back open against the outside wall so that the morning sunlight made a pool of light illuminating the worn and gritty doormat. The spinose texture of the outer edges of the mat gave way to a smooth patch the colour of baked earth in the middle where the passage of feet was heaviest. Margaret stood for a moment just inside the entrance to the shop letting her eyes became accustomed to the relative darkness inside. Other than the daylight which entered the shop through the entrance doors, the only other natural light entered through a row of small windows of opaque glass high up along one side of the building necessitating the use of artificial light on all but the brightest of days.

On the whole, Hemswell was a popular posting, but the shop nevertheless remained small and cramped. Apart from the counter where cheese was cut and bacon sliced, most of the shop space was given over to shelves. At one point there was an unexplained change in the level of the floor and here the shelves had been kept level by placing a small tin, its label now dirty and faded, under one corner of the shelving. Along the shelves tins, jars and packets were arranged: stiff cardboard boxes of washing powder with bright-sounding brand names; carbolic-smelling bars of kitchen soap in long yellow packets; bright blue tins of cat food; tins of sweet tasting Californian peaches in thick glutinous syrup.

Everything had been hermetically sealed. Factory jam, thought Margaret, factory jam and tinned vegetables; it all seemed so unsatisfactory. One year, at home, before she had married, there had been a glut of victoria plums from the tree which grew at the bottom of the garden – her father had fashioned wooden props to keep the heavily laden branches from breaking with the weight of so much fruit - and she and her mother had made so much rich, rubescent jam out of the fruit that the jars would not all fit in the kitchen larder and so a number of them had to be stored away in the sideboard in the dinning room, the vegetable dishes from the best service and the silver cake-stand being moved further along the bottom shelf in order to accommodate them all. Margaret half-heartedly selected her purchases – she had finally decided on macaroni cheese for their tea - and having eventually reached a compromise with Mark, paid for her groceries and a sixpenny bar of chocolate.

## *Chapter Ten*

The air felt clean and sharp and the sky appeared as if it had been newly refreshed with a deep, satisfying, clear blue trumpet-light. Aiden walked in the bright sunlight along the access road that ran behind the officers' mess. The refreshing air coursed about his face and neck and its sharpness penetrated the layer of warmth between his cotton shirt and the coarser material of his tunic.

Although the morning felt innocent of blemish, Aiden had a lingering sense of having been wronged. And feeling out of sorts, he felt put out upon hearing footsteps approaching behind him. He stepped up onto the kerb and turning smartly left started along the asphalt pathway which ran off at right angles towards the brick-built building which contained the briefing office. As he turned on to the path, out of the corner of his eye he caught sight of a red-haired, freckle-faced young officer hurrying to catch him up.

"What's this all about? Any ideas?" Geoff, his navigator, fell into step beside him. He spoke brightly in the same agreeable, but accent-less, tone that characterised Aiden's own speech and gave away his suburban origins; in all likelihood, he and Aiden probably shared remarkably similar upbringings. Geoff was amiable enough, but Aiden felt no closeness or intimacy with him.

"I'm in the dark just as much as you are, I'm afraid." Aiden made an effort to be agreeable.

"Oh. I thought you might have had some sort of inkling."

Geoff would have had a real shock of red hair, thought Aiden, had it not been cut to the regulation length, but as it was he blended in well enough.

"Pilots are no different." Aiden smiled at Geoff. "They only tell us what they think we need to know!" It was the utterance of a comfortable truism.

"You can say that again!" Geoff replied with feeling. But as much as they always grumbled to each other about being fed on bullshit and of always being the last ones to know anything about anything, in reality the men cheerily accepted this as a welcome, even a comforting, fact of service life; they earnestly believed that the men who commanded them exercised something akin to fatherly care over them.

Feeling aggrieved that Margaret now seemed to resent the way they lived, it was only with considerable effort that Aiden managed to give Geoff enough of his attention so as not to appear distracted.

If upon returning home at the end of the day Aiden loitered in the kitchen, despite having said that he would quickly go and change out of his uniform before tea, because he still craved to share with Margaret the wonderment of the things he came across during his working day, often she would smile sweetly back at him as if she thought he were being merely childlike before turning her attention back to the domestic task that his arrival had interrupted.

Aiden felt deceived. He wondered if at first she had fooled him and whether the astoundment she had so brightly and keenly offered him when he had talked at length of his life of flying had been no more than a series of small oblatory acts, albeit freely given, and now it was as if she thought motherhood had granted her possession of the moral high ground and that this now absolved her of the need to propitiate him in such ways. Aiden glanced at his watch; another five minutes and the briefing would begin.

"Where is everyone? It seems jolly quiet," Aiden said, more to himself than to Geoff, momentarily anxious that he had made some sort of a mistake about the briefing.

With only a few minutes to go, Aiden had expected to see a steady stream of aircrew arriving or a small knot of men in blue-grey uniforms standing about in an imperfect circle close to the entrance to the building, hastily finishing their cigarettes and chatting together whilst keeping a wary eye out for the familiar gait of the wing commander. But although Aiden was puzzled that there was nobody else but he and Geoff in sight, feeling preoccupied he also felt relieved that he was excused by their absence from the compulsion to share in the usual heartiness of the other men.

Apparently indifferent to Aiden's surprise, Geoff carried on talking pleasantly, "You missed a good evening in town!" But Geoff was simply doing no more than making polite conversation. "I wouldn't be at all surprised if a couple of the chaps are a bit worse for wear this morning," he added, as if this was a little daring. But Aiden looked surreptitiously at Geoff, a suspicion momentarily in his mind that Geoff might easily fall into this category.

Aiden rarely drank with his fellow airmen anymore, certainly not as a matter of course; generally he would now find himself quietly drifting to the periphery of any such group, as much as he sometimes felt a need to enjoy such companionship.

"I suppose that's somewhere else we're banned from?" His facetiousness and tone gently encouraged Geoff who interpreted them as a measure of Aiden's personal approval. Aiden continued amiably, "We'll soon be reduced to drinking with the other ranks, the way you lot carry on!" Geoff felt a warm glow as if his actions were somehow moving him a step closer to gaining admittance to a club he greatly desired membership of.

Aiden was never certain, on those rare occasions when he had been out with the other men to a pub or just along to the officers'-mess, whether it was his sense of guilt that made Margaret's comments to him when he returned home sound almost imperceptibly barbed, and in which case, feeling defensive, he would then neither admit to having enjoyed his evening nor to having been dissatisfied with it.

"It's just a spot of high spirits, really." Geoff spoke with an assumed modesty, as if he had just been vindicated, or he had just successfully carried out some difficult conjuring trick.

Making an effort to smile at Geoff, Aiden replied, "Oh is that what it is?" his exaggerated seriousness giving Geoff the opportunity he clearly wanted to elaborate.

"Harry was definitely three sheets to the wind!"

Aiden knew that the account would be heavily sanitised; the

younger officers had invented their behaviours for themselves and generally assumed that the married men could never have debauched themselves in any such ways. Geoff then added with obvious amusement, "Some of the chaps even had to put him to bed!"

There were two men in the squadron named Harry, but Aiden did not need to ask which one of them would inevitably be putting a brave face on his crapulousness this morning.

They had now reached the building. Aiden leant slightly forward, turned the door handle and pushed open the door. Stepping back and consciously smiling in an avuncular fashion, he courteously allowed Geoff to pass into the building before he did.

After the bright sunshine outside, the corridor seemed shrouded in relative darkness. Momentarily interrupting Geoff's account of the previous evening because it was on his mind, and also because knowing what Harry was like it was a sure-fire supposition to make, Aiden interjected, "And I suppose Harry had one of his pet theories about the briefing?"

Geoff began to reply, but then, as his eyes became accustomed to the lower level of light in the corridor Aiden cut him short with, "Well, something must be up!" For the briefest of moments Aiden's surprise and his employment of service slang bridged the carefully calculated distance between the two men, the tone of his exclamation suggesting a greater familiarity than was normally present between them: "Look, Snowdrops!"

Two military policemen stood silently outside the briefing room, one each side of the closed double doors. Their uniforms were sharply pressed and their boots shone so deeply that the windows across the corridor from their sentinel position were reflected in them. The leather belts of their uniforms and holsters looked sharply, zealously, clean. Paradoxically, Aiden was not used to seeing armed men and he found the sight of firearms rather unsettling. So inscrutable were they, that they gave an impression of a leashed force that was the servant of others and which trespassed on Aiden's sense of proprietorial familiarity with his surroundings. As if they had been silently reprimanded for being too frivolous, Aiden and Geoff entered the briefing room quietly, carefully, and unusually, closing the doors behind them.

The room already felt charged with a muted tension. It was immediately evident that only a small number of the squadron's crews were present but those that were had gravitated towards the middle of the room; the front and back rows, and the extremities of the middle rows, had all been left empty. Instead of the usual groups of friends chatting comfortably amongst themselves as they waited for the ordinary, predictable rundown of the day's activities, the crews conversed in hushed whispers.

"This is all a bit rum, don't you think?" Aiden whispered, sitting down in the row behind Harry, the other Harry, with Geoff following along close behind him. The chair Aiden sat in was diagonally behind Harry and Aiden leant forward and rested his arms on the tubular steel frame of the empty chair in front of him the better to talk to Harry.

With the air of a man who had been merely passing the time, Harry lifted his newspaper up from his crossed knee where it had been resting doubled over while he had been reading from one of its inside pages, closed it up, folded it, and placed it down on the seat of the chair Aiden was leaning on. As he did so he turned around to look at Aiden, "Well, they can't be posting us anywhere, or we'd all be here, wouldn't we?"

Harry was calmer, more steady, than most of the other men. Aiden's eyes automatically glanced down at the newspaper in front of him.

"That's what I was going to say!" Geoff said with an air of urgency.

Geoff was youthfully more impetuous than either Aiden or Harry, neither of whom took any pleasure in speculation when the matter could be grave, but Geoff was eager for his contribution to be valued.

"But I wouldn't have put it past them," Harry said in his customary measured tone, adding rhetorically, "We've only been here five minutes, but I don't suppose that would've stopped them."

Harry and Aiden had been posted to the squadron at the same time. Harry was older than most of the other men and a year or two older than Aiden. Also like Aiden he was married. Together, these two things, age and marriage, were enough to have moved both of them away from the domain of most of the younger men.

"I can imagine what Margaret would say if we were faced with *another* move so soon," Aiden said.

The two married men exchanged a private look to which Geoff mentally gave an unrealistically simplistic interpretation, but not wanting to court disapprobation from the older men and also being secretly a little in awe of the married state, he thought better of making any comment. So instead, he continued on his previous tack, "Last night not all of the chaps knew about the briefing! Apparently it's only for a number of particular crews!"

Aiden wondered if something momentous and percipient had happened in the world and he did not want to reveal his ignorance of it if it had; although their squadron had not been deployed in the crisis, Suez was still fresh in everybody's minds and there was therefore a shared tacit nervousness about the possibility of live operations. Aiden's eyes surreptitiously flickered down to the seat in front of him, but only the bottom half of the back page of Harry's newspaper was visible. He would not have been nervous of admitting any such ignorance to Dennis; they would even have comfortably shared in their ignorance together, quietly deploying a modest self-deprecating humour to carry them through the briefing having mastered the art of conversing in meaning-laden whispered monosyllables through unmoving lips.

"Sounds like the usual cock-up then, since we're not so particular." And then turning back to Aiden in mid flow, Harry continued, "No, although I expect if she's at all like Janet she'd feel more settled if we were sent back somewhere nearer home."

Geoff smiled at Harry's joke, but inwardly he felt in some vague, sensitive and indefinable way that the joke had at least in part been aimed at him.

"Fat chance of that," Aiden said in agreement with Harry.

"Not unless you want to fly a desk at the Ministry, I suppose?" Harry smiled at Aiden.

But Aiden felt he ought to be circumspect in front of Geoff and so he weighed his words carefully before replying, "Perhaps one day, but I can't see it just yet." But there was an unmistakable note of facetiousness in his reply.

"It's not what I joined up for." Aiden thought that Harry could probably have safely added that Janet accepted this state of affairs philosophically; Aiden always thought that there was a certain equanimity about her. Harry went on to say, "The houses don't help, do they? They're much the same wherever one's sent and it's not just that they're a bit on the small side, but what with all the moving about one just doesn't have the heart to do much with them."

"Or the gardens."

"No. I expect I'll just put a few runners in and that'll be about the lot. No point doing anything else really if we're just going to be sent somewhere else at the drop of a hat."

"Gardens!" Geoff exclaimed, eager to be included in the conversation. "At least I don't have to worry about gardens!"

"Oh you may joke," Harry began to reply, but at that moment the doors at the back of the room were opened abruptly and the wing commander strode in. The low hum of conversation ceased and the doors were smartly shut again by the military policemen.

The wing commander passed briskly down the aisle that ran through the middle of the chairs to the podium at the front. The men all stood up in the usual service fashion when senior officers entered a briefing room, pushing their chairs back with their calves as they did so, the chairs making hollow, dry, scraping noises on the wooden floor boards. Under the cover of the noise a number of the men coughed to clear their throats.

The men's nervousness quickly gave way to a mounting sense of excitement. Not only was the wing commander accompanied by their own squadron leader, but also by a mild-looking man of moderate height who was wearing a tweed jacket and grey flannels; civilian guests were rare on the airfield, especially attending a briefing. The elbows of the civilian's jacket had soft leather patches sown onto them; Aiden suspected that this had as much to do with the desire to conserve a favourite and comfortable item of clothing as anything to do with thrift or economy. The man's hair was greying about his temples, his face was amiable and his forehead carried a number of deep worry lines like so many furrows separated by soft, plump ridges. The morning sunlight streamed in through the windows along the eastern side of the briefing room and along with a few specks of dust which were drifting through the air, threw the three men on the podium into sharp relief.

The wing commander started the briefing in the usual manner. "Sit down please, gentlemen."

As he continued speaking, he made no allusion to the presence of the military policemen stationed outside the door as if enforcement of secrecy should be accepted as simply being par for the course, but the absence of any such reference worked on the men as if they had been brought to the realisation that the story that they were a part of was more serious or grown up than they had previously imagined and that in some peculiar way they would leave the briefing room feeling older than when they had entered it.

As the wing commander talked, the moderate looking man stood beside their squadron leader with his hands in his jacket pockets, apparently quite at ease and as if he were mildly distracted, unconsciously turning some item over with his fingers, a latch key or loose change perhaps.

"A detachment from the squadron has been selected to undertake a scientific task that is crucial for the future of our national defence." The wing commander had a powerful natural presence that projected to the corners of any room he was in, but today he exuded an additional, barely suppressed pride as he continued, "The task will demand an exceptional degree of skill and professionalism. I do not doubt that you men are more than equal to the task."

After his words of introduction, the wing commander turned and introduced the civil servant. A further flutter of infectious excitement passed through the room; he was from the Atomic Weapons Research Establishment at Aldermaston. He was one of the atom men, a boffin, and he therefore epitomised to the men all of the excitement, achievement and possibilities of the postwar new age. Without any further ceremony or preamble, the scientist, in a soft, almost dreamy type of voice, began to matter-of-factly explain the nature of the scientific task.

"I'm sure you men have heard all about Operation Buffalo which took place in October of last year at Marlinga in Australia where Britain's first live drop of a weapon in the kiloton range took place."

His words ran through them infectiously setting silent rumour running about the nature of the task ahead of them, the men sensing that they had been entrusted to take part in something which was of generational significance. "This next operation will step up the pace somewhat. It will be a series of live airbursts of hydrogen bombs, or thermonuclear devices, in the megaton range."

Without dwelling on the physics of the matter, the mild and gentle-looking civil servant casually went on to outline the awesome potency of the hydrogen bomb, the pulverising devastation of the shock wave, the flesh and bone vaporising white-heat of the fireball, all in the same understated, confident way in which he might have outlined the tactics for a school's first eleven cricket fixture. He continued quite matter-of-factly, "Aircraft from the "V" bomber force will be dropping the live devices."

For Aiden and the other aircrew, the language of the weapons scientist was laden with all the promise of godwords so that the prospect of being closely involved in some type of a grand atomic adventure offered them a heady mixture of redemption and modernity. "Your part will be to take samples from the mushroom cloud after each explosion." Despite the hideously obvious dangers, the mushroom cloud was a thrilling and potent icon of the brave new atomic age.

And as the golden godwords tumbled from his gentle lips, they worked a promissory magic on the flyers; as untempered boys they had had only the skimpiest acquaintance with danger. They made the short hairs on the back of their heads and necks stand up. They caused a fluttering sensation in the men's stomachs as if they were readying themselves for a giant leap over a dropping space of unfathomable depth. "The wing tip tanks on your aircraft will be modified with non-return valves to collect the air samples." There had already been rumours circulating within Bomber Command, but the men had never imagined that it would be they who should be participating and playing such a crucial role.

The scientist continued with his briefing. "Courier aircraft will fly the samples back to the UK within twenty-four hours." The men all sat in rapt attention; by passing their tongues over their parted lips it was as if they could already hungrily taste their participation.

One officer sitting two rows in front of Aiden was leaning forward with his elbow propped up on his crossed knee, supporting his head on one hand with his thumb curved up under his chin, his forefinger crooked around in a semi-circle in front of it and pulling on the skin of his chin tightly. Aiden felt quite sure he must have been completely unaware of how he was sitting.

Presently, the scientific officer handed over to their squadron leader, who was also notably more animated than usual, and who began to speak with a sense of creeping jubilation. But Aiden could not fully share in the excitement of the moment; he knew Margaret would be unhappy that he was to be part of the detachment.

"The Operation is to be known as Operation Grapple. You will be operating from Christmas Island in the South Pacific." Missing Margaret and Mark would be a legitimate emotion, but if he were honest he would also have to admit to feeling guilty about leaving them. "The instrumentation site will be Malden Island approximately three hundred and sixty five miles distant." But whether this was because Margaret would be sure to subtly insinuate that it was a boyish thing he was about to do, and he could neither be hard-hearted or indifferent to her, he was not certain.

"Nice euphemism for target!" Geoff muttered under his breath. Aiden did not reply. He wondered whether the other men had this curious and inexpressible dichotomy between their inner life and the outward, public show of feelings. "And actually quite precise, not really approximate at all!" Geoff added, in the same muted fashion as he had spoken in before. This was remarkably similar to the irreverent humour Aiden had once shared with Dennis but which had not really been cynical, and Aiden found himself feeling irritated with Geoff and thought, a little unkindly, that he could not imagine there being any conflict between Geoff's inner and outer emotional life.

"Preliminary drop dates have already been set; you will therefore need to begin making preparations for imminent departure."

Sensing the excitement spreading all around him, Aiden felt his sense of isolation steadily increase. Presciently, he imagined that telling Margaret about the forthcoming detachment would feel like he had to justify himself in some way, to apologise for his labours, for his discipline, and as the corollary, as if his maleness must be inferior to her femaleness.

"Valiants from Forty Nine Squadron are already on station, having worked up their routines using dummy weapons over the Orford Ness range."

He imagined the accomplished sigh with which she would greet him upon his return home this evening which would be intended to communicate to Aiden that her day must have been fraught when compared to his, as if somehow she unfairly carried some burden on behalf of them both. In all probability, as he began to speak she would sit down at the kitchen table, her shoulders rounded and her back curved and, protesting tiredness, initially hear him out in a disarming silence. Her adoption of the deportment of the defeated always made her seem so utterly unapproachable to him.

"You will all be issued with tropical kit." The squadron leader carried on speaking enthusiastically, as if he was extolling the virtues of their destination to them as being particularly good for their health. "Christmas Island is the largest coral atoll in the Pacific, although its dimensions are only about thirty-five miles east and west by twenty-four miles at its greatest width. In general the island elevation is only about ten foot above sea level, but to the east there are sand dunes rising to approximately twenty foot. Surrounding the island is a fringe of coral reef, several hundred yards in width."

Often, after crossing back across the landing having cleaned her teeth, she would slip into bed beside him and as one single event say goodnight to him and turn onto her side so that she was facing away from him. Then with one hand she would habitually pull the pillow down so that it tucked in neatly and firmly against her shoulder and then with the other pull the sheet up as far as her neck. She would then partially draw up her knees and rest her hands, one loosely on top of the other in the warm space in front of her body, nestling in upon herself. In some indefinable way her pose was more than unsexual, it suggested both vulnerability and defensiveness. It was an angry posture full of inwrought reflexes, so that he would be fearful of stretching out his hand to stroke her shoulder or run his fingers along her spine and he would therefore rather opt for safety and turn his back to her, away from the mingling smells of her minty breath and her hair, and quietly click out the bedside light. It was as if the rules they lived by were secretly fluid and he continually feared withdrawal of her permission to live in her protecting domestic bubble through some unwitting transgression of them.

The squadron leader now concluded his part of the morning's briefing. "You will transit through Aldergrove, Goose Bay, Namaro, Travis Air Force Base in California, Honolulu and from there on to Christmas Island. Your ground crews will go ahead to make preparations for your arrival."

Once he had finished, he turned his head towards the wing commander, who, standing very erect, acknowledged the handover with the very slightest inclination of his head. Then, in a tone of creeping triumph, the wing commander turned to address the men: "Gentlemen, would you care to join us for a cup of coffee?"

For a second or two, none of the men moved. But after a moment, the steel frames of the chairs once again scraping on the varnished wooden floorboards, the men all stood up; the usual form at the conclusion of a briefing was for the senior officer to simply dismiss the men who would then go about their ordinary duties. The men shuffled forward into the central aisle and made to follow the wing commander, the squadron leader and the scientific officer out of the briefing room and across to the officers' mess. The men had initially been silent as they had stood up but hushed and excited conversation now broke out between them as they started to walk.

"Well, what do you think about all that then?" Aiden said. He had naturally gravitated to join Harry as they walked, with Geoff tagging along beside them. A number of small white clouds now scudded across the morning sky, but they were not sufficient to interrupt the brilliance of the morning light.

"Aldermaston! So that chap might know Penney!" Even the naturally reserved Harry was not immune to the headiness of the situation. The press had affectionately christened Penney, Cockcroft and Hinton, the three men who spear-headed Britain's atomic programme, the Bold Bad Barons, and they frequently featured in the cinema newsreels.

"I suppose he might do," Aiden replied.

"You know, I had heard that a detachment from Forty-Nine was out in the Pacific, but everybody seemed to be keeping mum about what they were up to!"

The men walked on a few more steps, each busy with his own thoughts.

"At least we're not being posted," Harry then said, exchanging a knowing look with Aiden. He was sounding quietly relieved and was now much calmer, much more like his usual self.

"Do you think we'll get any leave in Honolulu?" Geoff chipped in eagerly.

"And what would you be wanting that for?" Harry said, gently ribbing the younger man in his customary fashion. "Thinking of shopping for a nice Hawaiian shirt?"

"Skirt more like it, I expect." Aiden sounded good-humoured enough, as if he was merely adding to the banter that marked the three of them out as belonging to the same tribe, but there was a hint of ill will behind his words, as if he was jealous of the younger man.

"Now now, Aiden, he wouldn't know what to do with it anyway." But then Harry suddenly added in mock surprise, "Oh look! He's not taking us in through the tradesmen's entrance. Oh very grand, I must say!"

They had turned the corner of the officers' mess, the wing commander, their squadron leader and the scientist a few yards ahead of the other men, and were heading for the main entrance of the building. They looked a curious procession; the two senior officers striding ahead, talking animatedly, the scientist uncomfortably trying to keep up with them while keeping one hand in his jacket pocket and the rest of the men, spread out, walking quickly in irregular bunches so that they appeared like blobs of flotsam jostling in an irresistible current.

~~~~

"I shouldn't get used to it, if I was you," Harry murmured wryly from behind his cup as he raised it to his lips. White-jacketed stewards served the coffee in an anteroom and, unusually, it was served in the bone china cups marked with a discreet squadron crest which were usually reserved for formal dinners. "Brown sugar even, where will it end?" Harry added, theatrically.

"Not to mention the cream," Aiden replied equally quietly. "And what do you think," he said looking towards the scientist without moving his head but so that Harry could see where he was surreptitiously looking, "A pipe man I should think?"

"Oh yes, I would say so," Harry murmured in reply, smiling conspicuously to the room as a whole.

"Look out, here they come."

The wing commander, with his unmistakable air of social ease, was circulating with the scientific officer introducing him to the members of the crews. After he had shaken hands with both Aiden and Harry, Aiden, casting a quick glance at Harry, noted with quiet satisfaction how the scientist absent-mindedly took out a nondescript pipe from his jacket pocket and proceeded to fill it with tobacco from a soft leather pouch, working the tobacco deep into the bowl with his thumb with careful, slow, precise movements. The scientist seemed perfectly content to let the wing commander lead the conversation.

"Quite an operation by the sounds of it, sir." Harry diplomatically struck up a note of polite enthusiasm, encouraging the wing commander to more small talk without having to express any particular opinion himself. Aiden, holding the saucer beneath his half finished cup of coffee in his left hand, his thumb discreetly tucked over the shaft of the spoon so that it could not slip and with the thumb and fore finger of his right hand just touching the handle of the cup, maintained the look of alert interest that they had learnt by experience was appropriate for these sorts of occasions.

This morning, the wing commander's enthusiasm far exceeded the demands of polite conversation and his voice continued to strengthen with pride as he continued to speak of the logistical achievements of the operation. He talked about the new airfield that had been constructed on the inhospitable island by the Royal Engineers, large enough to take the flight of Valiant bombers and all the supporting aircraft; the camp that had been constructed for the thousands of soldiers, sailors and airmen who were involved, even including a church; and how the Royal Navy shipped everything required for the operation, everything from cabbages for cooking to concrete for construction, half way around the world. "Largest inter-service operation since the war!" the wing commander exclaimed proudly.

Although he had only known him for a matter of weeks, Aiden had quickly developed a liking for the wing commander; he seemed to personify integrity. He had been heavily decorated for his part in wartime bombing raids, especially the precision bombing raids on the secret German V-weapons establishment at Peenemünde, and in some peculiar way, Aiden reflected, to men like him and the other older men of the squadron Operation Grapple must feel like the offer of some sort of redemption.

"Have the ground crews been briefed yet, sir?" Aiden asked at a convenient break in the conversation, when it seemed like the wing commander had started to look around to see if there was anyone the scientist had yet to be introduced to.

"Yes, they had their own briefings earlier this morning."

Aiden excused himself from the assembled company and left the anteroom to walk over to the hangars to look for his crew chief. There would inevitably be a lot of work for his ground crew to do in a short space of time, and Aiden had become adept at keeping his crew chief on side which made for an easier life.

As he walked past the station offices and the operations block with their gentle hum of orderly morning activity he wondered what words he would use to tell Margaret about the operation and whether trust should form a part of the conversation.

Aiden would have liked to have re-courted Margaret's enthusiasm; without Margaret's approval, it felt as if his every action and deed was illegitimate or improper. It was as if through marrying Margaret, he had performed some unknowing act of abdication, foolishly handing over some of his life energy to Margaret without understanding the implications of his action.

# Chapter Eleven

Back home it would be a mid-week day like any other and yet here too was a temptation for the aircrews to believe that today was not momentous after all; one-eighth cover of fair weather cumulus cloud with a light and variable surface wind was perfectly normal, almost invariably, tediously so, for the Pacific.

But today the sunlight appeared so bright to them that it seemed as if they could have been deep in the mind of God. It bounced back off the vast concrete runway that stretched out before them like an invitation to infinity, so that their retinas ached with a dull pain, and it transmuted the white reflective paintwork of their aircraft, that had been somewhat hastily applied on first deploying to the island, into an aura of blazing glory light.

And then there was a certain unreality to it all. In marked contrast to almost every other day, the usually busy concrete aprons, which provided the hard standing for all the many aircraft taking part in the operation, were eerily almost entirely devoid of personnel. The Shackletons, the lumbering piston-engined maritime patrol aircraft, had already taken off and were by now patrolling pre-arranged and well-rehearsed grid-like patterns to ensure that no shipping strayed into the live test area; the Shackletons' ground crews had therefore no need to remain on the aprons and the dispersals were now marked only by their abandoned-looking, functional but silent ground equipment.

Many other aircraft stood on the apron, but they were all quiet and deserted: Dakotas, used for communications and general transport, and affectionately dubbed Christmas Island Airways by the servicemen, the sun's heat already covinously shimmering off their white-roofed fuselages and hotly, fractionally, expanding their metal skins creating all manner of irregular and unnatural creaks and groans; other aeroplanes usually employed on fast courier duties back to the United Kingdom; heavier transports; the two of the four Valiants from Forty-Nine Squadron which were not to be employed on today's live drop; and, as absolutely nothing would be left to chance, the spare atmosphere-sampling Canberras from their own squadron, present in case of an aircraft going unserviceable.

The vast empty expanse of concrete, flooded with the hallucinatory sunlight of transitory, golden upland plains; the creaking aircraft forsaken to solitariness and lacking even their own ghosts; the minimal activity, like unimportant sparks of penance in boundless angel-light: all fuelled both a peculiar weight of abandonment and a disconcerting ontal proximity.

But the desertedness was rational; a safety plan had been put in place which involved the dispersal of all non-essential personnel in case one of the laden atom-bombers should crash on takeoff. Everyone on the island had repeatedly practised the safety plan until it had acquired the comfort of an accustomed drill; but mitigating against such a shocking possibility reinforced the gravity of the exercise, yet electrified each of them and increased their tingling exhilaration at being a part of it.

The crews of the Shackletons and Canberras had earlier attended their own briefing - a separate briefing having been held for the crews of the Valiants - and now, at the commencement of their task, they waited as if for a parade to wash their hearts. Today seemed like the enkindling culmination of all the labour, the slow discipline, his understanding of duty, and of the sacrifices Aiden had willingly undertaken since he had joined the RAF and he felt now that there could be no possible shame in being what he was before his son. Something deep and intuitive said to him that sons should understand what it was that their fathers did all day, what it was that gave fathers their particular elevation of mind or character, their cast of being; otherwise the sons would become suspicious of their fathers, and of other older men, and look for alternative truths about them.

The Canberras had been stationary at their holding positions along the taxiway parallel to the main runway since before the departure of the Valiants. At any time when irradiated by the sun's rays the temperature inside the bubble canopy of the Canberra's cockpit would rise rapidly. Now, inside the aircraft's cockpit the heat was intense. Aiden and Geoff sweltered inside their blue-grey flying suits. Aiden could feel his scalp clammy beneath the cloth flying helmet which fitted snugly beneath his hard outer shell-like protective helmet, and the sweat beading-up on his forehead, trickling down his temples and running along the snugly fitting edge of his oxygen mask. Inside his flying suit, the back of his shirt stuck to his back and he could feel the occasional trickle of sweat travelling erratically down his sternum. The inside of his upper thighs and around the area of his groin seemed damp and uncomfortable, briefly giving rise to the fluttering, niggling worry that his most personal hygiene may have been insufficiently vigorous.

The Valiants had cleared the runway a few moments ago at exactly nine o'clock. From their own holding positions Aiden and his crew had watched them go. Their takeoffs had been flawless, executed with precision and split-second timing. Like huge white bats the Valiants had risen-up and headed off into the voluminous blue sky, their engines casting a deep unsettling Olympian roar throughout the Pacific morning.

So great was the brightness outside their aircraft that when, having watched the Valiants' departure, and they had returned their eyes to their own flying instruments, momentarily everything seemed shrouded in darkness. But the cockpit retained its familiar, comforting, workaday smell of metal, lubricating oil and electrical insulation material so that it took them only a very few moments to fix their minds back upon their purpose.

Waiting for clearance to proceed to their own take-off position, their own engines, unlike the roar of the Valiants' engines when they had departed, gave out a constant anticipatory numinous whistle. Quite apart from the intense heat, sitting at the controls in the cockpit waiting for instruction, Aiden was far from comfortable: the metal bucket seat was purely functional and not designed for comfort and his life jacket was bulky around his shoulders and chest, especially between his rib-cage and his right arm where his emergency radio-location beacon nestled within it.

Although expected, even awaited, Aiden started slightly as the disembodied voice of the flight controller from HMS Warrior, the control ship for the whole operation, spoke suddenly in his earphones precipitating a prickling flush of anticipation in Aiden's lumbar region. Unconsciously touching his squadron scarf - both a superstitious talisman and his badge of pride and loyalty, which, as was his unforgoable ritual, he had carefully knotted about his neck as he had prepared for flight earlier this morning - Aiden released the brake and gently eased the throttles open a little wider. The whistle now glided evenly up a tone and the Canberra increased its speed to little more than a gentle walking pace, and taxied towards the head of the runway.

Once the end of the runway had been achieved, Aiden eased back on the engines' throttles, applied the brakes and with a pleasing precision the aircraft came softly to a halt at the exact point that Aiden had intended. The Canberra exactly straddled the broken white line that marked the centre of the runway and which guided pilots, helping prevent them from deviating from their course on takeoff. There was an intense silence in the cockpit; but it was more deeply fuelled than if it had simply resulted from the business-like concentration on the many technical tasks and checks that both Aiden and Geoff had to perform before any given flight. With a heightened sensory perception and his omnipresent secret fear of error or failure, today the pit of Aiden's stomach seemed poised as if he was about to be pitched headlong into an unknowable abyss.

The calm, assured voice of the flight controller spoke once again in his earphones. Aiden took a bibulous, steadying breath which he could feel to the depths of his diaphragm muscles and, with professional simplicity, acknowledged the clearance he had been given, and then confirmed that he was commencing his take-off run. He flexed his hands slightly within his flight gloves, the gloves moved with him perfectly, without friction, abrasion or chafing; they felt like a second skin. As much a part of a pilot's set of tools as any of the technically complex controls on a flight deck, their gloves were manufactured from extremely fine, soft, thin leather and gave pilots great dexterity and sensitivity at their aircrafts' controls. As he renewed his grip, adjusting the position of his hands on the control column, he thought epiphenomenally to himself that his gloves were so fine, supple and snug that they could be the gloves of a murderer, of a statesman or a priest.

Aiden and Geoff commenced their final pre-flight checks; Aiden, out of necessity having first fully applied the aircraft's brakes, opened the throttles as wide as possible, running the engines up to full power. The previously clinical whistle, so suggestive of merely simple clean efficiency, grew louder and louder with astonishing, heart-stopping rapidity until it achieved a cavernous, hurting roar. Then, after a matter of seconds, with the same suddenness, Aiden throttled the engines back. The resulting relative silence was infinitely more portentous than the thunder preceding it; it was like a hot, trilling wire entering the flesh.

For a moment, the Canberra stood hushed on its start point. To Aiden the aeroplane briefly seemed inconsequential or merely ephemeral, oppressed by the terrible, canescent sunlight on the vast expanse of the concrete runway; the runway was sixty yards wide and well over two thousand yards long. Aiden then confidently opened the throttles. The whistle grew louder and louder, higher and higher, a slow, even, considered glissando as the machine began to move purposefully forward; with all Aiden's discomfort now forgotten, the wire bit deeper. Ever since the bombing training had been completed well over a month ago, and all the squadrons taking part in the operation had been considered fully operational, they had practiced repeatedly and intently for this moment which gave them more than a mere confidence in their own technical ability. Their own *certainty* in their ability felt profound and invigorating, as if they had become warriors entrusted with a greater purpose, something that a grocer back at home, an engine driver or a dentist could not possibly do; it felt kingly.

As the Canberra gained momentum, each segment of the central white line disappeared in turn beneath the aircraft's fuselage. Slowly at first, then quicker and quicker, faster and faster, as if the aircraft were greedy for them. From his vantage point Aiden watched the runway speeding past beneath them and the individual white segments mesmerically blurring into an apparent locus.

As it rose up suddenly into the clean Pacific air, the aircraft distanced itself from its own shadow; the sharp black cross became smaller and smaller beneath them. As the aircraft accelerated up and away from the east-orientated runway, and crossed over the coast of the island at North East Point with the Bay of Wrecks on their starboard side, the Canberra's shadow became smaller and smaller. As a function of passing over the Pacific waves approaching to break upon the island, the shadow's outline became unfixed and moveable like jelly instead of enjoying the clear-cut lines it had enjoyed on the runway. Then, as the aircraft rose ever higher into the air, it became insignificant against the deep, clear blue tropical waters beneath them; and then to all intents and purposes its shadow disappeared entirely.

Geoff, as he would inevitably do at this point after any takeoff, matter-of-factly issued Aiden with the navigational bearing which would take their aircraft to its designated orbiting point, nearly four hundred nautical miles distant, where they would hold waiting for their instruction to take samples of the atmosphere following the air-burst. By now they had flown on this course so many times that Aiden hardly needed Geoff's prompt, but that was the discipline and the procedure and which they therefore unquestioningly followed.

All the orbiting aircraft listened to the controller's transmissions, so as they flew to their position they could hear the controller's instructions to each aircraft, the crews' replies and even the conversation between individual members of each of the flight crews, although such talk was strictly limited to the business of the day; the occasional service banter, usually present even if to a minor degree on any type of flight, was absent today as the crews all concentrated totally on the task in hand.

Without deviating from their course they flew straight and level between the elemental sea and sky towards their orbiting point. Aiden and Geoff checked the flight and navigational instruments, monitoring the health of their aircraft, their height, speed, bearing, their overall progress against their discrete but interrelated part of the complex plan for the day. In spite of the exhilaration that they felt, the tingling wire in their flesh, both experienced a mood of quiet introspection, or of silent communing as if something metaphysical constrained and directed them. Reaching their orbiting point, above them the sky was a well of cornflower blue and below them, and as far as the eye could see, the sun sparkled on the water. Aiden proceeded to fly the aircraft on the prescribed circuit at the prescribed height and prescribed speed.

At precisely the time he had been expected, the controller once again spoke to them through their headphones; a general announcement to all the orbiting aircraft at their many stations. Being now at forty-five thousand feet, and having completed an initial run to check telemetry, the Valiants would be starting their final approach. Indeed, over the radio, Aiden could hear Wing Commander Hubbard, the pilot of the leading Valiant, confirm his exact height and heading to Control as well as a short, factual conversation between Hubbard and the pilot of the grandstand Valiant which would be following Hubbard's plane on the approach to the drop. Although fully expected, the announcement nevertheless made the hair on the back of Aiden's head stand up on end, and reduced his back to bristling gooseflesh as he increased the grip on the control column and sought to bring the butterflies in his stomach under control; even repeated practice – and they had flown a full operational rehearsal the day before - could not have totally prepared him for the awesomeness of the day. Not having close-fitting anti-flash metal shutters inside the Canberra's cockpit as the Valiants had been fitted with, Aiden and Geoff now averted their eyes from the bright sky.

Eleven seconds before Hubbard's aircraft was scheduled to release the live thermonuclear weapon, the grandstand aircraft started its escape manoeuvre. Only one aircraft was required to perform the actual drop, but a second craft, the grandstand aircraft, following through the exact same routine gave another crew valuable experience of flash and blast and was also not without attendant danger; the high speed escape manoeuvre consisted of a sixty degree bank turn to port through one hundred and thirty degrees - close to the point of a high-speed stall.

The grandstand Valiant's aircrew may have been keeping radio silence for all the conversation which Aiden and Geoff could overhear over their own radio. There was only the occasional word concerning a correction to a control and the sounds of the crew members checking and counter-checking instrument readings, but after a few seconds Aiden heard the pilot of the grandstand Valiant affirming, in a quiet, collected, almost disinterested way, that his Valiant had completed the exit manoeuvre and that all was well. The controller politely thanked him and instructed him to return to Christmas Island according to plan.

The calm, factual manner in which the grandstand Valiant's pilot had made his report following such a demanding escape manoeuvre, and the way in which the controller with remarkably placid understatement had acknowledged him, engendered a feeling of immense pride within Aiden. It was as if their high-souled shared cause negated any need for displays of relief or excitement and to Aiden it also epitomised the attitudes and standards of the service and of the individuals within it.

When permitted by the controller to once more resume normal visual observation, the mushroom cloud from the live drop was already billowing dramatically upwards. At the point of weapons-burst, travelling at over six-hundred miles per hour, the Valiants were already nine nautical miles distant from the impact. At the point when the over-pressurisation wave, or shock wave, from the bomb would overtake them they would be twelve nautical miles distant. But not only had the Valiants been given a factory-applied anti-flash white finish, the thickness of which had been carefully calculated to an exact number of microns based upon the projected yield of the weapon, all the control surfaces had been strengthened to withstand the over-pressurisation wave, and special sealing strips, grommets and baffles had been fitted over any possible ingress for contaminated air. Upon the success of Operation Grapple rested the renewal of Bomber Commands' pride and reputation; the Valiants and their crews engaged in the operation would be sure to attract immense publicity and much was being done to ensure their safety.

Aiden had never imagined raw power of this magnitude. It

seemed illimitable like a terrible, all-consuming love or hate and gave the absolute lie to all studiously arrived-at thoughts of solipsism. The crews taking part in the operation had been briefed to expect a mushroom-shaped cloud, and some of its more probable features had also been explained to them, although now it seemed that the briefing had been woefully, if unintentionally, inadequate. The mushroom-shape had already become a popular icon of the Atomic Age, but its popular depiction in newspaper articles, even in cartoons, now seemed woefully inadequate, puerile or dangerously befooling. But perhaps nothing could have effectively prepared him for this moment and how foolish he now felt for even attempting to imagine the reality of it.

The mushroom cloud developed with a wildly captivating, twisting, worming stem of spumy, billowing smoke which from the distance of several nautical miles appeared curiously and deceptively static. At its base was a boiling cauldron mass of hellish reds, oranges and yellows. At its top, the mushroom shape wore a foaming white canopy stretching up to sixty thousand feet in the air, fifteen thousand feet higher in the sky than the height from which the bomb had been dropped just moments ago, with ice caps forming at the highest points. It was a smoking column of extremes or opposites; a metamorphosis of scorched and searing dust, mythologically short circuiting heaven to earth.

Aiden was predestined to aim their plane through the outermost edges of the expanding cloud. As he turned onto his new course, the shock wave hit them. It was unbelievably sudden and scary, and all the more so because the shock wave itself was invisible and thus they seemed totally at the will of some unseen and sturdy malicious force. The nose and the starboard wingtip of the aircraft were flung effortlessly and violently skyward as if the heavy craft were of no more consequence than a child's toy. Their instincts were to reach out with their hands to save themselves from falling despite the taut straps of their safety harnesses that now bit deeply into their collarbones and restrained them firmly in their seats. So violently, freakishly and capriciously thrown about were they that the instrument panel and control column appeared to jerk irregularly up and down in front of them, with all the frantic activity registering on the meticulously graduated dials appearing as a hopeless blur. Then, following the passage of the shock wave, the aircraft immediately lurched downwards like a fairground horror, and they felt themselves plummet, their stomachs sickly hollow, as if they were trapped in a doomed elevator. Acutely aware of their perilousness, of their butterfly fragility, they fought to regain control of the aircraft, to resume their course, and thereby to head into the expanding, boiling cloud.

Once inside the glowing gloom of the cloud, Aiden, having mastered himself, his face tinged with the grotesque netherworldly hues from the swirling clouds of particles that now bombarded the plane, held the aircraft steady sensing the heaving volumes of air that constantly threatened to upset the aircraft through his carefully feeling hands on the controls. Concentrating hard, he opened the vents on their wing-tip tanks and collected their atmosphere samples exactly as they had been instructed. Then as they emerged from the far side of the cloud, after precisely the prescribed amount of time, Aiden closed the tanks and asked Geoff for a bearing that would take them back. Without any hesitation, Geoff quietly and firmly replied. On his vector, Aiden then turned the Canberra to head back, like a bead in God's sky, to Christmas Island.

As they settled back down to the routine tasks of the flight back to Christmas Island, Aiden suddenly became aware of the shallowness and rapidity of his breathing. It was as if his body had put itself into a heightened sensory state ready to deal with the greatest of all possible dangers. Having now passed through fire, in itself this did not particularly surprise Aiden, but the fact that he had been quite unaware of it did. Aiden glanced back over his shoulder to where Geoff sat at his navigator's position and at that moment Geoff looked up from his calculations and caught Aiden's eye. Although most of Geoff's face was hidden by his oxygen mask, there was an unmistakable look of white animal fear in his eyes. Aiden raised one eyebrow enquiringly as he looked at Geoff, and Geoff replied by gently nodding his head. Reassured, Aiden turned back to the controls of the aircraft. Mixed with a smouldering jubilation at having successfully completed the task, he now felt excessively tired and had to concentrate hard on his flying even though the flight back to the island was merely a matter of routine from here on. Occasionally during the flight, he glanced back at Geoff busy at his navigator's station. Geoff was carrying out his job in his usual efficient way, but something about his bearing and his demeanour suggested that he was quieted and more reflective as if nothing deserved to be ever the same again.

Having obtained clearance for finals, they approached the main runway of the airfield from the west, flying in over Bridges Point with the bright playful lagoon on their right hand side. Looking down into the clear blue ocean as they descended, they could once more see their shadow as a tiny black cross growing to meet them. The shadow grew larger and larger and became more clearly defined as they neared the runway. As Aiden made a textbook landing it finally disappeared completely out of their view beneath them, finally fusing with the aircraft through the undercarriage wheels. As required by the operations plan for the day, Aiden then neatly taxied to the decontamination dispersal.

Only later did Aiden discover that during the course of the exercise something had gone gravely wrong with the exit manoeuvre and that the grandstand Valiant had almost been lost.

## Chapter Twelve

"Oh go on, be a sport!"

Harry was too unexcitable to be overly rebellious, but in a quiet sort of way he had never liked petty rules. Perspiring freely in the hot evening air, he leaned forward so that he could be heard above the general din. There was a note of mild exasperation in his voice; although it was not strictly allowed, he really could not imagine that anyone would mind and he would not have asked if he had seriously thought that the steward might find himself in some sort of trouble because of it.

Most of the men, especially those who had been directly involved in it, still felt a sense of euphoria following the successful live weapon drop. A second drop was scheduled for the end of May and operational readiness would be maintained through drills, practices and rehearsals, but the more commonplace, and frequently tedious, workaday routines inevitably remained large in their daily lives. A number of men would be returning home to be replaced by others and some could look forward to a few days leave in Honolulu, but key personnel, such as the crews of the atmosphere-sampling Canberras, would remain on the island until the series of tests had finished. As an antidote to tedium, when not on duty during the day, some of the men played cricket, the bright basting heat reflecting back off the crunchy hard-packed crystalline sand, and others developed unexpected hobbies. But officers and other ranks alike looked forward eagerly to evenings in the mess as their chief distraction.

There was an uncommonly thick press of people present this evening in the officers'-mess, even for a Saturday, and during the course of the evening the volume of noise had steadily increased as more and more men had gradually arrived. On the whole, their voices were high-spirited, not raucous, and like a muffling fug they densely filled the marquee that served as the officers'-mess defeating any attempted precision in communication. And although the entrance to the marquee stood wide open, the hot air and the static, stratified cigarette smoke that hung motionless within it steadfastly refused to circulate. By now Aiden and Harry were comfortably tight.

The steward once more politely protested that he was not really allowed to, but Harry persisted, "Nobody'll notice, and there's one in it for you, don't you know."

With a reproachful, baleful look on his face as if he felt he had been put upon, and that part of that feeling was that he was being cajoled by an officer, the steward grudgingly relented. He reached into his breast pocket for a small pad of pre-printed slips of paper. Then with a deliberate, sullen movement, he flipped open the pad and positioned a grubby and creased oblong piece of purple carbon paper between the top two pieces of paper and beneath them a dog-eared piece of cardboard to stop any indentation unintentionally being transferred to other sheets.

As if he had achieved a small victory, Harry straightened up and turned to face Aiden saying quietly but triumphantly, "There we are!" Then, with a sideways tilt of his head towards the main body of the room and speaking slightly louder than normal he added, "You can tell the new boys, can't you!" He then turned back towards the trestle table that served as a counter and, leaning forward, took the mess-chit that the steward ungraciously slid towards him.

"Do you have a pen, sir?" the steward asked with exaggerated politeness.

Shooting the steward a look and taking the pen that was held out to him, Harry said amiably to Aiden as he signed the chit, his left hand steadying the piece of paper, "Hate to think what our mess bills are going to look like. Sure to be questions asked in The House when we get home, I shouldn't wonder."

Aiden could not imagine Janet ever begrudging Harry a drink; there was an unmistakeable, enviable attunement between Harry and Janet.

"But what she doesn't know can't hurt her, eh?"

He smiled comfortably at Aiden, evidently not requiring a reply. Harry's tone was innocuous. Aiden and Harry did not really *drink* but nevertheless guilt still took the edge off his enjoyment; Harry would see nothing to hide from *his* wife. But, Aiden reflected, perhaps it was not guilt he felt but fear, but fear surely seemed too strong a word.

The steward turned away and placed the top copy of the chit in with countless others in a varnished wooden tray – the type of tray commonly found on a clerk's desk - which stood on a small battered table behind the main counter.

"I expect some poor sod has to tally all those up!" Harry added cheerily as he absentmindedly placed his own copy of the chit in his trousers pocket, roughly folding it twice as he did so, where it would probably stay until it felt fuzzy like an old bus ticket amongst his loose change.

As they waited for the steward, who was now reaching down beneath the trestle table, Harry and Aiden turned back towards the heaving mass of bodies in the mess. As old hands on the island they observed their fellow officers in a quietly amused and almost indulgent fashion.

"I see Len's here," Aiden remarked casually although it had actually been Geoff who had caught his attention; his carroty-red hair made him instantly recognisable. Geoff was clutching his pint glass, the beer slopping about dangerously, threatening to spill, as he talked animatedly to Len. It looked as if Len was tolerantly hearing him out.

"At least he hasn't got his bloody camera with him!"

Len was a keen amateur photographer and the phrase, "It's Len and his bloody camera," had passed into squadron folklore. Len took pictures of the men, persuading them to stand in relaxed, informal groups. He had taken a photograph of Aiden's plane in the decontamination dispersal. He took shots of the men going about their daily lives on the island. The men thought of him affectionately, secretly pleased to oblige, even to the extent of stopping what they were doing to re-group or pose so that the snap would be more life-like.

Harry was evidently the more garrulous of the two of them this evening, for apparently having dismissed Len from his mind, he continued, "When you stop to think about it, it's a bit odd really, isn't it?"

It suddenly struck Aiden, that tonight was actually like any other Saturday evening in the Mess: and it was really rather surreal.

The room was a hubbub of the usually staid and sensible officers dressed in the standard island evening attire of slacks and brightly coloured Aloha shirts. This particular evening-wear had developed spontaneously as a quirk of the posting. It was universally recognised as being a far from trivial affectation and the men had all become rather proud of it, feeling that it marked them out as being members of an elite club through their shared experiences and achievement. The men had become naturalised to the pattern of life on the island, but being on a desert island, standing in an army-issue marquee, drinking English beer and being dressed in exuberant shirts was really hardly very normal.

However, there were a few men who appeared ill at ease and who generally kept to their own small groups, tightly gripping their drinks and straining under the momentum of maintaining normal conversation as if they were uncertain whether they could yet properly abandon themselves to enjoyment. These were men newly posted to the island and to whom its particular ways were still a novelty. Generally, they lacked the obligatory Aloha shirt and stood instead in standard issue tropical kit.

"Poor lambs," remarked Aiden. "But I expect some kind soul back from leave will offer to sell them a nice shirt!"

"What's that?" Harry replied, occupied with his own train of thought. "Oh yes, like babes, aren't they, with nothing to wear but the clothes they arrived in. Nice little business opportunity for someone!"

"Just to make them feel at home, you understand."

"Of course, it'd be kindness itself!"

Aiden and Harry lapsed into a comfortable silence while they waited.

"But it'd be very nice, I'm sure," Harry suddenly continued after a moment or two, "Sipping a pink gin and watching the sun set over the sea, but that's not for the likes of you and me, old chap."

Aiden started. He had assumed Harry had previously been talking about the experience of spending evenings in their own mess, and he himself had started to mentally drift, musing upon his thoughts of why he should feel guilty about drinking. But suddenly twigging what Harry was actually talking about, he replied, "Ah yes, but it might depend on the company!"

He also wondered if he was a bit tighter than he had supposed himself to be, or indeed whether Harry was.

"Well, there's not that many of them there, of course, so it might be a bit too quiet for us. We wouldn't be used to it."

"Or we might just find it a bit too dull!"

"I really can't imagine what one would possibly talk about." Harry continued, "I mean, I can't see them being interested in how we manage to make ends meet on our wages, or what we might like to grow in our own little bits of garden and things like that."

The steward now surreptitiously slid a number of brown bottles across the table which he had brought out from the crates that conveniently nestled under the trestle table.

"Here, can you take a couple of these?" Harry said quietly.

Aiden put a bottle of Double Diamond in each pocket of his slacks.

"It's all a bit colonial really, isn't it?"

The senior officers' mess, about which they were speaking, was a wooden prefabricated building with a veranda which looked out to sea. It seemed a peculiar cross between a sour and astringent church hall and a down-at-heel gentlemen's club. Being reserved for the more senior ranks, group captains and above, no more than about ten men on the island were ever eligible to use it.

"I wonder how much is down to language? The differences, I mean, between them and us."

Aiden was wondering whether the senior officers would have understood Harry's comments about the mess bills in the same way that he had. He thought they would have. It was not a matter of class, he decided, or the worlds which they moved in, there were nuances of meaning which would have been intuitively understood by the majority of men. Most women, Aiden thought, would have understood perfectly well that such remarks were not derogatory, but they would have missed the overtones of affection, choice and duty that they contained or implied. Deconstructing his thoughts, the fact that Harry could utter the thought at all spoke volumes about the relationships involved, both between a man and his wife, but also between individual men.

"Sounds a bit deep for me, Aiden, especially after a couple of sherbets. Come on, let's get out of here, it really is too hot for words."

Their own mess was a complete crush. With army, air force and scientific staff all mixing together - naval personnel generally messed in port or on their ships - potentially a very large number of sweltering bodies had to be squeezed in.

"Think we're leaving in the nick of time; looks like a singsong's about to kick off." A pipe-smoking officer, who was looking remarkably at ease with the world, was making himself comfortable at the piano. "Good grief!" Aiden suddenly exclaimed, inclining his head towards a younger, fervent looking officer who had started doing the rounds; the younger officer had started to hand round song sheets. While singsongs were a regular feature of Saturday evenings in the officers'-mess, this was a new and rather worrying development.

"That definitely does it!"

Concealing the bottles of Double Diamond as best they could, they made their way across the crowded room, easing themselves between the tightly packed groups of men. Aiden followed closely behind Harry who, leading the way, held his right lower arm up from his crooked elbow so that his open hand was roughly at shoulder height in a friendly, familiar gesture implying he was looking for a way through. Occasionally, he reinforced the gesture with a pally word or a gentle touch on a man's shoulder when the men, too engrossed in their conversation or their beer, failed to notice their approach. In this way, they made their way out of the stifling marquee and into the cooler air outside.

Making their way the short distance towards the shoreline, they could hear the gentle waves breaking on the coral reef that surrounded the island. Once on the beach, they sat down heavily on the scrunchy sand, their legs stretched out in front of them, their arms supporting their bodies, their weight being taken on the heels of their hands.

"That's better," Harry sighed, "much too noisy in there. And what about that then, all those blinking song sheets! Too much like enforced jollity for my liking! Cigarette?"

Harry leant towards Aiden holding the slightly crushed packet out to him. Aiden took a cigarette then, in turn, leaned towards Harry with a lighted match. With the cigarettes lit, he blew out the match, pushed it sharply down into the sand beside him and returned the matchbox to his breast pocket. They sat back in silence for a moment, enjoying the quietness and the cooling onshore breeze. Aiden could feel the grains of course sand indenting on the palms of his hands.

"Here," Harry suddenly called out to Aiden, "Catch."

Neatly catching the bottle opener, Aiden opened one of the bottles of beer he now took out from his pocket. As he passed the opener back to Harry he said, "I expect our cloud samples are back in a laboratory at Aldermaston or somewhere by now."

Aiden had actually been wondering whether he resented Margaret for making him feel guilty. But not having Harry's seemingly innate ability for genial small-talk, or his gift for being able to unoffendingly deflect unwanted casual questions, he had spoken to avoid feeling rushed into answering any question from Harry which may have revealed something about his own train of thought, the subject matter of which he would feel insecure about another man knowing.

"Wonder what they do with them?" Harry replied, casually.

"Aren't you at all curious?" Aiden wondered whether Harry was really as disinterested as he appeared to be.

"Not really. Besides, they're not likely to tell *us* anything, are they? Fed on bullshit and kept in the dark, that's us. But I'll tell you what," he said more animatedly, "it'll make a fine story to tell your grandchildren one day. How we were here and all that, but buggered if I could find the right words for it all."

Harry fell into a meditative silence.

"It was beautiful, really." Aiden spoke hesitantly; he had thought twice about using the phrase to Harry, wondering, even if Harry did share the emotion, whether he would think it rightful to share thoughts about such beauty between men.

Harry initially made no reply, but remained semi-supine on the sand, his body limp and relaxed. Then he spoke haltingly, almost as if he felt ashamed, "Yes. It was, in a sort of grotesque way."

Encouraged, Aiden tried again, "Magisterial."

But there was a reluctance in Harry's reply, "Certainly."

Aiden sighed and both men continued looking straight out to sea, both known and guessed at in the darkness. The gentle, repetitive soughing of the waves on the edge of the impenetrably deep, unknowable ocean was lulling them as if by being where they were, they knew they were safe from any danger for the time being.

Sitting up straighter, Harry leaned slightly forward and to the left so that his left hand remained only partially supporting his weight on the sand. Balancing his cigarette gingerly between his lips and tilting his head backwards to avoid the drift of smoke from it, he could now delve comfortably into the right hand pocket of his trousers using his right hand. He pulled out the second of the two bottles he had been carrying, almost as if he had only just remembered he still had it with him.

"There, don't want to waste it, having gone to all that trouble to get it in the first place." Looking around at the expanse of sand as he offered the bottle opener to Aiden, Harry said, "Well I'm blowed, it's one of those crabs. I wonder where the little buggers come from?"

During their period of training after they had first arrived on the island, there had been a period of unexpected torrential rain which had made life for those men living under canvas – and there were about seven hundred tents and marquees on the island – rather unpleasant for some time. During periods of rain, land crabs appeared as if out of nowhere, scuttling through the low grass and the prickly shrubs, even in and out of tents, and then disappeared once more once the rain had finished. Aiden opened his second bottle and passed the opener back to Harry, but he wasn't really sure he needed another beer. Feeling that the evening was winding down, he said, "Sunday tomorrow."

"I expect they'll try to get a good turn out for church. Have to pretend to be asleep when the padre tries to drum up business in the morning."

The church was not part of Tent City; the Royal Engineers had constructed a church on the island out of prefabricated wooden sections and which would not have looked out of place as a railway mission amongst the dwellings and workshops of an English industrial town.

"Not sure I want any of that now."

Aiden never drank to excess and rarely drank with anyone other than Harry. It was not, he decided, that Margaret made him feel guilty, but rather that he feared her reproof. Women want men on their own terms, Aiden thought; and we give them permission to not understand our needs. Aiden knew that it would be fruitless to pursue this as a line of discussion with Harry.

"You know what, we could sling a couple of panniers in the bomb bays and make a special trip."

"Whatever for?" Aiden did not immediately follow Harry's train of thought.

"Shirts of course. You know, Honolulu and all that!"

Aiden smiled to himself. He found the thought of secretly filling-up two of the RAF's very expensive, technically complex, highly specialised medium bombers with colourful shirts highly amusing.

"Then we'd have to bring the oiks in on it. We couldn't do it without them." He replied, pleased to be joining in the joke.

But Harry had an answer to the problem of the ground crew. "Bullshit and threats should do it. It's what they're used to, after all."

"Time to hit the hay; I think I've had enough for this evening," Aiden said, grinding his cigarette out in the sand beside him.

"Righty-ho, think you're probably right."

Their co-ordination hampered by the effects of the alcohol, Aiden and Harry struggled to their feet, brushing the sand that still remained on them from where they had relaxed semi-sprawled on the beach from their trousers and shirts. There were a number of grains of sand on Aiden's palms which proved recalcitrant to removal.

Aiden had few friends outside of the RAF and like most of the men he knew, other than for his own family the circle he mixed in was largely defined by his wife's acquaintance. By degrees Harry had become Aiden's closest friend, but Aiden sensed that there would always be a distance or gulf between them, but not because Harry was mysterious or abstruse in any way. On the contrary, Harry was always remarkably easy going, straightforward and open. Now that Dennis had gone, Aiden doubted that he would ever again find himself in a friendship with another male where intimacies could be properly shared, valued and respected.

Leaving the imprints of themselves on the sand, Harry and Aiden began to walk back into camp. Aiden had come to the startling conclusion that Harry was rather like Aiden's brother-in-law; an ordinary man, not special, but in the case of Harry, he just happened to fly aeroplanes.

## *Chapter Thirteen*

Aiden ran his tongue around the soft flesh inside his mouth, particularly behind his lower lip. If anyone had been able to see his face it would have looked as if he were rolling a boiled sweet around his mouth with the tip of his tongue. He ran his tongue backwards and forwards several times, in part in an attempt to lubricate his parched mouth and in part to tactilely investigate the myriad small cracks that felt like sinewy threads that seemed to stretch down inside his mouth from his lower lip. It felt increasingly satisfying and peculiarly compelling to work his mouth, generating more saliva. He pushed his tongue deep down in front of his teeth until he could feel the thin film of gum that covered his jaw bone and the paste-like floury deposit that coated his teeth. Then he extended his tongue further afield; he curved his tongue up and slowly rolled the end-most portion of it across the concave roof of his mouth as if he were carefully wiping it clean. As a sensory diagnostic for cracking, flaking or other surface labial damage, he moistened his lips and then stretched them by gingerly pulling the corners of his mouth back. His stomach felt uncomfortable and gaseous, but as if it would be settled rather than upset by taking some breakfast, especially something wonderfully solid and greasy. Aiden opened his eyes carefully, as if this would be the final fingerposting as to his physical state.

"All right, old man?" Harry was sitting bare-chested in his khaki lightweight shorts on the canvas camp bed opposite his own. He did not look directly at Aiden but instead looked straight ahead. The camp beds were insubstantial so if he had sat on the edge his weight would have tipped it over. Instead, he sat with his weight in the middle, with his feet on the floor in front of him, his forearms resting on his thighs a little above his knees with his hands held loosely together. The canvas in the middle of the bed sagged beneath him so that he sat only two or three inches from the ground. His posture appeared mildly arachnid and his back excessively curved. His demeanour suggested a man who had awoken to find his body unexpectedly puny, and also that he had probably been sitting there motionless for some little time.

Aiden acknowledged Harry with a throaty sound that was somewhere between a cough and a grunt and then, after keeping his mouth shut for a short while, working his jaw up and down to generate more lubricating saliva, he answered a little thickly, "I think so."

Then, as if he were absent-mindedly making a general announcement, he said, "I need a slash." After a brief moment's delay as if he needed to collect his strength, he pushed back the bedcover and swung himself out of the bed. "Might see if I can get a shower at the same time," he added, clumsily groping for his towel where he had left it bunched up like a dishevelled mammal on the small table that the four men billeted in the tent shared.

"Righty-ho. See you in a bit," Harry replied, remaining quite still. The other two beds in the tent were already empty.

Aiden reached out and pulled up the flap of the tent. The sudden coruscation of the brilliant Pacific morning caught him unawares and he screwed up his eyes against the brightness. Eyes throbbing, he briefly stood in the entrance of the tent, holding the flap of stiff canvas in his hand, blinking stupidly until his eyes became re-accustomed to the habitual intensity of the light.

It all seemed a little unreal. Aiden made his way through the main camp along to the latrines. The vegetation had been cleared away from this part of the island, leaving an extensive pan of hard sand where the main camp had then been pitched. Although there were a large number of wooden prefabricated huts on the island, the living quarters consisted largely of hundreds of standard army issue tents, the khaki canvas having now been bleached by exposure to the bright sun, and laid out in a rigid grid pattern as if the services had sought to impose an unimaginative model of civilisation on the wild island.

Aiden zigzagged his way through the settlement of tents. The open flaps of tents, tied back in an attempt to circulate the air, offered peculiar windows onto ordered military souls. In one tent a man sat on a camp bed, carefully using a small wad of cotton wool to apply creamy Blanco to his leather belt with a precise circular motion, a grubby polishing cloth ready on the floor in front of him. Other men were busy organising their kit or making their beds to the prescribed, exacting, service fashion. He stepped carefully to avoid the guy-lines that stretched out from the corners of each rectangular tent, many of these ropes had items of clothing which had been pegged or draped there in order to dry quickly in the heat which regularly reached a hundred degrees Fahrenheit.

As he walked, the glare of the light became less oppressive and although he still felt a dull aching in his eye sockets and a heaviness in his head, walking encouraged his blood circulation and deep breathing oxygenated its flow and he began to feel somewhat brighter. Concerned about setting an example to Geoff, he began to feel a creeping sense of relief that he would not have to make the temple-throbbing effort required to bluff his way through the day, but he nevertheless remained feeling somewhat foolish and even slightly ashamed of himself.

The latrines in the camp were primitive and using them was incredibly unpleasant. The rough-and-ready toilets were no more than wooden seats on frames positioned over galvanised buckets. Each toilet was screened at the back and sides by sheets of canvas five feet high and therefore each cubicle afforded virtually no privacy. Although it was now no later than the normal breakfast hour, the imperfect cubicles acted as a suntrap and the stench rising from the buckets was already unspeakable.

Aiden, attempting to regulate his breathing to keep it as shallow and slow as possible, sat down on the hot wooden seat and pushed his khaki shorts a short way down his legs so that their waistband stretched around his marginally parted thighs. The enforced aprication and the trapped ambient, roasting, heat present in the nauseant cubicle reflected back off the ground and the canvas screens raising the sweat on his exposed flesh as if he were a discovered and unrepentant heretic.

He relieved himself of his night-water, first contracting his pelvic floor muscles and then, as his urine began to flow he gradually relaxed them again until the warm stream was comfortably controllable. Simultaneously, he leant forward from his hips so that his back markedly curved up towards his sunburnt neck and his shoulders. Partially protected from the view of others by the volume of his shorts pushed down over his knees as well as his hunched trunk, he surreptitiously slid his other hand down into his groin an inch or two just sufficient for his fingers to give direction to his pensile male organ so that the stream of urine struck against the inner side of the pail rather than gush splashily into the centre of it. By controlling and directing the flow in these ways, Aiden endeavoured to make his excretions as noiseless as might be possible. There was a rudeness to service life that did not seem to bother many of the men, an extension of communal maleness, or perhaps a discreet part of it, but with which Aiden remained uncomfortable.

There were boundaries to the communal maleness. Showers and toilets could ordinarily be relied upon to be a place of slaked fantasy or of simple immediate relief. It was no different for the men who were married; almost like a reward, Aiden felt, the state of marriage sanctioned occasional sexual relief with one's wife, but it could not regulate hot urges which could not be timetabled or allowed for. Logic told Aiden that not one of the men on the island could be immune from the sense of burning frustration that he so often felt, but not once had ever heard spoken about. The continuous, close proximity of so many other men and the showers and latrines that afforded no privacy, often meant sexual frustration often had to be endured for long periods of time, a powerful and dangerous distraction. Drink, tiredness, the repetitive military drills and, often arduous, routines could all help to take one's mind off sex for a while, and, perhaps, Aiden thought, that was what all the hearty singing in the mess last night had really been about.

But being hung over, relief of sexual frustration was not any sort of priority for Aiden this morning and deciding that he could really not be bothered queuing-up for a shower – water on the island was scarce - he made his way back through Tent City to his own tent.

He returned to find Harry bent over the collapsible washstand, his chin, neck and cheeks lathered up, squinting into a precariously balanced small rectangle of mirror that served them as a shaving glass, as he carefully scraped his razor up his neck, holding the blade against the direction of the growth of his stubble to achieve a closer shave.

"Isn't that water cold?" asked Aiden.

"I expect so," came the cheery reply.

"Sounds like you're about ready for some breakfast. I wondered if I would be dining alone this morning!"

"Now don't be fooled. It was a bit like playing dead in case the padre did his rounds."

Even given the diminutive size of the shaving mirror, Aiden could not miss the knowing wink Harry gave him. Presently, Harry lowered his face close to the surface of the water in the basin and cupping his hands together, noisily washed the residue shaving lather from his face.

~~~~

"Ah, sausages! That's what the doctor ordered," Harry said. Aiden and Harry knew all the ropes in the mess, they were old hands now; they could wheedle out extra cups of tea; they knew how to ensure that the stewards served them promptly; and this morning their plates were uncommonly full.

Having read the letter, Aiden sat absent-mindedly fingering the sheet of blue flimsy airmail notepaper. On the way over to breakfast, they had stopped off to see if there was any post. Life on the island was generally considered more tolerable because post was flown in each day.

Tossing the letter on to the table and cutting an inch or so off one of the sausages on his plate, he said, "How *can* she think they let

Hubbard bring his dog?" He placed the forkful in his mouth and robustly began to eat. Aiden had not really intended to let his exasperation creep into his voice, but Margaret's letter read as if she had addressed it to a miscreant or will-less schoolboy.

"How does she work that out then?" Harry had followed the downward flight of the letter and from where he sat he would have been able to read the neatly written words of blue ink if he had been so disposed. Harry raised one eyebrow.

"Thursday's photograph in the paper, apparently."

The photograph of Hubbard and his crew, with Hubbard's dog Crusty in front of them, clearly taken at an earlier date on a home airfield, had been released to the press for the following day once the success of the test had been known.

"If you don't mind my saying so, you do seem a bit peeved this morning. Could be the hangover, of course?" Harry looked shrewdly at Aiden, "But I expect if Margaret's at all like Janet, she worries the island is thick with women and we're getting up to all sorts of high jinx!"

Janet, Aiden thought, if he was any sort of judge in these matters, probably thought no such thing and Margaret should understand enough of the RAF's foibles to know that while it was possible to get away with a great many things, Hubbard would never have been allowed to bring his dog on the operation!

"She also thinks Hubbard looks dashing!"

"She wouldn't think that if she knew he indulges in painting-by-numbers, would she? Now it's just my opinion, you understand, but the image of a wing commander looking for his tube of number twenty-three so he can complete his picture of a cuddly puppy before popping off to fly his bomber is not particularly dashing!"

"He doesn't, does he?" It was true that a number of the men on the island had taken to painting-by-numbers to while away their free time.

"Oh yes, I have it on good authority, you know."

"Nothing from Janet, then?" The letter from Margaret had annoyed him, made him burn with indignation even, and he wanted to change the subject, as he did not think it would do to appear disloyal to her.

"No, it's my turn to write. But I don't think I'll mention too much about how we pass the evenings when I do." Harry smiled gently, but then after a moment he continued: "Now young Geoff, he *does* drink more than is good for him and what's more he shows no remorse about it when he does. Think you should be a bit careful, there."

"You've noticed too," Aiden replied quietly.

"But I haven't heard anyone else mention anything, yet, so we might be alright."

The implication was that a few well-timed words might straighten things out but a conversation of that type was quite beyond Aiden's experience. Aiden already felt a limited avuncular-like concern for Geoff, and clearly he could not afford him to be a liability; but Aiden intuitively sensed that his responsibility to him should rightly transcend something that could be considered merely a professional concern.

Harry offered Aiden a cigarette. With an involuntary shudder Aiden declined, "Not yet." Aiden put his knife and fork down on his empty plate and picked up his mug of tea and absent-mindedly cradled it in his hands, "Oh look out, here comes Len with his bloody camera!"

Harry was finishing the last of his fried bread. "Don't think I can cope with all that yet this morning. Probably time to get going!"

"One for the album! Hung-Over Pilots at Breakfast!" Aiden joked quietly, quickly draining the warm tea. Harry was not quite so quick and found himself in small talk with Len as he sat down in the seat vacated by Aiden; Aiden had made his escape by saying he had to write letters.

As he made his way back to the tent, Aiden mused to himself that everybody took photographs for granted but really there was a peculiar etiquette about them. Nobody particularly minded Len's snaps and stopping whatever he was doing to appear in them. People were happy enough to take their place in other photographs taken as a sort formal record, like for the squadron rugby or football team. But then there were formal portraits, which despite their formality seemed peculiarly intimate; Aiden tried to imagine what Harry would say if Aiden were to suggest that they sat together for a portrait. He had no doubt that Harry would think it very odd indeed. Perhaps Aiden really would go and write a letter.

~~~~~

Aiden felt ripped through by suddenness, and more than ever felt lonely amongst men. Having written his letter, he felt both dismayed and fearful at the reaction he felt sure it would be bound to produce. More than once he almost lost his courage and nearly tore the letter up, even thinking it would be preferable to burn the resulting fragments, and so decided to walk his letter then and there to the Post Office.

He had surprised himself with the content of his letter. He had started in a reasonable enough way simply replying to Margaret's letter, but as if driven by grief his outpourings had become quite savage. But having written it, he now believed that to take an easier but less honest path regarding Margaret would entail the loss of something essential of his self.

## Chapter Fourteen

The final live weapon drop of the operation had been on the Nineteenth of June and although they had been expecting to return home soon after, they had been given a mere forty-eight hours to pack-up ready to leave. For the purposes of gathering together the possessions they had brought with them three months previously, the time allowed to them was actually more than sufficient, but their sense of homecoming was one of remarkable rapidity, flying back into Hemswell a few short days after the conclusion of the exercise, and which left them feeling moderately dazed at the suddenness.

Sensuously, the summer morning approached perfection. Out on the wide sweep of the airfield there was hardly a breath of wind; the freshness of the air tasted luxuriantly cool and felt as if it could be poured silkily over the skin like a stream of soft rose petals; the high-up twittering of lazy-days skylarks filled the air; and a sweetness, reminiscent of summer hay fields, filled the air from the recently-cut airfield grass. It was the kind of day when men would be glad to be out in their shirtsleeves, not merely because of the summer heat, but to revel in the lusciousness of the day. But the small group of officers who were waiting out on the airfield were not in shirtsleeves; despite a quiet mood of celebration, there was a seriousness to their day.

"Are they coming yet?" a boy's excited voice demanded loudly. Service tradition dictated that after any significant deployment, families were also allowed out on to the airfield to greet the men when they returned.

The families had all dressed smartly, but they were not on a par with the officers. Without exception, the officers' crisp and pressed uniforms were sharp-edged with marching creases, their brilliant white shirt cuffs projected a neat half inch below their tunic sleeves as if the projections had been ruler-governed, their ties had been well-regulated and their highly polished shoes shone like wells of warming light. Margaret wore a simple, clean white blouse and a patterned skirt of swirling, sharply defined invaginated red buds set against a plain background, with an integral patent-look belt tight around her waist. Mark wore a white short-sleeved shirt, which Margaret had allowed him to unbutton once at his neck, grey shorts, and his hated sandals.

"Any moment now, I should think, Sweet Pea."

One of the officers who was standing close to them, barely turning his head, smiled at Margaret and Mark from beneath his peaked cap. Margaret, embarrassed, only gingerly returned the smile.

"But I want to see Daddy. I want to see Daddy in his aeroplane!"

The officer smiled once more, but this time exercised greater discretion and kept his eyes fixed on the horizon, where the other officers were also looking. Presently, an aircraftman hastened towards the group of officers, came smartly to attention and handed a piece of paper to one of them.

"They should be approaching the circuit any moment now, sir," the officer to whom the slip of paper had been handed in turn informed the wing commander.

A moment later, two aircraft could just be discerned low on the horizon, way beyond the airfield, rapidly curving around to the eastern end of the runway, a hazy trail of engine-smoke like a heat haze, barely visible behind them. These were the first two of the returning squadron aircraft. With obvious intent, the aircraft dropped lower and lower until they passed over the airfield perimeter fence at an altitude of little more than fifty feet. Had Margaret been watching the officers, rather than the approaching aircraft, she would have seen a smile of expectation on the faces of most of them.

Mark excitedly tried to wriggle his right hand free from the firm controlling grip of Margaret's hand, tightly contorting his fingers together in the attempt, and on failing instead used his left hand to point towards the approaching shapes and shouted out, very loudly, "Look!"

With their landing gear still retracted, the two Canberras visibly accelerated down towards the far end of the runway, and powered along it just a few feet off the ground, the concrete racing away beneath them. At a stunning speed, the aircraft silently streaked up towards where Margaret and Mark stood, rushing past them with the sun glinting off their paintwork, and with a full, deafening whoosh of thunderous sound following a split-second behind them as they banked away from the western end of the runway and turned to complete a circuit before lowering their undercarriage, deploying flaps and turning into their finals.

It was unbelievably exciting. Margaret unexpectedly found she had caught her breath, Mark was jumping up and down and exclaiming, "Wow! Daddy, Daddy, Daddy!" and the officers present, even the wing commander, perhaps particularly the wing commander, smiled and exchanged satisfied glances with each other; it was also in the best service tradition to beat up the airfield, as noisily as possible, upon returning from significant deployments.

The two aircraft, Aiden's and Harry's, completed their finals. Landing a few seconds apart from each other, they taxied towards their dispersals where the officers and the families were waiting. Reaching the concrete apron, an aircraft handler directed each of the aircraft with rhythmic backwards and forwards movements of his batons. As each aircraft reached its full-stop position the handler held both of his batons upright as a signal for the pilot to halt. The shrill whistle of the aircrafts' engines continued for a few moments before the pilots finally cut their engines leaving a voidful silence which seemed all the deeper for being laden with the quietly jostling expectations of the waiting families.

No further activity was apparent within the aircraft for as much as two or three minutes. Straightaway, the ground crews had secured the aircraft, placing sets of chocks in front of and behind the nose-wheel and the main undercarriage wheels beneath each wing of each aircraft. They had then opened and secured each aircraft's crew access hatch, below and slightly to the front of the bubble canopy. Meanwhile, the officers had approached to stand in a small loosely knit knot, close to the access hatch of Aiden's aircraft, marking time by talking quietly amongst themselves. The wives and children bobbed up and down straining to see, eagerly looking for any signs of the crews exiting from their aircraft, but exchanged few words between each other in case they should miss some important sign.

Aiden and Geoff, encumbered by their yellow life jackets, eventually climbed down out of their Canberra's access hatch, shortly to be followed by Harry and his navigator climbing out from their own aircraft. Aiden and Geoff both stood up straight for a few moments, forcing their shoulders back to relieve the stiffness in their bodies after the long flight from their transit base. At the same time they removed their flying gloves, tucking them under one arm, as they reached up to unfasten their flying helmets.

Once they had removed their flying helmets, and had mechanically, almost absent-mindedly, stowed their flying gloves inside them for safekeeping, they tucked their helmets beneath their arms where their gloves had previously rested. Aiden and Geoff then stepped forward contemporaneously with the wing commander stepping forward towards them. As they met, the wing commander animatedly shook Aiden's hand and then Geoff's, each time firmly holding the other man's grip in his own for an appreciable time, and exchanging kind and warm words with him.

The other officers in turn then shook Aiden's hand and then Geoff's. Several of them made some gesture, probably quite unconsciously, such as placing a hand upon Aiden's or Geoff's shoulder, as if they wanted to add something personal to underline the formal greeting. Although relaxed, this greeting was undeniably punctilious, and each man's pride in the achievement of squadron men was heartfelt. At that moment Harry and his navigator walked around the nose of Aiden's Canberra from their own aircraft and joined the gathering of their fellow officers.

Having greeted Harry and his navigator with the same degree of warmth with which he had greeted Aiden and Geoff, the wing commander now stepped back a pace or two and half turning back towards the waiting families, benignly beckoned them forward.

"Daddy!" cried Mark. Margaret finally permitted herself to let go of Mark's hand, knowing that there was no longer any ambient and present danger because Mark was so completely focused on his father.

Mark ran full pelt, way ahead of all the other people, across the short distance to where Aiden and Geoff were standing and excitedly threw his arms about his father's waist, seemingly quite oblivious to anyone else in proximity to him. Geoff, standing immediately beside Aiden, smiled gently and a little awkwardly down at Mark, as if he could appreciate the encounter for its tenderness, but nevertheless had not reached the point in his maturity where he could so easily be ensorcelled by another's child.

Margaret's greeting was more restrained, and also interrupted by two more of the squadron's Canberras noisily banking hard away from the runway having announced their arrival back home in traditional service fashion. For once, Mark took no notice of the jets, instead choosing to remain fixed about his father's waist, but Margaret briefly glanced skywards before kissing Aiden lightly upon the cheek and saying how much she had missed him. Then, politely and inclusively, she turned and asked Geoff how he was.

Having no child of their own to interrupt their embrace, Harry and Janet hugged, their arms unceasingly close about each other, relieved and reassured through the deep, familiar, physical touch, until Harry's navigator, Donald, also a married man, said good-naturedly, and pointedly so as to be deliberately overheard, "Steady on, old chap! Time enough for that!"

In good humour and newly full of soft relief, a number of the people around them laughed quietly and comfortably; of all the officers present, only Geoff remained unmarried and they all laughed as people might who understood the customs of a friendly type of club. Equally, they all appreciated Harry's very audible reply, "Well, I've never had any complaints about it from *your* wife!"

Janet smiled a private smile to Harry, equally sharing in the joke.

The wing commander, who was now taking his leave of the group, lightly touched Aiden on the arm as he passed him and called out amiably, as if reminding rather than commanding them all, "Ladies Night in the mess tomorrow evening. I'll see you all there!"

As they turned and watched the wing commander go, Aiden and

Margaret stood in the bright warming sunlight with Mark between them holding Aiden's hand. Beside them, Harry and Janet stood side by side, Harry with his arm about his wife's waist.

## Chapter Fifteen

"I want to get a photograph before we all get started!"

The wing commander had lost none of the enthusiasm he had shown upon their return to Hemswell yesterday morning and was now attempting to shepherd together all the officers who had been on the deployment. It promised to be an exciting evening: the officers wore their dress uniforms; the wives and lady guests, entering into the spirit of the evening, had all picked out their best evening frocks; dinner would be eaten off the best squadron china; and, a dance band had been engaged for afterwards.

"All get started doing what, I wonder?" queried Aiden facetiously; he felt in remarkably good spirits, considering everything.

"Well, in Geoff's case, I expect he means drinking," Harry quietly replied.

"Can't we just get everyone together?"

The men and their guests were milling around and not responding particularly well to shepherding, so the wing commander turned his attention to directing the hapless photographer; just for this occasion, a flight sergeant who in an unguarded moment had said he knew a little about cameras had been cajoled into taking on the role.

"At least it's not Len and his bloody camera."

The two men laughed quietly together. Janet and Margaret asked to have the joke explained to them but it patently was not as amusing as the two men had thought. Harry then said to Aiden conversationally, "The Old Man seemed pleased as punch yesterday." Then to Janet, "Oh, hold onto this," as he passed his pre-dinner drink to her to hold; the group was finally forming up. Consequently, Margaret and Janet could also be opportunely detached and introduced to the guest that Geoff had brought with him this evening.

As the group was marshalled together, Aiden said, "In some sort of peculiar way that I hadn't really been expecting I feel rather pleased too. It seems as if we've done something important, purposeful."

"And dangerous! But," Harry reflected, "I *do* think we have the right to feel proud of ourselves."

"Could you look this way please, gentlemen," the NCO said with a notable degree of consternation. He seemed uncertain as to whether he was allowed to be irritable with, or to raise his voice to, a group of superior officers who seemed too intent on their own enjoyment to pay much attention to his directions and so he kept one weather-eye on the wing commander as he went about his business of temporary squadron photographer.

"Eyes front!" Harry joked under his breath.

But in reality the men were happy enough to interrupt their conversations and look towards the camera, maintaining a convivial silence and appointing the appropriate look of relaxed poise and carefree smiles to their faces for as long as was necessary for the photograph to be taken.

There was a subdued wumph-like noise, an almost imperceptible tinkle of fracturing glass and a flash of light which left the men momentarily blinking and as they all started talking amongst themselves again the photographer called out, a rising inflexion in his voice, "One more before you disperse, please."

"One for the album!" Aiden said quite loudly. Harry and Aiden chuckled to themselves; they could happily accept a little glory and the implication that they had earned their place in the squadron annals. Aiden felt relieved to be in Harry's company this evening. More quietly, Aiden continued, "But it seems more personal, as if I've passed some sort of test."

"We'd miss you if you were to move on, you know," Harry replied in a measured, knowing tone.

"Smile gentlemen!" the photographer called out. As insurance against the first picture not coming-out, the photographer had changed the flash-bulb on his camera and was now ready to take another photograph.

In Aiden's experience, postings were things that were done to you, arriving completely out of the blue, and disrupted one's domestic arrangements dreadfully. The idea that he might actually solicit a new posting came as quite a jolt to him. He replied hesitantly, "I don't know that that's what I mean."

"You might want to move on to bigger things." It was said amiably enough, but it was as if Harry was asking to see whether he and Aiden were still of the same mould. "And talking of bigger things," Harry added quietly, inclining his head towards where Margaret, Janet and Donald's wife were talking to a younger woman, "Have you seen Geoff's latest bit of stuff?"

"Blonde as well!"

"Pretty. Too good for the likes of young Geoff!"

Geoff seemed to work his way rapidly through lady friends. This latest was very striking and carried an unmistakable air of confidence and savoir-vivre about her, as if she were no stranger to a world of ceremony and formal receptions. The men once again genially froze. There was a second wumph-noise, the same flash of light as before and some more blinking.

"I think we're about to meet her," Aiden said. He then added, although instantly regretted saying it, "I'm not sure that Margaret's type of energy allows me to be ambitious in that sort of way; it can be a bit draining."

The group began to break up, the men walking off in different directions as if some centrifugal force was spinning them away from each other. Harry and Aiden naturally started to gravitate towards their wives and Geoff and Donald, who had been standing together for the photographs in another part of the group, also began to move towards the women. But just as they reached them, the wing commander called out to them all again, "Chaps, just one more."

"Not more, surely, I need my dinner," Harry complained.

"This time with the ladies!"

The men paired up with their wives or their guests, and, after a flurry of activity looking for suitable surfaces on which to place their drinks while the photograph was taken, started to turn back towards the favoured spot below a large photograph hanging on the wall of a war-time Halifax bomber in night-time camouflage, its identification markings identifying it as belonging to their squadron.

"This is Kitty," Geoff said proudly to Harry and Aiden as they turned. With Margaret taking care to stay close at his side, Aiden reached forward and taking Kitty's hand lightly, smiled politely and said that he was very pleased to meet her.

The photographer ineffectually suggested where they should stand; the couples were required in two rows, but the group preferred to arrange it between themselves. There was a degree of inevitable banter, including Harry's suggestion to Donald that he should stand in the back row, furthest away from the camera, as he was the ugliest one of them all. Aiden, being one of the taller men, stood with Margaret in the back row, while Harry and Janet stood together in the front, close to where the wing commander and his wife proudly stood.

"Just as long as you don't think I'm standing here because *I'm* ugly." Aiden joined in with the banter.

"It must be on your account, mustn't it; Margaret's not ugly!"

Finally, following a deal of shuffling about and not a small amount of giggling and more laughing, they were all ready for the photograph.

"Smile ladies and gentlemen, please." There was an almost plaintive note in the photographer's voice as if he held out little hope of his request being complied with.

Looking towards the camera, Aiden noticed that Harry had surreptitiously slid his hand over Janet's backside; Janet remained complaisantly still. The photographer took his photograph and then as Aiden's vision returned to normal following the flash of light from the flash bulb, the group started to spin off once again into their own chattering groups. Janet, showing not a shred of embarrassment, paired up with Margaret. But Harry had evidently noticed Aiden's glance, whispering quietly to him as they walked off after their wives, "Her best feature, old chap," and winked at him; "very glad to be back, if you know what I mean!"

As they walked into dinner, Aiden speculated whether sex had provided the original motive power to Harry and Janet's relationship and whether their evident happiness had simply followed. He thought it all too easy to forget the urgency to couple and that it sometimes had little to do with anything as prosaic as the fear of being lonely.

~~~~

"Your wing commander's very proud."

Geoff's company had turned out to be disappointing this evening. But Kitty was sufficiently confident in herself not to require instant fixity, and being determined to enjoy her evening nevertheless, she had been directing more and more of her conversation throughout dinner to the other members of the party.

"Here, let me top you up." Harry had assumed the role of convivial host quite naturally and he now reached forward towards Kitty with the wine bottle. "Yes, I suppose he is."

"He's undoubtedly proud of our part in Operation Grapple." Aiden was pleased to join in the conversation.

With her glass only partially replenished, Kitty half raised her fingers from the tablecloth where her hand was resting; Harry would not dream of pressing her and, attentively, uprighted the bottle and returned it to its position in the middle of the table. Then with the slightest tilt of her head and momentarily turning her hand so that it was palm upwards, she said, "But all this, this is more than just a celebration for the sake of it, isn't it? It's not just an excuse for a goodtime?"

This smallest of gestures had managed to take in the whole room: the vivified parties of officers and their guests, the buzzing stewards and the dance band who were already setting up for when dinner should be finally cleared away. Aiden found himself pleasantly surprised at how refreshingly perceptive she was, unquestioning of their esprit and appreciative of the squadron's liturgies; and, she was not simply making a point under the cover of polite conversation of not noticing that Geoff was helping himself to more wine again.

"It's all about pride in the squadron and the service, I suppose," Aiden agreed.

"And personal pride, surely?"

"Oh, I suppose so," Aiden replied modestly, smiling at Kitty, "and I rather suspect that the Old Man feels it compensates him in some way."

"Oh, I see, for the war?"

"I think it was more than simple duplicity to him." Kitty clearly appreciated that a number of the men had seen active service in Bomber Command in the war and so Aiden's reply was perfectly adequate.

"And how about you, Harry, Geoffrey and all the other men who went out to Christmas Island?" Kitty said with interest, sipping her wine as if she were using the action to punctuate her conversation. "After all, you don't have the same history as the older men."

Aiden watched her full lips on the rim of her glass, and noted her flawless polished pink fingernails; he had been finding his pride quite lonely since his return from Christmas Island. At the far end of the room the bandleader was leafing through a sheaf of music, and one of the trumpet players looked quizzically through his mouthpiece, squinting as he held the mouthpiece up to the light.

"Such an achievement is the closest thing to perfection we're ever likely to experience and the Old Man licenses us to take the necessary risks to do it; he lets us soar." Aiden felt cosseted in sympathetic company as if there was no longer any need to feel guarded. In Kitty's company he found he could almost feel poetic. "But part of our pride is reciprocity; we can trust him not to let *us* down, we can believe in his honourableness."

Harry beamed across the table at Aiden as if he had put his own thoughts into words but more eloquently than he himself would ever have been able to, should he have ever felt brave enough to speak in this way – for it felt like a question of propriety, even amongst friends. Margaret, who had been seated next to Harry and had been closely following the conversation, took advantage of a moment's pause to ask Kitty, "And how do you know Geoff?"

"Oh, we hardly know each other at all, really," she replied brightly. "We met at a New Year's drinks party up in Town given by some mutual friends. I was really quite surprised to hear from him after all this time."

"And are you staying in Lincoln?"

Lincoln was a tidy step from the airfield, but Margaret thought Lincoln vastly superior to Gainsborough, which although not close, was their nearest town. Margaret had assumed that Kitty was a sophisticate who would prefer the best possible facilities that could be offered her.

"Oh no," Kitty smiled at Margaret as if she had been the victim of a curious misconception, "I'm staying just down the road; the inn's perfectly adequate."

"Did you come up on the train?" Harry asked.

"No, I drove myself. I have my own little car."

Margaret looked uneasy at this news.

"Ah, I see."

"Daddy bought me something fun to run about in!"

Kitty did not sound at all frivolous, rather she had sounded a little facetious as if her father had been the one who wanted her to have something fun to run about in, whereas she would have happily settled for something more workaday.

The white-jacketed stewards were now clearing away the white porcelain dinner plates, the vegetable dishes and the sauceboats, all the chinaware being marked discreetly with the squadron crest. As one of the stewards cleared, leaning forward between the diners and picking up each plate in turn with his right hand and then reaching back to pile the plates one on top of the other in his left, steadying the growing pile with his fingers whilst taking the weight of them on his wrist, another steward moved around the table, briskly sweeping errant crumbs away into a crumb-tray with a crumb-brush then critically repositioning the desert cutlery in front of each diner with an air of ceremonial aloofness which somehow seemed to economically imply that the guests could not possibly appreciate the importance of such precision.

There was a natural lull in the conversation as the stewards moved around the table. It being something of a novelty, there was a general excitement in the setting-up of the dance band and people would occasionally look up, craning their necks to see what was going on. Aiden had considerately leaned slightly to his right to allow the steward a space through which he could take his plate and was now discreetly returning to his previous fully upright position, when Geoff sought to fill the void in the conversation:

"Did I tell you there were coconuts on the island?"

"Yes, Geoffrey dear, you did."

Aiden was surprised that Kitty spoke so patiently. Geoff was making a sterling effort. He was sitting bolt upright in his chair with his hands on the table in front of him; his eyes were fixed upon his right hand, where the tips of his fingers were touching the base of his wine glass.

"Do you and Aiden have any children?" Kitty asked Margaret pleasantly.

"A boy, Mark; he'll be starting school this year."

"Oh how nice. And you, Janet?"

"No, we don't, I'm afraid," came Janet's gentle reply. As she spoke Harry cast her an unashamedly tender look. Smiling, she continued, "They've just never come."

"But it never really seemed so very hot on the island." Geoff's face appeared flushed. "That's because of the easterly trades."

Aiden caught Harry's eye.

"Is that so?" Kitty said gently.

"Don't you think, Kitty, that once a man has children he has a duty not to take risks in the same way as he might have done in his younger years?

"Oh come on Margaret!" Aiden spoke sharply. "That's an unfair question to ask since Kitty hasn't children!"

At that moment a steward brought along their desserts, placing a plate in front of each of them. Aiden, looking up, as always, marvelled at the steward's skill, of how it was possible to balance a row of laden plates from the hand to the upper arm and unfailingly manage to avoid accidents. Kitty, However, appeared to think nothing of it; the process was sufficiently familiar to her to be an everyday event.

"I'm sure Kitty is quite capable of saying if she thinks the question unfair, darling." Margaret spoke evenly, but there was a noticeable edge to her voice and Aiden caught an unmistakable dare-me-to look in her eye.

"Oh this looks good, doesn't it?" Janet interjected loudly, picking up her spoon and fork.

Kitty, sensing calculated manipulation, spoke cautiously, trying to sense where Margaret was coming from, "Perhaps."

"But don't you think it's simply a part of growing up? Accepting that one has responsibilities?" Margaret spoke pointedly as if she were determined to press the point, seemingly to the point of recklessness so that it was no longer possible to identify the key risk to the durability of the party.

Kitty answered Margaret neutrally, "I believe both husband and wife have responsibilities to a child, but of course their responsibilities may be different."

Harry had picked up his spoon and fork and was now studying them intently. Margaret, given the apolitical weakness of Kitty's reply, sensed that she was now firmly in control of the conversation. Anticipating the sweetness of moral victory, she looked directly at Kitty and opened her mouth to deliver another calculated blow.

But across the table, Geoff had misjudged and his elbow jerked off the edge of the table, his spoon fell from his hand onto his plate with a very noisy clatter and, unable to prevent himself, his head lurched forward in opposite action with the momentum generated as his elbow slid off the table. At the commotion, a number of other diners' heads turned to look at Geoff, and a silence spread about the tables immediately around them.

Simultaneously, Aiden and Harry looked up at each other. Harry raised his eyebrows, "Shall we?"

"I think we'd better."

Harry neatly replaced his fork and spoon from where he had so recently taken them up and, each of them gathering his own napkin from his lap and laying it down in a ruffled heap on the table, both men stood up, pushing their chairs carefully out from behind them as they did so. Moving with a sympathetic union, they stepped quickly round and behind Geoff, working together like familiar brothers with wordlessly synchronised actions.

Harry, the more powerfully built of the two men, slid his hands though Geoff's armpits until his forearms were in a position to take

Geoff's weight. With a grimace on his face from the physical effort it entailed, Harry lifted Geoff an inch or so up from the sitting position. As he did so, Aiden pulled Geoff's chair out from under him and manoeuvred it clear. Quickly moving back in beside Harry and Geoff, he took some of Geoff's weight, allowing Harry to pivot himself around to Geoff's left side, whilst Aiden supported Geoff on his right; from a distance they could have simply been three men standing together. The interest from the other tables started to diminish.

In a clear voice Kitty announced, "Oh, it looks as if the band is almost ready."

"Come along, Geoff, I think you need a breath of fresh air." Harry said loudly and jovially.

As much as providing an acceptable exit line for the benefit of their own party, Harry's words would be interpreted by the other men who were within earshot as one of their own was a bit tight, but it was being dealt with and that there would be no embarrassment. The other men would not think particularly badly of Geoff, most of them would be able to empathise rather too closely with the situation. But unbridled drunkenness crossed an invisible line, and as of yet, within the squadron, only Harry and Aiden suspected Geoff might have crossed it.

As they propelled Geoff towards the exit, Kitty leant across the table towards Margaret and said, "Geoff's lucky to have such good men looking out for him. It seems brotherly, clannish, in the best possible sense."

"Unless I'm very much mistaken," Harry said quietly to Aiden, "That's fifteen-all!"

"But I'm not sure about the rest of the innings, though."

"Now now, don't mix up your sporting metaphors!" Harry replied, quietly smiling at Aiden.

~~~

"We had a close escape tonight."

Aiden and Harry were standing together, smoking, outside the single officers' quarters in the rapidly fading evening light. They had conscientiously removed Geoff's jacket, had undone his top shirt button and loosened his tie, laid him on his bed and taken off his shoes, letting them drop to the floor with a clump-like noise, before pulling a blanket over him. Geoff had been quite docile and had not fought their help in any way and before Aiden and Harry had even left his room, he had been soundly asleep.

"Geoff did as well." Harry replied undramatically.

Relieved, Harry exhaled deeply and luxuriously, the smoke from his cigarette jetting out from his nostrils before dissipating in the warm summer night-air. Although they felt the pull of returning to their party as soon as they could, it had seemed the most natural thing in the world to reach for a cigarette following the strain of having to put Geoff to bed. In the distance they could hear the dance band in full swing in the officers' mess, the saxophones taking the lead on a perennially popular quickstep number with the brass adding accented backing figures.

"Geoff won't mind missing the music, bit old fashioned for him. He prefers beat numbers, I think," Aiden said casually, despite all the upset of the evening.

"He must have started bloody early, well before dinnertime to be in that sort of a state before we even got to the coffee." Harry spoke factually.

"I feel I've let him down," Aiden said, drawing upon his cigarette, the end glowing bright orange with the inrush of air, "We've known for ages he likes the juice a bit too much, but I've done nothing about it."

"Don't be too hard on yourself, old man."

"But he's my navigator," Aiden continued to speak quietly, but with more passion; he had a professional care for the safety of his aircraft.

"Yes, but don't you think that you, me, the others, all of us older men of the squadron ought to be looking out for him just as a matter of course?"

Aiden did not disagree with Harry and to his mind his previous statement had implied something very much like this, but he considered that it should have been he who should have taken the lead; although, and it was not a matter of his service training – that seemed strangely irrelevant - he felt ill-prepared, untutored, to take on such a role.

"Anyway, I expect that's the last we've seen of Kitty. She would have been a bit of a catch for him."

"Perhaps that's why he started so early today."

"Don't follow you, I'm afraid," Aiden replied.

"Well, she, or perhaps the idea of her, might have been more important to him than we all guess; because he drinks we tend to dismiss his feelings."

"Dutch courage," Aiden said as if this were a sufficient explanation.

"Something like that. Oh well," Harry ground the cigarette end out under the sole of his shoe with a twisting motion of his foot but glanced inquisitively at Aiden as he did so, "I suppose we had better get back."

"Yes, our party's a man down now; we'll have to look after Kitty as well."

"Oh, that one can look after herself!" Harry said breezily; it was clear to Aiden that Harry would never be troubled by a woman like Kitty.

Aiden had been thinking of Margaret. It being unlikely that they would ever meet again, it would not matter greatly if Margaret poisoned Kitty's perceptions, but he would remain cross with Margaret for her unfairness if should she do so. Feeling quietly ashamed, he also knew that he would not fight the unfairness as a man with a concern for his son should; not only would it be a solitary battle, but deep down he feared the loss that the regaining of a proper balance between the two of them could entail.

Walking back along the familiar pathways towards the officers'-mess, the growing darkness wrapping itself around them, Harry said to Aiden as if the velvet evening encouraged confidences between them, "I think young Geoff desperately feels the need for a good woman. I'm not saying that Kitty wasn't right for him, only that I'm pretty sure he'd be much the same whoever it was."

"That sounds like he needs someone to *pity* him!"

It seemed a shocking inference.

"Well, I really don't know," Harry ruminated.

But Aiden was put in mind of the evenings he had spent drinking with Dennis; while in those days they had never *drunk* in the same way as Geoff did now, there did seem to be a connection. It felt like they had been waiting for something to happen to *them*, and it seemed simply like an accident that he hadn't ended up being like Geoff.

Harry continued aloud with his own thoughts, "But unless he sorts himself out, he won't get a decent girlfriend, will he?"

"Well perhaps he'd rather have an indecent one instead!" Aiden smiled affectionately at Harry; despite the seriousness of the conversation he could not quite resist making the joke.

"He should be so lucky!" Harry said, returning the smile. "It's a bit of a conundrum, really, isn't it. Or, as we tend to say in the trade, a right old bugger's muddle!"

Harry paused briefly and automatically glanced both left and right as they crossed over an access road. Solicitously, he lightly touched Aiden on the sleeve as they stepped off the curb, as if he wanted to watch out for him. "Oh, I don't know. One needs to make a bit of an effort, I suppose."

Although he was not at all sure that it was what Harry meant, Aiden thought it was like Bill and Reg. They had laboured hard to achieve their purpose, and then along had come the popsies dropping into their laps almost because they *had* so laboured, although admittedly the war had forced their purpose on them.

After a while Aiden asked, "How did you and Janet meet?"

"Oh, it's not very exciting, I'm afraid. I used to play partnership whist quite a lot in those days; you see I was never clever enough for bridge!" Even though it was now quite dark Aiden could make out the gentle self-mocking smile on Harry's face. Aiden thought it sounded wonderfully companionable. "If you don't mind my saying so, and tell me to sod off it it's none of my business," Harry continued as if he wanted to say something before they gained the officers' mess, "but Margaret seems to have a real bee in her bonnet about you flying at the moment."

It was not a question as such, but Harry's mode of speaking cordially invited a response, but Aiden did not want to speak ill of Margaret, although opening up to Harry seemed particularly appealing. "It's just that she worries about Mark; she thinks flying's too dangerous."

"Well, it's not healthy." Harry shot Aiden a glance. "Goes with the territory, doesn't it? Not that it's my place to say anything really; I don't suppose we'll ever have children now," Harry added a little sadly. "But I'm sure having them must change things a bit?" Aiden could imagine that Harry would have made a splendid father.

"Well, yes, it does." Aiden could feel himself succumbing to the luscious temptation to speak freely to Harry, but merely added, although he felt deeply embarrassed at even alluding to the subject, "But it does seem to come upon you rather suddenly; a lot quicker than you plan it to, whatever you do about it, if you take my meaning."

By now they had turned onto the broad path which led up to the entrance of the officers'-mess.

"Ah, I see!" Harry replied knowingly, but was saved from the possibility of having to explain what he thought he now knew as the moment before he could reach out to open the door Donald came out of the mess and said brightly to them:

"Ah, there you are! I though I'd better come and check on the wounded."

## Chapter Sixteen

In her letter, Mrs Peabody, the landlady of the boarding house, had included some useful additional information with their booking confirmation: "I do a high tea for the smaller children at five o'clock, and serve dinner at seven." It had been last minute, but they had eventually found a boarding house with a vacancy. Aiden had high hopes that the change of air would be good for them.

Being situated beneath the eaves of the house, their family room enjoyed quietness. There were no other guests' rooms adjoining their own, and only occasionally could they sense the quickness of other families within the building; of a morning they might hear muffled sounds of children being hurried along to make haste down to breakfast, or sandaled feet running excitedly down the rather threadbare stairs and then the front door banging shut. The plumbing in the house creaked and groaned a little and the decoration was a little shabby, but Aiden thought that a soft flow of circumambient happiness unmistakably soaked through the house.

Aiden lay back with his head upon the pillow, his innermost private thoughts looping repetitively through his mind. His fingers locked his hands together behind his head so that his upper neck lay against his palms and his ears just touched the heels of his hands. Tucked inside the back of his unbuttoned collar, his thumbs pointed downwards so that he could feel the bumps made by his vertebrae within his neck. He could raise no sensible argument against Margaret's solicitude, but she had once again elected to stay with Mark during high tea; although lasting only three quarters of an hour or so, it could have at least created some private time and space for them.

Suddenly, the door handle rattled loudly and the door swung

wildly open and, high tea having now finished, Mark burst back into the room, Margaret following behind him. Aiden's conscious train of thought subsided into a base of feral incogitance which, like the bowling-over power of a deep sea swell, constantly lunged at him, sapping his energy.

"Gosh, it's hot up here." Margaret's tone irritated Aiden.

In his present subsultory state of mind it somehow managed to convey a sense that Margaret was surprised that he was able to bear the heat whereas she would have been *morally* right not being able to do so. He increasingly found such inflexions predictable.

"Tell Daddy what you had for tea, Sweet Pea," Margaret continued, as if she were prompting Mark solely for the pleasure it would afford her to hear him speak.

"We had blancmange for afters!"

"My, aren't you lucky! And did you have cake as well?" Aiden asked with theatrical incredulity. Mark nodded back. Margaret baked her own cakes, and apart from occasional cakes such as hot cross buns, she generally did not believe in shop bought ones; having fancy cake at each teatime was therefore a definite treat. Aiden went on to enquire very gravely, "Was the blancmange very, very pink?"

Aiden was looking sternly at Mark, but catching the affectionate glint in his father's eye, a broad gleeful smile spread across Mark's face. "It was very, very, very pink, Daddy!" Chuckling to himself, Mark ran and launched himself onto the lower of the two bunk beds.

Enjoying the novelty of sleeping on the upper bunk, Mark had turned the lower into a camp. Here, Mark kept the few toys that Aiden had been able to fit into their suitcases for him: a handful of cowboys and Indians, moulded unrealistically in blue and yellow plastic respectively; a number of farmyard animals; and, two or three die-cast Dinky toys, of which only a chunky green and yellow lorry retained its rubber tyres. Here also, when he was not out with Mark, lived Harris, the well-loved teddy bear, his fur worn to bare patches in places, together with one or two comics.

"Mind your head, Sweetie," Margaret called out to him absent-mindedly as she crossed over to the window. Upon returning to their room after an afternoon on the beach to find their room stifling with the August heat, they had thrown open the casement to let some air in.

Margaret parted the net curtains, stepped forward into the brightness and looked out, leaning her weight against the nursery bars which ran the entire length of the window. Letting the net curtains fall back into place behind her, she felt disjoined from Aiden and Mark, the phenomenon being exacerbated as facing more-or-less north the room consistently lacked generative sunlight and she therefore had a sense of darkness behind her.

The late afternoon was breezeless and the streets were now almost empty. Here and there shop-girls were making their ways home, sometimes with their arms linked, chatting and laughing together. Not far down the road a postman was collecting the last post of the day from a pillar-box, the iconic brightness of which attracted and held her eye. The front gardens of the villas and houses looked deserted and in the heat the hydrangeas looked dusty and the roses tired. From somewhere nearby, there was the sound of a lawn mower, the regular push and pull-back like the sound of a peaceful sleeper. It was a scene of order and familiarity.

From here Margaret had no sense of the sea. She did not mind not being able to see the sea for her own sake, but she minded for Mark. At this moment, she thought, lodged within the seaside town there must be thousands of holidaymakers, but at this hour they were nowhere to be seen. It was like a time for comfortable, private concealment so that the hot summer evening seemed pregnant with secret holiday life.

Aiden could not keep himself from watching Margaret silhouetted against the light even though her outline was gauzy and indistinct behind the net curtains. After a few moments of surreptitiously, guiltily, observing her, with an effort he called out pleasantly, "We've got an hour or so before we have to go down. What're you going to do until then?"

Turning away from the enveloping brightness at the window, Margaret could hardly make out Aiden in the dimness and she had to pause a moment while her eyes became re-accustomed to the bated light.

"I might write some postcards." On holiday, Margaret felt contented, peaceful, at this hour of the day. "Shall I do one to your mother?"

"If you like," Aiden replied neutrally.

It was generally Margaret who wrote their postcards. She found a particular satisfaction in carefully choosing cards, no matter how similar to each other they were, and writing routine greetings and news of their small doings was in itself an affirmation of holiday where nothing dramatic was ever required to occur.

Margaret crossed over from the window and walking around the foot of the bed, sat down on its edge on the side opposite to Aiden. Without needing any discussion, they had kept to the same sides of the bed as each had at home, Margaret instinctively placing their nightclothes under their respective pillows when they had unpacked on Saturday afternoon after they had arrived. Aiden stole a glance at Margaret as she sat down, appetently appreciating the shapeliness of her back, the pinch of her waist and the smooth curve of her buttocks where they gently sank into the blanket, the material of her skirt tautened with the motion of her sitting down. From her sitting position, Margaret bent forward and unfastened her shoes – Aiden hungrily watching the movement accentuating the orbicular curve of her backside – carefully removed them and placed them under the bed.

Sitting back up straight, she placed one hand either side of her hips on the woollen blanket – it had been far too hot for eiderdowns, but just in case, Mrs Peabody had insisted, they only had to ask should they want them – and pushed herself further back onto the bed and swung her legs up so that she was parallel to Aiden. Lifting her pillow up from the flat and using it in the manner of a cushion, she leant against the headrest. Knowing that Margaret would probably ask him what he was thinking about if he appeared to be doing nothing, Aiden similarly slid himself into an upright sitting position and picked up his newspaper from beside the bed where he had previously let it drop.

"There!" Margaret announced apropos of nothing as she settled herself by twisting her shoulders a little and pulling at the straps of her brassiere under the shoulders of her blouse until she felt comfortable. She reached out to the bedside table beside her for her pen and a small, flat paper bag which she had previously placed there. "Which one of these do you think for your mother?"

The paper bag had contained postcards that Margaret had bought that morning. Aiden glanced through the half dozen or so cards before saying, "She'll like that one, I think." Aiden had chosen an overly sunny aerial view of Swanage Bay with the cliffs in the background.

One of the cards that he had rejected for his mother was of the rock stacks known locally as Old Harry and Old Harry's Wife. Aiden thought of sending it to Harry and Janet, Harry would be sure to find it amusing - Aiden smiled to himself as he thought of Harry's loud, rather infectious laugh - and would probably pin it up in the mess. But humour requiring a more buoyant mood than he presently enjoyed, Aiden decided not to mention it to Margaret and continued to flick through the pages of his newspaper in a desultory fashion.

"Daddy, can we go to the castle tomorrow?" Mark asked, without looking up from his game; the plastic cowboys and Indians were perched precariously on the back of the green and yellow lorry.

Taking the branch train had been the final stage of their journey on Saturday. As was his habit, carefully consulting the railway timetable that he had opened out on the kitchen table, Aiden had worked out all the times and connections of the journey: he had worked out whether it was better to start from Lincoln or Gainsborough, or perhaps even Market Rasen, to travel down to Kings Cross; then they had had to cross London before catching the train from Waterloo to Wareham where they had changed for the branch line to Swanage. It had been a long and tiring journey necessitating an early start. He had especially allowed sufficient time to travel across London; besides having reserved seats from Waterloo, it would worry him if they were to arrive at the boarding house later than he had said they would, even though everyone would acknowledge that such things sometimes happened. "Mrs Peabody says they're quite close to the station. At least that's something." He had said, once again checking the details in her letter.

As the branch train had slowly rounded a curve, Mark had been excited to see the dramatic sight of Corfe Castle strategically commanding the gap through the Purbeck Hills. Long after the train had left the station at Corfe he was straining for a final view, his cheek pushed up against the carriage window.

"We'll go there one day before we go home." Aiden thought it would make a pleasant change from their usual routine which revolved almost exclusively around the beach.

"And do you want to send Geoff a card?"

"Yes, I should think so; we normally do."

Watching Aiden, Margaret said "Shall I address it to Kitty as well?"

Aiden paused for a moment before saying hesitantly, "Just ask how she is or something like that."

Margaret, inscrutably, looked back down at the postcard she was writing to Aiden's mother, her pen beginning to move once again as she neatly squeezed as much information as she reasonably could onto the correspondence portion of the card.

Finding nothing of interest in his paper that he had not already read, Aiden quietly folded it up and placed it back on the floor beside the bed and reached out instead for his paperback despite not really being in the mood to read it even though it was only light and insubstantial. After a moment he said, "I was thinking that perhaps we might buy a car."

"Do you think we could afford it?"

Margaret had not looked up from her postcard but Aiden caught the hint of sharpness in her reply.

"Of course, I'd need to look into it!"

They sat in silence for a few moments then Aiden pressed ahead with the proposal; it gave him something other than his brooding to think about. "It needn't be anything grand; something like a Morris Minor. Second-hand shouldn't be too dear."

"A family car?" Margaret asked, pausing in her writing and turning her head to look at Aiden.

"What else?" Aiden replied with rising consternation. "It would make going to see Ted and Daphne a darned sight easier and we could even come on holiday in it."

Margaret nodded ever so slightly and gently pursed her lips as if she was considering the argument. Aiden, sliding back into a lying position, picked-up his newspaper again, but only feigned reading it.

~~~~

"Come along, Sweetie, time to get you ready for bed."

On hearing Margaret's words, Aiden opened his eyes and looked at his watch; he must have drifted off, he thought to himself. His book was lying open face down upon his chest where it had dropped from his hand. One of the pages had been creased. Margaret was placing her written postcards in her handbag to post later.

"I guess we'd better be getting ready as well," Aiden said, feeling a little groggy from his brief sleep. He picked up his book and closed it.

"Do you want to go along to the bathroom first?"

This was not a question; it simply meant Margaret thought Aiden should use the bathroom while she got Mark ready for bed. Aiden sat up and swung himself round into a sitting position. Yawning, he rested his right elbow on his knee and rubbed his chin between the thumb and forefinger of his right hand like a man might if deciding whether he needed to shave but which was actually simply habit. Before going to the bathroom he picked up a towel from the hardback chair which stood on the linoleum in the corner of the room nearest to the door. The towels Mrs Peabody provided were scrupulously clean, but had long ago lost the downiness of new.

When he returned from the bathroom, Margaret had more-or-less finished getting Mark ready for bed and was tying the cord of Mark's pyjamas around his waist. Mark was standing in front of the bunk beds and his blue and white striped pyjamas looked so remarkably like Aiden's that Mark appeared as if he were a miniature version of his father.

While Margaret took her turn to go along to the bathroom Mark sat on the edge of the lower bunk looking at a comic while Aiden dressed for dinner. Aiden had brought a plain white shirt with him, his newest, to wear down to dinner in the evenings. By generally changing out of it again after dinner, he hoped it would remain sufficiently clean to last out the holiday.

When Margaret returned, Aiden turned to look at her. "I can't decide," he said pensively, "I think it really is too hot for a jacket." But Aiden was disappointed that Margaret must have changed her dress while she was in the bathroom.

"Well, while you're deciding, I'll sort the towels out!" She thought that Aiden was worrying far too much for a boarding house, but understood he would feel uncomfortable if other men wore jackets down to dinner while he did not.

Margaret picked up the towel Aiden had used and also having hold of her own, walked over to the window, parting the net curtains once more, and stepped into the golden brightness. She carefully spread the towels out along the window-sill, folding them as necessary, so that the little evening sun the room caught might aid their drying. This routine had become habitual and one or the other of them repeated it each evening before going down to dinner, and each morning before they went out for the day.

"I'll chance it without."

Margaret, having finished spreading the towels out and having returned back into the main body of the room, picked up her handbag in readiness.

"Come on little man, up we get," Aiden said, gently taking Mark's comic from him and helping him up the ladder onto the top bunk, where Margaret had previously turned back the bedclothes. "Time to snuggle down." Aiden tucked the sheet and blanket around Mark and handed Harris up to him. Mark, being a precise little boy, took care to tuck Harris in.

Rather than immediately settling down to go to sleep as Margaret would have preferred him to do, Mark turned over so that he was lying on his stomach propping himself up on his elbows; although it was quite distant, from the top bunk it was possible to look out of the window and see the station, a view that evidently fascinated Mark.

"You must promise me something, Sweetie. You mustn't get out of bed. Do you promise Mummy?" Aiden thought that Margaret was unnecessarily anxious.

"I won't, mummy. I promise."

But Margaret perpetually worried about Mark. Privately torturing herself with grisly mental tableaux, so intensely and vicariously could she imagine him suffering that she could make herself feel physically sick and so she longed and intended to *always* keep him close to her and would have even prevented him from growing up if she could.

"He'll be fine," Aiden said firmly. Mark always slept soundly. Not even the sudden, dramatic sounds of a busy airbase, such as the streperous and sudden booming engine noises of jet aircraft engaged in night exercises would wake him. Aiden was convinced that watching the station also hastened Mark to sleep; each evening when they returned to the room after dinner they had found him soundly asleep with nothing to suggest that he had ever left his bed.

Margaret and Aiden both kissed Mark goodnight and then just as the gong for the evening meal was sounding they turned, ready to descend to the dining room.

"Just a moment," Margaret said as they reached the door of their room, and turned back towards the bunk beds. Reaching them she quite unnecessarily again re-adjusted the sheet on Mark's bed.

"For heaven's sake!" Aiden exclaimed, already on a short fuse, and adding quickly, "We'll be late down" as he struggled to cover his rising exasperation.

Margaret made a final check that the covers were properly tucked in and lightly touched Mark's hair, before rejoining Aiden, casting him a look of enmity as she did so.

## *Chapter Seventeen*

"Let's turn back at the hotel." Margaret spoke unemphatically, as if she had merely walked far enough for this evening and now simply wanted to return to the boarding house. Just before speaking she had carefully linked her arm through Aiden's, so that their forearms rested together, and had gently leant her weight against him as if she were seeking a greater degree of intimacy. Then as she had spoken she had leant slightly forward so that the effect had been of her looking up into his face.

"Alright, then," Aiden replied reasonably and cheerfully, as if he were doing no more than happily indulging his wife's wishes. But then he added, "But I'm sure he'd be fine for a little while longer." He continued to employ the same reasonable tone, so that Margaret could not equitably take issue with him, but the undertone intentionally went beyond the simple reasonable answer that her request apparently only required.

As Aiden had expected, Mark had been soundly asleep when they had returned to their room after dinner, curled up into a ball and cuddling Harris, but Margaret had nevertheless remained uneasy about leaving him. She had wondered whether they should not rather stay in, perhaps, she had said by way of offering a compromise, taking their reading books with them down to the residents' lounge. But Aiden, with a feeling of rising trepidation as if his own happiness depended entirely upon her good favour, had counter-suggested saying they should put their heads around Mrs Peabody's door and say they were going out for a short walk and ask whether she would be good enough to listen out for him. Faced with his moderation, Margaret had hesitantly agreed.

Margaret's burden of concern did not ever have the strong flavour of being purely histrionic, but neither did he think that it was entirely innocent of affect when it suited her. But nevertheless, if he had managed to successfully insist they continue walking on further and there had then been some sort of crisis or problem, he would have felt unspeakably guilty. So, despite his carefully considered deployment of reasonableness, he *had* relented and in doing so once again felt the iniquity of there being a gulf between them.

"We shouldn't leave him for long." Margaret cleverly adopted the same reasonable tone, thereby making it sound as if the two of them were trying to convince themselves against extending their walk, rather than being engaged in some sort of struggle.

"Of course we shouldn't."

They had walked along Shore Road, beside the beach, for a short way, but had turned back before even reaching Victoria Avenue and headed instead towards the Old Quay. Aiden had hoped to walk out as far as the Point. Of all the walks they had found this holiday, walking out to Peveril Point was the one he enjoyed most. They had already been level with the pier when Margaret had spoken and therefore had been able to hear the music playing in the Grosvenor Hotel. Margaret had taken care to post her postcards in the first pillar box they had passed after leaving the boarding house.

They carried on in silence for a few steps before Margaret said in a tone that was almost jaunty, "Of course, you're not actually with him most of the time, but you have to be so careful. You only need to turn your back for a moment."

The unfair implication of a goodness and carefulness that eclipsed Aiden's own stung Aiden sharply but he said nothing. He did not want to be goaded into an argument with Margaret; without having any firm plan in mind he had hoped that the walk would give him a suitable opening with her, and as they had walked he found himself trembling like an adolescent. But Margaret seemed determined to assert the moral high ground over him and now added a layer of apparent malcontent.

"As much as I like being away, it's never a complete rest for me." Margaret almost imperceptibly emphasised the word me. "There are always little everyday things for me to remember: sorting the towels out, rinsing through any odd bits of clothing that need it, and then there's still Mark to look after, of course."

Across the road from the Hotel was a low wall or parapet. Having agreed to turn around when they reached the hotel, it seemed quite natural to stop walking when they had reached it. They looked out over the parapet through the dusk towards the bay. The water was calm and dark, and from where they stood they could neither see nor hear the miniscule waves gently breaking upon the beach. Then they turned, but rather than starting back Margaret surprised Aiden by sitting down on the edge of the parapet, facing the hotel, with her legs stretched out in front of her.

The hotel was a grand white building in a style that had been popular three quarters of a century before and which dominated this end of the bay and commanded a view over the town. Rich amber light filled all the doors and windows so that from the outside it appeared as a lambent pleasure palace for the well-mannered. Inside, Aiden and Margaret could see men in dinner jackets and ladies in fine evening dress deporting themselves with the air of those who were habitually accustomed to living at ease. Here and there, guests had spilled out onto the terrace in front of the hotel to continue their gossiping or their conversations blithely indifferent to the rank and file of unastonishing holidaymakers promenading in front of them.

"I thought you wanted to be getting back?" Aiden, feeling the situation running away from him, sat down on the wall beside her.

"In a moment." Then, pointedly, "Don't you think it would be wonderful to stay somewhere like this, to be waited on hand and foot."

"No, I don't! We've not been brought up to it!"

He felt infuriated with her and consequently spoke sharply. But in the silence between them that followed, Margaret appeared quite calm.

Presently she continued speaking as if Aiden had said nothing. "Crisp table linen; waiters at your beck and call; dressing up for the evening; the music and the dancing. We used to go dancing, didn't we?"

They could now hear clearly the music that they had first heard as they had approached the hotel. It did not appeal to Aiden. A small orchestra, probably no more than a string quartet, was playing light melodies, the arrangements predictable and undemanding, as if they were afraid of admitting to strong emotion. Ordinarily, Aiden would have thought that neither would it have appealed to Margaret.

"Not like this!"

When they had first courted, and even up to the time Margaret had become pregnant, not only had they listened to swing, they had danced to it. Margaret had learnt how to jitterbug even before she had met Aiden. They had preferred the American bands, such as Herman, Dorsey and Kenton, eagerly maintaining as enthusiasts and connoisseurs that there was a qualitative difference between them and their counterparts on this side of the Atlantic.

They had danced so hard, such was the amazing potency of the music: shouting at each other just to be heard; captivated by the riffing saxophones and their flowing, closely harmonised phrasing; excited by the screaming and punchy brass; transported by the tight excitingly expressive solos; lost to the pounding, sexy rhythm; and, feeling themselves red-alive and driven to each other, much more than if only sharing the sentiments and the big round sound of romantic ballads.

"Does that matter so very much?"

"I think it should," Aiden said sadly; it felt as if she had deliberately hurt him.

After sitting in silence for a minute or two, Margaret said quietly, "But can't you see the attraction?"

"Not really."

The hotel and the people in it did not seem to belong here. It seemed to have nothing to do with the seaside as Aiden understood it. It had nothing to do with wriggling one's toes in damp beach sand; nothing to do with having to find somewhere indoors if it should turn wet, plastic macs dripping; nothing to do with queuing for a table in a busy café at lunchtime. Aiden had felt quite confident at the start of their walk, but now he felt quite dejected.

"Come on, you're the one who wanted to go back," Aiden said tersely.

As they stood up ready to start back to the boarding house, Margaret said, "Kitty's from that sort of world, isn't she? Do you think that's part of her appeal?"

Particularly feeling reluctant to talk about Kitty, Aiden replied angrily, "I really wouldn't know."

They walked back in silence for a good part of the way. Then, having passed the pier and the Quay, they started to walk up the incline of High Street, with the intention of cutting through to their boarding house once they had passed the Black Swan public house.

"Aiden," Margaret began in a soft, coaxing voice, as if she regretted having goaded Aiden, "do you really want to buy a car?"

"Maybe," He replied defensively, not feeling particularly disposed towards any further discussion of the matter, not least because he was now suspicious of Margaret's motives for asking.

Margaret continued in the same gently cajoling tone, "Do you really think it would make our lives that bit easier? I can see that it would make visiting Ted and Daphne, or Mum and Dad that much easier, more convenient, so long as we could afford it."

Aiden did not reply and they walked on in silence as they climbed further up the hill and the dusk around them became deeper.

"And I suppose it would make everyday things easier," Margaret said more matter-of-factly, as if she were doing no more than giving reasonable further thought to the idea, weighing up the pros and cons, "Like taking Mark into town for new shoes and things like that. At the moment it's a whole morning or afternoon gone if we have to go in on the bus. We could be in and out in no time."

"It would," replied Aiden grudgingly, his jaw and face set rigid.

Aiden was looking straight ahead, determined not to look at Margaret. Margaret walked on for a few steps without saying anything, her movements were altogether more fluid, and she carefully gave Aiden a sideways quizzical glance through the deepening dusk in an effort to read his expression. Her own expression was slightly impish.

"And we could go out as a family, picnics and things," she said, and adding with emphasis after the briefest of pauses, "when you're not off flying."

"Oh for goodness sake, Margaret. Must we start all that again!"

Fearing that she had gone too far, she reached out to touch his upper arm, but Aiden repelled her touch, twisting his left shoulder forward violently and at the same time his face around his left eye screwed up in an involuntary spasm. In front of the Black Swan he stepped off the kerb to cross the road. She followed and they continued to walk in silence.

Then, as if she could not leave it alone, Margaret said quietly, "Is there any other reason why you want to buy a car?"

Aiden almost exploded with exasperation. "What else could there be!"

"But if you went off in the car I wouldn't know where you were. You're away so much from us as it is." Her voice was gentle, but definitely scoffing, knowing that Aiden was too incandescent with anger to effectively counter her. "I was just wondering," she continued, as if she enjoyed nettling him, "You see, you could be taking other women out in your car, doing who knows what with them, and I'd never know!"

"For heaven's sake, Margaret!" Aiden's voice was raised almost to the level of shouting. "When have I ever given you any cause to think like that?"

"This hasn't anything to do with Kitty having her own little car, does it?" Margaret went on to ask brightly with seeming innocence, but then fell leaden as Aiden replied with absolute acid conviction, his voice steely:

"I've had just about enough of all this. That's it!"

He felt as if he did not want to speak to her ever again and they returned to the boarding house in utter silence.

~~~~

Neither of them would allow their bitterness to interfere with their routines for saying goodnight to Mark.

Firstly, Margaret walked over to the bunk beds and carefully peered into the topmost. As if he had not moved at all, Mark was still soundly asleep cuddling Harris. Margaret carefully turned the sheet back away from Mark's face another inch or so and smoothed the turned-down portion over the pink woollen blanket which lay over the sheet. Then she touched the fore and middle fingers of her right hand to her lips as if kissing them, then placed them gently on Mark's forehead and whispered very quietly, 'Good night, Sweetie' before turning away.

Aiden then approached the bunk and placing his head close to Mark's, turned his face away from him so that his ear was close to Mark's face. Then, holding his own breath, he could be sure to be able to hear Mark's breathing. This was something he had done ever since Mark had been tiny. Not to do so would have been to court bad luck.

In silence, Margaret sat down at the dressing table, took off her earrings, picked up her hairbrush and began to angrily brush at her hair. Sitting on the edge of the bed, Aiden paused half way through untying his shoelace, his right ankle propped up on his left knee; he could *hear* the violence of the brush stokes as the brush tore through her hair. Convinced she could not see him reflected in the glass, he darkly observed her; sitting in her nightdress on the dressing table stool, her concupiscent form readily apparent, it seemed grievously iniquitous that he should feel driven to covet his own wife.

By the time Margaret had finished brushing her hair, Aiden, feeling totally dependent on the outcome of their struggle, was sitting up in bed pretending to read, surreptitiously watching even her slightest action. As she walked around the foot of the bed, her movements no longer flowed, they seemed angry as if she were consumed by indignation. Jerking the covers back, she climbed heavily and ungracefully in to her side of the bed. Aiden thought that she was making a point of not looking at him. Satisfied to continue fuelling the silence between them, Margaret picked up her book from the bedside table, her casual movement implying that *she* would have no trouble at all with concentrating on her reading.

Both of them were too upset to read, but neither of them wanted to make an excuse for turning out the light straight away, so for a time, both of them maintained the pretence of reading. After ten minutes or so, Aiden closed up his book. The only bedside table being on Margaret's side, he placed his book under the bed and then slid down into a lying position with his back to Margaret; he did not want to give her the impression that he was being conciliatory in any way by facing her. Soon afterwards Margaret shut her book, placed it on the bedside table and reached out to turn off the bedside lamp. There was a slight delay as she fumbled through the awkwardness of the switch. The moving bar that made or broke the electrical connection was too tight against the collar which held the lampshade in place; in a spirit of making do, at some time in the past the switch and bulb-holder had been cobbled together from ill-matching components. Having switched the lamp off, she lay down, but also with her back towards Aiden.

Aiden lay in the dark, wretched with dejection. He instinctively drew his knees up so that he was lying in a foetal position and placed his hands in the space or cavity created between his thighs and stomach. He placed his face close to the opening between the sheets savouring the warm beddy mugginess. Aiden knew that Margaret was not asleep; although she lay quite still, her breathing gave her away.

Not only was he miserable, but also whatever the outcome of this particular episode he knew he would be the lonelier for it. Margaret would no doubt confide completely in Daphne, thick with a watchful assumption of male wickedness, leaving Aiden feeling criminal, and he understood why some men feel compelled to turn to a journal or diary.

But presently, Margaret's body was no longer still and Aiden became aware that she was crying.

At irregular intervals her body was racked by spasms, the epicentre of which seemed to be either in her stomach or her chest. Simultaneously with these paroxysms, Aiden could hear short nasal or constrained throaty noises as if her convulsions were involuntary and that Margaret was fighting to control or conceal them. The subsultus gradually increased in regularity and force until Margaret's whole body was shaking.

Aiden felt glad that she was crying; it seemed only just that she should feel upset, and at that moment he vindictively and quite particularly wanted her to suffer and to be totally consumed by burning regret. But although still subject to his anger, he found it impossible to remain totally hard-hearted towards her for long.

At first he merely turned over so that he was facing her shaking back, but then he gingerly reached out and touched her. Soliciting no response, he slid over the bed and lay close to her so that her backside nestled snugly into the angle at his pelvis made by the trunk of his body with his thighs. He slid his left hand and arm over the slight paunch of Margaret's stomach and, working his way still closer to her, nuzzled his face into her warm neck. His right arm lay awkwardly beneath him, cramped along the mattress-side of his body so that his knuckles were resting against Margaret's right buttock. It would have felt natural to simply run his right arm under her so that they were lying comfortably together, but he felt insufficiently sure of himself or of Margaret's response to do so.

They lay nestling together in this way for a while, until Margaret was calmer and her body was no longer racked by crying. Aiden stretched his neck out so that they were virtually cheek-to-cheek, his head lying above her's; the position was uncomfortable for him, but by adopting it he could better sense her facial expression and gauge her emotional state.

Presently, Margaret said quietly, "I just wanted to tease you, like I used to. But then I couldn't seem to stop."

Aiden made no reply; despite his compassion, he felt sufficiently hurt not to want to lend any legitimacy to her actions by either dismissing them or by underplaying the impact they had had on him.

"I do love you," Margaret continued, quietly. Aiden wondered for how long he would be able to maintain his hurt silence. "You do love me, don't you?"

Ordinarily, after an upset, if Margaret asked this of Aiden he would reply in the affirmative in such a manner as to suggest his loving her was a given, and his tone of reconciliation would further suggest that it was therefore completely unnecessary to ask; it was part of the usual path of normalisation between the two of them, a comforting ritual. But tonight he continued to say nothing.

It seemed like they had been lying together in the dark for a long time until quite unexpectedly, their tense quiescence was broken. Aiden felt a single twitch of Margaret's behind. The movement was slight but unmistakable. It also appeared obviously pointed, and so Aiden tentatively and experimentally ran his hand up from Margaret's stomach where it had remained all the time they had been lying together towards her left breast, but he remained sharply alert to any sign from her that may cause him to instantly withdraw it again. But gently running his palm over her nipple, Margaret responded with a sharp intake of breath. Now more certain of himself, he drew his hand back down over her stomach, slowly and firmly tracing her contours and making the same deliberate tactile progress over her hip and down to her thigh. For a moment he let his hand remain there, his thumb tracing an imaginary arc backwards and forwards on her thigh in a soft stroking motion before running his hand further back down her leg, almost as far as her knee, sufficiently far to allow him to run his hand back up her thigh again, but this time beneath her nightdress.

Letting his hand pause momentarily on the flesh of her thigh, he drew up his right arm sufficiently to take his weight on his elbow and then lent forward to kiss her neck. Like a simple re-affirmation of right he kissed her lightly at first, but possessively, gluttonously savouring the smell of her flesh, but then burning with her having made him miss her for so long, he decisively slid his right arm beneath her and turned her head towards him and pressed his mouth hard against hers, suddenly aching to taste her, his right hand forcibly holding her head so that she could not move from him.

With an unguessed-at and urgent animal insatiability, he ran his hand up the back of her thigh, deliberately digging his finger nails into her flesh, enjoying the way she squirmed beneath his hand, wanting her to writhe beneath his touch, and buffered his hand firmly to a stop on her backside. Resting his thumb across the flesh on her left buttock, and resting the palm over her anus he pushed the fingers of his hand between her legs and into her genital passage. Margaret tried to turn herself over to face him, to position herself for their inevitably-used missionary position. But to her obvious and great surprise, Aiden withdrew his left hand but not to enable her to turn over, but to allow him the freedom of movement to purposefully roll on top of her, Margaret being forced to remain face down beneath his weight. In the same greedy suite of movement, he ruttishly levered her legs further apart with his ankles. Rapaciously, he savoured the sumptuous feel of her thighs and the pert curve of her backside. His dark brooding anger and lust mingled like thick, febrile blood so that he longed to penetrate into her and press her almost into oblivion.

As he entered into her, Aiden pushed her hands up on to the pillow beside her head. Tightly holding onto her wrists, he raised his upper torso up so that his arms took his weight, revelling in the increased traction and depth of penetration it afforded him as he thrust into her. Wanting no more of her than her availability to satisfy him, he used his weight from his pelvic thrusts as if to violently grind her into the bed beneath him, her bitten-back gasps a vindication and a delight. Aiden had the revelatory primeval and deeply satisfying sensation of his male energy smothering her. Regulating the depth and speed of his penetration maximised his sensual pleasure and hedonistically prolonged his own sexual enjoyment.

## *Chapter Eighteen*

Aiden took his cigarette from his mouth and exhaled the smoke through his nostrils in a leisurely fashion. He enjoyed taking morning coffee here. He rested his hand on the edge of the table and the smoke from his cigarette drifted up in front of them in a lazy, twisting motion. It was unusually early for coffee, not yet ten o'clock, but feeling unexpectedly exalted this morning, Aiden had taken a delight in a change from their usual routine. And being so early, they had been able to secure one of their favourite booths with the high-backed benches without any difficulty.

Savouring the aroma of the smoke as it drifted by her, Margaret said, "That smells good." She had indifferently stopped smoking a number of years ago but it occasionally suited her to ask for a taste from Aiden's cigarette.

"Do you want a puff?" Aiden held the cigarette out over the table towards her.

As if shy of a newly-hallowed object, she lightly touched his fingers as she took the cigarette from his hand. She carefully drew on it and handed it back to him. With the tingling rush of the nicotine, she smiled beatifically as if the ingrained presumption of something being unholy had been unexpectedly proved false.

Being a bakery as well as a coffee lounge, the warm life-affirming smell of fresh bread filled the air and a constant stream of local people came in to buy their bread so that by sitting here, holidaying seemed beneficially complected with the everyday and their idleness therefore purposeful. Summer wasps plagued the trays of sweet cakes laid out in the windows and the service the uniformed waitresses provided was merely as adequate as the majority of the customers expected. Aiden let the comforting atmosphere wash over him.

"Mother would like it here," he said quietly. "She'd call the waitress 'dear' and ask her if she had a young man, or some such nonsense."

Margaret smiled at Aiden and invitingly laid her hand on the table in front of her. The comfort-soft persuasory aroma of brewing coffee filled the air. Aiden, holding his cigarette between his fore and middle fingers, responded by placing his hand over Margaret's so that his two smallest fingers tenderly touched the knuckles of her hand.

"Are we going to the beach now?" Mark piped-up brightly.

As they did every morning on their way out after breakfast, they had picked up Mark's bucket and spade, still gritty with daily sand, from where it was kept in the front porch of the boarding house along with those belonging to the other children who were staying there, Mrs Peabody not worrying in the least about a little sand, a few seashells, or even a few rogue strands of seaweed, on her porch floor tiles.

"A little later, Sweetie. Daddy wants to walk out to the Point first."

"I don't mind. We could go there later."

Aiden spoke genially. It seemed to Aiden that at some time in the past, and he could not have said when or exactly why, he had taken upon himself the assumption that where holiday activities were concerned he should have no very great expectations for himself other than Margaret's and by practising a moderate self-effacement a peaceful holiday could be more-or-less ensured.

"But I want to go now!" Mark cried out petulantly, but Margaret chose to ignore Mark's protests and said with quiet determination:

"It won't do him any harm to wait a bit; I know how you like to watch the sea." And turning to Mark she said brightly, "We haven't had our coffee yet." She then added, her eyes widening as they did whenever she wanted to appease him, "And we're having cake!"

The prospect of cake had the desired effect.

Over time, at the very end of the Point, the upper, softer strata of rock had crumbled and been washed away through the action of the relentless sea, leaving a scarified platform of harder rock, exposed at low tide, lacerated and pitted, sharp and vicious. Here, the power of the running tides was horribly apparent; as the tide turned, tons of unforgiving water flowed in thick curtains over the treacherous rocks. Aiden found a deep instinctive fascination in watching the sea.

"And we must go to the castle; I promised him." Aiden spoke as if there had been some question of whether they would go to the castle or not.

"There's still tomorrow." Margaret had caught Aiden's tenor perfectly.

"I wonder what the tide's doing?" Aiden said rhetorically after a moment.

One day, they had seen a man in a rowing boat, trying to round the Point back to Swanage against the tide. He was a powerfully built man, but he could make no headway. They had watched in a kind of shocked paralysis for a few moments before understanding his awful peril, but before they could raise the alarm, another boat, a local fishing boat with a motor, had arrived and thrown him a line.

Presently, Margaret spoke again. "Do you think Kitty and Geoff will last?"

Ordinarily, Aiden preferred to be circumspect whenever Kitty's name was mentioned, but there seemed no edge to Margaret's question this morning. Although remaining wary, he replied after a brief pause with a more definite opinion than he usually would have ventured to give her. "Actually, I think there's a pretty good chance that it might."

At that moment their waitress arrived with a tray. There were cups of their usual hot milky coffees for Aiden and Margaret, and for Mark, a glass of milk which arrived with two brightly coloured drinking straws. The bright straws pleased Mark, and while Aiden and Margaret had scones, a Swiss bun with pink icing had been chosen for Mark. Mark decided he liked pink icing considerably more than he liked brightly coloured drinking straws.

Aiden and Margaret paused in their conversation while the waitress placed the drinks and cakes in front of them, making a special point as she did so of asking in a pleasantly exaggerated manner if the iced bun was for the young man. Then, after asking whether there would be anything else, she placed the bill in front of Aiden. Margaret smiled her thanks up at the waitress and Aiden casually glanced at her as she retreated, idly thinking to himself that the way the thick white loops of her apron strings hung down the back of her skirt and flounced with the rhythm of her walk emphasised her attractiveness. Aiden extinguished his cigarette in the ashtray in the middle of the table.

"I don't see what someone like her sees in him." Margaret said innocuously, continuing their conversation from the point where they had left off when the waitress had arrived. If Margaret had noticed the direction of Aiden's glance, she chose not to show it.

Laying in the dark last night, he had felt both wonderfully elated and deeply shocked. Such unbridled carnality was a previously unimagined, unsurpassable joy. But he had felt frightened at the sudden eruption of his voraciousness, which, like fury, he would have been *unable* to hold in check; on the dark side of lust, something disturbingly animal inside of him had been revealed and had actuated him. Unmentored and brought up in a Sunday-kind of isolation, he had worried that Margaret *should* feel violated, but she had lain in a kind of dreamy inertia as if she were perfectly content before she had fallen into a deep sleep.

This morning after waking, Aiden had initially watched her with incertitude but she had simply made no reference to last night. But her demeanour was unmistakably different towards him and by now he felt sufficiently fortified to intentionally give a careless-sounding reply. "He's got as much going for him as any of us have."

Manipulating conversations of any kind did not come naturally to Aiden and he was sufficiently homely to think that the politics of sex should be unnecessary between a man and his wife.

But Margaret did not rise to the bait, continuing matter-of-factly, "But look how he behaved at the Ladies Night!"

"I know, but perhaps she found something worth forgiving in him."

"I don't know what you mean."

"Just that perhaps he's gentler than you think," Aiden said

noncommittally. He had propped his elbows on the table and was cradling his cup between his hands in front of his chin, swirling the last drop of coffee around, savouring the smell of the thick liquid.

Aiden did not want to mention the conversation he had instigated with Geoff shortly after the Ladies Night; he felt it would be a betrayal of confidence to recount anything of the content and it seemed something curiously private between men. Lacking a mentor of his own, Aiden remained uneasy with the notion that he could legitimately make confidences which excluded Margaret. The conversation with Geoff had been difficult and Aiden had necessarily had to work hard at it. It was as if he was consciously labouring to do the work of older men: there was a drought of older men that Aiden himself could comfortably refer to, and his own experiences had impressed him as being woefully inconsequential to be a sufficient instrument of kindly persuasion.

"I was surprised when Geoff said that she had agreed to see him again."

Aiden felt pleasantly relieved. Margaret's tone was mild, but her expression suggested that she had not understood his reply. Deliberately choosing his words carefully so they could be construed in an inflammatory way, he replied, "Actually, I think she's very determined. Once she's made up her mind to something, I rather suspect that's it!"

But Margaret made no reply and feeling pleased with himself, he turned to Mark and said, "Come along Poppet, finish up your milk, it's time we were going."

"Here!" Margaret took out her handkerchief – Aiden could see a miniscule violet embroidered upon it – and holding it up to her tongue, dampened the corner of it. She leaned across to Mark, who was not quite quick enough to avoid her, and wiped away the remains of the pink icing from around his mouth.

"I'll go and pay."

It would not have occurred to either of them to do other than assume their usual roles; they were perfectly content with such divisions in their lives together. Aiden stood up and placed a few silver coins beside his empty cup and saucer. He wondered whether

Geoff had really understood when he had said that Kitty's pity should not be a sufficient motive for change.

Aiden crossed over the floor of the shop and joined the short queue of people who were waiting at the counter whilst Margaret, standing up awkwardly, unable to completely straighten her legs in the cramped space between the table and the bench seat, busied herself with checking that they had not forgotten anything. Then having quickly glanced at the coins Aiden had left on the table, her attention was mostly given over to organising Mark and brushing the cake crumbs from the seat cushion from where Mark had been sitting.

Margaret then successfully negotiated a deal with an initially reluctant and sullen-looking Mark whereby he agreed to carry his bucket and spade, and in return Margaret took charge of Harris - who had apparently decided to go to the beach with them today - as Harris could travel in the top of her beach basket. This was a reversal of the arrangement that had existed on leaving the boarding house, and Margaret felt pleased with her dainty victory thinking that for once she had got the better part of the deal. Taking Mark's hand, Margaret went to wait for Aiden outside of the shop.

Reaching the head of the queue Aiden handed their bill to the assistant and reached into his inside jacket pocket for his wallet. As he had waited he had been watching the shop girls as they fetched loaves, rolls and cakes, placing them in large white flimsy paper bags for their customers. He also followed the progress of the waitresses as they bustled about the tables taking new orders and clearing away the used crockery and as he turned away from the counter, pocketing his change, he happened to catch the eye of their waitress as she cleared away from the table they had just vacated. He briefly smiled at her and felt a tingling thrill of excitement as she lubriciously reciprocated as she deliciously leant with an exaggerated deliberateness over the table.

It came as a sudden subversive revelation that the waitress could have a whole very secret and deeply satisfying carnal dimension to her life. Aiden occasionally felt the loneliness of deep, aching lust for other women, much deeper than anything he ever felt for

Margaret. Such lust had always been unfathomable, all powerful like the heaving depths of the sea, and tinged with overwhelming sadness, imagining himself to be inherently guilty of all sorts of serpent-like inexpiable wickedness. So it was with immense private relief that he could now imagine the possibility of there being other, fully reciprocated, sexual lives, but the tragedy was, he sadly reflected, that he had only discovered a secret life of sex now.

~~~~

"But she *is* attractive, isn't she?" They were approaching the Point. Here, one or two larger Edwardian houses were set by the edge of the sea with a commanding view of the bay, their backs hard against the headland. As they had walked, Margaret had briefly pondered the generosity of the tip Aiden had left for the waitress and now she spoke in the manner of someone doubting a long held belief and seeking reassurance. The three of them paused, Margaret and Aiden looking out over Swanage Bay.

After a moment Aiden replied simply and decisively, still tempting her to anger, "Yes, she is. Very."

The idea had briefly flitted through his mind that Margaret had been referring to the waitress in the coffee shop, about whom he had been casually, but lasciviously thinking, knowing that he would inevitably soon forget her. Margaret seemed satisfied with his reply.

"Shall we sit for a while?" Aiden asked, wondering if attractive was actually a complex euphemism which men frequently failed to understand when the term was used by women about women to men.

Behind the Edwardian houses the land sloped up moderately but steadily, rising up to the high and dramatic cliffs above Durlston Bay behind them. The cliffs there were horribly giddy, with a vertiginous drop to the sharp and brutal rocks below; although Peveril Point separated the two bays, the concave shape of Durlston Bay was wide and broad, open to all the fickleness and steely elemental power of The Channel, on the edge of something elemental, seemingly unlike Swanage Bay. But here, where they sat, the grassy slope was pleasantly doted with copious brightly-eyed daisies and the air had a remarkable freshness or clarity far-carrying the sound of the eternally sad gulls wheeling above them.

"Why do you like it so here?" Margaret asked, "It's not just the sea, is it?"

Aiden sat with his feet together and his knees up. His legs gently splayed out so that his knees nestled into the crooks made by his angled elbows as his arms looped around his legs. His left hand loosely held his right wrist holding the loop of his arms together and keeping him in an upright sitting position. He felt more relaxed, more at ease, than he had felt at any time since before being deployed to Christmas Island. Margaret, attentively and sitting close to him, slipped her arm through his and rested her hand on the inside of his forearm.

"I imagine what it would be like to live in one of those houses," he began, certain that Margaret would be following the direction of his gaze, "but not on a day like today. I think what it would be like in winter, with the sash windows rattling in their frames, the house buffeted by gales and the wind roaring in the chimney." Pausing, he added pensively, "You haven't asked me anything like that before."

"They're lovely big family houses."

"When I imagine being there I'm imagining that I'm all alone."

"It sounds very romantic!" Margaret exclaimed lightly, as if turning Aiden's reflections into a conceit of her own. She shifted her body weight and laid her head on Aiden's shoulder as if she were merely able to respond to her own fanciful notion.

"Can I have Harris, please? We want to play."

Margaret interrupted her reverie to lift Harris out of her basket where he had been nestling in the beach towel, and handed him to Mark.

"There we are, Sweetie," she said casually, turning back to her thoughts.

From where they sat, the unremitting slope of the land away from the cliffs of Durlston Bay and down past them drew the eye and created a narrowing mental vista taking in Swanage Bay only. But Aiden's thoughts were wider, sympathetic to a broader awareness; the position of the houses with their backs to the relatively narrow headland with all the unpredictable savageness of The Channel beyond it somehow made their situation seem perilous, their security and their apparent solidity, dangerously false.

"More like a reminder of just how precarious everything can be," Aiden said quietly, smiling indulgently at her.

"You're talking in riddles this morning, dear!" Margaret replied amiably and then fell silent, seemingly content enough to be sitting quietly with her head on Aiden's shoulder. She then continued speaking, quite brightly, as if a thought had just struck her. "Does it matter awfully if I don't understand what you mean?

Aiden thought that she spoke as if she expected Aiden to reply lightly that it did not really matter. He almost succumbed to this invitation to regain a dishonest easiness with her, but he sensed they were at a pivotal moment and such a response would undermine the validity with her of his own thoughts and emotional responses. With genuine affection he lightly kissed the top of her head, her auburn hair on his lips feeling pleasantly warm from the sun. He rested his head against hers, enjoying their peacefulness together. But before he could formulate any reply advocating a new parity, Margaret suddenly sat bolt upright and cried out with the utmost alarm:

"Where *is* he!"

While they had been talking, Mark had been lying down on the grass behind them playing with Harris, holding him in front of his face, talking to him as if he lived and entreating him to walk though the grass for some purpose. But now he was nowhere to be seen.

In worried concert, Aiden and Margaret sprang to their feet. As if stupefied, they stood gazing about them in every direction straining their eyes for any possible glimpse of him as if they were bound to spy him, feeling that it should be impossible that he could be out of their view within such a very short space of time. But concomitantly, a feeling of panic spread through each of them. Aiden felt his heart rate quicken, and, like a terrified animal, the corners of his mouth drew back involuntarily, a savage inflow of air fuelled his instantly shallowed and accelerated breathing, dried the moisture on his teeth and parched the roof of his mouth. A shocking tremulousness spread about him as if his body could readily give out on him and reduce him to uselessness and ungovernable weeping.

"Mark! Mark!" Wildly, Margaret began to repeatedly cry out his name at the top of her voice and, toppling her basket over as she did so in her skittish fright, ran headlong up the slope towards the cliff tops.

Although knowing it to be patently absurd, but merely responding to his immediate shock, Aiden was momentarily pettily concerned with the items spilt from the basket – the thin, flowery beach towel, Margaret's sunglasses, her powder compact, sun lotion, and even her purse – thinking that he should pause to pick them up, but then fighting down the panic that threatened to engulf him, he began to claw back some vestige of his reason.

Initially, feeling that they should be acting together when faced with this awful adversity, he had been inclined to run pell-mell after Margaret. But then, he acknowledged to himself that a part of this reaction was his own fear of Margaret's criticism.

With tacit agreement from Aiden, even before he had been born, when faced with any divergence of opinion concerning Mark, Margaret would assume her own view to be the wiser, and, in all honesty, Aiden would not have seriously considered challenging her. Now, in this present predicament, not that he thought Margaret deficient in her purpose in any way, but believing he would serve Mark better than she, he courageously abandoned the easier option of simply following her up the slope. It would be more honest to himself if he ran in an altogether different direction; the situation was too serious, the risk to Mark too grave, to succumb to any kind of moral cowardice.

Leaving the contents of the basket where they lay, he therefore ran as fast as he could past the backs of the large Edwardian houses and further out towards the Point; both his instincts and his reason were telling him that this was the most likely direction for Mark to have taken.

The land rose a little higher closer to the Point creating a natural vantage point and Aiden kept on running up the incline until he stood at the top of it. The day was not yet hot, but he was perspiring copiously. Breathing deeply from the effort of running and from his fear, he looked seawards along the Point to where the remaining finger of rock crumbled jaggedly away into the sea. Out in Swanage Bay, the sea looked deceptively, wickedly, calm and peaceful, but he could see, and hear, that the tide had turned; thick and irresistible, occasionally rent viciously through by devilish edges, water, deep and thick like running lacquer, sucked and soughed it's way over the submerged rock table.

It was no real relief that Mark could not be seen in the water or even perilously close to its edge. Behind him, roughly in a south-west direction, lay the cliffs of Durlston Bay. This was the direction in which Margaret had run and so, trusting to her strong maternal power of care to search there extensively, he instead turned and looked back towards the west. His view of the town was partially obscured by the Edwardian houses, and also, on the Point side of them, by a complex of concrete bunkers, coastal fortifications for naval guns, which had been sunk into the Point during the war.

The bunkers, like strong concrete caves largely open on the seaward side, perched quite precariously above the bay, but achieved a low profile through much of their supporting infrastructure having been dug or tunnelled into the soil and rock. At the end of the war they had been locked-up, abandoned, but not slighted in any way, and Aiden had previously walked and climbed around those portions of the complex that remained visible, noting with the military man's quick eye for the detail of the site, how extensive were the areas which had been blocked off. These subterranean workings had presumably contained all manner of stores and accommodation but were now quite inaccessible. Soon, these burrowings would be all too willingly forgotten as belonging to a more perilous and intense time.

But Mark, too, had seemed to be drawn to the desertedness of the site. Perhaps it was no more than coincidence in that he liked to use the bunkers as his playground; the walls in front of where the guns once stood were an irresistible height for climbing upon and hiding behind and the bunkers behind made the perfect den or area to boundary a game of imagination. But Aiden also thought it was a place where the presence of ghosts, male ghosts, could be felt to linger; as if the peculiar camaraderie engendered by lonely watches, the exchange of surprising confidences, had left a soft spectral imprint or charge about the place.

Gazing down at them, the bunkers appeared quite deserted. The walk out to the Point was popular but presently there was nobody to ask if Mark had been seen, the headland around Aiden being quite empty. The wildest thoughts ran through Aiden's head. Apart from the understandable dread of Mark having been swept out to sea, or his body smashed and broken on the rocks, Aiden imagined that Mark, however impossible logic told him that this could be, had found his way into the blocked portion of the fortifications and was now stuck fast, injured or suffocating.

In his desperation, although it seemed like a step towards accepting that a tragedy must have occurred, Aiden was thinking that he must now run and raise the alarm and trust to the instigation of an organised search when out of the cool darkness under the roof of the bunker, Mark's head popped out. He waved happily and called out to Aiden, "Daddy, come and look. I've made a house for Harris!"

"Mark!" Aiden involuntarily let go a loud shout of relief, but Mark seemed quite unaware of any unusual emotion in his father's voice.

Aiden ran headlong down the rabbit-pitted and bumpy slope to the bunker, the treacherousness of the footing simply an irrelevance, and threw his arms around his son, exclaiming, "We were so worried about you!"

Aiden knelt in front of Mark hugging him tight. His left arm circled around Mark's lower back pulling him closer, while his right arm reached up his back with his hand curving over Mark's right shoulder, the smallness of his bones allowing the full depth of his shoulder to fit snugly between the palm and the fingers of Aiden's hand. Aiden wanted his son to cling to him, but in his arms Mark felt like a pliable sapling; his body gave and yielded to Aiden's embrace, but maintained a certain springiness as if he were indifferent to his father, not needing his father's comfort.

"Do you want to see what I've made, Daddy?"

Aiden began to untense as relief started to seep through his body. He could feel his son's whole shoulder blade through Mark's thin shirt. It felt smooth, tiny and puny as if it could have so easily been snapped apart; his boy-body seemed vulnerable, but untainted in any way.

"Of course," Aiden replied calmly, instinctively knowing that disappointment was simply part of a father's inevitable sadness. Releasing his hold on Mark, he continued, "But shall we find Mummy, first? She's bound to want to see as well!"

At that moment Margaret ran into the bunker, quite out of breath. There was another man with her, but he stayed in the background. Aiden stood up and turned towards her as she came in. It was quite evident that Mark was unharmed, but on seeing him, Margaret cried out with relief, "Are you alright, Sweetie?" and in her turn she now flung her arms about his tiny frame.

"Look at Harris, Mummy!"

"He's fine," Aiden quickly interjected. "He's just been playing."

Without acknowledging Aiden, Margaret released Mark from her hug, and dropping down and squatting so that her face was level with Mark's, she took his hands in hers and started to speak sharply to him. "Now, Mark, don't you ever…"

"Margaret!" Aiden quietly but firmly interrupted her, placing his hand on her shoulder. "Now's not the time."

Aiden did not disagree with the message, but thought that for now they should simply be happy Mark had come to no harm; there would be time enough to explain why he and Margaret had been so worried. Margaret fell silent and took a couple of deep breaths, and then as if she had come to an important realisation, still without looking at Aiden, she gently nodded her head in agreement.

Standing up, quite slowly, she carefully placed her hand on the back of Mark's head and in the same movement turned towards Aiden and embraced him, so that the three of them were tightly knotted together. They remained in the embrace for some time, unfazed by the presence of the other man, Aiden and Margaret feeling themselves calming more and more with each other's touch and the familiar smell of each other, until Mark, breaking away from Aiden and Margaret, said, "Come on Mummy, let me show you!"

Aiden and Margaret let their embrace slacken, but as they started to move away from each other, Aiden ran his fingers down Margaret's arm until his fingers caught in hers and they remained standing hand in hand for a moment before Margaret, glancing at Aiden, broke off to let Mark show her what he had made.

Sensitive to the interplay between the family members, only now did the other man step forward.

"I'm Simon," he said holding out his hand amiably to Aiden. He was a few years older than Aiden, the type of man Aiden would have ordinarily have passed in the street without giving a second glance to. "We saw your wife running, shouting out your son's name, and guessed that you had missed him and offered to help."

"I'm very grateful indeed," Aiden replied warmly, taking Simon's hand and grasping it firmly, holding onto it for much longer than he would ordinarily have done with a casual acquaintance.

"Don't worry, my wife's gone ahead to retrieve your basket and things, she thought that would help," Simon said seriously, adding by way of an explanation, "You see we heard your shout just now and presumed him to be found."

It seemed to Aiden that ordinary people tended to rally round with help, exerting tremendous effort, when it was most needed, perhaps as some kind of recompense for having dreadful unspoken muddles in their own lives that they did not have the courage to tackle. But for whatever reason it was offered, he was thankful for the kindness of ordinary people. Aiden and Margaret held hands once again and walked together out of the bunker and back into the brilliant sunlight.

~~~~~

"It isn't at all like in the pictures is it?"

The three of them were sitting at a table in the fish and chip restaurant. Aiden and Margaret had already finished their lunches, but Mark, as a treat, had been allowed ice cream to finish with and which he was still, workmanlike, carefully spooning his way through. Aiden had said that after all the excitement of the day he needed to eat something solid for lunch, something substantial, and that he really fancied fish and chips and that they were best from a proper fish and chip shop.

Aiden replied gently, "No, not at all." He understood Margaret's comment perfectly.

"I had expected, oh, I don't know, Mark to be all weepy or something."

Aiden picked up his cup and held it to his lips. He swallowed down the last drop of his tea having first swirled it around in the bottom of the cup, and then pulled a grimace. "Cold," he explained. The tea they had ordered had arrived before their lunch, not with it as they had expected; sensibly, Margaret had quickly finished hers, but Aiden had waited, as he preferred to drink his with his food. "I know. I felt it too," he continued, "But he didn't need us like that when we found him. As far as he was concerned he hadn't even missed us."

"But it *is* strangely disappointing," Margaret replied, speaking slowly and watching Aiden carefully as if she was fearful of his approbation. Suddenly sounding vulnerable, she added, "Does that make me very selfish?"

"I don't think so. It's just that what Mark needs from us isn't the same as you and I need from each other, it's a different sort of bargain and we shouldn't confuse the two things." Aiden craved uncritical comfort from his wife which is what would rightfully restore him after an upset. He looked across at Mark who was giving his full attention to his dessert; there was strawberry ice cream as well as vanilla.

For a minute or two neither of them spoke, both being busy with their own thoughts. Aiden then continued speaking but as if he had needed a little time to pluck up sufficient courage to speak. The depth of his emotion this morning had been another deep revelation to him; he had found his love for Mark was darkly terrible:

"I found myself imagining his terror if anything *had* happened and how he would have been all alone and to me that would have felt worse than any possible betrayal, him not understanding that we were not there."

Aiden found that his voice was quavering as he spoke; fearing that it could make him vulnerable in some indefinable way - he had not intended to reveal so much of his emotion to Margaret - and planting his elbow firmly on the table, he raised his left hand up and firmly pressed it in front of his chin, his forefinger curved tightly over his upper lip, in an effort to steady himself. Margaret, recognising the emotional state he was in, reached across the table to tenderly take his other hand. Knowing that Aiden would feel deeply embarrassed to display his emotion overtly, especially in a public place, she would not risk dislodging his left hand from about his face.

"And when I saw you running towards the Point," she said in a soft and kindly voice, "I felt so cross, angry, despondent even, that you could be abandoning Mark. But I was wrong and I'm so dreadfully sorry I felt that way." Pausing, she then added with a note of velvet finality, "I think you're very special."

Having regained his composure and sensing that Margaret had also offered him something raw about herself Aiden replied, "I'm not special."

"Yes you are, dear. Good heavens, you're a pilot in the airforce, not many men could do that." Most of the time it simply never occurred to Aiden that people might have an elevated opinion of him because of his occupation. "And you're a good father, and husband," she added quietly, but pointedly.

"No, really," Aiden protested lightly, buoyed up by Margaret's admission, "I'm just an ordinary chap, trying to do my best. Dealing with all the muddles."

"And I'm also sorry I don't always behave terribly well!" Margaret spoke lightly, with the familiar impish look on her face.

Sensing Margaret would understand that the moment of comfort had passed, Aiden withdrew his hand and took out his cigarettes. He drew one out of the packet, placed it between his lips and then reached into his pocket for his box of matches. Being meticulous, he never had to search through his pockets for matches, invariably returning them to the same pocket after their use. The match made a rasping noise as he struck it against the abrasive material on the side of the box. Then tipping the match gently downwards, Aiden let the flame grow, watching it as it grew into a bright triangle, yellow-orange at its tip, but colourless at its base, the match beneath it distorting, growing thin, brittle and black with the heat.

Having lit his cigarette, he waved his hand exuberantly in the air beside him to extinguish the flame, something he had done for as long as Margaret could remember. Tossing the match into the ashtray he took his cigarette out of his mouth and exhaled the smoke luxuriously.

"I'm quite ordinary," he insisted, smiling at Margaret, "And I always will be."

"But really, I only want ordinary," she said quietly. Aiden had sensed her contrition and felt pleased.

"Come on Poppet, time to go to the beach," Aiden said brightly, glancing up. It was now the height of lunchtime and the restaurant was very busy.

Gathering the bucket and spade, the basket with the beach towel and having made a final check for Harris, they stood up from the table and started to the door. Even before they had left the shop another family had snapped up their table, and besides them there were many others waiting.

Aiden laid his hand gently upon Margaret's back as if he were doing no more than guiding her towards the door. Mark walked along just in front of them but firmly within their orbit.

# Part Three

# 1964–1965

## Chapter Nineteen

Already positioning for its final approach, the Canberra flew in from over the sea. The air was moist and driblets of small grey wispy clouds of indeterminate shapes and sizes were being blown about with apparent haphazardness through the otherwise clear wash-blue sky by the stiff sea-windiness, so that it appeared to the two men that their aircraft would suddenly scud into an occasional handful of dusky smoke that momentarily enveloped them before dissipating magically along the fuselage of the aircraft, and they would once more burst out into the cold salt brightness. They passed high over the deserted beach. Renewed and washed primevally clean by the high-spring tides and piled up against the protective groins which stopped the drift along the coast, the bright pristine sands below them looked like a line of bleached napkins that had been neatly folded into triangles and carefully laid out expectantly along a table.

Gradually and evenly losing height, they covered the ten miles or so to the airfield in a few short minutes. As the aircraft descended, Aiden looked out over his shoulder and down onto the patchwork of fields and hedges below them, looking for the markers in the woody landscape that had become so familiar to him over the last three years that would confirm his trust in the aircraft's instrumentation. The horizon lazily tilted as they curved gracefully towards the mile-long expanse of concrete runway, returning smoothly to normal as the runway appeared pencil-straight ahead of them. Appearing tiny to them as they approached, three or four other silver aircraft, each with a thick yellow stripe around its fuselage and wings marking them out as training machines, were parked neatly in the early spring sunshine on the expansive concrete apron in front of the green hangars. The airfield's homely redbrick administrative and mess buildings were tucked snugly between the hangars and the main road, so that as they approached, the airfield looked like an isolated outpost built wistfully after home-counties architecture.

Unprompted by Aiden, the pupil-pilot called to the control tower to say he was on finals and distended the flaps beneath the wings, interrupting the lifting flow of air over the wing surfaces. The runway approached nearer and nearer. The fields and hedges raced past them faster and faster as they came lower and lower. Closer and closer to the runway surface they came, the twin jet engines gently whistling as the pilot reduced power, until the aircraft's undercarriage gently touched down and decelerated gently and elegantly towards the far end of the runway. Throttling the engines back to a minimum of power, the pilot cleared the aircraft away from the runway and, having received clearance from the control tower, along the taxiway that ran parallel to it until the brakes were applied and, the aircraft bobbing slightly from its own inertia as if it were taking a bow, it came to a halt on the apron precisely alongside the other aircraft.

Walking across the bright, expansive concrete apron, side-by-side with his pupil, heading back to the crew room for the final time, Aiden could not resist turning and taking an affectionate final look at the Canberra.

~~~~

They had found a house, an ordinary house. It was quite small, but it was their own. Aiden had first taken her to see it on a bright winter's day when it had been flooded with canescent brightness; sunlight had streamed unceasingly through the windows as if a perpetual golden peacefulness had been preordained for them and when they had shut the front door behind them the inset of stained glass in the hallway window had cast a coloured wavy pattern on the hallway floor. In their instant contentment it felt as if it had been the house that been quietly waiting for *them*. There had been a frost the previous night and their breaths had been visible in the air as they had walked from room to room, the bare floorboards grey and slightly gritty underfoot from the passage of outdoor shoes. In her delight, Margaret had occasionally touched the sleeve of his greatcoat with her fingers, relishing the feel of the soft woollen material or had quietly linked her arm in his as she had imagined arranging their furniture and placing particular pieces, ornaments and photographs here and there, on the mantelpiece, or on top of the bureau or bookcase. In her mind she had already planned outings for them together to choose everyday items for their new home, such as lampshades or the new milk saucepan she had been putting off buying for so long.

She had fallen in love at once with the turn of the stairs, and with the french windows into the garden, imagining her armchair positioned just so, so that she could look out of them when she sat down with a book after her lunch. In the kitchen they had told each other how they could imagine the three of them sitting down together to eat their daily meals, comforting food like steak and kidney pie, or cosy weekend suppers of poached eggs on toast with a pot of tea under a knitted cosy in the centre of the table. Margaret had lifted the latch of the larder door and peered into the cool blue interior and had thought of pots of homemade jam and preserves on the painted shelves. She had been quietly and evidently delighted with the house saying that she could not imagine anything ever being more perfect for them.

As they had walked through the empty rooms Aiden had felt quite content. He had impatiently wanted to gift her this happiness when they had first met. Precipitantly, almost before they had even started stepping out together, he had pictured her young and willowy in such a house, home-making, and had thought of how wonderful it would be to return to her each evening to simply glory in each other and to pass their time together in their own protective capsule of warmth.

So powerful had been this desire and thinking that it would somehow prove to her his love and expecting her most velvet empathy in return, he would frequently complain to her almost desperately that he could not be happy when they were apart. But quietly and creamily pleased at his unaffected simplicity, Margaret had sensed that such a tight bubble of exclusivity would presently have been suffocating to her and as tempting as it would have been to succumb to Aiden's heart-felt appeals to her reason that he could be as happy as Ted was in an ordinary job, she had made him miserable by saying that they would surely have a little house of their own in good time but for now she had better continue working for a little longer.

But looking at her on that morning when he had first taken her to see the house, looking at the way in which the corners of her mouth had now creased as she smiled and how serenity had informed her movement, her limbs a little thicker than they had been back then, he knew that she would not have been so content if he had been able to give her what he had wanted to at that time and that some regret had now seemed desirable or even essential.

There had been no key in the back door lock. Margaret had rattled the bulbous handle ineffectually and had worried that they might have to go round and see if the side gate was open instead, but Aiden, working methodically, had found it hanging on a nail in the larder so they had been able to unlock the door and walk out and look at the garden.

Brimming with child-like enthusiasm and eager for exploration they had stepped out of the kitchen door and into a narrow concrete space which ran the depth of the house between the side gate and the back garden. Just outside the kitchen door stood the coal bunkers; the downstairs rooms of the house were heated by coal fires, the bedrooms alone having gas fires which might be used to take the chill off the room on a winter's night. On one of the coal bunkers, the lid, which covered the aperture where the deliveries of coal were thunderously shot in, was broken. Aiden was sure he could mend it without much difficulty.

Even in winter the garden had contained the seemingly innate and comforting suggestion of longevity as if it would go on for ever. The flower borders, wild and abundant with last year's rich unchecked growth, had ballooned over the edges of the lawn and flowed over the edges of the narrow concrete path that ran almost the entire length of the garden. Margaret, transfixed with her own soft contentment, had walked out into the bright singing garden, her footfall gentle and steady, delightedly touching the plants in wonderment. Gently holding a leaf, an early bud, or a stem between her thumb and forefinger, she had been lost in abstraction as if the names of the plants would come to her from some deep ancestral memory. She had thought of powerful and scented blooms and luscious textures and shades that described the cycle of the year that was all-important to her: the shock of bright yellow forsythia announcing the onset of spring; the heady sweet scent of honeysuckle on a still summer's evening as dusk falls; the riot of colour of a clematis along the fence, its roots carefully protected against the strong sun by stray flints and broken half bricks pitched in the dusty soil; tall swaying golden rod giving the borders an architectural grandeur; clumps of earthy autumn colour like mauve Michaelmas daisies which she thought of as quintessentially English and which reminded her of leafy bonfire-smoke and wholesome earthy decay.

At the bottom of the garden, where the concrete path gave out, beyond an apple tree with spindly upper branches, the result of unchecked growth, stood a greenhouse whose wooden frame had been bleached to the colour of mouse fur by long exposure to the weather. Evidently the insides of the panes of its roof had once been painted white against the power of the sun, for yellowing flakes now littered the propagation bench, the stacks of forgotten terracotta pots and the broken seed trays. Beside the greenhouse and the garden rubbish heap, which was full of thick stalks and ancient brown compacted grass cuttings, there was a patch of ground with an air of pleasingly quiet dereliction, where it looked as if someone had once grown chrysanthemums. The greenhouse blocking their way, to step there they had to cross a corner of the lawn which had been worn bare by the continual passage of feet. Aiden had thought that he would rather use the space to grow some vegetables.

## Chapter Twenty

"I'll just finish this, and then I'll get started."

As they sat at the kitchen table, there was an occasional muffled splut-like noise from the oven followed by a diminishing hiss like a distant firework. The comforting, sweet smell of a joint of lamb roasting filled the kitchen. Margaret had already finished her coffee, but Aiden was finding it hard to get going this morning.

Sounding as if it would somehow provide him with added impetus, he added, "Well it makes sense to get it done before autumn comes and the weather turns." Despite a deep satisfaction with their life in their new home, a lingering legacy sense of feeling that he had to justify his actions to her persisted.

"And I must get on with the vegetables," Margaret smiled at Aiden, glancing up at the clock as she stood up. She did not mean the potatoes, which she had placed on the gas in her largest saucepan to par-boil when they had sat down for their elevenses; she felt put out if Sunday dinner was any later than half-past-one. Then, continuing an earlier topic of conversation, she added wistfully, "Perhaps we'll get back to Swanage again next year."

Aiden was listening carefully to the nuances of her speech; he thought it did not sound like a question. They had not managed a holiday this year; Aiden had maintained that what with the expense of moving they could not really afford one.

"I'd like that too, of course." Aiden said pleasantly enough; overly sensitive to her criticism, he was keen to affirm his commitment to their family holidays. Margaret had started to peel the carrots. He also retained a fondness for Swanage; they had been there three times now. "It's a good beach for Mark and everything you need is there, so you don't have to go anywhere else, not unless you want to, of course."

"You forget," Margaret said, smiling gently, almost secretly, to herself, "The beach isn't really that important any more!"

Pleased that he had managed to catch her smile, he replied, "I suppose that's true enough."

They had been relieved that along with Aiden's new posting they had managed to find a place for Mark at the grammar, a short bus ride away from their new home; with indigenous certainty both of them had felt that provincial schooling would have proved to have been inferior.

After a moment or two, all the while surreptitiously watching Margaret, Aiden said, "Surely it could go in the dining room." but he also added quickly, "I wonder if Mark's ready yet?"

Standing over the sink, Margaret did not look up from peeling the carrots. A long orange shaving of carrot skin, dirty with earth, curled up through the slot in the blade of the peeler and dropped into the water in the sink in front of her. As she rotated the carrot ready for the next pass of the peeler, the briefest look of irritation passed over her face, but her voice remained perfectly calm.

"He was upstairs finishing some homework just now."

Mark had only been back at school for a week. He had joined the school as soon as they had moved into their new house, early in the previous term; not at the beginning of it. But despite having worried about it throughout the summer, returning after the holidays just like all the other pupils had finally taken all the strangeness away.

Aiden continued sitting, not wanting to labour his point as he did not want to spoil the homely atmosphere, but he felt that if Margaret did not answer he could not lose face by letting the subject drop. By now there was a skin forming on the inch or so of milky coffee that was left in the bottom of his cup. But, finishing peeling the carrot and placing it on the chopping board, Margaret said evenly and without any hint of agitation, "Well, I suppose it can't do any harm there."

They were talking about a particularly eidetic photograph of

Aiden and Dennis. Both men were in service uniform and their eyes looked out of the picture vivaciously, suggestive of an unusual intimacy. Aiden had his arm around Dennis's shoulder yet it was not a snapshot; there was something majestic or timeless about it. The positioning in the house of the carefully framed photograph was a point of continuing contention. Once upon a time Margaret had admired the photograph, been sympathetic to it. Aiden would have liked to have put it out with the family photographs in the lounge, but Margaret had held firm in her continuing opposition to this suggestion. But as they lived more day-to-day in the dining room than the lounge, Aiden was actually pleased with this compromise.

"I thought we might ask Daphne and Ted over next Sunday," Margaret continued in a tone that suggested that there could now be no question about inviting them.

"That's fine by me," Aiden replied reasonably, careful that no hint of triumph should be present in his voice.

Aiden was fond of his brother-in-law although he still jealously resented the excluding thickness that persisted between Margaret and her sister, but since moving into their new home earlier in the summer they had only infrequently seen Daphne and Ted for this to be currently rancorous. Ostensibly quite different from each other, Ted and Aiden actually held remarkably similar values.

"Perhaps we'll ask them over for a weekend soon," Margaret said in a similar tone of reasonableness, adding, by way of justification and calculating that it should add weight to her argument, "it's such a long journey for them by public transport." Unlike Aiden, Ted had not learnt to drive.

"We could put it out after dinner, perhaps on the sideboard."

Aiden was mildly concerned to ensure that Margaret should follow through on her promise. The furnishing of the house and all that went with it was really her domain and it would be a relatively trivial matter for Margaret to stall in finding a place for the photograph; Aiden did not want to have to wait for another opportunity to raise the matter again.

"Alright," Margaret answered carefully, calculating that Aiden would then agree to Daphne and Ted being invited for a weekend. "But what do you think?"

"I don't mind. But you'd better let Mark know as they'll have to have his room."

"I'll phone Daphne and ask them," Margaret said with a hint of satisfaction which Aiden was perfectly content, even pleased, to let pass.

~~~~

In preparation, earlier that morning, Aiden had already moved the car out of the garage to give them sufficient room in which to work. Aiden fondly remembered watching his own father, a man who had applied the meticulousness and care with which he carried out his professional work to household maintenance and mending, even to the extent of carefully donning a carpenter's buff coloured apron to protect his clothes whenever he was doing a manual job, looping the apron strings right round his medium frame and tying it in a fastidious bow in front of him.

"Like this Dad?" Mark would no longer call Aiden 'Daddy' and was careful to always refer to him, a little stiffly, as 'my father' when talking about him to his friends at school. While Mark had been stood watching him, Aiden had already cut one piece of the timber by way of demonstrating the technique to Mark.

"That's right," he replied encouragingly. "But try shifting your body round like this."

Aiden felt a lush pride in teaching his son. Standing over the piece of work and steadying the tenon-saw against the crooked thumb of his left hand as Aiden had shown him, Mark had lined-up the teeth of the saw precisely against the pencil line that Aiden had previously carefully marked around the piece of wood with the help of a carpenter's square, carefully pressing the square firmly against each planed face of the wood and scribing his pencil hard up against the metal right angle, then turning the wood over to the next face and repeating the process until the lines on each of the four sides precisely met.

Standing behind and to the side of Mark, he placed his right hand on Mark's right elbow and his left hand on Mark's left arm and gently moved Mark a little to the side so that Mark's eye-beam looked directly along the thick top edge of the saw blade and so that his right hand which held the saw was directly in front of his lower sternum and directly beneath his line of sight.

"This way you have more control, it's as if you feel part of the work," Aiden explained.

Mark slowly embarked upon the projected cut and the heady resinous perfume of cut deal once again mingled with the smell of lawnmower oil and bicycles in the dusty, cobwebby garage. The saw cut began to stray away from the pencil guideline, but that did not matter to Aiden.

Encouraging Mark, Aiden said, "There, that's better isn't it? But you don't need to press too hard," the fine teeth of the saw were sticking in the cut, "let the saw do the work."

Aiden felt a tensile connection between his pride and the perilous yearning which would assail him from time-to-time; a yearning which would unexpectedly, almost violently, fill him with a deep and tender love for his son and which he intuitively knew equalled or surpassed anything a mother could possibly feel. An all-consuming and powerful emotion, at such times Aiden wanted to envelop Mark in his arms. But simply wanting to shield and protect him would be too simplistic an explanation of the feeling. Knowing such things to be sadly ephemeral, he wanted to immerse himself in his son's plastic innocence, the look and feel of his smooth porcelain-like skin, of his vulnerability and dependency, and of his wonderment at the world unbeclouded by the ambiguousness of the words whose slipperiness were already taking Mark away from the domain of the father.

Suddenly, the saw cut was complete. The measured portion of deal fell away and clattered onto the garage floor, but the cut was not clean; the piece had splintered leaving a jagged spindly tongue of wood on one of the lower corners of the portion of timber that remained clamped in the woodworking vice.

"Oh," exclaimed Mark, "does that matter?"

"Not really." Aiden smiled at Mark. Intuitively, to lighten the lesson, Aiden added brightly, "What homework were you finishing just now?"

It had only recently struck Aiden that there was a legacy of unfairness about his pride. Pride had always seemed part of the stock-in-trade of fathering but he had felt excluded from engaging fully in it. It had felt like longing to join a wildly peaceful and intimate scene surreptitiously observed through an uncurtained window, something ordinary, such as a father reading a bed-time story to his son in the flickering firelight, the boy, ears rosy-tipped from his evening bath and cosy in his dressing-gown, held in rapt attention by his father's certain words. But he now no longer felt excluded. The joyous participation in life was not just about rawness and excitement such as flying Lancasters or of being a part of something new such as Operation Grapple. But, he had resentfully thought, he could not be sure that he had won back this rightful peace or whether it had been granted to him by Margaret who had silently assumed its keeping.

"Geography. We had to write something about glacial features."

"We'll just clean up that saw-cut."

Glacial features always made Aiden think of maps, of flying over the Lake District in an ancient Airspeed Oxford during his training identifying the lakes and tarns, screwing up his eyes to read the tightly-packed contours on the Ordnance Survey map as they practised elementary navigation. He smiled to himself at the recollection.

"With sandpaper?" Mark enquired.

"I think we'll have a go with the rasp first."

"What's that?" Mark was not afraid to ask his father anything.

"It's a sort of rough file for wood."

Aiden looked about the workbench for the rasp and again thought of his own father. *He* would have identified all the tools he could possibly have needed to complete a particular job and have laid them all out neatly to hand, even to the extent of making doubly sure that his pencil was sharp.

Picking up the rasp he said, "You mean an essay?"

"Yes, but it's all in the text book. We just mustn't copy." Aiden could not decide if Mark was self-deprecating or simply modest.

"I'll just do this and then we can finish it off with a bit of sandpaper." Aiden rested the piece of deal flat on the workbench and, keeping the rasp square to the piece of timber, carefully worked away at the tongue of wood. "And how about the other boys?" Aiden enquired, trying to sound as casual as he possibly could. "Have you made any new friends this term?"

"It's the same ones, really. They're quite a good bunch on the whole."

Mark did not want to talk about his friends at school. The boys in his class had been impressed that Mark's father was in the RAF, and even more impressed that he had flown a variety of jets, although they had been disappointed that he no longer flew them. As an incomer anxious to court the other boys' approval, Mark had over-glamorised his father's career, claiming that his father had flown one of the Valiants on Operation Grapple and had dropped one of the live weapons. But he had quickly felt embarrassed about his claim, fearing the loss of credibility and fretting about how to correct the situation, and it seemed that to talk about his school friends would somehow make it more likely that his father should catch him out in the lie.

Aiden finished with the rasp and putting it down on the workbench looked about for some sandpaper of the right grade with which to finish off the job.

"Autumn term now; I suppose it's all rugby?"

Aiden would have preferred soccer, but the grammar school, with its elitist eye, preferred sports favoured by public schools, leaving football to the secondary modern boys.

"It's alright, but I prefer summer sports."

Mark had discovered the sheer exhilaration of competition. In part, this was his striving for excellence in the classroom. He revelled in those precious moments in class when he sat back having completed a piece of work, feeling satisfied from his cerebral exertion, breathing-in the quiet hot chalky atmosphere as the other boys around him struggled to finish, his neat script in his exercise book with its creamy paper the pleasing aesthetic evidence of his intellectual comprehension of a new concept.

But it was the thrill of competition on the sports field which excited him most of all; he had discovered that he could run. The electrifying feeling that his whole body was engaged in a mortal struggle was innately satisfying, and yet enigmatically remained beyond his description. From the moment he was called to his mark, the adrenalin rush cracked through his body. Relentlessly driving his limbs far beyond the point where they merely ached; violently sucking in enough air in greedy gulps to fuel his struggle; the heightened sensory sensations; the satisfaction of achievement; of winning through extraordinary effort: the exertion, the physicalness, was as much the imperative as was the competition.

"You could try-out for cross country," Aiden said, wrapping a quarter of a sheet of glass-paper around his sanding block. He did more than simply appreciate Mark's passion for running; the recognition that Mark had also successfully connected with something un-enunciably ferine within himself added to Aiden's sense of pride.

"It's not quite the same, somehow."

But Mark had been distracted, happening to look out of the window that was positioned in the end wall of the garage immediately above the workbench.

"Oh look!" he exclaimed. "Mum's gone all wispy in the garden!"

Aiden looked up. The father and son smiled at each other affectionately, pleased with their shared joke.

Margaret had evidently reached a point in preparing their Sunday lunch that now allowed her some time out of the kitchen between individual tasks such as basting the meat or the potatoes, for she was distractedly walking about in the garden with her secateurs in hand.

Margaret was not impulsive or impatient but she had lost no time in her start on the garden. Ever since moving-in, she had spent many hours on her knees wielding a trowel and a fork, systematically weeding and thinning, a small pile of drying stalks and shoots seemingly omnipresent in the sunny air beside her. To develop and nurture what had been planted before their own arrival at the house satisfied her sense of continuity so that much of her labour consisted of drifting around the garden, carefully pruning and shaping while all the time observing and noting each plant as it grew so that she might know the material she would have to work with over the coming years.

It had been Mark who had first coined the phrase, "Mum's all wispy in the garden," to describe this activity and it had quickly become an affectionate private joke between Aiden and Mark. This greatly pleased Margaret, and she took care to pretend not to overhear.

~~~~

Although he knew that there were bound to be times when he would regret it, Aiden had *chosen* to stop flying, as much as he had always loved it. And now that he had, reading the newspaper in the train, knowing that he could smoke a cigarette at leisure without fear of interruption, the smell of wet raincoats and stale tobacco in the railway carriage compartment on rainy days, even waiting in a queue, all this was so remarkably ordinary and safe.

Aiden had spent the last three years as a flying instructor, converting service pilots onto the Canberra who had previously been flying other types. It had pleased him that his last flight ever had been assessing the proficiency of one of his pupil-pilots and not a contrived joy-ride for his own benefit or amusement as so often seemed to be the case when pilots transferred away from flying duties. It had felt tremendously worthwhile and important to be able to teach and guide right up to the end.

Some of the inveterate flyers had found it hard to understand Aiden's decision to willingly give up flying, wondering if had harboured thoughts of Staff College, but the new routineness, the similarity between his own life and the people who lived around him was a source of quite specific and deep contentment to him. Although he remained in the RAF, his present posting was to an office up in Town. Like the majority of his neighbours, each morning he caught the train to London, where he worked quietly away all day at his desk.

This very everydayness was a tremendous relief to him as if he had passed through ritual and fire unscathed and through doing so had earned the right to peacefully provide for his family and to nurture his son. People must have felt something like this at the end of the war, he thought to himself: everybody had had their own private triumph and despair and must have enjoyed getting back to the mundane business of living. It was like there was a private joy in ordinariness. But the difference was, he ruminated, back then there had also been public ceremony which had helped people make sense of others' private strong emotions. Aiden had felt an anticlimax after his return from Operation Grapple. Outside of the squadron, there had been no ceremony for them; the Valiants' crews had been thrust into the limelight, while the crews of the Canberras had simply been asked to go on being normal.

Sometimes at the end of an afternoon Mark would ride his bicycle to the station to meet his father; Aiden invariably caught the same train home each day so as to be back in good time for tea. Mark would watch the dark green electric train slow down and listen to its distinctive whine as it entered the station and came to a halt. Aiden, together with hundreds of other commuters, would disembark, the carriage doors slamming shut with a comfortable "clack" behind them. The sound of their shoes on the hot asphalt-covered platform was like a great mass of dry leaves being blown along which increased in intensity as the crowd moved further along the platform. So densely packed were they that it would appear miraculous that none were precipitated off the edge as they funnelled onto the first treads of the footbridge which would take them over to the station exit. To Mark, his father stood out from the mass of people on the platform; he could always identify him as he edged forward.

Mark had cycled down to meet Aiden on the first day of the new school term. It had been a sunny afternoon, the air hot and dry. As they had walked back from the station, Mark wheeling his bicycle beside him, Mark and his father had talked.

"It's exciting somehow, the future."

"When I was your age the excitement was more for the moment, but our lives were quite different then," Aiden had replied.

"What was the most exciting thing you ever did, Dad?"

"Flying Lancasters, I should think." Aiden smiled indulgently at Mark, like most boys of his age would have done, Mark had spoken as if he assumed his father's life could no longer be exciting. "That felt like a real adventure."

"Not jets?" Mark sounded a little disappointed.

"No, not really."

"But isn't the speed exciting?"

"Speed isn't everything." Thinking that an explanation involving the redness, the rawness, of those days would be incomprehensible, instead he had turned to look fully at Mark and had said, "Do you want to go to Biggin Hill this year?"

Mark had not lost his love of aircraft. "Oh can we?" he had replied excitedly, a smile spread across his face. At that moment Mark had felt a strong imperative to hug his father but had quickly suppressed the instinct as being unmanly.

Mark enjoyed spending time with his father perhaps more than doing anything else in the world, although he thought of it as being a secret pleasure, one he would be tardy in admitting to his school friends.

## Chapter Twenty-One

In the past, in his capacity as an operational pilot, Aiden had attended a number of RAF At Home days. But on those occasions his attendance had not been a matter of personal choice. The RAF had its own unquestionable, and seemingly perverse, sense of logic and for reasons that were never totally made clear he would sometimes be required to ferry in his machine a few days before the show and not depart back to his home air-station until the following Monday or Tuesday. Although he had always tried his best to enjoy the atmosphere of the shows and had taken the professional flyer's interest in aircraft types that he did not usually come into contact with, the sense of having wasted his time - especially if he had merely flown-in an aircraft which was to be present in the static park and he had not taken part in the flying display - exacerbated his feeling of niggling guilt at being there.

In marked contrast, the planning for this airshow had been a delight and the anticipation of it had been a joy.

"When are we going, Dad?" Mark asked anxiously.

It was Saturday; the day Aiden and Mark had chosen to go to the airshow. Mark had been unable to sit still since finishing his breakfast and was restlessly moving about the kitchen fidgeting with this and that, first the salt and pepper pots and then with the handful of green tomatoes which had been set out to ripen on the window sill. From time to time he glanced anxiously skywards out of the kitchen window.

"Don't worry; we'll be there in plenty of time!"

Aiden was still seated at the kitchen table finishing his tea, his empty breakfast plate in front of him, swirling eggy lines indicating where he had carefully mopped up the last of the egg yolks with his toast. It seemed early to be up and about on a weekend, as if they were embarking quietly upon a secret campaign.

"Do you want to take a couple of apples with you as well?" Margaret glanced at Aiden across the kitchen and caught his eye, quietly sharing his affectionate amusement; it was as if they both felt that to be able to enjoy Mark's enthusiasm was a particularly precious and hard-won parents' prize.

Holding the hot handle with a tea towel, Margaret was tipping the boiling water out of the egg saucepan, holding the pan against the inside of the sink so that the hard-boiled eggs within it were not pitched into the sink along with the water. She held her head slightly back to avoid the rising cloud of steam.

"We might as well."

Aiden put down his nearly empty cup on his saucer and got up from the table to fetch the apples. A packet of sandwiches, some filled with cheese and some with corned beef and neatly wrapped in greaseproof paper, was on the corner of the table waiting to be packed.

"Can you put the kettle on for your thermos while you're up?" Margaret asked as she poured cold water from the tap onto the eggs in the saucepan so that by cooling quickly the edge of the yolks would discolour less. Aiden would have a thermos flask of tea to take with him, and Margaret had made up some lemon squash for Mark.

"Are you quite sure you don't want to come?" Aiden asked again as he picked up the kettle from the top of the gas stove and jigging it up and down in his right hand once or twice, attempting to judge whether there was sufficient water left in it to make up the thermos.

"I'll be fine here on my own," Margaret said using the same words as she had habitually used when Aiden was on the point of departing for an airshow when he had had no choice about going. But today her delivery of the words was fundamentally different. Her voice was soft, and her words entirely believable; but her words still had the power to create a peculiar and potentially distressing resonance within Aiden. "You go and enjoy yourself," she added in a tone that implied that Aiden was foolishly being overly solicitous.

"Well, if you're quite sure." He always needed to be quite certain of her.

"I've seen enough aeroplanes to last me a lifetime," she said smiling indulgently, serenely comfortable in her own rightness, as if she thought that Aiden had finally outgrown a childish phase as she knew he surely must do one day. "Go on, you'd better get going. You don't want to get caught up in the traffic."

~~~~

The suburbs ended abruptly; it was like they had crossed over a border and left behind them the codex of small events and quiet enthusiasms that engender a sense of belonging. Biggin Hill was not far from where they lived, but concerned about getting caught up in heavy traffic, they had left the house earlier than Aiden thought strictly necessary and had initially avoided the main roads, choosing instead to cut though and join the Biggin Hill road below Leaves Green. But he partially regretted his decision as the junction where they joined the main road was on a sharp bend so as to be almost blind and the seemingly incessant traffic coming from the direction of Bromley made it more difficult finding a gap in which he could safely join the flow of cars.

Sitting in the front passenger seat was a treat for Mark. Usually, when the three of them went out together as a family he sat in the back, generally behind his mother where there was more legroom as the driving seat had been adjusted so that his father was comfortable behind the steering wheel.

Once, when all three of them had been out driving together, he had seen his mother light a cigarette for his father, even though she did not smoke. She had carefully lit the cigarette from a match then having inhaled deeply, as if there was something deeply satisfying about the whole ritual, she had carefully placed the cigarette between his father's lips as he had continued concentrating on the road ahead. As she had done so, Mark had thought that his father and mother had exchanged a look which had seemed quite secret, but perhaps, he had later thought, it was not so much that the look itself was secret, rather that the look was about something secret.

Along the roadside as they came closer to the airfield, signs prohibiting waiting had been temporarily erected every hundred yards or so and policemen stood together in amiable knots. Here, through the sheer number of vehicles, the traffic gradually slowed to a crawl so that by the time the cars and buses passed the airfield buildings they were almost bumper-to-bumper. Growing up in an age when virtually anyone he would have considered to be an adult had lived through the war, Mark did not need to ask the significance of the Spitfire and Hurricane positioned as gate guardians at the main entrance to the RAF station, or indeed to ask why such shows were held regularly in September.

Airshow traffic being directed to continue along the main road, they continued past the airfield buildings and along to where the road ran between the end of the runway and the deep valley beyond the western end of the airfield. Here, Mark craned his neck enthusiastically to see if he could see any aircraft; in the previous few days, as Mark had become increasingly caught up in the anticipation of the show, the slightest sound of a jet engine had been sufficient to send Mark running to the window in the hope of catching a glimpse of the machine that had generated the exciting sound as it had arrived to take part in the display. But more often than not he had failed to see it; either it had passed by the time he had reached the window, or low cloud had hidden it from sight. During the previous week, there had been several days when low cloud and rain had threatened to spoil the coming weekend and Aiden and Margaret would be mildly amused to see Mark anxiously watching the weather forecast on the television set after the six o'clock news.

Eventually, the car having passed under the flight path to the runway and it having travelled a sufficient way further along the main road for Mark to irrationally worry that they may have somehow managed to miss the entrance to the airshow, a sign directed the continuous stream of cars up a barely-metalled track. Additionally, a traffic policeman was mechanically waving the traffic to turn off from the main road.

The cars passed slowly up the track between scrubby trees and thick brambly undergrowth until having just passed-by an over-sized, utilitarian-looking brick-built block of garages, they bumped up onto smooth concrete and once more emerged into the brightness of the summer day. Here, a string of bustling air cadets, with an unmistakable air of self-importance, directed the stream of cars across the concrete taxiway and onto the vast expanse of grass that lay beyond it. Mark eagerly looked both up and down the taxiway as they crossed it; every part of an airfield was magical to him and he wanted to miss nothing of interest or excitement.

Aiden carefully eased the car over the tufty grass. Great sections of this far side of the airfield, a considerable distance away from the main runway upon which the show was centred, had been roped off to form parking for thousands of cars. Seeing the rows upon rows of cars that were already parked, the morning sunlight glinting off curving chrome bumpers or reflecting off windscreen glass, Aiden had an uneasy feeling that getting out of the airshow this evening would take a very long time indeed, and, with a feeling of trepidation, he hoped that Margaret would not worry should they be late arriving back at home. As they approached the mass of parked cars, more air cadets, self-consciously smart in their blue-grey uniforms, directed them to park up close to the previous car to ensure that there would be plenty of room for all the cars that continued to stream across the airfield.

Not wanting to miss any of the sights and sounds, no sooner had Aiden brought the car to a halt than Mark was agitating to get going. All around them they could see families, or, just like themselves, fathers and sons, excitedly getting ready for the high-day: packets of sandwiches were picked-up; newspapers and sunglasses gathered; pockets were double-checked for wallets, purses and handkerchiefs as, they were undoubtedly telling themselves, it would certainly be a long way back to the car if it turned out that anything had been forgotten. In a far from isolated incident, bursting with untrammelled exuberance, two boys ran around the cars in front of Aiden and Mark, upper bodies bent forwards with their arms spread out backwards in imitation of supersonic fighter planes as their parents kept a wary eye on them.

Aiden leaned over to the back seat and picked up the bag which contained their sandwiches and flasks. The bag was a sort of cross between a shopping bag and a holdall. It had large looping handles and a tartan pattern on the sides and was used for occasions just such as these or for putting the last odds and ends in when they went on holiday. Adding their plastic macs, which had been put in the car at the last minute, to the bag, Aiden and Mark got out of the car and, Aiden having made doubly sure that he had locked both of the doors, joined the steady stream of people making their way through the parked cars towards the heart of the airfield.

As they walked, they could see the tailplanes of a number of aeroplanes towering above the marquees and stalls and the heaving mass of people. Some of the tailplanes were painted in camouflage and others were bright white or silver, but all of them had red white and blue tail-fin flashes. And even from this distance the dull thump of drums and a shrill wind-muddled cacophony of sounds shouted to them of parade and celebration.

Doing their best to avoid the patches of mud made sticky after the recent rain and the passage of so many feet, Aiden and Mark walked over the trampled grass and through the crowds soaking up all the sights and sounds of the day. Everywhere there was an atmosphere of carnival. In a display arena set up centrally in front of the two main hangars, military bands marched rhythmically back and forth to lively, patriotic music, the bandsmen attired in spotless ceremonial uniforms. Next, military motorcyclists displayed their skill and daring on their roaring, gleaming machines before a police dog display took its turn. Men and women dressed in the black uniform of the St Johns Ambulance Brigade patrolled through the crowd, their black canvass medical bags hung smartly over their shoulders. Yet more air cadets sold programmes and colourful RAF yearbooks. Stalls were selling tea and gritty instant coffee, ice creams, toffee apples and candyfloss, and newspaper vendors loudly offered a special souvenir edition of the local newspaper as a memento of the day.

But most of all Mark wanted to see the aircraft. So firstly, they crossed over from the display arena and looked in one of the hangars, cool and dark after the bright sunshine outside. Here, a number of aircraft from the Second World War, both British and German types, were stored, ear-marked for a permanent home in a museum. Aiden had not known that examples of such aircraft had been saved, but thinking it worthwhile for more than the sake of a mere story, he thought with a sense of awe of the men who had mortally battled in such machines even within his own lifetime.

But these aircraft were of less interest to Mark than they were to Aiden and so they joined the throng of people who cast admiring, even proprietorial looks as they made their way past the rows of aircraft lined up in the static park that were representative of the modern RAF. Here there were the workhorses of Transport Command and examples of training aircraft, but the most admiring glances were reserved for the sleek, elegant, swept-back-winged fighters – every inch of them looking like the mounts of space-age heroes - and the medium and heavy bombers. The shapes of many of these aircraft were as alien, as exciting and wonderful, as if they had been lifted directly from the pages of science fiction; here were new-age shapes that men could marvel at and which indulged the imagination's proclivity to riot.

Aiden would have suggested that he and Mark should go to the airshow even if he had not heard from Harry, who knew the station commander at Biggin Hill, that there was a possibility that a Lancaster might be there. Having been retired from service in a foreign airforce, as an example of the type it had been brought home privately by someone who had lost brothers flying Lancasters in the war.

Aiden felt a quiet thrill run through him when he saw it. It was on its own, drawn up on the edge of a deserted taxiway well away from the mainstream of the day's activities, but it had generated considerable interest.

There were knots of middle-aged men and women who had clearly sought it out and were standing around it and under its wings, affectionately or even reverentially touching the aircraft's metal skin. Some of the men and women were talking together, and occasionally one of the men would wave his arms or gesticulate with his hands to illustrate a point or help to recall a memory. But other men seemed more inspired to quiet introspection, standing alone, apart from even their wives, preoccupied with gaunt and unspeakably harrowing recollections.

If it had not been for this interest, the Lancaster would have looked neglected; the paintwork was faded and shabby, the paint had unevenly worn away on the leading edges of the propeller blades, the gun turrets had long since been removed as being unnecessary for its peacetime maritime patrol work and the resulting inelegant modifications to the fuselage appeared almost as a desecration.

"What are those markings?" Mark enquired, only mildly curious. Aiden had recognised at once that part of his excitement at seeing a Lancaster again was nostalgia and even briefly wondered whether this was one of the machines he had flown in his early days in the Service.

"French Navy. We sold them Lancasters after the war."

"I've only ever seen pictures of them."

They had stopped short, about a hundred yards away from the Lancaster. Quite unexpectedly after his mounting private expectations of the last few days, Aiden suddenly felt that he would be intruding if he were to join the men who were clustered around it; it would have felt presumptuous.

"Apparently this one's privately owned now."

"Oh." Mark thought for a moment; Mark preferred to compartmentalise his knowledge and the idea that a military aircraft could be privately owned was a novelty to him. Presently he continued, "But why?"

The question took Aiden aback, but he did not have to think about his response. "Because it's a tremendously grand and loving gesture," Aiden said kindly and smiled at Mark.

"Oh." Mark said again, but this time uncomprehendingly and then fell silent.

"I haven't seen one for years," Aiden said a little wistfully, more to himself than to Mark. "I don't suppose there's very many of them left."

Mark had heard his father talk about how he had lost his best friend in an accident involving a Lancaster, but he did not connect the story in any emotional way to the aircraft that was in front of them and after a few moments he said, "Can we go on? There might be some more to see."

"Okay," Aiden replied, silently pleased that the men who were looking over the Lancaster did not look like heroes, but just like any other ordinary middle aged men in sports jackets who no longer had any appetite for the fight.

Aiden realised soon afterwards that his expectations of the day had been unfair. Mark had, quite naturally, been more interested in the modern jets. Aiden had never thought of himself as being hasty, but he now felt increasingly anxious to tell Mark the story of his life.

Towards lunchtime they made their way along to the side of the runway in plenty of time to find themselves a good place from which to watch the flying display in the afternoon. Mark wanted to be as close to the runway as possible. Aiden spread his plastic mac out on the grass and they sat close together on it to eat their sandwiches, hard-boiled eggs and apples. Mark's lemon squash tasted strongly of the polythene plastic container it had spent the morning in, so much so that Mark did not want to finish it and they carried the last of it with them for the rest of the day.

The flying display was the highlight of the show and although service tradition was omni-implicit, the airshow was clearly a celebration of the current. Their picnics finished, empty paper bags and apple cores put away, the crowd stood in rapt attention pressed tens-deep against the barriers that lined the length of the runway and straining over each other's heads and shoulders the better to watch each participating aircraft as it thundered down the runway and rocketed skywards to take its part in the display. They tilted their heads upwards, craning their necks and squinting their eyes, following every movement of each display item, watching every possibly moment of the aerial display of dexterity and power. It was a pride-engendering egalitarian experience to the spectators, a mixture of pageant and tattoo; a f te of comforting strength.

There were exciting displays of aerobatics and formation flying, even from the fast jets. When the Canberra displayed, Aiden squinted up at the aircraft in the afternoon sun trying to make out the squadron markings. Mark was uncertain which of the aircraft he enjoyed the best. Among his favourites were the thunderous, full-blooded and potent Lightnings, their tail fins decorated with a virile, flamboyant red-and-white checkerboard design. They were the dream of every schoolboy, blending raw power with heroic devil-may-care. But just when he thought nothing could possibly better them, the Vulcan, latest of the "V" bombers, stole the show and quite took Mark's breath away. Powering almost vertically skywards from a touch-and-go with a deafening, sickening fulmination into the unfathomably deep blue sky, it shook every particle of the ground beneath the crowd's feet with the thrust from its four immensely powerful engines. And then, as the Vulcan levelled off into horizontal flight, a heart-twisting alien delta shape high up in the sky, the ground suddenly stopped shaking, people's flesh and internal organs stopped pulsating and vibrating, and it seemed as if there was a sudden, god-like, post-apocalyptic silence. It was all quite unbelievably magical.

At the end of the afternoon, Mark, sated with excitement and ruby from his father's company, watched as the ground crews secured the aircraft for the night; he wanted to remember every detail of the day. The crowds were moving off towards the car parks and the queues for the excursion busses were already thick like wadding. But Mark lingered as long as he could and Aiden uneasily indulged him until together, with the smells of spent aviation fuel and cut grass heavy in the hot air and their skin reddened and taut around their foreheads by their day in the September sun, Aiden and Mark eventually made their way back across the stubby grass to their own car.

Aiden had been quite correct about leaving the airshow; moving no more than inches at a time - and there were times when the queue of cars that they were in did not move at all for a whole quarter of an hour - the mass of cars crawled towards the inadequate exits. Initially, as they had got going Mark had talked more enthusiastically and animatedly than Aiden could remember him doing for a long time, wanting to talk about and re-live every moment of the day. But eventually, he fell silent, satisfied and tired, and by the time they reached home he was fast sleep.

It was dark by the time they arrived home. Margaret greeted them in the hallway as Aiden guided the oscitant and stumbling Mark through the front door and said that he would put the car away a bit later. Margaret leant forward and kissed him lightly on the lips and reached forward and gave his hand an affectionate squeeze saying, "Did you have a good day? I expect you're hungry."

The house felt snug and cosy. Margaret made them a pot of tea as she prepared Aiden and Mark something on toast for a late supper. The kitchen light cast a sphere of amber heart's-ease over the kitchen table, and Aiden, cradling the cup of hot tea in his hands, savouring the smell and the sweetness of it, lent back in his chair contentedly as Mark animatedly recounted all the day's events to Margaret. Margaret, patiently and serenely, heard him out, encouraging him with her soft words and quiet interjections of wonder. And catching Aiden's eye, she smiled privately and intimately back at him.

~~~~

It was at about this time that Aiden first started to occasionally feel ill. At first he merely felt off-colour and somewhat tired. But then it seemed as if the tiredness, present from the moment when he awoke, and his persistent lack of energy could no longer simply be explained by the fatigue induced by doing a new job and by travelling up to London each day to do it, so that Margaret insisted that he should make an appointment to go and see the doctor.

## Chapter Twenty-Two

"Shall I make you a cup of tea?" Margaret said, trying not to sound overly concerned. She had taken care to be in the kitchen at the time when Aiden usually arrived home from work and she had been relieved when she had finally heard the reassuring click of the side gate being opened. She had already pre-filled the kettle. Towards the end of the week Aiden would now inevitably feel very tired.

"I almost missed my stop." Aiden sounded shocked. Pushing the back door shut behind him, he had gone straight over to the kitchen table and slowly eased himself down onto one of the kitchen chairs in the manner of someone whose limbs were stiff and heavy as they might be from unaccustomed manual labour. He looked cruelly enfeebled, gaunt and his skin had an unhealthy pallor, as if it were pellucidly grey. "I woke up suddenly and the train was already pulling into the station," he continued with consternation. "I don't even remember drifting off!" Aiden fell silent, staring sadly down at his hands, cupped together on the table in front of him.

Having lit the gas beneath the kettle, Margaret blew out the match and placed it in the shallow pottery dish – a cheap seaside memento she had taken a fancy to on one of their holidays in Dorset – which they kept beside the gas stove for that purpose. For a moment, a tiny wisp of smoke continued to rise from its blackened, bulbous tip.

Usually he crossed the kitchen and kissed her when he first came home, and so she gently asked him, "Do you want to sit in one of the comfy chairs in the other room? I can bring your tea in to you when it's ready." Margaret did not want to sound as if she pitied him.

"No," he managed a weak smile, "I'm happy enough here."

Not only did he treasure the reassuring warmth and the homely cooking smells, he enjoyed watching Margaret in the kitchen. He loved the glimpses of Margaret's shapely wrist or of the erotogenic nape of her neck as she inclined her head over the sink, or, watching her movement, he imagined the feel of running his hand around her naked waist. It had been a deliberate part of his routine ever since taking up his new role, that when he returned home from work he would sit in the kitchen drinking a cup of tea quietly watching her while she finished preparing their evening meal, and without giving herself away, Margaret liked the earthy certainty of knowing that he was watching her.

Involuntarily, Aiden suddenly shivered.

"Do you feel cold?" Margaret asked tenderly. But it was not a cold day and the kitchen felt pleasantly warm from the heat given out from the oven; Margaret had made a casserole for their meal. "We could have a fire this evening," she said as she poured the boiling water onto the tealeaves in the teapot.

"I'm just a little chilly."

There was a chink as Margaret put the lid on the teapot. She continued to be very frightened and craved the healing comfort of spending the evening in front of the fire with Aiden. They liked to sit together in the two armchairs in the dining room, one on either side of the hearth. The arms of the chairs were worn almost threadbare and one of them sagged a little in the middle of the seat. Margaret imagined them sitting quietly reading in the downy glow of the standard lamp as the glowing powder-topped coals sang and the ash dropped silently through the grate, or perhaps she might pick up her knitting again, although there had not seemed very much point in it of late.

After a moment, Aiden said, "I'll go and light it in a minute, then. So it can be getting going. But I'll have my tea first though, if that's alright."

Ordinarily, if it were merely chilly he would have thought having a fire to be too extravagant. But this evening he felt defeated.

He then asked, "Where's Mark?"

"Upstairs. He's doing his homework."

In their unspoken division of labour, the lighting of fires had always been a task generally reserved for Aiden. He found the art of balancing the tent of kindling on the scrunched-up newspaper and feeding-in just the correct size of coals as the flames began to take a hold and lick around the edges, to be fundamentally and peculiarly satisfying.

"He's a good boy, isn't he?" Aiden said, distractedly. To have saved him from the effort, Margaret would have willingly lit the fire instead of letting Aiden do it, but she knew how he detested feeling useless.

Smiling at him, Margaret placed a cup of tea in front of him and then turned back to the gas stove to put the potatoes on.

Aiden immediately stirred his tea and then took a sip of the comforting hot, sweet liquid hoping that it would revive him sufficiently before Mark came back downstairs; he wanted to hide his illness from Mark, intuitively preferring to present a wholesome image of fatherness to him. He then sadly reached out for the post that had come that morning; maintaining his ability to appreciate his wife's comeliness currently seemed exceptionally cruel to him.

Last of all he opened a small, flimsy brown envelope. When it had landed on the doormat with the rest of the post that morning, Margaret had thought, as she had picked it up, that it appeared so slight that a single gust of wind could have carried it away so that the receipt of it had seemed dangerously haphazard. Mildly curious about it, he first inspected the typewritten name and address – the typeface of the capital letter 'P' appeared worn as if the typist had had to use some small degree of force to reproduce correctly the second line of their address – but the letter did not really look important, too inconsequential to be anything dreadful. Turning the envelope over, he picked at the corner of the triangular gummed-down flap sufficient to tear up a small section of it that was just large enough to make a gap for him to insert his finger, and then, running his finger along the top, opened it up.

"Whatever is it?" Margaret exclaimed loudly, forgetting herself, she had been unable to keep the alarm out of her voice; Aiden's face had turned ashen as he had unfolded the single, diminutive sheet of paper and read it, letting the envelope fall onto the kitchen table as he did so.

"They've recalled me. They want me to go back," Aiden said with simple dread, re-reading the letter to make absolutely sure.

"When?" Margaret looked aghast.

"Monday."

Margaret unconsciously put her hands up to her face in horror at the awfulness of the implication of being recalled to the hospital at such very short notice.

## Chapter Twenty-Three

With its rather ordinary hope of regeneration, it was an unspeakably cruel spring day. It had seemed a long journey by public transport but Aiden had felt too ill to manage the drive.

They stepped down from the platform at the back of the bus. Aiden, with a look of frustration, stepped down awkwardly, grasping the grab-rail which had been worn to the colour of tarnished thruppenny bits by the gripping of countless hands. Margaret had been relieved that there had been space inside; Aiden would not have made a fuss if they had had to have travelled on top. The conductor reached up and rang the bell. The two notes sounded in rapid succession, and the bus drove away leaving them standing in the shattering quiet of the countryside.

The bus-stop was immediately opposite the entrance to the hospital and for a moment they stood still, stealing themselves as if they had been managing to delude themselves into believing that the end of the journey had been in some sort of doubt, until the act of alighting from the bus had chased away any such emollient self-deceptions. The wind felt quite cold now and they each pulled their coats closer. Aiden felt himself thin and diminished in his greatcoat, and Margaret absent-mindedly pulled at the belt on her coat.

"We don't want to be late," Margaret said glancing at her watch, as she looked up and down the road, her external nicety for punctuality secretly giving way once more to her pullulating internal terrors so that she unintentionally sounded brusque and abrasive. There was no traffic to be seen in either direction.

"No, we don't," Aiden absent-mindedly agreed with her; so great was his dread he had not caught her tone. Automatically, Margaret held out her right hand to take Aiden's left. Aiden kept his right hand tucked into his greatcoat pocket.

They crossed over the road and started up the avenue they had to walk up to reach the hospital buildings. At its start, at its junction with the main road, there was a small or lodge or gatehouse, its presence suggestive of there being a great house further up the driveway. But a clothes line of pegged-out laundry blowing in the wind, the vegetables growing in its bit of garden, and the peeling paint on the window sills all suggested that this was now a very ordinary private dwelling having nothing now to do with any great house, and that perhaps the great house might have even gone.

Aiden remembered the way from his previous visit. They passed a number of austere-looking brick-built blocks. Each of these blocks was identified by a combination of block capital letters and numbers which had been painted in sharp gloss paint on regular-sized squares of contrasting background colour above the bright red fire-buckets which stood beside the entrance doors to each block. It looked as if these more recent buildings had been unforgivingly superimposed on the gentle parkland that had been here before, as if daring anyone to challenge that this new arrangement was not more useful and more democratic, than the sensibilities that had caused it to be created in the first place.

"This is it," Aiden said unnecessarily as he opened one of the double doors which gave access to an entrance hall, and letting Margaret pass through before him. They had not spoken since they had got off the bus. The entrance hall had retained its moulded plaster ceiling, which on their first visit had struck them as being incongruous; this part of the hospital had once been the great house, a large gothic mansion built a hundred years ago by a railway magnate, or so Aiden had been given to understand.

"Oh yes," Margaret said rather too brightly, "we go through here, don't we?"

Margaret made her way towards a door on the left hand side of the room, in front of which an official-looking notice had been positioned which asked all visitors to report to reception on their arrival and helpfully had a large arrow pointing the way.

Passing through the door, they presented themselves at the reception desk. The clerk sitting behind the desk looked up as they entered and said smartly, "Good afternoon, sir. Can I help you?" Aiden slowly drew out his letter; he had been keeping his hand securely on it in his pocket as if it had been some sort of valuable permit that would prove disastrous if lost.

"I have an appointment."

The clerk took the letter from Aiden and having carefully looked over the details contained within it, ran his finger down the first column of the neatly typed list that was positioned in front of him. Having found Aiden's name on his list, he efficiently made a neat pencil tick beside it. Addressing Aiden by his rank and handing the letter back to him, he pointed out the direction they should take, "You'll see some chairs outside his room. If you'd care to wait there until you're directed to go in."

The institutionalisation of the great house had been accomplished thoroughly and walking along its corridors, they felt a long way away from the spring sunshine outside. Margaret placed her hand on a cast-iron radiator. It was luke warm and a gloss grey like virtually every other surface they could see: the floor was covered with sanitary grey linoleum; the wood panelling on the walls had been painted grey; and, the ceiling had even been painted grey, albeit of a lighter shade. Some way ahead of them the corridor terminated and where it did so light flooded back towards them as if there were a portal or a door open to the sunshine just out of sight so that the doctors, nurses and patients, walking between them and the end of the corridor appeared to be spectrally hovering over the highly polished floor, the light bouncing all around them off of the hard glossy surfaces.

They found the consultant's room off a quieter corridor. The chairs were hard-backed and uncomfortable-looking. Aiden sat down languidly, his right hand still tightly holding onto the appointment letter. Margaret sat down next to him and after a moment's hesitation - apart from the nurses who could occasionally be seen about the corridors, Margaret had not seen any other women in the hospital –

she reached out for his hand. Taking her hand Aiden gave it a tender squeeze and continued to hold onto it, their fingers tightly interlaced. Presently, Margaret lifted his hand and placed it upon her lap and at the same time she slipped her other hand over it as well, asexually and elementally pressing it down into the dip formed between the roundness of her thighs beneath her coat, cupping her hands around him as if invaginating his hand between protecting coverlets.

Presently, a nurse stepped out of the consultant's room and, looking directly at Aiden, said his name. Aiden withdrew his hand from Margaret's comforting clasp and with a sharp intake of breath stood up, his entrails suddenly turning traitorously cold and watery. And as he followed the nurse into the room Margaret was left grimly wondering how she would ever cope with the business and habit of living if she did not have Aiden to rely upon.

There had been no room in the nurse's manner to entertain the idea that Margaret might have accompanied Aiden into the consultant's room and so she remained sitting on her chair until eventually an orderly brought her a cup of tea. As she sipped her tea she marvelled approvingly at the orderliness with which people conducted their lives even at times of adverse circumstances or worry, dutifully following official instructions and directions, passing along corridors quietly and waiting patiently in queues.

~~~~

"I understand your wife's come with you today."

The consultant spoke gently and unhurriedly as he leafed through the sheaf of papers of various sizes and colours that constituted Aiden's medical notes as if he were looking for something in particular rather than simply giving Aiden space to assimilate his news. He was a kindly-looking man, who, Aiden imagined, was probably close to retirement.

Thickly and slowly, Aiden replied, "Yes."

He could not engage in even undemanding conversation for the moment; he now understood how serious his illness was and how it would inevitably, and with such dreadful certainty, end.

"I think that's best," the consultant said avuncularly, surreptitiously watching Aiden as he turned over the pages. "It's a dreadful shock, and having family around helps tremendously. It's what we do it all for really, isn't it, family?"

Aiden looked up at him and nodded slowly, blankly, in reply. He noticed that the consultant's ears were quite hairy.

The nurse had conducted Aiden into the consultant's room and had then discretely retired, carefully closing the door behind her. The consultant had introduced himself, holding out a soft warm hand to Aiden, and had then invited him to sit on the chair which had been drawn up in front of his desk. Through the casement window, behind the consultant's head, Aiden could see the pale sunlight on the springy turf of the lawn in front of the house and the bobbing heads of daffodils worried by the chill wind. And as the consultant talked to him about the results of the tests he had had just a few days ago and what it all meant, Aiden had suddenly found that he was unconsciously pressing his knee and lower leg hard against the desk and had desperately wanted something to tightly grip hold of.

"It's not strictly by the book," the consultant said lazily, in a distracted type of voice as he peered over his glasses as if he found one of the pieces of paper of particular interest, "but I could give you something, if it would help?"

What if some of those slips of paper miscarried, as surely they sometimes must, Aiden thought, did people never then find out the truth?

"I was a medical officer on bombers during the war," the consultant continued speaking, as if he had not noticed Aiden's silence. "I used to dole out stuff. I'm sure you know all about wakey-wakey pills, but there were plenty of other things as well." His voice was almost dreamy now. "I simply tried to somehow get the chaps through it all."

Aiden wondered if without the pieces of paper there really could be any truth.

"No, I'd rather not," Aiden finally found his voice.

"I'll tell you what," the consultant put down the piece of paper and pulled his prescription pad towards him and started to write,

"I'll give you this just in case. These are just for the pain, but they're probably a lot stronger than anything your own doctor would prescribe. Back then, of course, there was always the threat of LMF." The consultant reverted to his previous train of thought. "I always thought that was particularly cruel, so we always did what we could to avoid that."

"I'm not frightened," Aiden said quite sharply.

"It was as much about class as anything else, really," the consultant continued amiably, simply smoothing over Aiden's testiness as if he had not even noticed it. "My father was a grocer. I always liked the orderliness of the tins and packets on the shelves, you know, soap powder and sardines and things. They looked so attractive and homely. But there were always those in authority who thought that unless you'd been to the right school and all that sort of thing, then you couldn't possibly have what it took to be courageous. Lot of nonsense, of course." His words trailed off quietly as he watched Aiden.

"When we converted to Lancasters most of our instructors had been on ops. They spoke to us about what it was really like; they were just ordinary chaps," Aiden said, feeling the consultant was waiting for some sort of reply from him.

"Brave men. At least the newsreels had that right. But the public were always given a rather rose-tinted version of it all. We all seem to applaud being fooled for the common good, I suppose we see it as some sort of willing stoic conspiracy; we're terribly good at that in this country." The consultant smiled wryly and gave up the pretence of being interested in Aiden's medical notes. "You know, the RAF today reminds me of the types in Bomber Command back then, or at least amongst the aircrew it does, ordinary chaps, although I'm not so sure about the top brass; not that you see much of them, of course, but they make their presence felt, even here."

"Yes, they were brave men," Aiden agreed.

"But tell me about what you did on Grapple," the consultant then said, adding quickly and reassuringly, "Oh, it's alright."

Aiden's facial expression had betrayed the concern about secrecy that had been instilled in him from his very earliest days in the airforce and that he had become habituated to think of as being not just prudent but institutionally desirable.

"I'd been on Canberras for a while, by then. Following on behind the Valiants after the weapons drop, it was our job to fly through the mushroom cloud and take air samples."

"You *actually flew* through the cloud!" the consultant exclaimed.

"It was extraordinary," Aiden spoke quietly. "It was really very frightening. I was terrified, actually. It was all I could do to carry-on. It was like looking into the churning abyss. Rather like seeing the end of the world."

Aiden had always believed that these thoughts should be kept firmly to himself and he had never before admitted the extent of his terror, and, ashamed, he now looked down at his hands where they were laying limply on the desk in front of him.

"Those men in the war, they were all absolutely terrified," the consultant said softly.

"But it's not the same; they faced far greater danger, night after night."

"Perhaps, but you *have* faced danger and taken great risks."

"We understood about the risks. You see, nobody really knew how the aircraft would handle in such conditions."

"I didn't mean that," he smiled gently at Aiden. "I meant about the dangers of the cloud itself, of what was in it. Did nobody say anything to you? It's not as if nobody knew."

Aiden sat staring down at his hands, feeling quite wretched as the implication of the consultant's words sank in. He then said weakly, "But we trusted. Why shouldn't we have?"

"At the end of the war I think it was Churchill's victory speech that did it for most of the men. When Churchill mentioned everybody else's contribution to victory, but omitted to say anything about the men of Bomber Command, they knew then that they had been sold-out short, betrayed even." Aiden found himself picking up the prescription that the consultant had slid across the desk. "There's all sorts of courage, you know, and most of it's private," the consultant said quietly, but firmly.

After a short pause Aiden said, "What will happen to me now?"

"I'm sure the service will look after you the best it can." The consultant was an honourable man. "But you must understand our business here is making servicemen fit again and so I'll be referring you to a civilian hospital for the rest of your treatment." The consultant seemed to understand that this should seem like a body blow to Aiden, for he added, with genuine feeling, "I really am so dreadfully sorry."

~~~~

There was no cause to worry on Mark's account; they had made arrangements in case they were late back. The mother of one of his school friends had ruthfully understood saying that of course Mark could stay with them after school and Margaret had said they would telephone when they got home.

But Margaret wanted to believe that her house and garden held recuperative powers, that the peacefulness and calm domestic routine must surely make Aiden whole again. So sitting outside the consultant's room, she had fretted in case they missed the next bus in which case they would not be home until after teatime and that would make the evening seem unsatisfactory. So upon seeing his face when he emerged from the consultant's room, intuitively knowing what he had learnt, she momentarily failed to understand he could not go home immediately, but instead needed time to recover his equilibrium.

The spring sunshine was weak but on coming out of the gloomy house it seemed candidly bright and for an instance Aiden and Margaret stood slightly dazed and mole-like, blinking, looking out over the grounds of the hospital. Slipping their coats on over their shoulders, they walked together amongst the daffodils that grew out of the lawn in front of the house and which seemed to go on forever. Despite their recent shock, they could still marvel at them; there were great swathes of golden trumpet-heads, like carpets of sprightly announcing angels, all moving as one, strong, but giving in the breeze, and yet smartly springing purposefully back upright again.

"Does it make any sense to talk about generations of flowers?"

"I've never thought," Margaret replied softly, measuring her words carefully; she did not fear Aiden would crumple with his news, but she felt distressed and uneasy with herself for making the assumption that he would be comforted in the way *she* imagined he would. As they walked, she once again took his hand.

"Because if one can, then I can find some sort of sense in them."

"I don't know that flowers are about sense," Margaret smiled tenderly.

"But just look at them all, there're so many. I couldn't even begin to count them." He paused briefly, before adding, quite calmly, "You know, I'm not frightened of death itself."

"I know you're not, dear. You're a brave man!" She squeezed his hand tenderly; their fingers were intertwined. But then, as she continued speaking, her voice sounded strangely solemn, or theatrical, "We'll face it together when the time comes, like lovers; you wouldn't want the end to be merely companionable."

"But without the jealousies lovers feel, I hope," he replied sharply, shivering involuntarily in the chilly air, having surprised himself at his reply.

The daffodils bowed down, as if in supplication, as the breeze passed over them once again. At times Margaret still craved a kind of wounding intensity and Aiden briefly wondered if she had taken umbrage in what he had said. But she did not reply and so he continued, "But they can't have all been planted like this, all these yellow bell-heads. Such a profusion. Each year, or generation, more of them must grow, not for us but to fulfil their own purpose, I suppose."

They walked on together in silence through the sea of bobbing flowers until Aiden said grittily, as if it were both a difficult admission for him to make and a deeply unpleasant thought, "Although, I think the prospect of un-relievable pain is quite frightening, terrifying really."

"I think it might be a little strong to impute purpose to flowers, don't you?" Margaret spoke playfully, knowing the strength and humour in Aiden's character, but thinking that she had never heard Aiden admit to being frightened like that. He had feared fatherly things before, but it seemed somehow shocking, unmanly even, that such a man might ever be so terrified of pain.

"Waking up each morning and knowing it will never get any better. Knowing that eventually I'll want to scream and cry out uncontrollably. It seems so damnably wretched." Then, breathing out a big sigh and watching Margaret carefully he continued, but much more slowly, "But he's given me a prescription which should help, you know, as it becomes worse," adding quietly, as if more remembering something to himself, "unbearable."

They had now walked the length of the lawn and had joined one of the paths that had been cut through the gardens after the hospital had been built and had been smoothly macadamised so that invalids would find walking along them easier.

"How long until it gets too awful?" Margaret could not meet his eye. She did not want to use the word 'unbearable'; people, she thought, good people as well as silly people, all used the word 'unbearable' when they really meant no such thing at all.

"A matter of weeks." Aiden struggled to keep his voice even.

"Oh, Aiden!" On making her abyssal, anguished exclamation, she suddenly stopped walking and pivoted around on her clumsy shoe to face him.

Although her mouth remained closed, her jaw fell and her face turned powdery white, washed slack with ruinous shock. Her face appeared unnaturally elongated and distorted. The corners of her mouth dropped and the flesh about the top of her neck no longer looked taut and beach-firm. Taking out her handkerchief, one of her pretty ones with a violet embroidered on the corner, she quickly wiped the corner of her eye, scrunched it back up into a ball and pushed it back up her sleeve.

"Oh, my love, please don't cry." Aiden pulled her towards him and enveloped her in his arms. Margaret made a single deep, involuntary sob, but then took a sharp, deep intake of breath and resolutely clamped her mouth shut tight. Slowly she exhaled the air from her lungs, forcing her self to take control once again. Aiden relaxed his arms, but still held them loosely about her shoulders.

"You sounded just like Trevor Howard when you said that." She laughed as she sniffed loudly and reached again for her handkerchief. "You know, when they're on that station!" She wiped the left hand side of her nose and then her right before again screwing up the hankie into a ball.

They stood together for a moment, Aiden with his arms about her, conscious of her warmth, of her dolour, and of the chill air blowing around her which made her seem all the more alive. Margaret stood with her handkerchief held tightly and contingently in her clenched hand until presently Aiden gently dropped his arms and they began walking again.

"It's not that I'm *frightened* of dying," he said after a moment, "but I do feel an incredible sense of disappointment."

Despite the chill they sat down on one of the benches that were placed at regular distances along the path. Here and there recuperating patients sat, pale in the spring sunshine. They were mostly young men, huddled in their greatcoats, or with blankets tucked over their knees, who sat silently and moved very little so that they appeared like outlying runéd rocks.

"You must try not to worry about Mark, he won't forget you; you've always been such a good father to him."

They looked back at the rich daffodils they had walked through. Most of the shrubs in the bed behind them had not yet started to bud and looked dismal, skeletal and bare.

"It's not just that I won't be there to see him grow up. On its own that's simply quite selfish, really. But after today I realise more than ever just how much he needs someone in whom he can safely put his trust."

"I'll always be there for him," she said soothingly, with an effort concealing the hurt at the implication she had taken.

They sat in silence for a while and Aiden squeezed Margaret's hand as if to say he had not intended to imply Mark could not trust her and Margaret squeezed his hand back and hoped he would explain. But Margaret had also started to feel cold from her bouldering shock, and was worrying about preparing the vegetables for their evening meal and so could not help but start to fret a little, feeling that they ought to be thinking about catching their bus home, and would have been content for Aiden to continue his explanation as they walked on.

But Aiden, apparently indifferent to the chill and intent upon working through his train of thought, continued sitting, until eventually he spoke again. "You see, that chap in there even talked about Grapple."

"What did he say about it?" Margaret replied, still worrying about their bus.

"He was drawing a sort of comparison with the war, I suppose. He talked about courage and LMF. You know," Margaret was looking slightly puzzled, "they could put men on the charge of Lack of Moral Fibre, if they flunked it, if they couldn't face going on ops anymore. He was an MO on bombers back then, apparently."

Absolutely horrified, she said, "But surely he wasn't saying that you, Harry and all the others lacked courage!" But for the briefest of moments, thinking of how Aiden could be so physically frightened, the thought had flitted through her mind that there could be some secret truth to the charge.

"No," Aiden said quickly, smiling at her. "Quite the opposite, I think. He was thinking about how the bomber crews back then felt let down, or worse."

"And he thinks the same about Grapple?" Margaret spoke slowly. As a service wife, she was fully familiar with the private hurt of the wartime bomber crews.

"It's all about trust. *We* trusted in what we were told about Grapple and our part in it all. We trusted the men who commanded us." Margaret sat in silence, weighing-up the gravity of what Aiden was saying. Aiden continued, "The cloud. He seems to think there was something awful in the cloud that's caused it and it seems to me all that was kept from us. There was always secrecy, but we could accept secrecy when it was partnered with honesty. But there was never deceit."

"Is that what he thinks?" her voice was now no greater than a horrified whisper.

"Oh, I think he's an honest man and if anything his suspicions would travel no further than to error or mistake."

Margaret placed her hand in his and they sat in silence for a few moments. Margaret realised as much as Aiden how awful was the inference from the logic of Aiden's thought.

"But who would have *known,* your squadron leader, the station commander?" Margaret spoke urgently now.

"I just can't believe that they would have known anything. I think it must have gone pretty high up, you know."

"Well, what about the scientist who was at the briefing before your deployment." Margaret was angry now and eager to find a culprit. "You know, the pipe man. He must have known!"

"Oh, maybe," Aiden replied casually, feeling sure that the amiable scientist must have known all about the physics of the explosions, but had been only explaining what he had been asked to. "Just now, back in the consultant's room," Aiden continued, "I wondered what would happen if just one of those pieces of flimsy paper in my record had been lost. Would my illness appear to be just some sort of randomness?   Betrayal really does appear very easy when people simply do as they're told."

Leaning slightly back and to one side so that he could reach awkwardly into his jacket pocket, Aiden slowly drew out a packet of cigarettes. Taking one out, he tapped the end of it several times on the packet, even though he had smoked tipped cigarettes for a number of years, and then reached back into his pocket for his matches. "Do old men everywhere have their dark secrets?" he said with a sudden bitterness as he exhaled a long jet of blue smoke and waved the match in the air to extinguish the flame.

Aiden suddenly felt a great wave of exhaustion passing over him as if it was his thoughts that had induced a sense of deep shock rather than the news he had received today. Along with this realisation came a deep sense of wanting to go home. "I'd like to stay at home as long as I can."

Now feeling in accord with each other, Aiden and Margaret rose slowly from the bench and once more pulled their coats about them. Aiden cast a brief look back at the old house and, choosing the path which took them past the solitary servicemen on the other benches, they walked out of the hospital grounds and on to the bus stop to wait for the bus which would take them back home again.

## Chapter Twenty-Four

Mark felt compelled to follow the progress of the two prefects. Even from a distance he had noticed them immediately they had set out from the school buildings. They had walked purposefully across the empty playground where the broad expanse of grey asphalt shimmered in the intense afternoon heat and then out onto the bright playing field. Walking solemnly, side-by-side, they looked like morbid crows as if they should be cloaked in dark midnight colours. As he watched, they walked directly to the part of the field where the games lesson was in progress, increasing Mark's sense of foreboding, and headed straight towards where the games master stood.

The games master had been on the verge of blowing his whistle. He was standing in the centre of the playing field beside the running track with a line of tense and poised boys spread out on their marks. But there was something of dark prognostication in the prefects' demeanour and as they approached, the games master took the whistle out of his mouth and turned his full attention to them.

He was still holding onto the whistle when, in answer to a question from one of the prefects, he swivelled around and pointed towards the sandpit where Mark and a knot of other boys were taking turns at high jump. With a sudden plunging sensation in his stomach, Mark felt quite certain that it was he who was being identified. The games master watched as the prefects walked in the direction of the sandpit. At the same time he absent-mindedly blew his whistle to start the race but only when the prefects arrived at their destination did he finally turn his attention back towards the activity on the track. Mark was so certain that it was he that the games master had been pointing out that he stepped forward as the prefects arrived.

"Your mother's here. Your father wants to see you."

The prefects hovered uncertainly near the edge of the sandpit, their smart uniforms and highly polished shoes sharply incongruous amongst the spilled sand and all the paraphernalia of sport. For all their apparent maturity and pride they did not appear comfortable discharging their duty; one of them remained awkwardly silent throughout its execution, the other betrayed a nervousness so that his words sounded unintentionally gruff.

For a moment, Mark did not know what was happening; the distant shouts and cries of the boys dotted over the playing field and those richer, closer sounds of the boys in the group of high-jumpers spiralled out of his awareness to be replaced by a peculiar rushing noise which filled-up his ears.

A long time afterwards, he had realised that although at the time he had thought the statement had been totally unexpected, the effect it had had on him had been so great because quite the opposite had in fact been true. He realised that he must have overheard and on some level understood some of the pointedly opaque words and phrases which had been spoken between his father and his mother around this time, or those words spoken between them and the noticeably increasing drift of visitors who had called at the house throughout the spring and summer.

"Get changed and meet her by the School Office."

Out of nowhere, there appeared a thick metallic taste in Mark's mouth.

Mark had felt shocked when shortly after being taken ill, Aiden had been admitted to hospital, although his Uncle Ted, who with his Auntie Daphne had arrived unexpectedly at that time and eager to be cheerily helpful, had awkwardly told him that he should try not to worry.

Always feeling compelled to act upon any official instruction, he unhesitatingly started back toward the changing rooms. As Mark ran quickly back over the playing fields towards the school buildings, the games master watched him go.

As Mark passed the curved end of the oval running track, the boys who were racing were nearing the end of their final lap. Without exception the boys all wore well-laundered, uniform white cotton singlets and shorts. A band of colour, a distinguishing house colour, was woven into each of the boy's singlets, but to all intents and purposes the boys appeared as a single homogenous group.

He felt terribly exposed as he ran across the grass and as he ran he silently rehearsed his clumsy defences to himself in case he should run into other prefects or teachers who, unaware of any unfolding calamity, should challenge his right to be absent from lessons. And fearing the charge of solitariness, he worried that his peers must be slyly watching him, judgmentally noting his deviation from the afternoon's usual activities.

Margaret was standing outside the school office staring out of the window. As Mark approached her he was shocked at quite how motionless, how absolutely still, she was. On reaching her, she silently pressed him close, indifferent to the fact that her arm had also clumsily enveloped his duffel bag which contained his athletics kit. A cup of tea remained untasted on the low table in front of the window.

"I didn't know if I should have showered," Mark said looking down at the floor. The bell for the afternoon break was just sounding and he wanted the awkward moment to end. "They usually make us after games."

Mark had hurriedly changed back into his school uniform. Afterwards it was with a sense of shame he recalled his quickness was due to his sense of set-apartness rather than through any intention of joining his mother as soon as might be possible.

As they stood together by the window, the school secretaries, visible where they sat in the office through a hatch with sliding glass doors, did not once raise their eyes from their typewriters. Margaret simply said, "Daddy wants to see you."

After a moment, when he realised how deeply frightened he suddenly felt, Mark said, "But we're going to go home first?"

"I'm afraid we don't have time to, Sweet Pea." As Mark had grown up, at least since Mark had been at secondary school, she had instinctively avoided the term of endearment which she had once used habitually.

"But what about my bags!" Mark cried out in alarm.

Apart from his duffel bag, Mark also carried a smart leather briefcase into which during the course of the day, lesson by lesson, he would carefully pack all the exercise books and textbooks he would need for his homework. Margaret, not wanting to have to impress on Mark the urgency of the situation, and feeling increasingly anxious about taking an unfamiliar bus route and having to look out for the hospital, said as evenly as she could manage, "I guess we'll just have to manage together as best we can, Sweetie."

At the sound of the passage of feet in the corridor behind them, Mark withdrew from Margaret's embrace. Margaret made the pretence of looking for something in her handbag, but took out her handkerchief as indifferently as she could manage and wiped her nose. Screwing up and keeping hold of the handkerchief in her hand, she snapped her handbag shut again and said breezily, "We must get going; we don't want to keep Dad waiting, do we? You must help me find the right bus!"

~~~~

Once they were on the bus and Margaret had paid their fares, taking her change and slipping the coppers back into her purse, Mark had settled-in staring out of the window with his briefcase on the floor tucked under his legs and silently nursing his duffel bag on his knees. Margaret, sitting beside him next to the gangway, had been unable to settle. Almost as soon as they had started she bobbed her head up and down looking out anxiously for any sign of the hospital. Then she had made a mistake. They had jumped up much too early, and had got off the bus a stop too soon and had ended up rushing along the pavement in the blazing afternoon heat, Margaret tightly grasping Mark's free hand, and running up the steps into the hospital building.

"This isn't the way!" Mark suddenly cried out in dismay.

Breathing deeply, he had stopped dead in the deserted corridor; unexpectedly, once they were out of the main atrium Margaret had turned left into the long main corridor that travelled the length of the hospital.

"It's alright, Sweetie!" Margaret said, she also catching her breath and trying her best to keep her emotions from affecting her voice. "They've moved Dad to another ward, that's all."

When Aiden had first been admitted to the hospital it had been to a general ward which had a smell of antiseptic which cut to the back of the throat like frosty air.

"But why?" Mark asked loudly and insistently.

Although he had initially been deeply apprehensive, Mark had not disliked the general ward. It might have been somewhat austere, but it was never bleak; nurses crisply bustled around the bright, spotlessly clean ward and any number of the men swapped their newspapers, and chatted about the cricket. During precious visiting times wives and knots of children pressed about the beds with bunches of cut flowers from their gardens or allotments and brought out plump, fleshy grapes from where they had been tucked into brown paper bags until it was once again time for the women's handbags to be snapped tightly shut and the children's coats buttoned. Sensing the camaraderie, it had seemed a surprisingly cheery, hopeful place to Mark. Here, somehow, it had felt possible for him to adjust to the shock of having to visit his father in hospital.

"It's just to give him a bit more privacy at the moment," Margaret said mustering as much lightness into her tone as she could. She had turned to face him, intuitively thinking that by doing so she would seem to be more in earnest. She felt desperately anxious to press on and although she knew that she was not providing any great degree of comfort to Mark, she did not want to say anything which would undermine what she had agreed with Aiden as that would seem to her as being disloyal.

Mark stood where he was looking hot and dejected, his briefcase hanging limply at his side. His lips were curiously puckered-up as if they were covering over his tightly clenched jaw; he looked as if he might dissolve into floods of tears at any moment.

"Come along Sweetie," she implored, feeling quite wretched that she could not make everything seem better for him. "We really must get along to see Daddy, now."

Margaret briefly flirted with the intoxicating and milkilycomforting idea that she never should have agreed to him having to suffer any dreadful ordeal such as this. But then after a moment, and looking curiously grown-up, Mark took a deep breath and as he slowly exhaled, as if he were carefully controlling the exit of air through his slightly parted lips, he slowly nodded his agreement as if he now understood the need to willingly accept the labour of a difficult but necessary task. Taking his free hand once more, Margaret and Mark started walking silently down the corridor, Mark's briefcase banging against his knee as they went.

It was between the normal visiting times; the afternoon session had finished a long time ago, so that not even the most persistent of stragglers remained anywhere in the hospital after the bell had sounded, and the evening session would not begin until after teatime. Without the bustle of visitors coming and going along the corridors, Mark found the desertedness of the hospital corridors disconcerting. Occasionally they passed a nurse walking purposefully, or a white-coated orderly pushing a pyjama-and-dressing-gown-clad patient in a wheelchair, but this probative activity produced an uneasiness in him, as if it were evidence of his unsanctioned presence and which was similar to the feeling he had experienced earlier that afternoon in school.

For a minute or two they walked along the corridor with its thick layer of white glossy paint on the walls and its uniform signs giving directions to the various wards and to any number of disquietive-sounding hospital departments, until, briefly glancing at the name of the ward, although she was quite certain that she was right, Margaret turned to the left and pushed open one of a pair of glass-panelled doors. She held the door open with her stretched-out right arm and then lightly placing her hand on Mark's left shoulder, she gently propelled him into the ward in front of her. Mark found himself standing uncomfortably in front of a small nurses' station where, day or night, a shaded lamp provided a welcoming pool of soft amber light. This ward consisted entirely of private rooms, set on each side of a short, sunless corridor which ran back at a right angle from where they now stood.

Unconsciously smoothing down her uniform over the front of

her thighs with the outstretched palms of her hands, a nurse stood-up from the desk as Margaret and Mark approached and stepped smartly forward to meet them. The nurse had clearly been expecting them. She greeted Margaret politely and efficiently. As if he had been previously excluded, Mark uncomfortably inferred from the nurse's sympathetic concord with his mother that Margaret must have already made a number of visits to this new ward.

The nurse then turned to Mark and said pleasantly in her practised, professional carer's tone, "Hello Michael. Have you come to see your father?"

Mark felt an awful flutter of panic. He was not yet old enough to realise that it did not matter whether he corrected her mistake or not and she evidently did not expect a reply for she was already turning her attention to Margaret once more, "He's quite lucid at the moment, considering everything," she was saying, matter-of-factly. But Mark desperately sought to correct her in case some lasting wrong was created.

"I'm not Michael. My name's Mark," he said, his voice throaty and quiet.

But she had already turned away from him and showed no indication of looking back, "That's right, dear." The rebuff was completely unintentional but to Mark it was crushing making it feel to him as if to the nurse his presence was no more than a second thought.

"Can we go in?" Margaret asked, meekly accepting the authority of the nurse without question. A relaxed approach to visiting was applied in this ward; at the point of crisis visitors would arrive or depart at any conceivable hour. Knowing the way, Margaret led Mark along to one of the doors in the corridor behind the nurses' station.

Here in the individual rooms there was a different qualitative feel from the general wards. As if in direct challenge to the stuffy claustrophobia of illness, each room was airy and sparsely furnished. There was only a tubular steel-framed bed, a bedside cabinet, an upholstered easy chair with wooden arms and the smallest of cupboards which provided the only space for clothes or other personal items; on a previous visit Margaret had already sadly taken

Aiden's jacket and trousers back home with her. Unlike in the general wards, the curtains were quite gay, with a repeating pattern of green foliage on a plain white background, but in the air there was an odour like decaying chrysanthemums.

Aiden's room felt surprisingly bright after the dim corridor. A shaft of rutilant sunlight fell on the bed from the window, like a bridge or a ladder, the brightness exposing everything within it to intense scrutiny. Flecks of dust drifted inertly in the golden light.

Mark had only seen his father a few days ago and he was now appalled at the rapidity of his decline. His father's emaciated body, propped up on his pillows and riddled through with cancer like the lettering in a stick of seaside rock, seemed to hover over, rather than lie upon, the bed. His stick-like arms poked out of the blue-and-white striped pyjamas and terminated in crabby hands that rested like those of an old man on the turned-down sheet. It looked as if his cheeks had been artificially reddened. What Mark saw did not fit with his image of fatherness, which was still immortal, giant or demonic even.

"Say hello to your father," Margaret prompted.

Shocked, Mark could only mumble a greeting and did not want to approach his father. He now felt quite ridiculous, stupid even, carrying his briefcase and duffel bag and dearly would have preferred to have taken them back home before setting out for the hospital, and in his mind he bitterly reproached Margaret for not letting him do so. Not knowing what to do with them, he awkwardly placed his briefcase in the corner of the room by the door, and swung his duffel bag off of his shoulder and placed it neatly down beside the case.

Mark then sat down miserably on the bed below the spot where the bedclothes hid his father's feet. The bed was higher than his own bed at home and to sit with his feet on the floor he had to sit stiffly on its edge. Finding this uncomfortable, he tried leaning his elbow and lower arm on the rail at the foot of the bed, but this felt clumsy and awkward, and to slide into the middle of the bed so that his legs could stretch out across the mattress would mean embracing the terrifying space of illness.

For a moment, Aiden did not even acknowledge him, so that

Mark, with his terrible new awareness of his father's condition, was intensely frightened that he may have been sedated against the pain to such an extent that speaking would prove impossible, or that he may not even be aware of his presence.

But then presently Aiden stirred and spoke thickly. "I expect your mother has told you that I'm not at all well." Then as he continued speaking he became more lucid, "I'm afraid there's no easy way to tell you this, but I'm not going to get well again. Do you understand what I'm saying to you?"

Aiden paused. Mark found he could not answer, but bowed his head, unable to meet his father's eye. The slight, everyday words strung together in this way created a meaning that was cruelly unequivocal. It was as if they had been metamorphosed through the fire of speech into adamantine semantic blocks; too heavy to move and too large to see much beyond. "I won't be coming home again," Aiden said quietly but exercising a surprisingly strong degree of control, as if he wished to ensure that there could be no possible misunderstanding. "I had thought whether I should try to find a softer way to say that to you. But then I considered that to do so would have been no kinder. You need what I have to say to you to be hard and sharp."

Margaret reached out for his hand where it lay on the bed covers. She knew that he had much more that he wanted to say to him but thought that what he had already said must be the most important and that it would not matter greatly if Aiden was not able to say any more.

"Shouldn't you rest now, my love?" Margaret said solicitously, gently caressing his hand; she greatly admired his courage for wanting to tell Mark himself.

"What would I be resting for?" Aiden replied slowly, managing the faintest of smiles at Margaret. He had not found it difficult saying any of this to Mark; he considered it simply a loving duty.

Aiden then took a number of measured breaths. But this was not the husbanding of a valetudinarian's strength but a preparatory exercise, so that when he spoke again his voice was not loud but held an unexpected and controlled passion:

"Do you see the flickering firelight?"

The unexpected words startled Margaret.

"Do you see the flickering firelight, here in this room?" he continued. "The bright snapping tongues of reds, oranges and yellows licking the immensity of the darkness beyond. And can you smell blood and fear, here in this room?"

His words sounded disturbingly wild to her, out of character, and for a moment Margaret worried that the drugs that had been administered to him to control his pain must have made him hallucinate or his mind wander. But then, she considered, they did have a kind of measured, dramatic quality.

Ever since the day earlier in the year when she and Aiden had walked amongst the daffodils in the hospital grounds Margaret had dreaded this day. She knew that there was nothing she could do to put it off and each new, additional day was therefore both a bonus and a trial to her. But on hearing Aiden's unexpected words and having convinced herself they were not the product of palliative drugs, she suddenly felt quite ashamed as she realised that she was so startled because she had a deep presumption that an end such as Aiden's would be full of pathos.

Aiden continued speaking, his voice sounding stronger than Margaret would have thought possible:

"The smell of blood and fear as we disguise our faces with smears of berry and wood ash. Can we know what it is like to tread so dangerously?"

The words carried an unexpectedly deep resonance and although Mark had said nothing while Aiden had been speaking, he now sat up on the bed with his arms behind him supporting his weight and looking straight ahead, alert, his nostrils flaring as he breathed deeply, as if Aiden had struck a seam of precious innate wildness that ran deep within him and that he had not known that he possessed.

"That's how it should all begin," he said to Mark, "sitting in the glow of the fire with all the older men, listening to the rhythm of the dark."

Aiden paused and for a few moments none of them felt that they could say anything. From outside of the hospital, the distant, gentle hum of the summer afternoon's orderly suburban traffic reached them, at odds with the charged atmosphere within the room. Margaret found she was trembling, as if she believed herself to be in the presence of a dark, potentially threatening facet of Aiden's self.

"But it sounds so awfully primitive!" Margaret voiced, barely at more than the level of a whisper, as if she were saying something shocking.

"Yes it's primitive," Aiden said as if he were savouring a taste that was almost too strong to palate, "the agnate need to nourish and to be nourished, sitting in that tight circle around the fire with all the old men, the uncles and grandfathers." He then added vehemently, "But now I feel cheated."

Margaret realised that not only had she really expected today to be filled with pathos, she also now recognised a deep expectation of wrapping herself around Mark and comforting him, of taking him back home again to cosset him and keep him in perpetual safety.

"Of what, dear, of seeing Mark grow up?" Margaret said steadying herself. She was no platitudinarian and so she realised the inadequacy of her question virtually as soon as she had spoken it.

"Seeing Mark grow up," he echoed Margaret's question back to her, rolling the syllables of her words around his mouth like so much soft creamy wine as if he were contemplating their meaning. "Mark will grow and flower into a potent and fallible man, full of vim, heart-felt immortality and the capacity for making all sorts of vibrant mistakes. I wanted to be able to marvel at that blossoming. But I have been cheated of all that."

"By whom?" Margaret replied, her voice trilling with emotion; faced with such an unknown, she feared that somehow Aiden might want to implicate her.

"I suppose at first I thought I had been cheated by some deity; after all, there didn't seem to be anybody else to blame, nobody else seems to have the gift of quickness and death in quite the same unjust manner."

Although she was tensely relieved at the apparent direction of Aiden's thoughts, Margaret felt uneasy with the irreverent sentiment; she had not expected theological uncertainty today. But perhaps, she reasoned, and not knowing how deep her own was, faith was easily shaken in an age of bat-like almighty aeroplanes and raw atomic power, so she was not dismissive.

"At first?" she said, wanting to be absolutely certain.

"Because even now, after everything, I can't really believe in an unkind God, but then, deep down I know I won't see him grow up," Aiden said with a note of finality.

There was silence in the room as Margaret contemplated what Aiden had said. The silence seemed all the more intense for a background rumbling noise that had a deep subterranean-like quality and which permeated into the room from the corridor outside and which was accompanied by the rattling of teacups and saucers.

When Aiden finally spoke again, he was speaking boldly once more and seemed to be speaking once again as if for Mark's benefit, "But look around you. The old men have all gone and here in this room there is no flickering firelight, just dust floating in angel light and a day like butterfly wings."

Mark was still sitting up straight, but was now looking intently at his father.

"I think you'll have to speak more plainly," Margaret said, not unkindly, as much for herself as for Mark.

"I think he'll understand one day," Aiden said quietly, smiling weakly at Mark and adding simply, "It's about trust, really."

"Oh!" Margaret said, surprising herself with the intensity with which she spoke, thinking that she now knew what lay behind what Aiden was saying and realising that it had made a tremendously deep impact on her as well as on Aiden. She added quickly, "It's the Atom Men isn't it?"

"I suppose so, in a sense."

"But you know that I'll be looking after him!"

Margaret now felt uncomfortable about where the conversation might be going and looked uneasily at Aiden.

"I know you will. But it's not the same," Aiden said firmly. Although he had no intention of showing it towards Margaret, Aiden felt an irritation with a womankind who considered that the canon of child rearing and nurturing was exclusively their own. He realised how close he was coming to upsetting Margaret, what such dangerous territory this could be, but nevertheless, he added in the same strong tone of voice, "He needs to serve his apprenticeship in maleness."

Although already highly charged, the tension in the room intensified sharply.

Aiden was convinced of a specific male need that went beyond the demand of ordinary affection, something that was hard-wired into the mortal machine. It went greatly beyond the simple biological imperative of needing to know that one has forged a link in the chain of generations.

"And I suppose you think that's something only men can do for him," Margaret said sharply.

She was far from convinced, believing that the existence of such innately different male and female perspectives threatened her cherished view of total intimacy as being the ultimate state, and thought it would be an unspeakable tragedy if the afternoon were to end on a sour note.

"This is when the old men in the firelight should teach him not to be frightened of his wildness," Aiden replied steadily, but now looking tired, "Of how to safely take risks and to guide him so that he will not be blighted by his life's choices."

Margaret darted a careful look at Aiden; she wanted to know what he had meant by being blighted by life's choices. She wondered what he might think he knew but was nervous of what reply he might give if she asked him directly.

The shaft of yellow sunlight had moved round by now. It no longer illuminated Aiden or Mark but brightened a square of the greeny-grey linoleum with a deep golden intensity, the shadow of the window's transom and mullion dividing the square of bright light and looking like a leaning or a distorted cross.

"But you will speak to Harry for me?" Aiden then said, urgently. "I know I can count on Harry."

Margaret, carefully watching the expression on Aiden's face, slowly nodded her head. She was relieved that the moment of danger seemed to have passed. "Yes, of course I will," she said slowly and squeezed his hand. "And there's Ted," she added. "He'll do his best for him."

Ted, of course, was family. Aiden lay back on the bed feeling as if his life energy was almost entirely spent, the motes of dust randomly floating in the bright shaft of sunlight like barbated ideas in the minds of sharp angels.

At that moment there was a gentle knock on the door and opening it, the nurse put her head into the room and said in a tone that suggested she had no doubt about just how comforting it was bound to be, "I've brought you a nice cup of tea."

As Margaret sipped her tea she said, "I'd better take Mark along back home in a moment. Daphne and Ted should be getting there at about the same time if we go soon. They're staying of course, so they'll be with Mark this evening and I'll be able to come back just as soon as I can. Daphne can get Mark some tea; we've got eggs in the house."

"But you must make sure you have something before you come back. You have to look after yourself, my love."

"Oh, but you mustn't worry about me!"

Mark noticed that his mother was tightly holding her bunched up handkerchief in her hand once again.

Mark thought these words sounded so wonderfully and refreshingly mundane, so perfectly ordinary, as if his mother and father were casually discussing the domestic arrangements they would make so that they could attend his school play, or go to the church bazaar.

Feeling a little disappointed or deflated, as a part of her would have liked to have comforted Mark in the way she had previously imagined, Margaret put down her cup and saucer on the bedside table. Then she unnecessarily smoothed and re-adjusted the turned back portion of the sheet on Aiden's bed before saying to Mark, "Say goodbye to your father." Then she hastily turned away, tightly clutching her handkerchief, and went to retrieve Mark's briefcase and duffel bag from the corner of the room.

## *Chapter Twenty-Five*

As expected, in the middle of the fiercely sunny afternoon, Daphne and Ted arrived. Mark hung back, standing in the doorway into the front room as Margaret opened the door in answer to their knock. Daphne, leaning forward out of the glare while Ted stood beside her holding their shabby suitcase, embraced Margaret, silently enveloping her, as if under the circumstances she thought that her usual cheerful manner of greeting clearly wouldn't do. But after a moment she confessed to Margaret, in a gush of guilty relief, that actually they were parched and dying for a cup of tea after a journey that had been dislocated by all the usual small anxieties that come with the business of changing trains and of waiting in the hot summer dust for connecting buses. Margaret had been airing out the front room; although the food was to be laid out in the dining room, the lounge would also be needed.

Under the pretext of there being so much that still had to be done Margaret had been fretting for Daphne to arrive and, although she had known it was really far too early for them, she had been looking out for her and Ted ever since lunch time, glancing up from her dusting if anyone should walk past the house. But in truth there was not that much that could be done: the baker would not be delivering the finger rolls until the morning as they had to be fresh; Margaret had baked sausage rolls earlier in the day; a fruitcake had been made yesterday; and, she had made a trifle in the large cut glass bowl that had been a wedding present but she could not put the cream on it until tomorrow.

"What about the ham then?" Daphne persisted.

"No, we walked down to the shops earlier to fetch it, didn't we Sweetie. It's crumbed; it looks nice."

They were sitting at the kitchen table drinking the longed-for cup of tea and Margaret had put some Lincoln Cream biscuits out; the kitchen did not catch the full force of the sun until later in the afternoon.

"So for now it's just a couple of sponges?" Daphne said in a business-like, but not unkindly, manner.

"Well, yes, I suppose so," Margaret answered slowly as if she suddenly felt uncertain, doubtful of her own arrangements.

"We'll have those done in a jiffy, won't we?" Daphne said, implying only that everything was under control. There was only the smallest amount of tea left in her cup but she nevertheless placed it carefully down in the saucer and reached out across the table and gently laid her hand over Margaret's; she realised that Margaret would be relying on having plenty to do today.

"Ted," Daphne then said, as if a thought had just occurred to her, "be a love would you, and check what there is in the sideboard?"

Ted was sitting quietly drinking his tea and had just taken a second biscuit. He was content to let the two sisters dominate the conversation, as they usually had when they were all together, even before Aiden had died.

"Do you suppose it'll be enough?" Margaret sounded worried.

Daphne glanced around the kitchen looking to see if Margaret had taken the margarine for the sponges out of the fridge.

"Don't fuss so," she replied kindly, giving Margaret's hand a gentle squeeze, "people are coming to pay their respects, that's the main thing. Anyway, it'll be plenty!"

Margaret sat quietly for a moment, and then, after sighing loudly, said, but now sounding much brighter, "Well, shall we get going then?"

Margaret, Daphne and Ted all stood up. Having cleared away the teapot and the teacups, Ted unbuttoned his cuffs, rolled up his shirt sleeves and started to run water into the washing-up bowl, placing his index finger under the stream of water as soon as he had turned on the tap so that he could feel when it began to run hot, while Margaret and Daphne set about making the sponges; Daphne chose eggs of a uniform size, and Margaret turned the gas on to regulate the oven.

"It wouldn't do him any harm to do a bit of drying up," Daphne said softly to Margaret, thinking that she was far too indulgent.

But Margaret replied, "We'll manage."

As Daphne had confidently predicted, the sponges had taken no time at all to make and the first two of the baking tins had quickly been put on the middle shelf in the oven. Ted, who was still on self-appointed washing-up duty, washed the mixing bowl, sieve and wooden spoon and Daphne dried them up vigorously with a blue and white tea towel. Having completed their chores, they felt free to go and sit in the lounge. Margaret and Daphne sat together on the sofa, while Ted and Mark took the two armchairs.

Margaret initially seemed lost and worried with her hands for something to do, but Daphne breezily started to talk about happier times and so Margaret finally gave herself up to soothing talk, turning sideways in her seat the better to talk to Daphne, her left leg hard up against the front of the sofa and her bottom pushed right into the corner of it. Occasionally, she fiddled with the braid that edged the seating cushion.

And as they talked, sadness and happiness seemed peculiarly wedded to each other like a bimetallic strip. As emotion flowed through the house and in and out of each individual's private memories, first the one extreme would momentarily dominate and the atmosphere of the house would seem to bend to it, but it was inevitably silvered with its opposite emotion and each recollection or expression could so easily induce the opposite bend, so that the atmosphere in the house became uniquely charged.

Mark felt rosily included; at each softly washed seaside-like recollection of his father, many of which sounded so rolling and fresh to him and at which Margaret sadly smiled or looked tearful, her handkerchief held tightly damp-balled in her hand, it was as if he was being unexpectedly upbuoyed and sustained; he had hung vaporously about the house since his father had died not quite knowing what he should do, and without any direction of how he should be.

"How about another cup of tea?" Daphne asked looking around brightly at them all, cheerily interrupting the comfortable silence they had fallen into. "It's time for the other sponge to come out, anyway."

"Right-oh," Ted said, sensing Daphne wanted him to stir himself and pushing himself forward in his seat and getting to his feet he added, "I'll just take the case up."

Thinking about the jam for the sponges, Margaret said, slightly concerned, "I've only got raspberry. Do you think that's alright?

And temporarily, the spell was broken.

~~~~

As on his Uncle and Aunt's previous visit a few days ago, their suitcase was placed in Mark's bedroom and Mark was exiled to sleep on a camp bed in the dining room with the table pushed back against the wall to make enough room. The curvature of the camp bed under Mark's meagre weight and the sheets and blankets over him made a warm, muggy tunnel which even under the present circumstances seemed cosy and something of an adventure.

As his mother did not know how to, his Uncle Ted had put the bed together saying it was a small thing but he was very glad to be of help. The large oblong box of thick cardboard with big orange-brown metal staples along the join which ran the length of one side, and which Mark still found difficult to manhandle, had been brought out from the under-stairs cupboard and the component parts slid out of it and assembled, his uncle kneeling on the floor. Mark, as if he wanted to learn how to put it together for himself, had happily squatted down close beside his uncle; the slightly stale smell of cigarette tobacco perpetually hung about his Uncle Ted, like it had with his father, but even allowing for this similarity, his uncle had a quite individual grownup sweetish smell about him which Mark found almost as appealing as his father's.

Mark awoke while the dinning room still wallowed in deep subaquatic grey light and not knowing whether he should get up or not, uncertain of what he should do, he spent a long time worrying and watching the dining furniture as it spectrally took shape and colour in the growing light. Waking this morning felt rather like how waking had felt the morning after he had seen his father for the last time; he intuitively felt that the regular comforting routine that the house usually enjoyed had been ominously abandoned. He had been lying awake for so long by the time Margaret came needlessly into the dining room to wake him that he felt ravenously hungry, as if he had been out running a race rather than lying in the half-light listening to her crying upstairs.

The kitchen was cooler than it had been the last few mornings at this hour. Breakfast was cooked and eaten at a slower pace than the slightly hurried pace of most workaday mornings; although Margaret worried that she still had a lot that she had to do. There was bacon. The slightly sweet smell of frying lingered in the air and the dripping bowl stood on the draining board with a fresh pool of fat in it, translucent and marbling as it cooled. The four of them sat at the kitchen table, Ted sat freshly-shaven and anxious to keep his shirt clean which for now remained open at the collar and with his already-thinning hair carefully combed and slicked across the top of his head.

"So is it just Mum and Dad who are coming here first?" Daphne Asked.

But, taking them all aback, Margaret said, "Aiden always used to think it was quicker by tube, you know, from Liverpool Street."

When visiting either Margaret and Aiden, or Daphne and Margaret's parents, Ted and Daphne habitually got on the bus to travel across to Charing Cross to catch the train for the final leg of their journey.

"Oh Peggy!" Daphne exclaimed, laughing. "You are a scream sometimes! Never mind about all that. What about the cars?"

"And Audrey." Margaret managed a smile at herself.

"Oh yes, of course, she must come in the cars," Daphne said more quietly; she felt guilty she had momentarily forgotten Aiden's mother. "Anyway, Ted thinks so, don't you love?"

"What's that?" Ted was cutting his slice of fried bread.

"Bus or Tube?"

"Oh, I don't suppose there's much in it, really," Ted said amiably. Then, thinking that he really should try to include him more in the conversation, he turned to Mark and said in a large round voice as if he were announcing a bonus, "And what about you, young man? Another day without school!" But as he said it he realised that it was the wrong thing to have said and that he sounded false or unnatural, just like anyone else who was uncomfortable talking to children. He keenly regretted that he struggled to strike a chord with his nephew, indeed it felt more like failure as he was Mark's godfather; he felt ill-equipped to look out for his godson or watch over him should there ever be the need. Then, trying to push his regret aside he remarked casually to Margaret and Daphne, "It's just what you get used to, I expect."

After a short pause Margaret added: "And I thought I'd do a few of salmon as well. I'm fairly sure I've got a large tin in the larder."

"I don't think you really need to, Peg," Daphne said gently, humouring her.

Elsewhere, in other houses in the suburb, there was an unusual eagerness or anticipation to the day. Out of albescent-smelling airing cupboards freshly laundered and ironed shorts and singlets were taken down, matched with spotless plimsolls and stowed neatly away in duffel bags.

"It's my school sports day today," Mark said sadly.

"It's not the feeding of the five thousand, you know!" Daphne ran-on. "We're not a big family and I don't expect many of Aiden's colleagues will come back."

"Oh Sweetie, I'd quite forgotten about Sports Day. I'm sorry," Margaret said tenderly, turning to Mark, "I'm afraid it just can't be helped."

"I suppose some of the people in the office will come out of a sense of duty," Daphne continued.

"Harry and Janet'll come back. You remember them, don't you? And I don't really know about Geoff."

"Well, I suppose so." Daphne sounded unconvinced.

"You need to go and clean your teeth, Sweetie," Margaret said to Mark.

Disgruntled, Mark slid out of his chair; he felt irritated at being reminded to clean his teeth and, momentarily feeling resentful, he was embarrassed that his mother had reverted to calling him by his old pet name since Aiden had died. Equally, he had been looking forward to participating in his sports day.

As Mark started off down the hallway towards the stairs, Ted got up from the table and started clearing away the breakfast plates, leaving Margaret and Daphne talking together at the table while they finished their tea. He crossed over to the sink and piled the plates up on the draining board. Then he paused and looked out of the window. A sad spindly geranium and a number of Aiden's shirt-collar-bones stood on the tiled window-sill in front of him, and one of the tiles was cracked. Placing his hands on the sink to steady himself, he leant forward so he could see a wider field of view than would otherwise be possible.

"If anything, I thought perhaps we could do with a drop of scotch," he said casually over his shoulder to the two women. Ted had found a bottle of sherry in the sideboard that had hardly been touched as well as half a bottle of gin. "I'll pop down to the off-licence in a bit," he added, more to himself. He thought that most people would probably have a sherry when they got back to the house, but he didn't know about the RAF types; for his own part, he thought that scotch was too celebratory a drink for such an occasion.

Ted felt a little anxious, even though the sky was bright blue and the sun was shinning brilliantly; not only was it cooler, the morning had a different feel from the last few mornings: the outlines, textures and colours of everything in his field of vision from the coal bunker with the newly-mended lid and the flaking paint near the back door to the creosoted fence at the bottom of the garden, the branches of apple trees in other gardens and the roofs of more distant houses, all stood out fresh and clean so that every detail seemed strangely clear and sharp.

"Whatever you think best, love. We'll leave all that to you; men are so much better at these things!" Daphne replied, smiling secretively across the table to Margaret, as if they were sharing a private understanding or cleverness.

"I keep thinking about it, Daphne."

Once left to themselves, there was a much harder edge to their conversation this morning; their sisterly closeness was almost insular in its intensity.

"He wouldn't have wanted to upset you," Daphne replied. "It would have been so unlike him to be inconsiderate."

Their conversation had turned once more to the penultimate time that Margaret had seen Aiden alive, the time when she had taken Mark in to see him in the hospital, and to the conversation that had so disquieted her.

"It left me feeling as if there must have always been depths to him that were quite unknown to me; it made me wonder whether I'd been right after all." Part of her unease was a fear that she might not have been able to read Aiden as well as she thought she had.

"But you know I never saw it, Peg," Daphne sought to reassure Margaret; they were going over well-trodden ground now. "As far as I could ever tell Aiden never gave cause for other women to speculate. And although it may have all been a bit peculiar he probably just wanted to say his goodbyes to Mark in his own way, and, goodness only knows, that's understandable enough."

Margaret was silent for a moment, contemplating what Daphne had said to her. "But it does worry me. What do you think he meant," Margaret glanced over at Ted and conspiratorially lowered her voice, "when he said about choices?"

But Ted was still looking out of the window; each individual leaf on each tree and each tile of each roof could be seen in sharp relief as if everything had been cut out with a scalpel from clean new clay and brightly painted for the new gaze of children. Now there was a slight breeze. Ted thought that it somehow seemed trivial and disrespectful to worry about whether it was likely to rain.

"Well that's another thing altogether," Daphne replied, also quietly, and she too glanced over at Ted. She had a hard, pragmatic tone to her voice. "It's not really their concern, is it, children, and anyway, it turned out all right in the end; so no harm was done!"

Before getting up from the table, Margaret and Daphne briefly squeezed each other's hand, as if signifying that their conversation had come to a definitive and satisfactory conclusion.

~~~~

As they walked to the station, fathers from other homes admired the vivid splashes of colour and inhaled the fragrance of the bright July flowers in the gardens they passed, content to be part of the commonwealth that had produced them. Then they smelled the keen fresh air and wondered if they should have picked up an umbrella from the stand in the hall before leaving the house. Sensing that the long hot spell of weather may be broken, mothers, pausing in their morning routines, thought ahead and planned what precautions they should take against the possibility of rain at the sports day that afternoon.

## Chapter Twenty-Six

Outside the west front people stood about awkwardly in small groups, as if they were foreigners who did not know the customs or were uncertain of the local ways. The groups did not mix much. Here and there, and far many more of them than Margaret had thought likely, clusters of blue-grey service uniforms relieved the monotony of the sombre funereal clothes. For the most part, existing wardrobes had furnished the needs of the mourners. Having shaken the vicar's hand, yet more mourners emerged into the afternoon light and looked anxiously skywards, worried about the cloud that had started to bubble up.

Although none of them were very old, the graves around the redbrick church were generally overgrown and many of them tipped at rakish angles into the weeds and wild flowers. The graveyard had always been too small and had been closed to new burials for a good number of years now, so that after the church service the party necessarily had to journey to a cemetery a short distance away for the committal.

Presently, when it was time to move off, the mourners, in sharp contrast to their previous uncertainty, quickly gathered their own small parties together and hurried towards where they had parked their cars before the service. Some of the women, not many of whom habitually wore them anymore, checked that their hats were properly secure. Some of the mourners who had come from further afield did not know the way and needed to follow others, and some, irrationally, suddenly felt nervous of being left behind.

The vicar travelled in the leading funeral car with Margaret and Mark. There was little to say between them; even if they had been regular church-goers Aiden and Margaret had not lived long enough in the parish for there to be any great familiarity. Presently the car moved off at a walking pace behind the hearse. The vicar stared fixedly out of the window while Margaret, doing her absolute best to remain calm and steady, held on tightly to Mark's hand.

A short distance down the road and still in sight of the church, the cortege momentarily slowed to a halt to allow the funeral director to regain his seat in the front of the hearse. After this, the hearse and the gleaming black curvy saloons, followed by a remarkably varied assortment of cars, joined the main road, but turned away from the heart of the suburb with its neat local railway station and parades of friendly shops that Margaret was forever quietly enamoured with.

The cortege began to gradually increase its pace and Harry, his car tucked in close behind the black saloons, reached across and gently patted Janet's leg just above her knee and called out amiably over his shoulder to his passengers in the back, "Alright back there? Michael's being very good!"

Janet, sensitive as ever to Harry's mood, caught his hand in hers for a second and squeezed it tight saying quietly, intimately, "Are *you* alright?"

And Harry, who thought that many things were unjust, setting his jaw tight, managed a nod by way of a reply.

~~~~

There was great excitement at Mark's school; sports day was getting under way. All morning, the tension had been increasing; from the time when the headmaster had made his announcements in the morning assembly, including the special arrangements that had been made for when lunch was to be taken, through a persistent and unusually indulged buzz of chatter in each classroom, to the final preparations being completed out on the sports field.

Those boys who would have ordinarily been having their games lesson that morning had been directed to bring out the long wooden benches from the gymnasium and a number of chairs from the school hall and position them alongside the running track. A wooden table for the trophies had been carried out to the playing field by two of the boys, who had leaned and lurched taking awkward steps with the weight and bulky mass of it straddled between them. The table had been placed prominently near where chairs had already been positioned for the governors, the headmaster and his guests. The running track's chalky lines had been re-marked, the sand pits freshly raked, sports equipment brought out from store, and a line of hurdles had been stood regimentally inside the track for when they would be needed.

Any number of boys now milled around like excited, straining colts as school masters with billowing gowns and hardboard clipboards consulted their lists of participants for each event and marshalled the first starters to their places. Prefects bustled about importantly. Smartly turned-out mothers streamed across the playing field clutching their handbags, precautionary light raincoats thrown over one arm, their summer shoes making little or no impression on the yellowing grass, as they looked about them for familiar faces and wondering when their boys' races would be run. The first race was due to commence at any moment, and as a prefect rang a handbell to gather everyone's attention a few isolated drops of rain began to fall, enough for some mothers to check inside their handbags for mackintosh head-scarves, and people began to be worried in case the day should be spoiled.

~~~~

Outside the cemetery, the mourners disembarked from their cars and surreptitiously adjusted their clothing. History felt quite different here. On first leaving the church, the cortege had followed the straightness of the road, which ran along the line of an ancient field boundary, past the snug suburban houses that Margaret thought of as being so perfectly suited to the area that they seemed to be all but indigenous. But to reach the cemetery they then had to travel a short distance along an arterial road, which was bordered by an estate of light industry with its alien smells of light engineering and factory-produced bread. The cemetery served the souls from a number of suburban parishes. It was quite flat, efficient and somewhat featureless.

As they walked down the long broad path through the cemetery, past the water tank where slimy jam-jars could be dipped for water for flowers that had been brought, the clouds became darker and the warm air became still and palpable like folds of silk. Margaret turned to her brother-in-law and said, "I don't know what you do about tipping, men are so much better about these sorts of things, would you take charge of it?" Ted, conscious that his suit was now a little shabby through age and wear, reluctantly agreed.

Nearing the end of the path, the mourners turned off the smooth macadamised surface; it was clear in which direction they should go. Straight grassy paths cleaved between the graves at right angles, but generally the mourners preferred to zigzag their ways through the grid of graves until they reached the virgin open space that remained covered with spiky grass.

The vicar, who had strode on ahead, was standing by the newly-dug grave and looking over the heads of the mourners as they approached, a book held in readiness in his hand. A green canvas tarpaulin covered the mound of sticky clay from sight. Aiden's family, friends and relatives filed into the cramped spaces between the graves, trying their best to avoid standing on those that were still new, where the earth was still soft and spongy. Where there was no other room, they dotted in clumps over the rough undisturbed grass. Now and then, some of them cast quick anxious glances towards the sky.

The vicar now opened The Order for the Burial of the Dead, the flimsy pages fluttering back and forth in the rising breeze as he waited for everyone to finish gathering, and unconvincing glints of reflected light sparked busily off the gilded edges of the pages. And as he began to speak, isolated drops of rain began to fall which, perceptibly wincing, he wiped from the pages of the book with his plump forefinger.

Dutifully and well enough meant, the vicar attempted suitable words to both satisfy the quick and to venerate the dead. Making his preparations for the funeral, he had called to offer his professional sympathy and to understand something of Aiden. His eulogizing emphasized Aiden's love and commitment to his wife and family, and how he had never flinched in carrying out his duty to his country.

Harry, who had taken the news of Aiden's death badly and was standing a little away from the first tier of mourners, whispered irreverently to Janet, "They never mention all the bloody muddles at these things do they, the little buggers."

Janet, uncertain as to exactly which little buggers Harry was referring to, nevertheless readily agreed with his sentiment, but kept looking respectfully ahead.

Then a moment later, Harry again whispered to Janet, "Do *you* think Mark's lonely?"

Startled, Janet involuntarily turned and looked at him.

"I mean," Harry hissed, "I know there's not many children in that family and now the poor little sod hasn't even got his dad! But I really don't think that's what Aiden could have meant."

Janet quietly shushed at him.

"Oh, alright," he responded, even quieter than before. "But don't you think there's an element of farce. And anyway," he added, "in the end it turns out that his country did bugger-all for him!"

At the sports day, one of the masters, his black gown billowing out behind him, marshalled the third year relay race teams to their marks imploring them to hurry in case the weather should turn against them. The mothers strained for a closer view, some of them even standing on tiptoe to peer over the shoulders of other mothers who were standing in front of them; the schoolmasters allowed themselves the rare indulgence of overt enthusiasm; the boys shouted out bold words of encouragement to the boys from their own houses who were competing. Then, as the boys who were to be first off took their positions in their lanes, anxiously checking the spread of thumb and forefinger against the chalky mark, tensing their thigh and calf muscles for instant flight, the pitch of feverish excitement increased before the spectators all fell tensely silent and a wave of anticipation passed through the whole school: the timekeepers stood with their thumbs nervously poised over their stop-watches; the marshals and the stewards stood waiting in their positions; and, the finishing tape was stretched out taut and ready.

The pistol crack suddenly rent the air and set the six boys running pell-mell along the track. Legs pounding, and chests heaving with the gargantuan effort of pulling in enough air to oxygenate their pulsing blood, their faces distorted with their grim determination, they pounded the track like war-trains heading for the front. At the cemetery, the words continued, lost amongst the swirling clouds and the splats of rain that now came with an increasing frequency and smote the mourners' cheeks like barbs. Now the baton had been handed to the next boy. His task completed, the first bearer freewheeled and, relieved, cast himself down upon the damp grass knowing he had done his absolute best. Then, after allowing himself only a brief moment of respite and deeply drinking-in the cool air, he rolled over and supported himself on his elbows for the satisfaction of seeing the other stages of the race.

Then the words stopped and Aiden's coffin was committed into the dark. The breeze died down and the sun came out again, the bright sunshine flooding the cemetery with gorgeous light; thankfully, the rain had come to nothing after all and it looked like it would turn out hot again. Margaret now let go in a wild blackbirding of grief making everything legitimate for her. Sobbing deeply and uncontrollably and without her realising it - her contracting diaphragm muscles forcing spasms of deep soundless pain from her - she doubled over and Daphne and Ted supported her and stopped her from falling.

A boy from Mark's house was the first through the finishing tape, his arms spread high and wide in ecstatic jubilation, and a cheer for the victors went up from the whole school. The watching mothers all applauded and the schoolmasters smiled self-satisfied smiles and heartily congratulated each other. Mark, deeply jealous of his mother's grief, found that he wanted her arms about him and for her to say something abundant to him that would legitimise the boys' cheering and laughter.

Gradually, people now slowly started to drift away and the undertakers began to move the flowers closer to the grave. There was much discussion about who exactly would be coming back to the house; people wanted to understand who would be coming, and to ensure they were properly accounted for in the cars. As they made and re-made their arrangements, the men shook hands with each other. The figures in uniform occasionally allowed themselves to place a hand on another's shoulder as they did so or mutually allowed a pause in the handshake itself extending its duration, more like their hands were held together, implying both an intimacy and a broader channel of communication in its own right. Not being as constrained as the men were, as a matter of course the women generally allowed themselves greater contact with each other as if proximity was a natural precondition to their intimacy.

## Chapter Twenty-Seven

To get ahead of themselves, they had done everything they possibly could before they had set out. But despite this, upon their return from the cemetery Margaret had rushed straight into the kitchen like a mad thing. Without even pausing to change out of her shoes, which had a tendency to pinch, she had seized her apron and inclining her head forward as she reached behind her lower back, she quickly looped the strings around her lumbar region and tied them together in a tight bow.

"I expect everyone must be ravenous!" She had loudly declared; the funeral had been at an awkward time, disrupting the usual regularity of their meals so that the funeral refection seemed neither one thing nor the other to her.

She had seemed eldritchly imbued with boundless frenetic energy, turning her attention to other household matters as well as to the food. "Be a pet, Daphne, go and open a couple of windows in the lounge, would you; it gets so hot in there!" And then, calling out after Daphne, she added as an afterthought, "And tell Mark that he can sit on one of the kitchen chairs and to leave the others for the grown-ups!"

Earlier in the day, Ted and Mark had carried the kitchen chairs through to the lounge to provide extra seating.

Ted was in charge of the drinks.

"Perhaps not everyone will have a sherry," Margaret said, anxiously. There were not really enough sherry glasses to go round. Her mother and father had brought their own half a dozen glasses with them this morning, carefully wrapped in a tea towel balanced carefully in their basket on top of the extra packet of assorted biscuits and other oddments they had thought might be wanted. These, together with the five Margaret and Aiden owned – one had been broken last Christmas – and the three or four not-quite-sherry glasses that had been all next door could offer to borrow was all that could be managed. Before they had left in the cars, the glasses had been wiped and put out on a tea tray and the tray rested on top of the washing machine; with all the various plates and dishes jostling for space, clear surfaces were at a premium. Margaret added, "Perhaps you should offer the men a scotch."

Countering Margaret's preponderant tone, Ted replied quietly, but firmly, "Let's just see how it goes."

He was carefully pouring the sweet, walnut-coloured liquid into the glasses, initially under-filling and then going back and carefully topping up, meticulously dribbling a few extra drops into each glass.

"I've done the french windows as well," Daphne announced, coming back into the kitchen. "People can go out into the garden now if they want."

"There," he said, having finished pouring. "I'll take these round."

Ted picked up the tray. It had a craftiness about it epitomised by its beaded handles that a less straight-forward man might have found incongruous for offering round a serious toast. Feeling a peculiar personal hollowness at the loss of Aiden, he was quietly determined that he should not be overly directed by either Daphne or Margaret today.

"Do you need any help in here?"

Janet's head had appeared around the kitchen door.

"No, it's fine, thank you Janet," Margaret said artificially and contrived a bright smile at her.

"All under control!" Daphne added breezily; she rather felt in her element. Margaret and Daphne, aided by their mother, were busy in the kitchen taking the tea towel covers off the plates of rolls and sandwiches, washing the salad and lifting the cakes out of cake tins. A baking tray of sausage rolls was waiting to go in the oven once it had regulated so that they might be warmed right through before they were taken through and laid out with the rest of the food on the dining-room table. But Janet hesitated in the doorway.

"I could put the kettle on?"

"It's alright, Janet, I'm making some tea for those who want it."

"Well if there's *really* nothing I can do…" Janet looked searchingly at Margaret, and was on the verge of turning about to go back out of the kitchen when Margaret gulped back a huge sob and wiped the back of her hand across her eye, her knuckle lingering in her eye socket.

"Oh Peg!" Daphne said softly, clearly distressed for her sister and she stopped what she was doing and gently touched Margaret's elbow with her fingertips. "Come along and sit quietly in the lounge. We'll manage alright in here."

"But there's ever so much to do!"

But Margaret nevertheless allowed herself to be guided out of the kitchen, Daphne's hand loosely cupped beneath her elbow, down the hall and into the front room.

Seeing the two of them come into the room like that with Janet following on behind looking concerned, Kitty instantly jumped up from the armchair she had been sitting in. "Come and sit here," she insisted.

She had vaguely been following the conversation between Geoff and Harry. Together with Donald and one or two men from Aiden's office, they had drifted into a knot and been seduced by the rosy attraction and safety of talking shop; with the exception of Mark, most of the family had formed their own small groups in the dining room. Donald, who had not yet heard Geoff's news, had been impressed.

Sitting back down beside her on one of the kitchen chairs which had been placed in front of the window, Kitty added solicitously, ostensibly speaking to Geoff, "We'll look after her!"

Geoff, hovering just in front of the armchair with a glass of sherry in his hand, darted a look at Kitty, "Of course we will. But you're not too hot there, are you?"

It was the middle of the afternoon and the sun streamed in from the west. The chair Kitty was sitting in appeared as if brightly burnished, catching the full force of it, and the room was bathed in a bright, captivating, bewraying light.

"I'm fine," Kitty replied, quietly content at Geoff's attentiveness.

Kitty then asked Margaret, "Can we get you anything?" She had always considered Aiden to be an uncommonly decent man.

"I'll bring you some tea along in a bit, Peg."

As Daphne went back out to the kitchen, Margaret looked down at her lap and suddenly said, "Oh, my apron!"

Kitty, being an insightful woman, understood how Margaret would not like to be seen wearing her apron when in company. She had thought it unspeakably cruel that Aiden should have been so terribly ill when he had only recently, and finally, come into passable contentment.

Margaret leaned forward and reached behind her back to undo her apron, and while watching Margaret closely, Kitty said, "I thought you'd be interested, we've asked Harry to be a godfather. It was Geoff's choice, of course."

Geoff heard his name spoken. "What's that?" He and Harry were still talking about the ins and outs of Geoff's new posting. Sitting close by, Mark was enthralled by the talk about the "V" bombers Geoff would be flying in, but equally, he derived great satisfaction from being on the boundary of the group of men.

"I was saying," Kitty emphasised, "we've asked Harry to be a godfather."

"Actually," Geoff looked uncomfortable, finding it an awkward topic for the day of the funeral, "I would have asked Aiden."

"Now you've gone and cut me to the quick!" Harry cut in amiably in the style of an Ealing comedy, "There was I thinking that you'd chosen me for my wit and charm, but it turns out I'm merely second best! Positively wounded, I am!"

Harry could have felt disappointed, but instead he had felt honoured at being considered a sufficiently able stand-in for his friend, even if the substitution had been accomplished a little clumsily.

"Well, it certainly wasn't for your good looks!" Geoff retorted, recovering his composure.

Harry smiled back at him and a gentle ripple of laughter passed through the group; happiness and sadness seemed joined together once more.

Ably directing the conversation, Kitty joined in, "We wanted to choose *appropriate* people."

"People who we could be confident would look out for him; like Aiden always looked out for me," Geoff said, his manner becoming embarrassed. But Kitty looked decidedly pleased that the conversation had taken this turn.

Geoff looked down and past his glass of sherry which he was simultaneously tilting and turning around awkwardly in his hand, the surface of the liquid making an ellipse at a point near to the rim as the glass rotated.

Studying his feet he continued, "I know us chaps get embarrassed about this sort of thing, but I think it should be said. There was one conversation in particular when I thought he was going to give me a real bollocking. It wasn't long after we returned from Christmas Island. And to be quite honest, I'd been indulging in the old juice a bit too much. I suppose we all did back then."

Geoff paused to let his words acquire an authority of their own. Harry felt no need to contradict him; it was important to let Geoff maintain his self-respect.

"And he would have been right to," he continued with the air of a man who has an admission to make, or who is ashamed at the remembrance of some past episode in his life. Growing increasingly pink, Geoff stumbled on, "But instead, he talked about understanding the wildness in each of us, about solitary struggles and how men need to soar." The silence between the men grew markedly awkward. "And," he added with a glance outside of the immediate group of men, "the things that can stop us. Actually, I think I was shocked; talking about men's intimate feelings like that was so *alien* to me, so utterly unexpected!"

To each of the men, Geoff's words sounded incredibly personal, resonating with something ancestral and wordless deep inside of them in a shockingly intimate way. Feeling a peculiar and familiar set-apartness each man looked awkwardly down at the carpet for what seemed like a long time, fearing to catch each other's eyes. This was something that was difficult to explore in a sunny front room where dust floated slowly by in the brightness.

The conversation with Aiden shortly after the Ladies Night had been an impellent for Geoff to approach Kitty and although he had been sincerely contrite she had recognised in him a particular resolve, as if he had broken the persistent addiction to harmony, which had meant that, even had she wanted, she could never have dictated the terms of their relationship.

Then with impeccable timing, Harry broke the broody silence saying blithely, "You do talk a load of bollocks, old chap." And the tension in the group of men was suddenly dissipated and they could each look about himself again.

"Harry!" Janet cried indulgently, and pointedly glancing over towards where Mark was sitting, added: "You're not in the mess now!"

"Ah, tea! Just what the doctor ordered!" Harry said, looking pleased with himself and winking at Janet.

Daphne had come into the room carrying a tray laden with teacups. As she passed a cup to Margaret she announced generally, "And the food's all out in the dinning room if you'd like to go and help yourselves."

"Do you think anyone will mind if I go and lay down for a bit?" Margaret said to Daphne as she took the cup of tea from her and placed it on the end of the mantelshelf beside her. She had suddenly felt the burden of the conversation.

"Of course not. I'll bring you up something to eat in a bit."

"Today was always bound to be a strain," Janet offered in her most reassuring voice as she reached out a hand to help Margaret up from the armchair.

Once on her feet Margaret expelled the air from her lungs in a long sigh as if weariness had suddenly overtaken her, and she then picked up her cup of tea.

And as Margaret made her way out of the lounge and towards the stairs she heard Harry saying in a tone that surprised her and struck her as being full of love, "And now, young man, how say you that you and I go and get ourselves something to eat? And did your Dad ever tell you about Operation Grapple?" Adding with infectious, zealous, amazement so that Margaret could imagine the wide-eyed expression on his face as he said it, "About how we flew our aeroplanes right through the mushroom cloud!"

~~~~

"I don't know that I really want anything, thanks Daph." Coming upstairs quietly after a while, Daphne had brought a plate with a few sandwiches and a sausage roll on it for Margaret but had been fully expecting that Margaret's appetite would not be up to much.

"I'll just put them here, then," Daphne said, moving the alarm clock to make enough space for her to put the plate down on the bedside table. Margaret had moved the clock to her side of the bed after Aiden had been admitted to hospital.

Daphne sat down on the edge of the bed beside Margaret so that her bottom was almost level with Margaret's hip and so that by rotating her upper body through an eighth of a turn she could then more-or-less look directly at Margaret as they spoke. The bedroom seemed privily dark when compared to the rest of the house, especially to the bright, sunny lounge downstairs; when she had come up, Margaret had closed the curtains against the inveigling brightness before lying, fully clothed, on the bed and despite the warmness of the afternoon had pulled the blanket up over her.

"I wondered if you might be asleep," Daphne said in a conversational tone.

"I don't think I could at the moment." Enjoying a peculiarly close communion with her sister, Margaret understood that Daphne was really asking her a question. "It was all just getting a bit much for me down there, you know, everybody talking about Aiden like that."

Daphne continued matter-of-factly, "There's plenty of cake left." She thought that the prospect of the sweetness of cake might cheer-up Margaret more than sandwiches would. "Perhaps you'll come down in a moment and have a piece after everyone's gone. Mum and Dad'll stay for a bit to help clear up, that's alright, isn't it?"

"People aren't going already are they?" Margaret said sounding surprised and shocked at herself. "I should come down."

There had been no need to answer Daphne's question; it went without saying they could rely upon family and there would have been no need to defensively peacock her grief in front of them.

"No need, not unless you want to, of course. Mum's down there and I'm sure Ted can find people's hats and things."

"It's one thing when you and I talk about him," Margaret said seriously, "but it's quite another hearing Geoff talking like that. It made me realise there's all sorts of things about him I didn't know."

"Oh Peg," Daphne said gently, "we've been over all that so many times now, haven't we?"

"Oh, I didn't mean *that*!" Margaret said with an emphasis that surprised Daphne, and went on to say, "Perhaps it's not so much that there's things I didn't know, I don't think I really mean that; I suppose I just feel numbed about it all. But it's as if in the last couple of years everything had started to be how it should and it just seems so cruel that he's been taken away from me!"

While Geoff had been speaking when they had all been downstairs in the lounge, Margaret had been surprised to find herself feeling unmistakably jealous, but she had not at first been able to place the object of her jealousy, only that it was clearly centred on something to do with what Geoff had been recounting about Aiden. "It was like Aiden had finally grown up." Margaret continued, troubled with her thoughts. "I don't mean that he was childish before, I don't mean that, it was more like he had finally come to grips with what's really important."

Then, as she had been lying in the bedroom, not even closing her eyes, she had realised why she had felt the way she had. Margaret had been utterly content with her quiet life with Aiden, especially since the time when he had finally stopped flying and they had moved into their own little house, and thinking their home was the rightful centre of their existence any other dimension to Aiden's life should have been relegated by him to a merely tolerated second division.

Margaret suddenly said earnestly, "He *was* really happy, wasn't he? There's nothing more important than family, is there? I am right, aren't I?"

Believing she had ordered their lives - although Aiden had not given up flying as she had calculated he would once she had fallen pregnant - it was as if she also thought she had an inalienable right to know or deduce everything that went on in his life.

"It goes without saying, doesn't it?" Daphne replied, wondering what exactly it was that Margaret doubted.

Aiden had once seemed so tinglingly exciting to Margaret that it still made her smile, almost regretfully, to think about it. When she had first met him she had quickly forgotten any inculcated notions of conducting a purely chromatic love affair with him. She had found his being a pilot unashamedly romantic; deep within him there had been something untamed so that it seemed as if she had been playing dare with appetising doom. Consequently, he had been a splendid catch for her to work on.

"I always thought he would simply change alongside me. You know, once we were married," Margaret said, a little regretfully.

"And the little nudge didn't really work out as planned, did it?" Daphne replied kindly, smiling at Margaret. "I suppose I was lucky really; being that little bit older than Aiden, Ted got all that sort of thing out of his system when he was in the army in the war."

"Oh he's *such* a lamb, Daph," Margaret said approvingly, returning her smile.

"You remember how at one time he thought he'd like to stay on in the army, even volunteering to go out to fight the Japanese as part of Tiger Force, not that he got any further than Aldershot, of course, but you wouldn't think so to hear him talk about it now, would you?"

"But at least he had a safe war; it wasn't as if he had a shooting war or anything. That's the main thing, I suppose."

"All the more strange that he wanted to go out and fight the Japs. There's no telling with men."

"Do you think he guessed, and that's why he carried on with his flying?"

"I don't see that it's all that important to men."

"Why did I worry he'd find out, then?"

"Did you?"

"Ever since that time at Swanage."

They sat in a familiar silence for a few moments until Daphne, while all the time looking intensely at Margaret, said slowly and carefully, as if she were finally conceding a point that had been under discussion or disputed for a long time, "But she *is* beautiful, isn't she."

"I was forgetting; you haven't met her before, have you?"

"But she's different from us, Peg; I think she has a different way of seeing things and perhaps that's why you worried so. I don't think I could ever *really* get on with her, not properly."

They lapsed once more into a silence, but this time more contemplative as if they were considering their own natures, until Daphne said, "It sounds like people are starting to go, but nobody'll mind if you don't want to come down."

"No, I'd better come and say goodbye. It *is* good of everyone to come. But I think I'll put my slippers on; those shoes really aren't very comfortable."

And as Margaret sat up and pulled the blanket off her legs Daphne said to her slowly and cautiously, "There was a card, you know, from Dennis's parents. Audrey said so. It was sent to *her*."

Margaret swung herself around so that she was now sitting on the edge of the bed alongside Daphne, and slipped her feet into her slippers.

"That's better. I wonder why, and after all this time as well. It doesn't seem at all likely, does it?"

Pushing herself up from the bed with her hands, Margaret got to her feet. Quite unconsciously, she smoothed down the front of her skirt and then bobbed down so that she could see her reflection in the dressing table mirror.

"Audrey seemed quite touched by it, really," Daphne said with soft detachment, as if the matter could be of little possible consequence.

Gently patting her hair just above her right temple to make sure that it was in order, Margaret then said, equally vaguely, "Oh, I see." Then, with more spirit, she continued, "I won't be sorry when everybody's gone; I don't want any more mysteries today. Is that just *too* ungrateful?"

"No, Peg, I expect you'll just want to be quiet for a bit now after all the upset of the last couple of weeks." Daphne got up from the bed and stepped over to the window. "Shall we let a bit of light in?"

Daphne parted the curtains and pulled first the right hand one so that it ran along its track and buffered to a halt, and then repeated the process for the left hand one. Then, carefully parting the nets, she placed her hands on the windowsill, one each side of her waist, and looked out of the window, the net curtain falling veil-like behind her. After a moment Margaret came and stood alongside her. They stood close together so that their hips and shoulders were touching.

"Perhaps you and Mark can just be quiet on your own, just the two of you," Daphne said positively.

"That sounds nice and peaceful; just what we need!"

Outside, the street was flooded with bright, heavy golden sunshine so that the street appeared richly settled. The neat hedges bordering the front gardens on each side of them and across the road the clipped front lawns, the pavements and tarmacadamed road-way, all looked still and dusty in the corporeal light. It was that peculiar in-between time in the afternoon when all the children had returned to their homes from school but the fathers were still absent at work.

"It looks as if you should be able to see into people's lives from up here, somehow," Daphne said.

"It seems very bright, almost too revealing."

But Daphne replied, "Do you think so? Apart from the few cars parked outside, there's nothing to tell that we're all in here today, is there?"

They stood together for a little longer before turning and going out of the bedroom. They crossed over the landing and started to descend the stairs, Margaret walking ahead of Daphne.

On seeing Margaret coming down the stairs, Harry called up to her, "I'm afraid we've got to be making a move, Margaret."

"Oh, and are you going as well, Geoff?"

The hallway seemed uncommonly full of people. Apart from Harry and Janet, Geoff and Kitty were also preparing to take their leave, Kitty cradling Michael in her arms as Geoff, still uncertain of the detail of the duty, busily checked that they were leaving with all the necessary paraphernalia of travelling infants that they had arrived with. Standing close to the front door, Ted was conscientiously carrying out the duties of a succedaneous host and Mark was standing uncertainly on the periphery of the group.

"They're staying with us tonight," Harry said, answering for Geoff. "They can travel on in the morning; they've got a lot further to go now Geoff's back in the wilds of Lincolnshire. Besides," he said dryly but with a glint in his eye, "you wouldn't want to be out after dark up there, would you now?"

"Harry!" Janet affectionately admonished him.

"Well, I mean to say, they've all got webbed fingers and toes up there. I say," he added suddenly looking dramatically at Geoff, "you *have* checked Michael's fingers, haven't you?" Then adding darkly, "I know where you were posted last year!"

As Janet gave an audible sigh as if to say that she thought Harry was quite incorrigible, Margaret was struck with the thought that fond as she was of her, Janet was also different from her and Daphne; she would have hated Aiden to have made such a remark, even allowing for the dryness of Harry's manner which meant that no one was ever in any doubt that he was not in earnest.

"Oh, is this anybody's bag?" Margaret asked as Janet, having gathered up her handbag, was leaning forward to kiss Margaret goodbye.

"Oh, that's mum's," Daphne interjected. The extra packet of assorted biscuits could still be seen poking out of it.

"Well, we'd better all be off then," Harry said, taking Margaret's hand and taking his turn to lean forward and kiss her lightly on the cheek. "Rum old do. But we'll keep in touch, Margaret; I've promised Mark I'd come and see him again, if that's alright."

As Geoff and Kitty stepped forward to say goodbye to Margaret, Harry, in the same generous, fraternal tone of voice that had so surprised Margaret earlier in the afternoon, made a point of calling Mark forward to him. He then said to Mark, full of mock ceremony, "And now, young man, would you do me the honour of letting me shake your hand?"

Mark, appreciating the spirit in which Harry spoke, momentarily forgot his lingering sadness and feeling that all his subsistent awkwardness must surely pass, took Harry's hand with equally mock solemnity. It was as if he intuitively knew that in the company of such men he could one day be truly effervescent once again, or that he might possibly float away through the clouds like magic.

"And about your mum's trifle!" Harry added seriously to Mark. "I'll tell you what, I've seen trifles all over the world and they just don't compare!"

Mark could not help smiling broadly at Harry, it was almost as if he wanted to loudly giggle, and he imagined that he must be standing up a little straighter than he usually did. He felt a joy and a vivaciousness stirring inside himself similar to that which he had felt when spending time with his father, although there was an unmistakable qualitative difference in the sensation, as if Harry was inviting him to joyously follow him to the ends of the earth.

Harry stepped back and ushered his party towards and then out of the front door. Each of them in turn said goodbye to Ted who was standing with his feet just on the edge of the doormat, leaving enough room for them to pass through. Harry was the last of them to leave. Drawing level with Ted, he turned to him and held out his hand.

"Well, thanks for everything, old chap," Harry said amiably, gripping the hand that Ted had held out to meet his own. Then, before Ted could reply he added, "Perhaps next time we come down you and I can take Mark out somewhere?"

But Harry's question did not sound conditional in any way, it was quietly insistent and rather as if it were a firm invitation. Rather than letting Harry's hand drop, as he would routinely have done when saying goodbye, Ted remained holding onto Harry's hand; he was deeply aware of its glorious communicative warmth, and its soft inviting fleshiness about its palm and the meaty folds between his thumb and forefinger where their two thumbs remained locked together.

"Well, yes, I'd like that!" Ted replied, brightly. He felt surprised, taken aback, as if he had been improbably caressed by a numinous understanding. Ted had marvelled at the kingly ease with which Harry had been able to talk to Mark this afternoon and felt certain that in the company of Harry he would be able to do the same. The two men stood together for a moment, looking into each other's faces, all the while their hands remaining tightly locked together. Then, with an almost imperceptible nod to each other, as if some pneumatological understanding was passing between them, they relinquished their grips and slowly dropped their hands and Harry turned away and stepped out through the front door.

And with a brief glance back at Margaret and Mark, Harry raised his hand up in a casual parting wave, his palm open wide and his fingers held loose and relaxed, and then he was gone, down the front garden path and out into the effulgent brightness of the suburban afternoon.

# The Letters

*Hemswell,*
*Lincolnshire,*

*16th May, 1957*

My Dearest Aiden,

*It really is quite exciting. It was in all the newspapers this morning, the main headline news and as I am sure you can imagine everyone here seems to be talking of nothing else! There was a picture in the paper – I think the same one was in all of them – a photograph of Wing Commander Hubbard and his crew. They are pictured standing together in a formal sort of grouping in front of his aircraft and his spaniel is with him! I should not have thought he would have been allowed to take his dog! I must say, Hubbard looks quite dashing, really.*

*It was disappointing there was no mention of you and Harry and the rest of the Squadron, I am sure your part in it all was just as important, although the papers did make a big thing about it being a great success for Bomber Command. There was no picture of the mushroom cloud, which was disappointing. But I do worry about you, my darling, I am sure what you are doing must be very dangerous.*

*Your last was about ten days ago, now, but I expect I'll receive one very soon, as I'm sure you'll be writing to tell me all about Wednesday just as soon as you can. But I expect you and Harry are taking advantage of being away from Janet and me and are having a high old time with the rest of the men! I expect Wednesday was very exciting. Are there really no women on the island? I can't keep an eye on you when you're so far away!*

*We are ticking over here much the same as usual. I catch the bus into town once a week and change my library book and shop for odds and ends, and last week, as a special treat, I took Mark to*

the pictures. It wasn't a terribly good main picture, actually
something rather silly about natives in the jungle, but Mark
enjoyed it anyway. It probably sounds rather silly to you, but it is at
times like that I miss you most of all. It probably sounds mundane,
but I do so love doing things like shopping for things for our home
together.

   The other day I had a letter from Daphne. She and Ted should
be in the house in Enfield very soon and as soon as you have some
leave after you get back I have said that we will go and stay with
them. It sounds very exciting!

   You've been away such a long time now, I do wish you would
hurry up and come home, it does not seem fair that I have to be on
my own and I get quite lonely. But I must say, when you're away on
deployment, everyone in the Squadron does rally round so; apart
from Janet and the other wives of course, I have had a number of
visits from your superior officers to make sure that Mark and I do
not need anything which is rather nice and the company makes me
feel more appreciated, some of the attentions are quite flattering,
really. Mark misses you terribly, although I must say he is quite the
little soldier.

   It is not that I am not terribly proud of you, you must know
that! It gave me such a warm glow to read about the operation in
the newspaper this morning and I count myself so lucky to have a
husband like you.

   Look after yourself and come home safely to me. Write soon.

Love,

Margaret.

*Christmas Island,*

*Sunday, 19th May '57*

*Dear Margaret,*

*I read your letter this morning at breakfast. Being Sunday, and I don't have so dreadfully much to do until later, I thought I would write you now. I would have written earlier but quite apart from my duties keeping me busy, I have not been able to quite settle to anything these last few days, perhaps it is something to do with Wednesday, a lot of the other men seem to feel pretty much the same.*

*It was something I shall always remember, a truly seminal moment. For our part, everything went according to plan. We took off shortly after Hubbard's aircraft and the other Valiant, and then flew on to our holding position. When the Valiants had done their bit we flew through the edges of the cloud taking samples of the atmosphere. Then we flew back here to Christmas Island.*

*Put like that it doesn't sound very much, but the passage through the cloud was extraordinary, and despite all our training, I see now it could never have totally prepared us for the real thing. The violence of the passage was so much more than any sort of turbulence I've ever experienced; we seemed to be thrown about in the air as if we no longer mattered to God and had to find our own direction.*

*The cloud was unspeakably awesome. At first when I saw it, it looked like a very dark ripe apple with a snowy white sauce poured over it. But you cannot imagine the size and the appearance of the cloud once it had formed-up, fifteen thousand feet higher than the bomb-run! It was a boiling mass of cloud with devilish colours at its base. By the way, I hear Hubbard's dog, Crusty, is actually staying with Hubbard's people in Norwich for the duration.*

*It was humbling and sobering. I am not sure I could find the words to properly describe it, but when he is old enough to understand better I feel I should try to tell Mark all about it. It feels like a duty to do so, a male-duty, not just because it is a part of my own story, but so that in some peculiar way he can learn from my experience.*

*I felt a tremendous sense of purpose and pride. It felt remarkably* feudal *as if I was fighting for something undeniably just, certainly something far greater than myself. What we are doing is dangerous, and I know you would keep me from danger, but you must allow me my choices. It is not as if they are unreasoned, as much by you as by me, or at least it seemed so in the past. It feels as if you want to bind me to the ground, but then I would not be the person that you married or the person you married because of what he should become.*

*I have said before that there are no women here and do not know why you should feel the need to ask again. To be quite honest I am sure I and all the other chaps would like there to be women – men always like there to be women around - but that does not mean I need ever betray you. Of course I find other women attractive, but you credit me with nothing but base animal instincts.*

*Women often seem to claim they are not simply physically attracted to men, but that there must be something more, but I wonder whether this is the whole story and not just a trick to imply they're morally superior to men!*

*I know that last paragraph or two will make you cross. But I do not want to believe you can have so little trust in me.*

*Please do not arrange anything with Ted and Daphne yet as I do not know when I shall get leave when I return, it will probably be quite soon, but I really cannot tell. And although you may not believe it, I miss you and Mark very much indeed and I think it would be more important for us to try and get away for bit rather than seeing Ted and Daphne. Perhaps we could go to the seaside. Mark would love that. Why do you think it is alright to make these arrangements without asking me first? Do I matter so very little?*

*This letter has taken longer to write than usual, and I really do have to go now. I do love you so much and that is why I had to write these things.*

*Love,*

*Aiden*

*Hemswell,*
*Lincolnshire,*

*27ᵗʰ May, 1957*

*Dearest Aiden,*

*At first I did not know what to make of your last and I am not certain that even now I really know, but it upset me greatly. It seemed so riddled-through with anger that I was tempted to think the operation has affected you deeply in some way that is not readily apparent or obvious.*

*But I have been thinking about what you said, indeed I have been thinking of little else since I received your letter last week. I do not honestly know if I feel angry with you or guilty with myself, or some sort of mixture of the two. I feel numbed. How has all this managed to creep up upon us in this way? And if you have felt like this why have you not said anything before?*

*I'm afraid I could not follow you when you wrote about seeing the atomic explosion. You have never been one to gush so I'm sure your description was understated but your words were enough for me to imagine how dramatic it must have looked. But I cannot recognise the emotions you described; women, and particularly mothers, must think differently about such things. It seemed so very war-like, and whilst I can appreciate how awesome it must have looked, such sentiments appear to me quite mawkish or dismal.*

*Perhaps this is why I do not understand what you think Mark would learn from it; of course I can understand that it was spectacular, an important moment in history, even, and for that reason you want to tell him all about it and he should have a pride in your being there, but surely that is reason enough. There seems to be nothing peculiarly male about wanting to do that; I can't see that men could have any peculiar emotional understanding that women do not have.*

*Surely you must know that Mark has been my purpose ever since he was born, and that is why I would keep you safe and out of harm's way. Is it a measure of how far we have grown apart if I have to spell out to you that it seems unreasonable that you should put yourself in danger because you need to be here to provide for me so that I can look after Mark? It saddens me greatly that you could be so selfish as to put yourself before your son and myself; it makes me feel like an accidental wife!*

*Oh Aiden, I wonder how many other couples feel this way? We were never so overly passionate that we excluded all else, but when we first married we seemed to be in our own special place where we would laugh so and our evenness, our everydayness, seemed to be our great strength. Perhaps it is just that we have grown up.*

*I do not know if I were really teasing you about there being other women or whether I really thought you were keeping something from me, and I am sorry if it upset you as I would not really do that for the world, but sometimes I do not really know if you love me and that makes me feel so dreadfully insecure.*

*As for Daphne and Ted, couldn't we go and see them as well if it were at all possible! After all, she is my sister and I do so want to see her settled.*

*Please write soon, my love. I hate it when we are all at sixes and sevens with each other.*

*Love,*

*Margaret*

## *Author's Note*

*Out of the Clouds of Deceit* is a work of fiction, but I have endeavoured to be as historically accurate as I could reasonably be. For the experiences of bomber crews in the Second World War that appear in chapter two, I have drawn upon a number of true recollections published in the superb book *Tail-End Charlies* by John Nichol and Tony Rennell. This book should be required reading for all those wishing to understand the horrors and the comradeship of the crews who took part in the allied bombing campaign; my words could never be as harrowing as their own.

For all its importance in post-war military history, its logistical achievements and sheer scale, relatively little seems to have been written about Operation Grapple. Much of the background detail I have used has come from Group Captain Kenneth Hubbard and Michael Simmon's book, *Operation Grapple, Testing Britain's First H-Bomb*.

Apart from a number of secondary sources, I am indebted to Andrew Dennis of the Department of Research & Information Services at the Royal Airforce Museum who willingly answered specific questions I had concerning RAF training, terminology and Operation Grapple and who also ably filled-in the gaps in my knowledge concerning 76 Squadron who operated air-sampling Canberras during Grapple.

The responsibility for any technical or historical inaccuracies remains entirely my own.